Sugar's Sweet Allure

Khalil Rahman Ali

To Bakish
May Allah Bless to keep you
Eam

HANSIB

*Published to coincide with the 175th anniversary of
the arrival of Indians in the Caribbean, 1838-2013*

Published by Hansib Publications, 2013

Hansib Publications Limited
P.O. Box 226, Hertford, Hertfordshire, SG14 3WY
United Kingdom

www.hansibpublications.com

ISBN 978-1-906190-66-8

A CIP catalogue record for this book
is available from the British Library

Printed in Great Britain

To Manjeet, and Sonya, for their love, encouragement, and help. To my late parents Rahman Ali and Sahidan Mohamed, for their guidance and all the opportunities they gave me, my brother Nasimul, and sister Razia. To my late grandparents, and all of my ancestors who had made the journey as Mustafa Ali and others did in "Sugar's Sweet Allure". To all fellow Guyanese, wherever they may be.

PREFACE

The fifth of May 2013 marks the 175th Anniversary of the arrival of Indian indentured labourers in the then British Guiana, to work on the sugar plantations. These migrants were intended to fill the gap in the labour force on the sugar plantations, upon the ending of African slavery in 1834. The Indian labourers had been enticed by recruiting agents in Northern, Eastern and Southern States of India, to enter into contracts of three to five years, with the option to return to India.

The journey by sea was perilous, and many of the passengers lost their lives. Then, upon arrival on their allotted sugar plantations, the labourers had to endure incredible hardships. However, as conditions improved, most of the migrants decided to stay on in the colony. They had begun to forge new lives amongst the former African slaves, other indentured labourers from Madeira and China, and, the indigenous Amerindian people.

This story sheds light on the beginnings of a new multi-religious, multi-cultural, and multi-racial community in the colony. Similar migrations of Indian labourers had also occurred to the British colonies of Trinidad and Tobago, Jamaica, and Mauritius, as well as several other locations, for the same purpose of working on the sugar plantations.

This book will be of interest to the millions of descendents of the migrants in the Diaspora. It is a story that has largely gone untold in this way. It is about a young labourer who ran off to find work along the Grand Trunk Road across Northern India, with the intention of saving enough money to then return to his village to ask for the hand of his childhood sweetheart. He eventually followed the same journey as the indentured labourers before him, and found himself in British Guiana, in 1845. Will his dreams be fulfilled?

CONTENTS

PART 1

THE GRAND TRUNK ROAD

1.

Forbidden love

Mustafa Ali was perspiring profusely as he waited impatiently for Chandini Sharma, the love of his life. Their *Muslim* and *Hindu* liaison was strictly forbidden by almost everyone in their village. He crouched low behind some sage bushes just outside the six feet high brick walls surrounding the compound of her family home. It was about eight o'clock in the evening, and the only visible source of light was the bright full moon. The temperature was unusually cool for January 1843, in the State of Uttar Pradesh in Northern India.

"Chandini... Chandini, are you there?" he whispered above the din made by hundreds of crickets and mosquitoes. He was very wary of being heard by Ballu, the watchman and guard of Chandini's family home and compound. Mustafa kept as still as possible, and decided to wait a little longer so as not to arouse any suspicion in Ballu or his guard dog which was fast asleep. The mongrel was tied securely to a short wooden peg in the hard ground by the main gate.

Ballu was never the most vigil and alert of watchmen, and was known to drift off into sweet slumber through the night whilst on duty. No one from the large household ever seemed to check on him or his equally lazy canine companion through the night. This approach to security by Ballu, a short and chubby man in his late forties, allowed Chandini, at sixteen years old, the youngest child of the Birendra Sharma family, to sneak past him and out of the compound, to meet her Mustafa, who was eighteen years old.

This night was crucial for the two young lovers as they wanted to meet for one last time, to plan their elopement. They would creep slowly through the sage bushes beside a pathway, as they had done many times over the last few months. The pathway led to the edge of a great stream that flowed past their beautiful, serene village near the town of Kanpur. They would nervously hold hands, tiptoe down to the water's edge, and sit on one of the *ghats* with their feet dangling into the cool, soothing water as it slowly and silently ebbed along. There was a great mango tree whose branches provided cover over the *ghat* in the evenings, and welcome shade during the bright, hot, and sunny daytimes.

Mustafa was about five feet and nine inches tall, of dark brown complexion, and appeared to be older than his age due to his work as a labourer in the village, and the local sugarcane plantations. Chandini was petite, about five feet tall, fair, and always wore a captivating smile which exuded a sense of mystique. Their relationship had begun as innocent children playing amongst others in the village square. However, as they grew older, their friendship was frowned upon particularly by the village elders, and their own families.

Their clandestine meetings were normally restricted to about half an hour to an hour at most, for fear of being discovered, particularly by anyone from Chandini's family, or the servants of the household, including Ballu. They would hold hands and whisper about how much they felt for each other. About the first time they looked at each other, and became aware that the little glances they exchanged meant more than friendly acknowledgement, and mutual respect.

Mustafa was the youngest of Hussein Ali's seven children, all of whom worked on the sugar plantation owned by Birendra Sharma, Chandini's father and the *Zamindar* of the village. The work in the sugarcane fields was tough, and included cutting any grass or unwelcome weeds from the undergrowth whilst the young sugarcane plants were growing through to the time of maturity, and readiness for harvesting. The grass and weeds were manually cut using a hand-held "grass knife" which was a sharpened and jagged half-moon shaped iron blade, securely wedged into a wooden handle. A two feet long sword-like machete or "cutlass" was used to cut the sugarcane stalks at about six inches from the base. The cut stalks would be tied into bundles using the long grass-like leaves of the plant. The bundles would then be packed onto two-wheeled bullock carts, and taken for processing into sugar. Mustafa always took great pride in carrying his grass knife securely tied to his hip with a string which was tightened around his waist. He had learnt the art of weeding from one of his most experienced brothers.

The village was a small enclave of two-roomed low-level wooden houses which were spread out in a loose circle away from the square. A large banyan tree provided natural shade in the middle of the square.

Wooden seating was constructed around the base of the tree where the village elders would normally sit discussing all manner of issues affecting village life. This was also used as the central meeting point for the villagers, where the *Zamindar* and other prominent members of the community would gather around to hold meetings, hear disputes, and, deliver judgements on family matters brought to their attention. Some of the village elders held sessions of story-telling which fascinated the children and young people. The very young children used the square as their main playground where they chased each other tirelessly, only to be scolded by an elder when the noise became too distracting. Mustafa and Chandini, when they were very young, often joined in the play, and sat in to listen to the stories which were normally narrated just after sunset.

The Sharma's house was the most substantial property in the village, with two floors. There were four bedrooms on the upper floor, and the flat roof was also often used as a place for sleeping during the dry and cool evenings of summer. The majority of the three hundred villagers were Hindu, who lived in the low level houses about one hundred yards away from the square, and the Sharma's house. The minority Muslims lived in a few similar structured houses a little further behind. The Sharma's house was flanked on either side by a large *Mandir*, and a *Mosque*.

Hussein Ali's family were Muslims who tried their best to practice their faith by learning to read the Holy Qur'an in *Arabic*, and observed *namaaz* five times each day even when they were working in the sugarcane field. They fasted through the holy month of *Ramadan*, and gave *zakaat* to the poor whether or not they were Muslims. Those who could afford to do so, and were fit enough, undertook pilgrimage to Mecca in Arabia, at least once in their lifetime.

Birendra Sharma was a Hindu of the *Brahmin* caste who, although not as learned in Hinduism as a *Pandit*, ensured that his family followed the tenets of *Sanatan Dharm*, and obtained knowledge through study of the sacred Hindu texts such as the *Vedas*, the *Ramayan*, and the *Bhagwad Gita*. The family also served the village community selflessly. Indivar, the eldest at twenty-two, was being groomed as the successor to his father, and at the same time, studying to become a Pandit.

The Sharma family had funded the village's only Mandir which was built by the people mostly during the gap between harvesting

13

times. Everyone with a skill, including stone and wood carving, carpentry, masonry and roofing, was contracted to work on the building, and its grounds. The Ali family also helped to build the Mandir. Likewise, when Hussein Ali's grandfather had started to build the first and only Mosque in the village, everyone including the majority population of Hindus, worked on the building and gardens. The *Madrasa*, which was built alongside the Mosque, was used as a facility for young Muslim boys and girls to learn *Arabic* and *Urdu*, and, the tenets and practice of *Islam*.

The Mandir also served as a school for young Hindu boys and girls to learn the Hindi language, to conduct prayers in the ancient *Sanskrit* language, and, to master the art of Indian classical music, singing and dancing. They learnt to sing Sanskrit *Shlokas* and Hindi *Bhajans*. Everyone in the village was able to communicate in their local *Bhojpuri* language. They were also beginning to learn some English words through contact with the British who had been extending their growing influence across the States of Uttar Pradesh, Bihar and Bengal in Northern and North-Eastern India.

Both Birendra Sharma and Hussein Ali were mutually respectful of each other, and shared a common dislike for the new masters; the latest in a long line of invaders to their beloved country. They both relied on each other to collaborate, and to be prepared to resist the British as much as possible, as their ancestors had done against the Marathas, the Mughals, and others before them.

In one such battle against the Marathas, their fathers, who were also very close friends, took up arms, and fought their enemy with all their might. Hussein Ali's father always stood beside his friend in battle, and when he was savagely slashed by a Maratha soldier's lance across his chest and arms in trying to shield his wounded friend lying on the ground, he begged Allah for mercy, and his friend to ensure that he looked after his family back at the village. This final pact between the two friends included an understanding that their families would continue to follow their different paths to God, and that there would be no inter-marriage of their siblings, and others to follow. The Ali family would also continue to honour their financial debts to the Sharma's, by working on the sugar plantation.

This mutual respect between the Sharma and Ali families continued with Birendra and Hussein often meeting at each other's homes to discuss developments in the village, and any pressing political matters, such as the growing influence of the British in India, and how best to deal with this, every step of the way.

On one such occasion, when Birendra Sharma visited his friend's home, everyone present at the time, was allowed to welcome their guest respectfully, and then leave the family sitting room area. Hussein's wife, Batool, who was a petite lady of forty-six years of age, silently served the two men cups of hot green *chai* which had been brewed over a large cooking stove made of bricks and clay. She also left the friends, and sat outside the room in the courtyard, where she began to sift some rice in a tray made of the leaves of the coconut palm tree. Mustafa decided to stay in the adjacent room, and listened into the conversation between Birendra and Hussein.

"Hussein *bhaiya*, I need to talk to you about your youngest son Mustafa," Birendra announced before sipping his *chai* from the beautifully decorated glass mug he cupped in his hands. This immediately alerted Mustafa who leaned closer to the wall in an attempt to hear more clearly.

"Birendra *bhaiya*, what has he been up to now?" asked Hussein looking a bit perturbed.

Birendra said, "I have heard that he has been secretly meeting my daughter Chandini. And I am worried that the two of them have strong feelings for each other."

Hussein put his cup of tea down slowly, and bore a look of great surprise. He said, "This is the first time I am hearing of this, and I am concerned that such a thing can happen when we have both tried to encourage our families to respect each other as friends. Have you scolded Chandini about this?"

Birendra shook his head, and said that he preferred to discuss the matter with Hussein in the first instance, and hoped that they would plan the best way to deal with the situation together. They both knew about the mutual pledge they shared, and therefore any prospect of a marriage was not even contemplated.

"Hussein *bhaiya*, maybe you can talk to young Mustafa, and confirm what has been going on. Also, please do not tell anyone about our conversation, especially your sweet daughter Aleemah who has been passing secret messages between the two of them when she comes to work at my house."

Aleemah, who was nineteen years old, was very close to her best friend Chandini, and was always providing Mustafa with advice. She was smart, very inquisitive, and always sought information and knowledge about everyone and everything going on in the village. She was acutely conscious of her family's obligations to serve the Sharma family, and although she never displayed any resentment, she wished that someone in her family would break free of this type of bondage. She once told Mustafa that, like the meaning of his name, he was the "Chosen One" to go on to liberate the family.

She advised Mustafa that as long as he stayed in the village, he would never progress beyond being a good sugarcane cutter and general labourer just like all the other four brothers of their family. She actively tried to encourage him to leave the village, go to one of the large cities anywhere in Uttar Pradesh or Bihar, become learned, earn wealth, and to lead the others out of their plight.

"Birendra *bhaiya*, I will ask Mustafa. Can you tell me how you have come to know about this relationship?" Hussein asked his friend in a more hushed manner.

Birendra leant forward and whispered, "I overheard your daughter Aleemah making plans with Chandini for her meeting with Mustafa one evening. Apparently, they meet at the *ghat* beside the mango tree by the village stream."

Mustafa did not quite hear this properly but he heard Aleemah's name mentioned by Birendra, and he realised that he should not allow her to remain involved in his communications with Chandini.

Hussein said, "I will ask Mustafa, and if this relationship is true, I will tell him to stop meeting with Chandini immediately. I hope that the boy will listen to me. He is of age to get married now, and you may be able to help me find a suitable girl from here or another village. In the meantime, I also hope that you will keep an eye on Chandini."

Birendra said, "Thank you Hussein *bhaiya*. I know that you are a man of your word, and I will ask Ballu the watchman to look out for me. I will also make sure that none of my family members, especially Mahaveer, my youngest son, who is too protective of his two sisters, get to know of our plan."

Hussein took another sip of his tea, and asked Birendra whether there were any other matters to discuss.

Birendra said, "Hussein *bhaiya*, I am very happy with the way that this year's sugarcane crop is growing, and I am looking forward to a good yield. I expect that all the workers will be available, and especially your four sons. I want to grant you and your family, one extra share of rice as a gift for all the hard work that you do for me, and my family."

Hussein was delighted with his friend's gesture, and rose up to embrace him as they concluded their meeting. Birendra then walked slowly past Batool in the courtyard, and respectfully said goodbye to her. She looked up for a moment, and smiled in acknowledgement.

Mustafa kept out of sight of his parents and sat down on the *matya* in the room, in quiet contemplation. He knew about the strict separation and prohibition of inter-religious relationships between young men and women of the village. Harsh punishments were meted out to any couple who dared to cross such lines. His and Chandini's relationship was strictly forbidden, and could end with severe repercussions for both of them, and their families.

2.

Run Mustafa run

"Mustafa... Mustafa... are you there?" whispered Chandini who did not hear Mustafa's earlier calls. There was no reply, and the only noise she heard was from a slight shuffle amongst the bushes only a few yards away. Mustafa slowly and quietly stood up with his arms outstretched. He had a small cotton bundle of clothes which was tied with a piece of string, and secured to his right wrist. He held his arms outstretched and walked towards Chandini. She also stood up, and smiled with great relief that her beloved was there as expected.

"Oh my Chandini," said Mustafa excitedly as he smothered her in a tight embrace. She rested her face against his chest. They stood unmoved for what seemed like a lifetime until Mustafa whispered.

"Chandini, we must not go to the *ghat* tonight. Let us go somewhere else so that no one can find us."

Chandini asked, "Why Mustafa, did you also learn that my father knows about our relationship?"

Mustafa said, "Yes, I overheard your father speaking about this with my father. They are both against this, and plan to stop us from meeting ever again."

"What will we do? It must be Aleemah who gave our secret away," suggested Chandini.

Mustafa said, "Chandini, I have not told her about tonight, and I hope that no one else knows about this meeting."

They walked quietly away from the path that led to the *ghat*, and holding hands, helped each other to overcome the higher grassy area towards another tree in the village orchard, using the light from the full moon to guide them. They soon reached a spot within the orchard, and sat down beneath one of the mango trees. Mustafa looked back towards the *ghat* to make sure that they were not being followed.

He said, "Chandini, we must go away tonight. Far, far away from this place. No one will approve of our liaison, and I will never be able to live here without you."

"I feel the same way, but my brothers, especially Mahaveer, will make my life unbearable. I am very scared of running away with you, and if we are caught, they will kill me," Chandini pleaded, as tears welled up in her almond eyes which glistened in the light of the full moon. Mustafa held her small face with his rough labour-worn hands as gently as he could, and implored her not to cry.

He said softly, "Be brave. We can do this together and if we go now, we will be too far away before they realise we have gone. They will never be able to catch up with us, or to find us."

Chandini said, "Mustafa, where can we go? We only know this village. People everywhere know my father, and sooner or later, someone will see us and inform him."

Mustafa said, "I have heard of many large cities along the Grand Trunk Road, and we could either go west towards Delhi or Amritsar, or east towards Varanasi or Calcutta." He tried to sound very positively about his knowledge in an effort to convince her that this would be the right thing to do. He continued, "I also heard that although in some parts, the road is dangerous, there are many places where we can hide safely. People are very trusting, and we could take work as we travel along."

Chandini said, "But Mustafa, you are talking about very long distances, and I do not think that I have the strength to face such hardship. Maybe you can go, and when the time is right, you can come back for me. I shall wait for you for as long as it takes."

Mustafa realised that Chandini was very scared of the consequences of being found with him. If he left her now, it would be almost impossible for them to be re-united again in the future. Chandini knew that their separation was inevitable. She turned to Mustafa and said that he must be brave, and to pray constantly for their safety that night, and forever.

"Mustafa, please say these prayers for me and we shall be protected at all times. I know that you will do your *namaaz* like a good Muslim. But can you also say this *mantra* every morning at first light?" asked Chandini with her hands clasped. She then softly recited the *gayatri mantra* which she had memorised from the lessons at the Mandir and by practice at her home. She said the *mantra* three times, and he repeated the words slowly, committing them to memory: "Om Bhur Bhuwah Swah. Tat Savitur Varenyam. Bhargo Devasya Dheem Mahi. Dhyoyo Naa Prachodayaat."

Chandini then explained the meaning of the *mantra*, still whispering, "Oh God, thou art the giver of life; the remover of pain and sorrow. The bestower of happiness. May we receive thy supreme sin-destroying light. May thou guide our intellect in the right direction."

Then suddenly in the distance, the sound of frantic barking caught their attention. They both turned around towards the Sharma compound, and their worst fears were realised. The barking dog was accompanied by the sound of human voices, and the flickering light from hand-held lamps were visible in the distance. This must be a search party, and before they could get any closer, Chandini hugged Mustafa with great urgency, and with tears gushing from her eyes, she pleaded with him to, "Run Mustafa run! Please go now! I shall wait for you forever!"

Mustafa turned, and opened his mouth to say something to her, but the words could not come out. He looked towards the lamps in the distance, and started running away in the opposite direction. Chandini also could not say goodbye, and just slumped to the ground sobbing loudly. She did not attempt to hide from the search party, and simply allowed them to find her. This would give Mustafa more time to escape further away.

He ran as fast as he could along a track he would normally use when heading to work on the sugar plantation. The track led through to the bank of the Grand Trunk Road, and he headed eastwards. After running for about five minutes, he began to feel very tired, and was breathless.

He slumped to the ground, and started to weep loudly. He kept muttering Chandini's name and turned around once more with the faint hope that she would have changed her mind, and run after him. But there was an eerie silence. No more sound of a barking dog or humans shouting aloud. Many a time, he contemplated returning to his beloved, and to face whatever was in store for them both. Each time he recalled her pleas to pray for her, and to hope that they would be re-united.

Meanwhile, Chandini stood up to reveal herself to the search party. She quickly recognised Ballu and his dog. Then she noticed Mahaveer.

He wore an angry frown as he approached his sister, and said, "Chandini, where is Mustafa? Where did he run off to? Tell me!"

Mahaveer became more agitated, and only seemed to be concerned about finding his prey. Chandini ignored him, and sat there weeping silently. Mahaveer shouted at her once more to find out about Mustafa's whereabouts, and grabbed her arms firmly, shaking her in anger.

"Let go of me! You have no right to touch me! Go away and leave me alone!", Chandini shouted angrily as she tried to free herself from his firm grip.

Mahaveer could not restrain himself, and shoved her back to the ground. He was a very strong, and powerfully built young man who prided himself as the one who would fearlessly protect the family's honour at any cost. Chandini clasped her head for fear of being hit by him. He then turned to Ballu, and ordered him to lead the search in the direction away from there, towards the main road. Chandini saw that they seemed to have guessed at the correct direction to which Mustafa had headed. She shouted, "No! He did not go that way! He headed back to the village to get his clothes!"

Mahaveer, Ballu, and the dog ignored Chandini, and headed back towards the village. The two men ran hard to keep up with the dog which was now relishing the new hunting responsibility. Mahaveer was too intent on catching Mustafa, and did not seem to care about Chandini who was left to fend for herself, and to make her way back to the family home.

She looked into the distance where Mustafa had run towards, to see whether he had made good his escape. She also wanted to make sure that he was not returning to stay with her. After a few moments, she realised that he had drifted away as she had urged him to do. She stood up, and without dusting her clothes, she slowly trudged back towards the village.

When she eventually reached the main gate to her home, she saw Mahaveer and Ballu standing in her way. The dog continued to bark at her, but was firmly held on his leash by Ballu. Mahaveer said quietly, "So you have lied to us. You must be very proud of yourself for protecting that useless scum. How could you do this to me? And, to your family? Have you no shame? Do you care what everyone will think and say about the Sharmas?"

Chandini kept her composure, safe in the knowledge that she had protected her Mustafa, and gave him the chance to be well away from everyone, in particular, the vengeful Mahaveer. She did not answer any of his questions, and was not afraid of Mahaveer's attempts to intimidate her into giving him any information. He raised his right hand and lashed out at her, but failed to hit her as she managed to sidestep him. She then eased past Ballu and the dog, and headed to her room.

Mustafa wearily got up from the clump of grass he sat on, wiped away the tears from his eyes with his cotton shawl, and started to walk further away for as long as he could see, through the light from the moon. He kept to the edge of the road, and could see no sign of anyone else. He broke into a jog, and tried to cover as much distance as possible until he was too tired to go on for the night. He knew that he had to avoid as many villages as possible so that he would not be recognised by anyone.

When he felt that he had travelled far enough, he decided to find a safe place to sleep. He soon came upon an open-fronted shack with its roof made of dried coconut palm leaves. It was only about ten feet long, and ten feet wide. It was one of the outlets which were used during the daytime hours from dawn to dusk, as a stop for *chai* and light meals for travellers. No one was in the shack, so Mustafa felt at ease about lying down on the table used as the serving counter. He assumed that the vendor would be someone from the nearby village, and thus, he should be undisturbed at least until the next morning. He planned on having a good rest, and then proceed further away before dawn.

"Hey get up! Who are you?" shouted the vendor, pushing hard at Mustafa's back as he lay on the table. It was dawn, and Mustafa had failed to get up, and move on as he had planned.

"Who? What?" mumbled a groggy looking Mustafa as he tried to rub the sleepiness away from his tired eyes. In a few moments he was fully awake, and jumped up from his lying position, almost falling over the edge of the table. He quickly composed himself, and without replying to the stranger, he grabbed his bundle of belongings, and smartly stepped out of the vendor's range. He then broke into a steady run. The vendor was more relieved that the intruder had run away, and did not bother to chase after him.

3.

The long walk on the Grand Trunk Road

Mustafa kept up a brisk pace of walking alongside the right bank of the magnificent Grand Trunk Road known as "The Long Walk", still heading eastward. He passed by village after village which idled sleepily beside the maturing sugarcane fields. The occasional bullock cart creaked past him in either direction. He always made sure that he covered his face with his shawl, to avoid being recognised and also, to prevent the dust that was being raised by the carts, from entering his eyes, nostrils or mouth. Other strangers walked past him without acknowledging him. He began to tire as the sun cast its increasingly warm spell along the dusty road.

He finally stopped at the edge of a stream, and repeatedly used his hands to cup some water to wash his face, and then sprinkled some onto his head, arms, upper body and legs. His leather sandals were very dusty, and he gently kicked at the water with his left foot and then his right, in an effort to wash them. Mustafa felt very hungry, and looked around in search of any edible fruits. He saw some ripening *ber*, an Indian berry with brown edible skin and sugary white flesh. Then he positioned himself to push at the slender trunk of the tree, and shook it vigorously until some of the ripened fruit fell to the ground. He quickly gathered them up, and put a few handfuls into his shawl. He sat down under the shade of a large mango tree, and ate all the fruit. Although this was not enough to satiate his hunger, he felt better for it.

He had no money, and decided to continue walking along the road in the hope of finding a *chaat house* for some *chai* and snacks. He felt that he could offer to work for the vendor in exchange for some food. It was now mid-day, and the sun was unbearably hot. He was very relieved to find a *chaat house*, and greeted the vendor who was busy trying to serve his half dozen customers.

"*Chacha Ji*, can I help you please?" asked Mustafa as he put down his small bundle.

"Can't you see I'm busy? I have no time to talk. Just join the people at the back, and everyone will get what they want," said the elderly vendor without looking at him.

"But *Chacha Ji*, people will walk away from here, and go somewhere else to get their food and drink. Please let me help you," pleaded Mustafa.

"If they wish to go, they can. They all love my food and *chai*. So, shut up, and wait patiently like all the others," said the unrelenting vendor.

Mustafa then asked one of the customers, "Do you want to wait here any longer? You must be hungry, and the next *chaiwallah* is only up the road."

The man shrugged his shoulders, and quietly endorsed the vendor's statement. "This place is the best, and we all love to come here."

Mustafa started to contemplate his own advice to move on to the next vendor a few hundred yards away, when much to his surprise, the old man turned to him and said, "Young man, come over here and help me. I cannot give you money, but you can have some food and *chai* for your effort."

Mustafa dashed behind the serving counter, and started serving up the *chai* and snacks with great enthusiasm and energy. When all the customers had been served, and there was a lull in trade, the vendor gestured to Mustafa to have some food and *chai*.

"Who are you?" asked the old man firmly.

"I am Mustafa Ali. Thank you for helping me."

The old man smiled, and asked, "Where are you heading to? You seem to be a little lost. Are you running away?"

Mustafa sipped some *chai* as he thought of an answer. He said, "I am travelling east to find some work for a few months, and to make some money. Then I hope to return to my village to help my family."

The old man said, "You do not have to go so far away. You can stay with me here, and after a while you may enjoy the work. It will be a very great help for me. You see, I am now too old to continue doing this work, and I have no family to pass the business on to. Besides, I like your business attitude. One day you will become a very successful businessman."

Mustafa served himself some boiled, spicy *channa*, and *aloo paratha*. The food was very tasty, and he appreciated why the customers loved it.

"Me a businessman? Never! I am a good hard-working canecutter, and labourer. I cannot trade like you," said Mustafa with a contented smile.

The old man adjusted his shawl over his left shoulder, and looked at Mustafa straight into his eyes. He said with a frown, "I am not a successful businessman. Yes, the customers come here because they like my food, and my service. But, they also pay very little for my *chai* and food. That's the real reason why they put up with me, and this small *chaat house*. Is that being successful? I am still not able to earn very much from this business. Maybe someone with your energy and savvy can make this into something much bigger. I wish I had a son like you."

Mustafa smiled and nodded in appreciation of the old man's honesty. He thought about the offer for a while, and when he finished his plate of food and his second cup of *chai*, he stretched out his right hand, and grasped the old man's right hand firmly.

He shook his head, and said, "*Chacha Ji*, I feel that I can trust you, and I am happy to try this kind of work. If I become good as a trader, I may stay here for a long time."

The old man smiled contentedly, and beckoned to Mustafa to help with the washing up of the dirty plates and cups. They both cleaned the *chaat house* before the sun began to set. He then led Mustafa back to his small house in the village which was about two hundred yards away from the main road.

The house had one wooden front door, and two small windows. There was a living room which also served as a sleeping area with enough space for two beds. The beds were made of wood, and without the comfort of a mattress. When they were not in use, they were stacked upright against the wall. The kitchen area was tiny, and had a mud-based cooker and some basic utensils.

Mustafa asked the old man about his family, and he replied, "I have no one except..."

Before he could finish speaking, the door was opened, and in walked a beautiful young woman. The old man continued, "... my daughter, Sita."

Mustafa was taken aback. The young lady clasped her hands, and bowed slightly towards him, and then reached down to touch her father's feet with respect. The old man touched her head, and said, "Bless you my *beti*. Please meet my new worker, Mustafa Ali."

Sita was of light brown complexion, and about the same height as Chandini. Mustafa could not believe his eyes. How could there be any one else like Chandini?

He clumsily clasped his hands, and mumbled "Namaskaar" to greet Sita. She nodded, and smiled nervously, then moved towards one of the beds. Mustafa reached across, and grabbed the bed by the two legs at the top, and pulled it down to rest on the dirt floor. He then reached for the second bed, and placed it beside the first.

"There. Two beds for two people," said Mustafa as he backed off nervously towards the door. "I... I cannot sleep here. I will go into the courtyard and sleep there."

The old man reached out towards Mustafa, and said, "No, you can use one bed, and I will sleep on the floor inside the house. Sita will not mind."

Mustafa could not accept this, and said that if he did not sleep outside, he would leave the house, and stop working for the old man.

That night, Mustafa could hardly sleep for more than a few minutes at a time as he kept thinking, and dreaming of his Chandini. He wondered how she was coping. How she was being treated by Mahaveer, and the rest of her family. How his own family must be cursing him for running away, and letting them down so much. How everyone else in the village must be reacting to his sudden departure. Then he consoled himself with the thought of finally finding a useful job by which he could work towards making a good living, and then be in a position to return to Chandini, and his family.

"Mustafa... Mustafa... wake up! Get up!" shouted the old man as he prodded Mustafa just as the sun began to rise. Mustafa rose up, rubbed his eyes, and stretched his arms aloft whilst yawning. He heard a voice from the house quietly chanting the *gayatri mantra* that Chandini had asked him to recite first thing each morning. It was Sita, and he also quietly recited the *mantra* three times. The old man looked at him with some surprise, and asked him where had he learnt this from.

Mustafa did not reveal the source of his knowledge, but said that he had heard it as he passed by the Mandir in his village each day to and from the sugarcane fields. He then walked off towards the village pond, did his *wuzu* and performed his *fajr namaaz* on the neatly cut grassy area. The *fajr namaaz* is the first of the five daily prayers in Islam.

He then returned to the old man's house to accompany him to the *chaat house*. Before they left to start the new day's trading, Sita had cooked some *roti* and *daal* for their breakfast. Mustafa could not resist the aromatic side dish called *aloo choka*, made with mashed potato and several spices including crushed ginger, *jeera*, red chilli powder, turmeric, and salt.

They all tucked into their meal quietly, and then drank some hot *chai*. Mustafa complimented Sita for the delicious meal, and noticed that her mannerisms were very similar to his beloved Chandini's.

The old man saw Mustafa's observance of Sita as she collected the used plates, small bowls, and tea mugs, to wash just outside the front door of the house. She used some clean water kept in a *matka*. When she had finished washing the dishes, and the flat metal plate used for making the *rotis*, she laid them on a wooden plank to dry.

"Sita, could you please show Mustafa what supplies we need to take to the *chaat house*? Black *chai* leaves, milk, coal for the cooker, some *aata*, *aloo*, and the spices," said the old man as he washed his face and mouth with the remainder of the water from the *matka*.

Mustafa noticed the small pool of used water settling so close to the house, and he suggested to the old man and Sita, "I should dig a drain to take this water away towards the stream"

The old man sighed, and said, "Oh please help us with this. I am just too old to dig such a drain in this hard and dry soil. Thank you, my *beta*."

"I will start digging the drain after today's trading is over, and before the sun sets," promised Mustafa as he picked up the two large bags of the supplies that Sita had packed.

"Sita, when you have finished the housework, washed the clothes, and cooked, please take some rest, and we will see you when we return," said the old man as he walked off slowly beside Mustafa.

After about one hundred yards, Mustafa stopped as his arms began to feel the strain of the heavy weight in the bags. The old man offered to help him, but Mustafa refused. Then, after a short rest, he resumed carrying the load.

"My *beta*, I am so happy that you are with us. Sita and I have struggled to fetch this load every day, and it was becoming more and more difficult for us. Besides, she is a very young girl who works so hard to keep our home clean. Your help will do us a lot of good."

Mustafa nodded, and grunted in agreement as he ploughed on for the next one hundred yards to the *chaat house*. When he finally reached the door at the back of the premises, he dropped the bags down, and immediately opened up the front hatch for business. Soon, they were set up and ready for the first customers of the day. Mustafa poured himself and the old man some water to refresh them after their joint effort.

"Raam Raam maharaj!" said the first client who ordered his *chai* and *roti*. Mustafa brewed the *chai*, and poured it with some fresh milk, into a glass. The old man quickly made the first batch of *rotis*, and they served the contented customer.

The man sat quietly, and looked out towards his buffalo cart to make sure that it was still tied securely to a stake in the ground. The buffalo stood beside the cart, and was chewing at its meal of newly cut grass.

"So my friend, where are you heading to so early?" queried the old man.

"Oh, I am going to Mr Birendra Sharma's sugarcane plantation for some work, and hope to stay there for the rest of the harvest. I heard that he needed more workers this year, and he pays very well."

Mustafa felt tempted to join in with the conversation, and would have loved to agree with the stranger. But he kept quiet, and tried to avoid eye contact with the man, for fear of being recognised.

The old man said, "Yes, I have heard about Mr Sharma. People have always sung his praise. It is very good to have people like him to help take care of us, and our families. It would be unthinkable for anyone to show Mr Sharma anything but utmost respect."

Mustafa again felt like joining into the chat in order to put the record straight as far as he was concerned. Thankfully for him, the customer finished his snack, and left quickly. Mustafa began to feel uneasy, and thought that perhaps he was still too close to his village. He was worried that sooner or later, his identity would be revealed.

The old man noticed Mustafa's disquiet, and asked if he was alright. Mustafa nodded and set about washing the plate and glass used by the customer. The *chaat house* soon became very busy, and they both worked extremely hard to cater for their customers. At the end of the day, the old man beckoned to Mustafa to lock up, and they soon began to slowly walk to the house.

When they reached the house, the old man noticed that Sita was not there, and he started to call out for her, "Sita!... Sita!... Sita!" There was no reply, and the old man became very concerned. He then asked Mustafa to accompany him towards the nearby orchard to search for her.

They soon found her sitting beneath a large mango tree beside the small stream that flowed gently past the orchard.

"Sita *beti*, are you alright?" asked the old man anxiously.

Sita was visibly upset, and said, "Pa... I... am unhappy because Mr Thakur came to the house yet again, and tried to put pressure on me to marry his son."

The old man stretched out his arms towards Sita, and beckoned her to move forward to embrace him. She dutifully rose up, and slowly stumbled towards her father. They embraced, and she began to weep inconsolably. He urged her to stop crying, and tried to reassure her that he will handle everything. Mustafa stood by quietly observing the pair, and decided not to intervene. The old man turned to him, and said, "You see, this is how people are trying to take advantage of an old man. I have warned off Mr Thakur, and his good-for-nothing son. Yet they try to put pressure on us. We have nowhere to go for help. Not even the headman of our village is willing to intervene, and deal with Mr Thakur and his family."

Mustafa continued to listen, and preferred not to respond. He thought that he had only recently faced his own relationship problem with his family, and Chandini's family, and was not prepared to get involved in this situation. He nodded respectfully, and started to walk back towards the house. The old man and Sita followed closely behind him.

That evening, the three of them sat quietly eating the meal prepared by Sita, and soon retired to sleep as the dark night drew in. Mustafa had a restless night, and kept thinking about whether he should continue to stay with the old man and Sita. Perhaps he should allow the storm to subside for a while, and then make up his mind.

Very early the next morning, Mustafa rose up, washed his face and mouth, and picked up the hoe which was lying outside the house. He then carefully marked out the length and width of the drain he had promised to dig. He hacked away within the markings, and soon the drain began to take the water away from the stagnant pool. He continued to carve the neat drain through to the edge of the stream flowing beside the village, and the water from the pool finally trickled away.

"Well done my *beta*," said the old man as he walked out into the front yard of the house, and inspected the new drain. "Let us hope that this drain will become a mirror of how all our problems will go away. Please come in, and have our meal before we go off to the *chaat house*."

Mustafa was very pleased with his construction, and smiled at the old man. He washed his muddied hands and feet over the new drain, and watched the water making its way very quickly down towards the stream.

Sita was already up, had done her *pooja* and recited the *gayatri mantra*, before preparing the first meal of the day. She was very subdued, and did not greet Mustafa as she had done every morning. This behaviour troubled Mustafa, and he was unsure as to how best to handle the situation. He could not recall Chandini ever having ignored him in this way.

However, before he could greet her, the old man said, "Namaskaar Sita and Mustafa. Let's eat and go to the *chaat house*. Today is Friday, and there is normally a bigger crowd to feed. Sita, you will need to come with us to help with the cooking and cleaning up."

Sita and Mustafa nodded in agreement, and shortly after their early morning meal, they packed the extra provisions to take to the *chaat house*. The three of them made their way quietly, and without speaking to each other.

No sooner had they opened the *chaat house*, and started to prepare the food, the rush of customers began. Mustafa noticed that many of the men were as young as him, and carrying their cane-cutting tools. They were travelling together as small working gangs who would move from one sugarcane plantation to another throughout the weeks of harvest. He tried to listen in on their conversations, and heard that they had been travelling and working from very far into the east, close to the border with the neighbouring state of Bihar.

Interestingly, they even talked about how the English *Massa* was using agents to recruit field labourers from all the way through Uttar Pradesh, Bihar and Bengal, to take them to work overseas, for good money, and on long contracts. The men seemed to express great interest in this as the money offer was better than they were earning each year in their States. They had the option to return to India after their contract ended. They would be much richer men than they were able to be currently.

Mustafa was tempted to join in with the conversations, but yet again resisted to do so. He simply continued serving and clearing up whilst the old man and Sita continued to work in silence. The crowd gradually slackened off to almost a trickle, and when the final customer had left, the old man asked Mustafa and Sita to take a break to share some refreshment with him.

"So the English are looking for workers," commented the old man. Mustafa nodded.

"Who do they think they are, to come here in our country and take everything from our people? They now want to take our people away from here as well. We must teach our young people to resist this," said the old man, who was becoming more agitated as he directed his concerns to Mustafa.

The old man continued, "We have a lot of work here in India for everyone. What will happen if our young people leave us for such a long time? We are too old to do all the more heavy work in the plantations. Will they ever come back when they have their wealth? Will they ever be the same good Indian people if and when they do return? What kind of person would leave their families in the villages, and never return?"

Mustafa listened intently as the old man continued his argument, "And what of our young daughters? What will happen to them when all the young men go away? Who will marry them, and look after them? Our young men should stay here to help everyone, otherwise our villages will suffer, our plantations will die, and our peaceful lives will be destroyed. What do you say Mustafa?"

Mustafa said, "This is the first time I am hearing of this offer. I really do not know what to say on the matter. The young men in the working gangs seemed to be very keen to accept the Englishman's offer of more money."

The old man raised his voice even louder as he continued to make his case against the recruitment. "So, what happens when the workers get fed up or become ill, or really miss their families here in India? They will not be sent back immediately. At least here they can leave their gang, and go back to their home village if they are not happy, or, they get news of any problems back home. And, what about their food? What will they get to eat in these faraway lands?"

Mustafa and Sita sat quietly as the old man spoke with such passion against the enterprise. Then Mustafa interjected, "But *Chacha Ji*, we workers have the same problems here. We are given shelter at the *Zamindar's* village. The people treat us with suspicion, and prefer not to mix with us, as we may be of lower caste or Muslim. Our food is very basic *roti* and *daal*, and some vegetable curry. If we get injured, we do not get good treatment. And, our money is not very good. Besides, some people are used to being away from their families for months."

The old man seemed to accept Mustafa's response, and then turned to Sita, "*Beti*, what do you think? Do you agree that our young men should go away from here to places they know nothing about? How can they trust the white man, and his greedy wish to rule over all of us?"

Sita gracefully fixed her cotton shawl over her left shoulder, and without looking at her father directly, said, "I do not agree that people should leave our beautiful country. They can do better somewhere else in our own country, and come back with enough money to live well. Many people and their families have so much debt here that some of them kill themselves when they cannot pay the moneylenders."

Mustafa agreed with Sita, and seemed to be impressed with her argument. The old man, clearly frustrated that his reasoning was not making the desired impact, brought the discussion to an abrupt end by saying, "It is getting late now. Let us close up, and retire for the day."

That evening, Mustafa lay awake or half-asleep for most of the time until falling into a deep slumber just before dawn. He was restlessly contemplating the discussions about young labourers leaving their homeland to venture abroad, into unknown territory that lay oceans away from Calcutta. The old man's anguish could easily be the same as his own father's or Birendra Sharma's back at his village. Will Chandini ever support him or forgive him for going so far away and for so long? Can the old man be right in his estimation of the situation? Was he being selfish in his attitude towards the young labourers, or the English? How can the old man come to such conclusions when he had not spoken to anyone who had experience of such a contract? Does Sita reflect the same impression as Chandini would? Oh, for Chandini's thoughts at this time! Will she wait for him for such a long time?

Mustafa woke up suddenly as a *mor* bellowed out its loud call in the village. He mopped his brow and face that was in a sweat, and was about to get up off his bed when he heard the voices of two men approaching the house.

It was Mr Thakur and his son whom Sita had complained about. Mr Thakur was a thick set dark man of medium height, with fierce eyes, and a large black moustache which he proudly shaped upwards at the ends. His son was of similar build, without a moustache, but with similar large and wild eyes. The two men were standing in warrior-like poses, holding six foot long sticks threateningly, as if they were spears.

"Who are you?" Mr Thakur asked Mustafa whilst pointing his stick towards him.

"This is Mustafa, our Sita's intended husband!" shouted the old man walking purposely towards Mr Thakur and his son.

"Are you mad?" queried Mr Thakur. "This cannot be allowed here. He is Muslim and Sita is Hindu. I have come here once again to demand your daughter for my son, even though we are higher caste than you."

The old man took courage from Mustafa's presence, and said, "You have heard what I said. I will never accept you and your good-for-nothing *bandar* of a son into my family."

Mr Thakur was utterly enraged by this, and shouted, "How dare you call my son a *bandar*? I will give you one more chance to come to your senses, and get rid of that scum you are taking for your daughter. If you do not agree with our offer, we will come back, and give you all a good thrashing."

They raised their sticks in a threatening way as if they were about to attack the old man. Then they turned away, and stormed off in anger. Sita had heard the commotion, and ran out from the house. She reached out, and hugged her father as she sobbed loudly.

Mustafa stood in utter amazement at what he heard from the old man and Mr Thakur. He calmly picked up his bed, and placed it against the wall of the house. He then went inside to pack his belongings into a small bag, and started to walk away without saying goodbye.

"Mustafa... Mustafa... please do not do this. Please do not go away. I only said this to put Mr Thakur and his son off. Sita and I need you here," pleaded the old man as he freed himself from Sita's embrace, and stumbled towards Mustafa, with tears in his eyes, and arms outstretched.

Mustafa kept walking away purposefully and briskly as the old man struggled to catch up with him. He stopped momentarily and said, "I cannot believe that you had such intention for me to take your Sita. I like her very much, and respect her as much as I do you. She is like a loving sister to me. You have been so kind, and helpful like a good father." Mustafa could not contain his emotions, and continued to walk faster and further away from the old man.

"Please my *beta*, I beg of you to stay with us for as long as you like. You do not have to marry Sita. We are so afraid of the Thakurs, and any other like them who just wish to ruin us," pleaded the old man. He could no longer keep up with Mustafa, and stopped suddenly, slumping unto his knees and cupping his face in his hands, crying loudly. Sita ran to him, and also fell to her knees as she embraced him.

Mustafa looked back briefly over his left shoulder, and after pausing for a moment, he pressed on moving further and further away. He had clearly made up his mind to continue on his long walk, eastwards.

4.

The reluctant Holy Man

Mustafa walked steadily for long periods of time, stopping at every opportunity, to rest, and to drink water from any stream or clean looking village pond. As night was approaching, he sought shelter beneath a large banyan tree in the middle of a village which was unknown to him. He had never travelled thus far from his own village.

The great banyan tree stood like a massive shelter over a large area, and had some wooden seats constructed all around its thick trunk. No one was around, as the villagers had retired to their houses when darkness fell. That night, Mustafa slept blissfully and deeply despite a slight chill in the air. The tree provided good cover, and a feeling of safety. The light from the full moon seemed to dance amongst the leaves, and flickered onto his well-covered body. The stillness of the night was only disturbed by the chattering crickets. Occasionally, a moth would flutter about Mustafa's head as if to inspect the stranger, and it would then fly off into the distance.

As soon as the dawn chorus of *mors*, cuckoos, cockerels and cattle started their daily racket, Mustafa woke up, and quietly headed to the *ghat* by the village stream. He performed his *namaaz*, and decided to return to his resting place under the banyan tree, for a little more respite, before continuing on his journey.

Soon, a few of the villagers approached the stranger in their midst, and started to enquire as to who he was. Mustafa just sat there with his legs crossed beneath his trunk in a basic yoga pose. He began chanting the *gayatri mantra*, followed by passages from the Holy Qur'an. The villagers became more curious, and soon it seemed that the whole village population of about two hundred souls, gathered around the still figure of the stranger. They were whispering amongst themselves, and then decided to ask the headman, the Pandit, and the *Imaam*, to try to obtain some response from Mustafa.

Mustafa continued to recite his prayers, and ignored the delegation that stood before him. The three wizened souls greeted him with their own customary salutations.

"Raam Raam," said the headman.

"Asalaam O Alaikum," said the Imaam with his right hand outstretched.

"Namaskaar," said the Pandit, clasping his hands respectfully and bowing slightly.

Mustafa repeated in good Arabic diction, the first chapter or *surah* of the Holy Qur'an, "Bismillah ar Rahman ar Raheem. Al hamdu lillaah hi rabbil aalameen. Ar Rahman ar Raheem. Maaliki yaw middeen. Eeyaa ka naa budu, wa eeyaa ka nastaeen. Ehedinas siraatal mustakeem. Siraatal lazeena, an aamta alaihim. Ghairil maghdoobi, alaihim wa laa dwaa leen." The English translation is, "In the name of Allah, the Most Beneficent, the Most Merciful. Praise be to Allah, the Lord of the Universe. The Most Beneficent, the Most Merciful. The Master of the Day of Judgement. You alone do we worship and you alone do we turn to for help. Direct us onto the straight path. The path of those whom you have favoured. Not the path of those who earn your anger, and not the path of those who have gone astray."

The Imaam, and all the Muslims gathered at the scene, uttered the Arabic word, "Ameen", meaning Amen. They were very impressed with the stranger's beautifully rendered *surah*. Mustafa then surprised everyone by reciting the *gayatri mantra* three times, and all the Hindus present were in awe of him. They clasped their hands in dignified respect.

The headman tried once again to obtain a reaction from Mustafa, apologising for disturbing his prayers. "Oh Holy One, please tell us who you are, where have you come from, and why have you chosen to bless our village with your presence?"

Mustafa continued to maintain his steady vigil without responding to any of the promptings of the villagers, and their three representatives. He coughed slightly, and this immediately caused the Imaam to take action.

"Someone, quick... bring our *bhaiya* some milk and some food," ordered the Imaam.

Within a few minutes, a plate of *roti* and vegetable curries was brought, and laid gently at Mustafa's feet, by an elderly lady. A young man brought him a glass of hot milk. The Pandit turned to the crowd, and raising both hands above his head, he waved everyone away. They all dutifully obeyed his instruction, and walked away, still muttering amongst themselves.

The Pandit then turned towards Mustafa and said, "Please *bhaiya*, do eat and drink. You must be starving. When you are finished, please come with me to the Mandir. You can stay there for as long as you wish."

The Imaam intervened with, "Oh no, you must come to our Mosque. We have better living quarters there. It is free at the moment, and you can stay and pray with us."

The headman also felt obliged to make his own offer for Mustafa to stay at his large house where he would be well looked after by his servants.

Mustafa opened his eyes, and looked closely at the three men. Then he spoke. "Thank you all so much. I cannot accept your offers, and if you do not mind, I will stay here under this tree, and when I am fully rested, I will leave."

The Pandit pleaded, "Oh Blessed One, please do not leave us. We have been waiting for a visit by such a Holy Spirit for so long. We have so many problems here that only a wise person like you could give us the best advice. It has been predicted by our holy calendar, that a great calamity will descend upon us within the next few months. How can we prepare for such an event?"

Mustafa said, "I am sorry. I cannot help you or advise you. I am not a Holy Man. I am Mustafa Ali, and I am a labourer looking for work."

The Imaam said, "My Brother in Islam, you are indeed the Chosen One. You have been sent here to help us all. Why do you deny this?"

The headman reached out to hold Mustafa's hands, and said, "Mustafa, my *bhaiya*, please stay with me, and we can discuss what needs to be done to save our village, and our people."

Mustafa rose up and said as he began to walk away, "I must insist. You are all wrong to assume that I can help you. I am not a religious person, and I do not know any more of Hinduism or Islam than you do. So please let me go in peace. Just keep praying for divine help from God, and do the right things to protect your homes and families."

The Pandit said, "Hey Raam! There you are. We were warned that a Holy Man will come to our village and deny us three times. Mustafa, you must be this blessed person. You must stay." The headman and the Imaam nodded in agreement.

Then, just as Mustafa began walking away, a huge thunder struck in the darkened sky above, followed by sharp flashes of lightening, and a torrential downpour of heavy rain. The headman grabbed Mustafa's left hand, and hastily led him to the comfortable shelter of his large house which stood a short distance from the centre of the village. The Pandit tried to open his large umbrella, but soon gave up with the idea as the rain lashed wildly at him. He also ran for cover behind the headman and Mustafa. The Imaam, a much older figure, tried desperately to keep up with the others, and was completely drenched.

Within a few minutes, they all arrived safely at the headman's home, frantically trying to shed the water from their heads and bodies. The smartly tiled floor in the hallway of the house soon became wet with large puddles of rain water around each of the visitors.

The headman ushered them into an area where they could sit on some ornate hand-carved wooden chairs. "You see Mustafa, we have not had rain as heavy as this for over two years now. You have truly blessed us, and as Panditji and our Imaam have said, you are special to us. We have to make sure that you stay here, and help us with your divine presence."

A maid quietly brought a pot of hot *chai* for the visitors. The headman gestured to his guests to take a drink whilst he removed his wet shawl, and handed it to the maid. She bowed slightly, and retreated to the kitchen. The headman said, "So your Holiness, will you stay with us at least until we are out of danger of what is to befall us?"

Mustafa, whilst relieved to be out of the rain, said "Please sir, do not address me as a Holy person. As soon as this storm ends, I would like to go on my way. I am truly sorry that you have suffered so long without rainfall. But now it seems that all of your prayers have been answered by this storm."

The Imaam caressed his long, grey beard and said, "Mustafa, my Brother in Islam, unless this storm subsides, this village will be flooded, and we are not properly prepared for such a calamity. This may be the start of what we most feared will befall us."

The maid returned with a tray of four plates of rice, *daal* and *channa* curry, and gracefully invited the group to eat. They each took one plate, and without hesitation, started to eat the meal. The storm continued well into the night, and as the wind and rain lashed against the rattling windows and main door of the strongest house of the village, the three representatives continued to convince Mustafa to stay, and to see the crisis through.

Mustafa thanked the headman for his hospitality, and asked him for a space to lie down. The headman was overjoyed, and offered him his own sleeping quarters. Mustafa declined, and said that he would prefer to sleep on the ground. The headman, Pandit and Imaam, were struck by the stranger's humility, and were becoming even more convinced that he was indeed a special Holy Man.

Later on, the three men slept near to Mustafa, and kept an eye on him, just in case he decided to get away from the village. But this was not possible as the rainstorm became more relentless, accompanied by a howling wind, booming thunder claps and dazzling lightning flashes. No one was prepared to venture out into such a storm.

Mustafa closed his eyes and tried to sleep, but this was punctuated by the clap of thunder, and the loud snoring of his hosts. He thought about being mistaken for a Holy Man. Could this be true? Was he some kind of soothsayer or *Fakir*? Why was he being put through this experience? Was this his fate? Was this his purpose on earth? Why was everyone he met on his journey, trying to hold onto him, and stopping him from moving on? What was his purpose?

The Imaam was the first to wake up the next morning, and he quietly started to pray. Mustafa, still groggy from a rough night of disturbed sleep, joined him and when they completed their *namaaz*, they embraced each other as is customary at the end of Islamic prayers. The Pandit stopped snoring, and woke up to do his *pooja* prayers as Mustafa and the Imaam sat silently in respect. The headman continued to sleep through the prayer sessions, and everyone waited patiently for him to wake up.

Mustafa quietly opened the main door, and peeped outside, only to find that nearly everyone from the village was standing forlornly in the courtyard, which was covered by a few inches of water. The whole village had been flooded by the storm. When a few of the villagers caught sight of Mustafa, there was a hush, followed by smiles on their faces.

"Hail Mustafa!" shouted one old man at the head of the group. They all repeated, "Hail Mustafa!" This caused the headman to spring up from the floor. He rushed out into the courtyard, almost knocking Mustafa to one side.

"You see... He saved us! He is a Blessed One! We have the rain, the water, but no disaster!" cried the headman with his arms aloft.

"Hail Mustafa!" shouted the crowd in response.

"O Blessed One, speak to us!" pleaded the old man moving forward towards Mustafa, with outstretched arms.

Mustafa tried to ignore them, and as he turned to go back into the house, the Pandit and the Imaam held his arms aloft, and then guided him towards the crowd.

"Please everyone," began Mustafa. "The storm had nothing to do with me being here. I just happened to come here looking for some rest, and something to eat before I continue on my journey. Please go back to your homes, and try to help each other to clear away the water. I can help you to do this by cutting drains through towards the stream, to take the water away. I am not a Holy Man. I am just a labourer who would like to be left alone."

The crowd applauded Mustafa's statement with such enthusiasm, that it became clear he would not be allowed to leave the village as he intended. They were utterly convinced that his presence in the village was a divine intervention, and the answer to their countless prayers. The more he denied his assumed status as a Holy Man, the more they considered him a man full of humility, unlike other *Saadhus* who regularly passed through the village on their way to pilgrimage to Allahabad and Varanasi further east into Uttar Pradesh.

Mustafa decided not to engage with his new followers, and proceeded to lead the work of clearing the slowly subsiding water. He quickly surveyed the level and extent of the flooding, and started to mark out the best route of the drains to be dug. Soon, everyone was hacking away at the barely visible soil, and as the work progressed through the morning, the water receded considerably. Effectively, a drain was dug from every house, directly towards the stream.

When the new drains were completed, and all the water flowed away, Mustafa told everyone to make sure that they kept the drains clear of rubbish, and fast growing weeds. The headman appointed a few of the villagers to take control and responsibility for this task. The villagers stood in admiration of Mustafa, and applauded him whilst chanting, "Mustafa! Mustafa! Long live Mustafa!"

Everyone was very tired and as was customary, they all gathered together in the village square. They squatted down where it was dry enough, and enjoyed a welcome meal which was prepared, and served at the headman's expense.

As soon as night fell, they all slowly drifted away to their homes, safe in the knowledge that they would be able to sleep on dry beds and floors. The sky was clear, and there were no storm clouds in sight. An eerie stillness descended on the village once again.

Mustafa chose to sleep out in the open under the banyan tree, and surprisingly, no one insisted on him taking shelter elsewhere. Perhaps the three wise men realised that he would be too tired to continue his journey that night.

"Hello *bhaiya*," whispered an old man wearing a white turban and a long, neatly kept beard. "Sat Sri Akal."

"Sat Sri Akal," replied Mustafa as the *Sikh* gentleman took up a seat beside him.

"I have seen how you have helped our people here. You remind me of one of our Sikh Holy Men. I wish to thank you on behalf of all our Sikh brothers and sisters here, for your kindness and humility. Please stay as you are. You are not a Holy Man, but as our Guru Nanak said, you are God-fearing and full of Truth."

"Thank you *bhaiya*," whispered Mustafa. "I appreciate your gratitude, and I am glad you do not think like the others."

The Sikh man smiled gently, and handed Mustafa a neatly written note. He said, "Please take this with you, and when you feel the need for some solitude, say these simple words called the Mool Mantra." He proceeded to slowly and quietly recite the *mantra* in the Punjabi language, pausing to explain the meaning of each line or phrase.

"Ik onkar. There is only one God.

Sat naam, karta-purakh. His name is true. He is the creator.

Nirbhau nirvair. He is without fear. He is without enmity.

Akal murti, ajuni. God never dies. He is unborn.

Saibhang gur-prasad. God is self-illuminated. He is realised by the grace of the true Guru.

Adi sach, jugadi sach. God was everlasting in the beginning. God was everlasting when time came into existence.

Hai bhi sach, Nanak hosi bhi sach. God is everlasting now, Guru Nanak says God will be everlasting."

Mustafa thanked the Sikh man, and stood with some reverence and respect towards the stranger.

"Young man, please take such simple beliefs and understanding wherever you go. You will always find peace, and people who will help you. I know that you will not stay here, and I believe that you have a purpose in this world. So, I bid you farewell and may Allah or Rab or Bhagwan go with you." The Sikh man wiped some tears of joy that had welled up in his soulful eyes. He clasped his hands, and after bowing slightly, he turned, and walked quietly away into the darkness.

The next morning, before anyone was up for their prayers, Mustafa slid away from the village, unnoticed. He was soon back onto the Grand Trunk Road heading eastwards. His stride quickened as he set a very purposeful and fast pace for himself. From time to time, he looked over his shoulders to check on whether anyone from the village had been following him. The dark road was silent behind him as it was ahead of him. The Long Walk beckoned once again for the Reluctant Holy Man.

5.

Spiritual cleansing in Allahabad

Mustafa turned around quickly as soon as he heard the creaking of a badly worn wooden axle of a bullock cart that was following in his direction. The bullock was a fully grown animal, powerfully built with a huge pair of horns, and almost entirely black except for a small white spot in the middle of his forehead, between his large staring eyes. The bullock pulled the two-wheeled cart, and its driver, with utter ease through the sheer power of his front and hind legs.

The bullock snorted, and shook his head as he neared his latest spectator who had paused to allow the vehicle to go by. Mustafa raised his right hand, and gestured towards the driver, asking for him to stop. The driver seemed to be expecting this interruption, and calmly invited Mustafa to climb on board, and to sit beside him.

Mustafa would have much preferred to sit quietly at the back of the eight feet long cart. The reason soon became obvious when the bullock lifted up its messy black tail, and unceremoniously dumped a full load of fresh dung onto the road beneath him, followed by a mini waterfall of pungent urine.

As soon as the bullock completed its early morning ritual, the driver gently prodded him with a short stick. Without a fuss, the bullock continued his job with much ease despite the additional weight of Mustafa on board.

"So, where are you heading to my *beta*?" asked the driver, who did not seem to be so old as to refer to Mustafa as his "*beta*".

"I am going as far as you can take me," replied Mustafa, grateful for the lift.

The driver said, "Well, I am heading to Allahabad, which is only a few more miles from here. We will stop soon to have some *chai*, and to feed Rustum, my faithful friend, with some fresh grass. He always likes to eat and drink soon after his early morning sh.."

"Yes, I can see," interrupted Mustafa, who was still recovering from the stench of Rustum's expulsions. Rustum snorted, and shook his head as if to suggest how pleased he was at his well-timed gesture towards his new passenger.

"I have never been to Allahabad," pointed out Mustafa. "What is it like?"

"It is a large and very busy city. I wish that one day I will go there, get a job or learn a new trade, and make enough money to buy my own house with sufficient land to plant some vegetables and fruits. Sorry, I am telling you more about myself than about the city," said the driver, smiling at his own error.

"No my friend, I have the same hopes, but I do not know where I will end up. So there must be a lot of people living in Allahabad. How are they towards strangers?" enquired Mustafa, keeping an eye on Rustum's rear end.

"In my experience, the people are normally very busy with their daily lives, but when you get to know them well, and to deal with them in business, they are very friendly and willing to help," said the driver as he gently prodded Rustum forward.

The cart jolted ahead, and its pace quickened as Rustum's response took effect. The dry dust on the well trodden path on the road lifted, and formed a small cloud trailing behind the two-wheeled vehicle. The creaking of the axles became louder under the greater stress being imposed by the new speed. The driver and his passenger both felt the urgency as their bodies vibrated in line with the bounce of the cart's wheels over the rough terrain. Occasionally, this became more uncomfortable when one wheel would suddenly sink into a deep groove made worse by continuous traffic. Most times the driver would see whether there were such dips or holes in the road, and would expertly avoid them.

"We are the best drivers in all of India," declared the driver. "And, Rustum is much admired everywhere we go, for he is a beautiful bull. He is in much demand, you know. I just cannot bear the thought of selling him for any price."

Mustafa said, "Maybe he can earn some extra money for you, by using him as a stud bull. More and more farmers are doing this, and everyone benefits from improved stock."

"You seem to have a good brain for business, young man. You seem to be able to spot a good opportunity. Is this what you are aiming to do?" asked the driver.

Mustafa said, "No, I prefer to work as a labourer on the plantations. This is what I know best, and I have the strength to keep doing this kind of work for some time yet. Maybe when I am tired of doing this, I may consider the easier work of buying and selling goods."

The driver said, "Doing business is not really easy, young man. You worry all the time, about buying the right kind of goods, at the right prices, then having the customers who are prepared to buy your goods, and, you have to manage your takings well enough to be able to pay your suppliers, your taxes, and your expenses for living."

"You seem to know a lot about business," observed Mustafa. "How come you are not a businessman?"

The driver paused for a moment as he steered Rustum away from a deep indentation in the road.

He said, "Well, it is not easy for you to notice. But I am a businessman, and I am on my way to pay some merchants in Allahabad, and to take some new stock to sell at my small shop back in my village."

Mustafa said, "Oh, I see. This is how you do it. What happens if you do not sell some of your goods. How do you pay the merchants? Do they take the unsold goods back?"

The driver replied, "You see, you are talking like a businessman. There is an understanding I have with the merchants who will take unsold goods back at a lower price, as they do not charge me interest for the money I owe them. Today, I have done very well, and I am not taking back any old unsold stock. It is very important to be able to choose the right goods that you feel will be sold well. Besides, I do not charge my customers any more than is reasonable for me to pay my debts, and have a good life. You cannot afford to be greedy as a businessman."

Mustafa nodded as he listened carefully to the driver's advice. Soon, they arrived at a small stop off point where both Rustum and the driver could get some rest, and have their mid-morning snacks. Rustum was freed from his shackles of the harness that secured him to the cart, and began to tuck into a bale of freshly cut grass. The driver beckoned Mustafa to join him for some welcome snacks and *chai*.

"So, what else can you tell me about Allahabad?" asked Mustafa, as he took a seat on the roadside bench of the *chaat house*.

The driver, a slim man in his twenties, stroked the mall stubble on his chin with the fingers of his left hand, and said, "I do not know about history, but it is a very famous city that was built way back in time. It used to be known as Prayag, because it is the place where the great Ganga, Yamuna and the unseen Saraswati rivers meet. Even Lord Rama stayed at the ashram of Sant Bhardwaj, which is in Allahabad."

Mustafa said, "Yes, I have heard of the great Hindu pilgrimages, and I think that this year happens to be the time of the Maha Kumbh Mela, which occurs only once every twelve years. But we did not see many pilgrims along our route."

The driver said, "This is because they are already at the *Sangam*, and are preparing for the mad rush to plunge into the cold water at the meeting point of the rivers. If you are lucky, you may be able to reach this point, and bathe there. I hope to do so on this trip, and pray that I would be cleansed of all my sins, and be able to start a new life."

Mustafa took a sip of his *chai*, and turned to the driver, saying, "But I am a Muslim, and the only place of pilgrimage for me is Mecca in Arabia. I would not be allowed to do this at the Mela."

The driver smiled, and said, "Do not worry. People from all religions go there. It is a truly spiritual experience, and also very special to be there on such a historic occasion."

Rustum rudely interrupted the discussion by snorting loudly enough as if to attract the driver's attention, and to signal that he had finished his meal. The driver sprang up immediately, and took a bucket of clean water for the bull. He patted the left side of the animal's thick set neck, as Rustum lowered his huge mouth into the bucket, and began to noisily slurp the water, until he drank most of it.

"Well, we must get on our way," said the driver, as he lured Rustum back to his position between the arms of the cart, and securely buckled the harness over the broad back of the animal. He then invited Mustafa back on board, and smiled as the young man took care to avoid Rustum's large rear end.

The driver hopped on board, and prodded Rustum forward. This time the pace was a lot more sedate, as everyone seemed to prefer allowing their meals to settle down in their stomachs. As they approached the great city of Allahabad, there were more carts, elephants, camels, walking pilgrims and other people ahead, stirring up a large cloud of dust. The noise was also very loud, as animals and humans seemed to compete with each other, to be heard. Some *Saadhus* lined the way towards the *Sangam*, showing off their different approaches to sacrifice and worship.

There were completely naked *Saadhus*, covered in grey ash, with long matted hair. Some stood on one leg only, and others were in elaborate contortions of legs and arms locked together. Some had moustaches which had never been shaved. Others smoked what appeared to be some kind of exotic grassy drug, and exhaled large clouds of smoke that temporarily engulfed them, and all who were standing or passing nearby.

People paused by some *Saadhus*, and sought special predictions from ancient scrolls of astronomical readings and charts. One *Saadhu* showed his incredible strength by lifting an iron bar with only his bare teeth. Another stood on his head whilst balancing a heavy iron pot on the soles of his feet, and did not blink or move, as the throngs passed by.

The driver skilfully steered Rustum, and the cart through the massive crowd until he found a suitable spot to secure them. Mustafa hugged the driver, and thanked him for the lift.

He then turned to Rustum and gently stroked the animal's neck. Rustum seemed to appreciate this gesture, and he gently lowered his head as if he was bowing to his master. They then parted company, and Mustafa carefully avoided bumping into any one as he headed towards the *bazaar* area of the city.

Mustafa marvelled at the impressive stone buildings which seemed to cover a vast area ahead. He admired the beautifully carved arches and windows of the living quarters, and the ornate sculptures of various religious characters and scenes from ancient Hindu epics. The streets were all cobbled, and well worn over centuries of traffic by people, livestock, and carts.

He slowed down to look at the colourfully decorated shops and stalls of the *bazaar*. There was an impressive array of goods for sale, including freshly made garlands of yellow and orange marigolds, statues of all sizes of the various Hindu deities and their consorts, such as Lord Rama and Sita, Lord Krishna and Radha, Lord Shiva and Parvati, and many more. There was also, a vast collection of saffron-coloured shawls, and other multi-coloured robes. He marvelled at the displays of assorted Indian sweets, multi-coloured bangles, gold and silver bracelets, various food grains, succulent and juicy fruits, and other items which the pilgrims and other visitors were keen to purchase. He noted how spiritual and material pursuits seemed to co-exist, side by side.

He felt that the *bazaar* presented him with the best opportunity to find a job, and to settle into the city. So, he quickly moved from one stall to the next, asking for a job, but to his great surprise, he failed to obtain an offer. Perhaps his luck would change if he took a ceremonial bath in the holy rivers, alongside the other pilgrims.

Mustafa obtained a saffron-coloured turban and shawl, and made his way towards the long lines of people waiting to walk towards the waters' edge. Without warning, he found himself pushed along with a massive surge of people, and ran into the swirling water, which was very cold. He dipped his head below the surface of the water, and as he emerged, his turban had disappeared up stream.

Mustafa was now shivering with cold, and turned to make a quick exit back up the slope he had just hurtled down from. He narrowly avoided being caught up with the waves of pilgrims rushing downwards, and was mightily relieved when he finally reached the safety at the top of the river bank.

He walked purposefully away from the enthusiastic crowds of pilgrims, and headed towards a part of the city that appeared to be more tranquil. He felt very relieved to be away from the mayhem, but he was still feeling very cold. He needed to get his sodden clothes dried as soon as possible, and to find a place to stay, before nightfall.

Mustafa approached a clothing merchant, and asked him for a job so that he could buy new clothes, and a pair of new sandals. The man generously obliged as he saw the young man becoming more uncomfortable.

"You can have any new clothes you wish, young man. You have been truly blessed by the sacred waters of the *Sangam*, and it is also a good omen for me to offer you these clothes as a way of sharing in your good fortune." The merchant pointed Mustafa to the multiple choices of headwear, shawls, shirts, *dhotis*, and sandals.

Mustafa made his selection, and quickly put on his new outfit after abandoning his tired-looking, wet, and ragged clothes and sandals. Unfortunately for him, he was not able to secure a job with the merchant, and after thanking him, he continued with his search. He moved on towards the less crowded area of the city. As he strolled past the magnificent new Christian Church, called The Holy Trinity, which was opened about four years prior, he was approached by a young Englishman.

"Hello young fellow," said the Englishman.

"Are you speaking to me?" asked a surprised Mustafa, as such a polite contact was unusual between the new English masters and the local Indians.

The Englishman said, "Yes, I noticed that you were interested in our new Church. Why don't you come in and have a look?"

Mustafa was a little hesitant as to whether or not he should take up such an offer. He looked up at the impressive spire, and scanned the robust outer stone walls of the magnificent building. The concreted pointing that showed off the well carved stonework was much neater than any other religious buildings he had seen. The grassy surrounds looked a bit tired, and in need of a good trim.

The Englishman was about six feet tall, of slim build, and red in the face due to exposure to the hot climate of Allahabad, and the less comfortable clothes he was wearing. Mustafa accepted the invitation, and followed the Englishman, taking care not to walk ahead of his host.

The Englishman said, "My name is John Turner, and I work for the local priest here."

Mustafa replied, "My name is Mustafa Ali, and I am looking for some work. I notice that your garden around the Church needs to be cleared and looked after. Do you have a gardener?"

John Turner said, "Well actually, this is the main reason why I stopped you. I noticed that you are carrying a grass knife, and I assumed that you might be a labourer or gardener."

Mustafa looked up to catch the eyes of his host, and said, "Yes, I am a labourer, and I know a lot about gardening, weeding, planting and harvesting. I can even do drains. I would love to do this work for you at a good fee, including a clean and safe place to stay."

"You also seem to be able to drive a good deal, my friend," said John Turner with an ironic smile.

Mustafa said, "Oh, and I will need some helpers as this job is very big. I mean, that by the time I trim one end of the churchyard, and get to the other end, it will all grow back. If I have at least one assistant weeder, we can keep on top of this, and the churchyard will look clean and beautiful at all times."

John Turner was duly impressed by Mustafa's commonsense, and ability to argue his case. He wondered whether he was doing the right thing to offer the job to this smart young man, lest he should become more than a handful in the future.

He said, "You can start today if you wish, and I will show you where you can stay. We do have another young man who could become your assistant. But you must promise me that you will not over-burden him with all the work whilst you look on as his boss, and foreman."

John Turner then led Mustafa up the short walkway through the huge and imposing neatly carved wooden front door of the Church. Mustafa bowed slightly as he entered the cool, silent space, passing the rows of neatly carved wooden benches that faced the ornate, and beautifully decorated pulpit. He marvelled at the multi-coloured stained glass windows depicting scenes of religious importance.

"John *Sahib*, can anyone come in here to pray?" asked Mustafa, quietly.

John Turner said, "No. Not everyone. Only if you are a Christian. But you can come here to visit, and when you have learnt about our Lord Jesus Christ, you may wish to become a Christian, and worship here."

Mustafa decided not to enter into a religious debate, particularly as he did not wish to cause any misunderstanding with his new boss. John Turner arranged for him to meet Peter Thomas and his wife Mary that very afternoon. Mustafa accepted the offer to board with the young Indian family in their lodgings attached to the Church. Peter agreed to act as Mustafa's assistant in the garden and grounds of the Church. He and his wife were very humble and friendly Christians who had only recently been converted from Hinduism.

The young couple were in their twenties, and seemed to be very content and happy with their new way of life, serving the Church, and its growing community. They were both quietly spoken, with good English which they were learning from priests at the Church, and at "Sunday School", which took place after the regular Sunday morning worship. They were proud to have been baptised and married at the Church, and fortunate to have jobs with accommodation there. Mary worked as an *aaya* to John Turner and his family, whilst Peter was learning to become the gardener.

Mustafa spent that first evening conversing with his new acquaintances, and tried to discover as much as he could about the couple, and how they were being treated by John Turner, and other members of the Church. Peter and Mary shared their much anticipated supper with Mustafa, before they all retired to their respective rooms. Mustafa confirmed with Peter and Mary that he could read his *namaaz* within their home, and was very impressed with their calm religious tolerance.

Early next morning, Peter and Mustafa walked around the churchyard after having had their breakfast. They agreed on who would undertake each task, the times for taking breaks for rest and meals, and, how Mustafa would report on progress to John Turner. They then launched into the huge task of weeding the overgrown lawn areas.

Mustafa was happy with Peter's commitment to the task, his good standard of weeding, and the efficient approach to clearing up the cut grass and other rubbish. Within the first week, they managed to produce a very clean garden around the perimeter of the Church. It was much admired by John Turner and the congregation. Indeed, it became fashionable for the Church members who were mostly English, to stroll around the newly maintained garden, admiring the plants, flowers, shrubs, and neatly trimmed grass. Mustafa and Peter were shown much appreciation and respect for their dedication, and hard work.

Mustafa began to feel very settled in, and satisfied with his new environment. One Sunday morning, he was very surprised to be invited by John Turner, to join Peter and Mary, and the other members of the Church, for Sunday worship. Mustafa was taken aback by this apparent change of stance by John Turner. He was not asked about conversion to Christianity, and did not know about the Christian prayers and hymns.

He was greeted at the main door as all the members of the congregation, and felt a sense of pride as he took his place near the back of the Church, alongside Peter and Mary.

Peter showed Mustafa how to follow the proceedings, and assured him not to worry about the actual prayers and the singing.

Mustafa found some difficulty in understanding the English spoken by the Priest, whose voice boomed out along with a chilling echo through the vast ceiling and walls of the building. The singing of the hymns was also new to him, and he listened quietly. At the end of the service, John Turner invited Mustafa to his room, and offered him some tea with English scones.

"Well my friend," began John, "I must say to you, that I have been very pleased with your work, and the way you have contributed to the maintenance of the Church grounds. Everyone has been very complimentary about this, and even Peter has said that he enjoys working for you, and being in your company."

"Thank you, John *Sahib*," replied Mustafa bowing slightly, with his hands clasped in respect. "I am happy with Peter and Mary who have treated me very well. I regard Mary as my sister."

John Turner stroked his small, neatly trimmed greying beard, and said, "I am keen to keep you here for as long as I can, and would like to know whether you needed anything more from me or the Church, to make things better for you."

Mustafa continued to be very surprised, and impressed by John Turner's wholesome attitude towards him. This was his first encounter and relationship with one of the new masters, and seemed to run contrary to the impressions he had been given until that moment. He felt at ease with John Turner, and was prepared to trust him implicitly.

He said, "John *Sahib*, thank you very much. I am quite happy here, and I am not short of anything. But, since you asked, will you allow me to continue to attend for English lessons at the Sunday school? Peter and Mary have helped me to improve my reading, writing and speaking in English. This has helped me to speak to everyone who comes to the Church, especially about the garden."

"I hope that you do realise that in order for you to do so, you will need to be baptised as a Christian. Will you be prepared to do so?" asked a smiling John Turner.

"John *Sahib*, I already believe in Jesus Christ as a Prophet of Islam. We Muslims know him as Esa. Besides, I do not agree with yet another conversion. My ancestors were all Hindus before they were forced to become Muslims by the Moghul invaders," reasoned Mustafa.

John Turner listened to the young man intently, and could not help feeling some empathy towards him. He said, "Mustafa, our Church offers everyone a new and peaceful way to worship God. No one is forced to become Christian against his wishes. We try to look after all our members of this grand Church. You can see how Peter and Mary are happy and content with their lives. As you already have so much love for Jesus or Esa, you should have no problem in accepting the Christian way."

"John *Sahib*," interrupted Mustafa. "You say this with sincerity, but your whole aim is to convert us all to Christianity, and to make our country English. I already respect our Hindu traditions, our Sikh peacefulness, and I am proud of my Muslim upbringing. I believe in tolerance towards all religions of the one God."

John Turner knew that his attempt at converting Mustafa would be very difficult to achieve, but was not prepared to give up at this stage. He said, "I hear what you say, and as an exception, I will grant you your wish to continue to attend the school. But I have to tell you that you will not only be learning English there. You will be taught a lot about Christianity."

"Thank you, John *Sahib*. I do not mind learning more about Christianity, but I will never accept conversion," said Mustafa firmly, but with a wry smile.

6.

The Recruiting Agent

Sundar Das was a short, thin Bengali man of very dark complexion, who lived alone in rented accommodation just about two hundred yards from the Bhawanipore Depot in the City of Calcutta, in the State of Bengal. He took great pride in wearing a saffron coloured *dhoti*, smart black leather shoes, and used a finely polished walking stick. He sported a large, carefully groomed moustache which made him appear to be much older than his thirty years. He strode with an air of confidence bordering on arrogance.

He was delighted to hear that, after a few years of the suspension of the shipping of Indian indentured labourers to the then colony of British Guiana on the mainland of South America, the recruitment of workers was to be sanctioned to re-commence in early 1845. He was after all, a very successful Recruiting Agent for the initial shipment that took place in 1838.

At that time, he had quickly learned the art of persuasion, and was able to recruit members of the Dhangar tribes from Chhota Nagpur in the hilly areas of West Bengal. These comprised a fair proportion of the people who were enticed to enter into contracts to leave India, and to work on the sugar plantations in the colony. The others were from the villages nearer to the Depot. The Dhangar people were called "Hill Coolies".

Sundar Das employed much cunning, and targeted potential recruits in places such as the *melas* and in the *bazaars* of the City. He spun a tale of great promise for his victims, of light work, decent accommodation, good food, clean clothing, free medical care, friendly bosses, and above all, much better pay than they were used to as labourers on the sugar plantations in India. The recruits would have to travel to the colony by ship on a free passage, and had the option to return to India whenever they chose to do so. He did not elaborate on the vast distance by sea, the length of time for the voyage, and the conditions they would face on the journey, and on the plantations.

The Dhangars were of low caste, and were poorly regarded by their compatriots. Their clothing always seemed to be dirty, and they were not regular bathers. They came down from the hills looking for any kind of work, and were willing to accept low pay, offers of food, and places to sleep. They were easily impressed by Sundar Das's upright stature, and convincing language. He used his cane as an instrument to emphasise his speech, and would make a point of speaking loudly in order to attract more listeners who may happen to be passing by. No sooner had he started his session, a small crowd of potential victims would assemble, and listen intently with some respect.

He was confident enough to allow the listeners time to consider his offer, and to return to hear more if they were interested. Those who returned to listen to him would be more willing to accept his proposition, and they were the clients Sundar Das waited for with some relish. He duly returned to his chosen podium in the *bazaar* only two days after his first session. To his great surprise, the audience which was made up mostly of the Dhangars, almost doubled in number. There was a considerable amount of animated discussion amongst the crowd, and he tried to call them to order by tapping his walking stick firmly on the wooden soapbox that he stood on.

"My good friends and gentle listeners, *Namaste* to you all!" shouted Sundar, as he drew attention from his audience. "I am truly happy to see so many of you here today. Obviously, you must be very interested in what I said two days ago. The offer of work in the colonies of British Guiana and Mauritius, is very attractive, and better than any of you or I have seen in this State."

At this point, a tall, dark and angry looking younger Dhangar tribesman stepped forward as if he was formally nominated to speak on the crowd's behalf.

He said, "You are lying to us! I have been to British Guiana. I can tell you that everything about this work, and our contract was bad."

Sundar Das was taken aback, and tried to respond immediately, but the Dhangar spokesman and the crowd would not let him prevail. The young man continued, "First of all, we were treated like animals on the ship. There was no good food, no proper water to drink, a lot of punishment from the white sailors, who hated us. Many of us were sick as soon as we were on the ship. There was no doctor and no medicines for us. Many people died, and when this happened they were just thrown into the sea. The white men beat us for everything. We were feeling very bad, and sad to leave our homeland."

The crowd listened intently, and fixed their angry gazes on Sundar, which made him become more visibly nervous. He decided not to stop the spokesman for fear of antagonising the crowd more than they were already displaying.

The Dhangar spokesman continued, "When we reached British Guiana, after weeks on the sea, we were put in groups, and sent off to different places. We lost some of our friends, and we became more frightened than when we were together on the ship. I went to a place called Vreed-en-Hoop, and let me tell you, we were very badly treated there. Two of our friends ran away across the big river, and we never heard what happened to them."

Sundar looked on, and kept shaking his head from side to side, trying to express great empathy with the spokesman, and with the crowd. The spokesman continued, "The place was very hot, with a lot of nasty insects biting us all over our bodies, day and night. There were large red ants, lots of sand flies, and worst of all, vicious mosquitoes which made us all very sick. This was very bad for us even though we have flies and mosquitoes here in our country. We had no proper houses to live in, no comfortable beds, and the food rations were always a problem for us. The work was not easy for the men and the few women who were with us. Many of our men died there every year. We were very lucky to come back to India. Why do you ask us to go there again?"

This gave Sundar a welcome opportunity to respond as best he could. He needed to be very careful with his answer, and it had to be convincing.

He said, clasping his hands together as if in prayer, "My friends, I am so sorry to hear of this bad experience. I have also heard these stories before, and let me say that I was very angry with the English *Sahibs*, and told them that I will never work for them again unless they can properly honour everything they now promise. It was because of such bad experiences that they had to stop shipping our people abroad. They have now made new arrangements for us before we go on such journeys again."

"So what are they offering us now? How can they improve on the treatment they gave our people?" asked the spokesman amidst a huge volume of collective groans from the crowd.

Sundar said, "First of all, no one will be forced to take up a contract to work if they do not want to do this. Anyone who wants to go, will be properly examined by a doctor at the Depot, and will not be allowed to travel unless they are very fit. You will receive good provisions whilst you wait to travel, and for the whole journey at sea. A doctor will also travel on the ship with you, and you will be well looked after. When you reach the country you are going to, you will be given better treatment."

Neither the spokesman nor the crowd was convinced by Sundar's new offer, and demanded to hear more. "And what about people like you, who kidnapped our people and forced them to take this contract?" asked the spokesman, shouting above an encouraging "Haa!" from the crowd.

"My friends, I am not one of those agents who behaved so badly. Anyone who does this from now on, will be severely punished by our courts," promised Sundar, as the crowd erupted in mocking laughter. By now, the audience had grown even larger, and the Dhangars were outnumbered by the locals.

Sundar was quite worried as the crowd became more aggressive towards him. He knew that he had failed to convince them about the new promise of better treatment. However, he decided to persevere, and not to give up on his potential earnings. He knew that if interest from the Dhangars waned, he would have to work on the local villagers in Bengal, Bihar, and even further west, in Uttar Pradesh. He started to plot his moves to recruit from amongst the agricultural working gangs in these States. The better targets would be the younger, fitter men who had experience of working on sugar plantations, and were used to being away from their families for weeks and months at a time.

Sundar continued to speak after the spokesman raised his arms and pleaded with the crowd to stop laughing, and to listen. "Please believe me when I say that this time, I will only ask people who really want to do this work. I will make sure that you are given the best protection. No one will take advantage of you. I will go now, and if any of you wish to join me, I will pass by here tomorrow morning. *Namaste* to you all."

Sundar then quietly slipped away from the mocking crowd, and returned to his lodgings. After helping himself to a good meal of *roti* and fish curry, he packed some clothing in a small case, and spent the rest of the day relaxing, and thinking about his new recruitment tactics.

Very early the next morning, he met his landlord, and paid him some additional rent for the next three months, and thus secured his tenancy for his return from his new recruiting mission. He was careful not to disclose to anyone where he was heading to, and the nature of his business. Recruiting Agents tended to be very secretive, and kept very few friends, if any. Sundar Das was no exception. No one knew where he came from, who he was, and most importantly, what he did for a living.

He picked up his case and walking stick, and strode confidently away from his home towards the *bazaar* area in the hope that new recruits would be waiting for him. As he slipped past the deserted podium of his last speech, he began to relax, and his pace slackened into a more measured stride. After another fifty yards, he noticed someone walking briskly towards him, and he suddenly recognised the person as the spokesman of the Dhangars. Sundar could not avoid the man who stopped just in front of him, and raised his right hand to signal his wish to speak to him.

"*Namaste*, my friend," said Sundar nervously.

"*Namaste*. You did not give me and my people a chance to tell you more about our sufferings in British Guiana. I was one of those people badly beaten in Vreed-en-Hoop, Demerara, for complaining about our conditions there. We were being driven to work as if we were African slaves, for very long hours every day. We were never given much rest, and sometimes we were made to work for extra days."

Sundar noticed the spokesman's eyes beginning to well up with tears, as his hurt became more visible. He placed a calming hand over the man's shoulders, and tried to assure him that he also felt his pain. The spokesman took off his shirt, and showed Sundar the gruesome markings left by the lashes he received on his back.

He said, "You see, these marks were bleeding by the time the white man stopped lashing me with his cat-o-nine tails. Every lash opened up new cuts on my back and arms. But I am a strong and proud man, and I did not scream or cry like the others. Then when he finished lashing me, I fainted as they untied me from the post under his house.

They took me to the sick house, and there again I saw our people being treated like dogs. Some of them were being forced to eat meat against their religion."

Sundar was also visibly upset by the young man's account, and he offered him some comfort by saying, "I am so very sorry to hear about this, and I will make sure that the authorities who run the ships are told the truth. This must not be allowed to happen again."

The young man persisted, "But why are you still trying to help the white man to do this to our people? Why do you not stop taking us to that wretched place? Everyone who came back from that hell, do not want to go there ever again. Nor do we want any others to do so."

Sundar shrugged his shoulders, and sighed heavily. Then he made the spokesman an offer.

"I feel for you my friend. Perhaps the only way you can help to change this attitude, is to join me, and work for me to recruit the best and most suitable workers to take up the new offer. I will pay you very well."

The young man paused for a moment, and was quite surprised by Sundar's offer. He stretched out his right hand, and shook Sundar's hand with a firmness that emphasised his sheer brute strength. Sundar winced from the handshake, and said, "Oh! Thank you. I promise to look after you, and you will see that things will change for the better for all who take up the new offer. By the way, what is your name?"

"My name is Mohan Lall," answered the young man, thrusting out his large chest with great pride.

" Mohan, my name is Sundar Das. We can become a good team which can make a lot of money, and even employ more helpers in the future. Let us go and get a few things we will need for our journey."

Mohan Lall nodded, and started to walk beside his new boss feeling very important through his new status. Sundar kept quiet for a while, and thought of how he will manage this unplanned change to his strategy. He looked across to Mohan and as their eyes met, they both smiled at each other.

7.

Diwali in the City of Lights

It was October in 1844 when Mustafa finally reached Varanasi, after having spent most of the last year at the Holy Trinity Church, tending the garden and doing odd jobs as a caretaker. He developed a better command of English through the Church's Sunday School, and had learnt a lot more about Christianity. However, John Turner had failed to convert him to Christianity, and instead, the two became very close friends. His keepers, Peter and Mary Thomas became more established members of the Church, and were particularly saddened by Mustafa's decision to leave, and to continue his quest for betterment elsewhere.

Mustafa was always intrigued about Varanasi, the City of Lights. It became a magnet for him, and he wanted to know why the city was the holiest place for Hindus, and also attracted other pilgrims including Buddhists, Sikhs, Jains and Muslims. It was known to be the oldest continuously occupied city in the world at that time. Can there be a more spiritual place than Allahabad?

He took every opportunity to talk to fellow travellers along the Grand Trunk Road, and was told to expect great wonders, and surprises in Varanasi. Hindus would give up all their material wealth and other attachments, to die, and be cremated at one of the great *ghats* beside the River Ganges which flowed past the city. They believed that they would attain instant *moksha* or enlightenment. The very old, and widows of all ages, would go to Varanasi to spend their final days in deep meditation or yoga, to perform daily ritual bathing at the *ghats*, and to listen to sacred recitations of ancient texts in the enchanting Temples.

The stone *ghats* at Varanasi stretched along the entire waterfront, and whilst some were gradually eroding, most remained in better condition, and were well used by the worshippers. The believers regarded the waters that flowed in the Ganges as holy *amrit*, and despite the presence of many pollutants, this never deterred them from dipping their whole bodies several times in one session.

The pilgrims would enter into a spiritual tour of the five most important *ghats* of the Panchtirthi Yatra, or five crossings. These were the Asi, the Dash, the Manikarnaka, the Panchganga, and the Adi Keshava. At the Asi *ghat*, the River Asi flowed into the River Ganges, and the pilgrims would perform a ritual bath followed by an offer of prayers at the imposing smoothly carved stone *shivalingam* which represented the source of creation. The Manikarnaka *ghat* was larger than the others, and was the main cremation ground. The dead were placed on carefully assembled funeral pyres made of wooden logs, and set quickly alight through the use of camphor which also helped to significantly reduce the unwelcome smell of the burning corpses. The crackling fires produced plumes of dark smoke which lifted into the air, and was then blown away in the direction of the sacred river's waves. The pilgrims would offer prayers, and then move onto the other four *ghats* of their holy trail.

The Panchganga *ghat* was the site of the baptism of Kabir, the Sufi saint, who was venerated by Hindus and Muslims. Overlooking the *ghat*, was the Mosque of Alamgir which was built by Aurangzeb, the Moghul Emperor, over the remains of an ancient Vishnu Temple. Beside the Adi Keshava *ghat*, or the "Original Vishnu", the River Varuna flowed serenely into the River Ganges. This inspirational journey from the River Asi to the River Varuna, through the five *ghats*, represented the true spirit of Varanasi, and of personal fulfilment.

The original Kashi Vishwanath Temple, known as the "Golden Temple", because of its gold-plated spire, was then visited by the pilgrims. Prayers were offered at the Jyotirlinga, through which Lord Shiva, the Hindu's Master of the Creation, demonstrated his majesty over all.

Mustafa, upon arrival in Varanasi, entered the narrow winding streets that were populated with every semblance of Hindu worship, and devotion. *Saadhus* and Pandits were offering sessions of palmistry, astrological readings, herbal cures for aches and pains, mystical recitations to ward off evil spirits, and, prayers to cure mental depression. There were also Muslim *Fakirs* who were either begging or offering their own brand of treatment for physical and mental ills.

Some men were collecting money to buy logs for the cremation pyres, as they cried out loudly to show their deep pain at losing their loved ones. Upon receiving a sizeable amount of mostly silver coins, they would securely tie this with their cotton kerchiefs or towels, and disappear from the area. Mustafa noticed this after falling prey to the trickery, and then tried his utmost to resist giving any more money to other beggars along his way to the riverside.

He found himself periodically ducking to avoid the large flocks of pigeons which would sweep up and down in their majestic flight formations from the rooftops of the houses along the way. The *kabootar baz* who owned the racing pigeons, were proud of their control and influence on their prized assets.

Mustafa continued his tour, and he was amazed at the large numbers of monkeys allowed to roam freely around the vicinity of the Temples. The pilgrims seemed to be able to go about their business, unaffected by the crazy antics of the animals. They kept their food well hidden, to avoid the attention of the thieving monkeys who were expert at snatching any items of interest without being caught. However, no one did them any harm because they were regarded as sacred animals in the Hindu religion. The epic *Ramayan* recounts how the monkeys were the army of Shri Hanuman, who helped Lord Raam to defeat the villainous Raavan, and rescue his consort Sita from the villain's clutches.

As the day began to draw to a close, Mustafa could see the beautiful spectacle of the large full moon reflecting a darkened red hue as it took its place over the calm waters of the River Ganges. Then, as the sun finally disappeared, the glorious lights of the clay *diyas* and lamps flickered all along the riverbanks. Some of the lit *diyas* were placed carefully on the water where they floated off, bobbing along gently into the distance. There were thousands more lit *diyas* and lamps placed in the windows, and door ledges of all the city's Mandirs, Mosques and dwellings. Varanasi thus became the delightful City of Lights.

It was the time of the *Diwali* Festival of Lights, and many more pilgrims and visitors such as Mustafa, were out and about offering sweets to each other. During this festival, the Hindus celebrate the triumphal return of Lord Raam and Sita, to the Holy City of Ayodhya after the defeat of the mighty villain Raavan. The residents of Ayodhya lit the rows of *diyas* to allow Lord Raam and his party to see their way much more clearly through the darkness of the evening.

Mustafa found shelter in a small room in one of the blocks of houses away from the riverside, and was able to witness the new dawn. A beautiful red sun steadily rose over the River Ganges. Soon, the flickering lights of the diyas and lamps gave way to the brighter and warmer rays of the great life-giver. Everyone, regardless of their faith, paid homage and welcomed in the new day as others had done for thousands of years.

Varanasi was symbolic of a vivid representation of contrasts; of life and death, of sunlight and moonlight, of the pious and the trickster, of the washed and the unwashed.

Mustafa offered his *namaaz*, ate a light breakfast, and sat quietly on the weathered stone step of the Panchganga *ghat*. He reflected on his journey away from his beloved Chandini, how he nearly succumbed to the charms of Sita, his spiritual encounter as a mistaken Holy Man, his ritual cleansing at the Sangam, and his exposure to Christianity in Allahabad. Varanasi was a good place to stop, and to take stock of one's life. However, his experience of the city would not be one of finality as it was for many of the pilgrims. He realised that his personal mission to make his fortune, could not end in the mysterious Varanasi.

Diwali also marked the start of a new year in the Hindu tradition. People had cleaned their homes, wore new clothes, and lit their *diyas* and lamps to welcome in Maa Lakshmi, the Goddess of Wealth, into their lives. Devotees performed *pooja* to Maa Lakshmi, seeking the end of darkness, and welcoming the goodness that light brought. Mustafa also benefitted from the generosity of a rich merchant who gave him some new clothes, a sweet shop owner who donated food and sweets, and, another who offered him a job. He humbly declined the latter, as he had intended to move on from the city. As soon as the day began to cool down in the later part of the afternoon, he set out once again on his journey.

He had become a stronger person, bigger in build, and fitter both physically and mentally. He also appeared to be more confident, and less fearful of anyone, and any challenge. The Grand Trunk Road was much busier with many other travellers heading in either direction. Obtaining a free ride was thus more difficult, as more people were competing for limited spaces on the bullock carts. Mustafa bided his time, and made his move when he saw the best opportunity approaching.

The bullock cart stood out most impressively from the others. It was longer, with four wheels, and had a robust roof to provide shelter from the elements. It also had two wooden benches secured at the opposite sides of its tray. At the front, a *Saadhu* like figure sat beside the driver who was often striking at the rears of the two bullocks, encouraging them to make better progress. Mustafa spotted some space on the two benches, and timed his mount onto the moving vehicle, to perfection. He found a seat next to a dark and muscular young man who did not object to the stranger's claim. There were fourteen other passengers who turned to look at the newcomer.

Sundar Das looked at Mustafa, and then at Mohan Lall who was sitting beside the young man. The driver cracked his whip against the thick sides of the two bullocks, and the cart lurched forward causing all the passengers to bump into each other before they settled back into their positions. Varanasi, the City of Lights, slowly faded into the distance as the cart moved further away.

8.

Terms of Engagement

The bullock cart, with its passengers, made considerable progress along the Grand Trunk Road, well into the State of Bihar. It stopped in order to give the animals and the driver some well deserved rest. The passengers climbed off the vehicle in an orderly manner, and stood silently alongside each other, beside the road.

Sundar Das and Mohan Lall approached the passengers whilst the driver unshackled the bullocks, and took them for their meal of freshly cut grass and some water. Mustafa noticed that there was one young woman amongst the other passengers, and she appeared to be very nervous. Sundar Das spoke quietly to her, "My *didi*, are you well? Please follow me to have something to eat and drink."

Without replying, the young woman immediately followed him towards the *chaat house*. Mohan Lall then asked the men to do likewise, and they all retired to the establishment which was very similar to the one that Mustafa had worked in. The air was filled with the enticing, and irresistible aroma of the spicy food on offer.

Sundar Das, standing proudly with his left hand on his hip, and his cane touching the hard ground, said, "My friends, please eat and drink as much as you want. I am paying for everything, and I want you all to be happy, and to feel strong. We still have a long journey ahead of us before we reach a better resting place in Calcutta."

Mustafa, upon hearing this, interrupted Sundar, "Excuse me. I have only taken a ride with you all, and I am not one of your party. So, if you do not mind, I will pay for my meal and if you wish, I will also give you some money for the ride. I do not know who you are, and I do not know your business."

Sundar looked at Mustafa closely, and said, "I am Sundar Das. My assistant, Mohan Lall and I, work for a Recruiting Agent in Calcutta. We have found these young and agreeable men, and woman, who are willing and very happy to travel with us to Bhawanipore Depot in

Calcutta. They will join a ship that will take them to work overseas for good money."

Mustafa said, "I have heard people talking about this contract, and how they have been treated badly by you, and your masters."

Sundar said, "So have I, my friend. So have I. But let me tell you that my assistant here has been to British Guiana, and just look at him now. True, he was mistreated but he now feels that things will certainly change for the better. The new arrangements and contract are to be put in place to make sure that no one suffers as those people who had travelled in the first ships. I see that you carry a grass-knife. Are you also a labourer looking for work?"

Mustafa replied, "If everything is so good, then show me the contract, and I will determine whether the offer is good or not."

Sundar Das was taken aback by Mustafa's apparent arrogance and forthrightness. He had never encountered a potential recruit who could read English, and who was also prepared to look at the details of the contract.

Sundar said, "Let us all settle down to have our meal, and to rest for a while. Then we can discuss the labour contract with each other. I want you to appreciate that this is a good deal for all concerned, and it is much better than previous arrangements."

Mustafa listened intently, and decided to take up Sundar's offer of a free meal, and the rest. Mohan Lall returned from his strenuous effort of helping the driver with securing the bullocks to a sturdy post, and providing them with their refreshments.

Mustafa was encouraged to sit with Sundar, Mohan and the driver, whilst the others sat at a larger table, sharing food from two trays of rice, *daal*, vegetable curries, and yoghurt. They then quenched their thirsts with some cool water.

Sundar Das said, "So tell me, young man. Who are you, and are you looking for work?"

Mustafa said, "My name is Mustafa Ali. Yes, I am an experienced labourer, and come from a village near to Kanpur in Uttar Pradesh. I want a good job that will give me regular pay, so that I could save enough money to go back home, and look after my family."

Sundar smiled, and said, "I am very proud of young people like you. You see, all my people here have the same kind of hopes and wishes. I promise you that you will never regret joining them, and you will achieve much more than you have ever dreamt of."

Mohan Lall and the driver nodded in approval. However, Mustafa was determined to extract more information from Sundar, and he was not prepared to be deflected. He pressed on with his enquiry, "Please tell us more about what is on offer for this job."

Sundar looked around at all his recruits, and said, "The contract is for five years, and for labouring work on the sugar plantations in British Guiana or Mauritius. You will only have to do light work for a set number of hours each day. You get a good break for food and drink, and the pay is very good."

Mustafa interrupted Sundar and said, "Forgive me, but you are still not giving me enough detail about this contract. I think that you may be hiding something."

Sundar kept his composure and said, "My friend, everyone will receive good medical checks and care before they are allowed to leave Calcutta. Then they will get good food on board their ship. When they reach British Guiana or Mauritius, they will get a weekly allowance of food provisions, some blankets, some clothes, and utensils. Most of these people here with me, do not have these basic things right now. They are hungry, are ill-treated by their *Zamindars*, and they are forced to leave their homes and families, in order to find good work, money and betterment. So, why are you so adamant, and still cannot see how good this offer is?"

Mustafa asked, "What about the pay?"

Sundar replied, "The rate is five rupees per month, and this is way above the two paisa per day you earn here in India, if and when you get work. This contract gives you steady work for five years, and at the end of that period of time, you can get a free passage back to Calcutta. Believe me, most of you will never want to return here to yearly floods, famines, and, other hardships imposed upon you by your *Zamindars*."

At last Mustafa felt that he had heard a reasonable argument for the contract, and nodded in approval. Sundar Das, Mohan Lall and the driver smiled at each other. The other passengers continued with their own animated conversations.

Shortly afterwards, a scuffle broke out amongst the men as one of them tried to grab the young woman in an uncompromising way. She resisted his over-zealous and physical approach, and shouted at him to let go of her. Two of the other men jumped on him, and wrestled him to the ground. The young woman ran off towards the shack beside the *chaat house*. Mohan Lall intervened, and soon had the fighting men under control. Sundar then stood up, and followed the young woman into the shack.

Mustafa preferred not to become involved in the brawl, but kept a close eye on Sundar's movements. He felt that Sundar, being the opportunist, was up to no good. About fifteen minutes later, Sundar emerged from the shack still trying to fix his loosened *dhoti* and ruffled hair. He tweaked his moustache as he sheepishly made his way past the onlookers, and took up his place at the front of the bullock cart.

Sundar said, "Mohan, get the bullocks ready, and let us prepare to move on."

Mohan and the driver obeyed their master, and hurriedly re-established the bullocks under their harnesses. They then ushered the passengers back onto their seats in the cart.

The young woman emerged from the shack, also nervously adjusting her *sari* and hair. She then took her place away from her protagonists, and sat beside Mustafa. She wiped away some tears from her dark eyes. After a while on the journey, Mustafa decided to speak to the young woman, and asked her, "Are you all right?"

She did not respond immediately, but after a short time, she said, "Yes, I am fine. What else can I say when I am alone amongst people who are only interested in abusing me. You men are all the same. You see someone like me, and you think that you can have your way with me."

Mustafa said, "I can assure you that I am not like the others. I am more concerned about why you are on this journey which will not be safe for us men, let alone someone like yourself."

"Thank you, *bhaiya*. I can see that you are a very respectable person. You seem to be very educated, especially in the way you were pressing him for the facts. My name is Ishani, and I lost my husband only one year ago."

Mustafa said, "I am so sorry."

Ishani continued, "I ran away from my in-laws who were insisting on me to do *sati* on my husband's funeral pyre. They never liked me, and blamed me for bringing bad luck to their family, who were all depending on my husband's earnings. I had to leave when they were all taking turns to abuse me, and beat me for things I never did. This man found me, and saved me from ending up as a prostitute in the *bazaar*. But I do not trust him. He also keeps forcing himself onto me every time he gets the chance."

Sundar turned around to look at his passengers, and said aloud, "My friends, we are going to stop over at Sasaram for a day or two! Then we will head for Bodhgaya, near to Gaya!"

Everyone seemed to ignore Sundar's announcement, and carried on with their conversations. Mustafa contemplated on how cleverly Sundar Das had manipulated the situation by giving the otherwise docile young men a drink of alcohol that helped to spark the commotion, whence he could "rescue" Ishani from their sexual harassment. He thought of confronting Sundar about his relationship with Ishani, but desisted as she had not complained about the incident. He felt that he needed to keep on the right side of Sundar and his henchmen, until the right moment presented itself.

The ride on the Grand Trunk Road continued to be very bumpy, and uncomfortable as the bullocks pulled the laden cart with all their combined might, and as fast as they could. Thankfully, the cart was full, and there was no reason to stop to pick up more passengers.

Sundar and Mohan took turns to look back into the cart to check that they had not lost any passenger as other recruiters had experienced on the journey to Calcutta. The agents would have people such as Mohan Lall, to remain amongst the workers, keeping their spirits up, and reinforcing the benefits of the contract. Some agents would "sell" their recruits to other agents, in order to cut their losses from runaways.

In order to lessen the utter boredom of the long and uncomfortable road journey on the bullock cart, one of the young men began singing a local Bhojpuri folk song to which the others provided choruses, clapping their hands in perfect unison. Then as soon as the first singer reached the end of his song, another would introduce a similarly familiar rendition. Mustafa and Ishani also joined in with the singing session, but Sundar Das, Mohan Lall and the driver did not, as they were not familiar with the folk songs of Uttar Pradesh and Bihar.

They did, however, offer some Bengali folk songs which were more melancholy in lyric, but quite melodious in tune. The others could only listen quietly until one of their own songs was introduced. Morale was clearly lifted for the passengers, and this became the normal pattern for each part of the remaining journey until the next stop.

9.

The paths to enlightenment

Progress of the bullock cart was very impressive, and Sundar Das decided to head straight to Bodhgaya, thus ignoring Sasaram. As they neared this traditional place of pilgrimage for Buddhists from all over India, Ceylon (Sri Lanka), Tibet and the wider world, a quiet calm descended upon Sundar. He was a Hindu, but also had a deep respect for Buddhism.

"My friends," said Sundar, "I am so proud to bring you to this place of enlightenment. This is where Gautam Budh sat under a *peepal* tree or *bodhi* tree for several days, and became the "Awakened One", the "Compassionate One", the "Light of the World", the "Supreme Buddha"!"

Everyone was quite surprised at Sundar's apparent new awakening, and particular interest in sharing his knowledge about Buddhism. They remained silent as if they were monks on the pilgrimage, and kept observing the constant movement of holy men around the Mahabodhi Temple complex.

"We must go and pay our respects to the Statue of Buddha in the Mahabodhi Temple, and this will give us new vitality that will help us on our own mission to betterment," announced Sundar, as the bullock cart drew to a halt. As soon as the bullocks were securely tied to a watering hole, everyone was invited to descend from the cart and follow Sundar, Mohan, and the driver. Mustafa walked beside Ishani as they made their way over the narrow cobbled stone streets leading to the Temple.

Although the ancient stonework of the Temple was quite impressive, the building and its surrounds were in need of much repair. The party passed by hundreds of saffron robed Buddhist monks sitting in quiet contemplation beneath and around the large *peepal* or *bodhi* tree. Its large spread of branches and leaves were extended to provide welcome cover from the searing heat of the sun.

The base of the Temple was large, and gave support to its magnificent tapered pyramid shaped spire. Four towers at the base provided a sense of great strength, and balance to the structure. The pilgrims were prostrating themselves around this large base, before slowly making their way over several stone steps, to offer obeisance to the statue of Buddha within the Temple.

Sundar and his party refrained from doing the prostrations, and walked silently in an orderly and single file, straight towards the statue. Here they bowed respectfully, with some uttering their own prayers. Mustafa simply nodded his head whilst clasping his hands, and moved on towards the exit. It was yet another moment of spiritual respect, and awareness that he was pleased to encounter on his journey.

"Mustafa!" called out Sundar. "Can you see how beautiful and peaceful this place is? We all have to suffer this cycle of birth, suffering and ultimate death. But Gautam Budh has shown us all how to escape this fate. We must overcome our egos to free ourselves from this terrible world."

Mustafa thought for a moment, and responded with, "So, tell me why so many people, who know and practice their religious beliefs, can still seek to cheat other fellow human beings?"

"Do you think that I am one of those people?" asked Sundar.

Mustafa replied, "It is not for me to judge you. But it should be a warning to us all. We must always try to practice what we know to be good for ourselves, and all other beings. I am very pleased to know that you have a spiritual side. Your enthusiasm has made me become more interested in understanding what Buddhism is all about."

Sundar said, "I am sure that everyone in our group would be pleased to hear more about this faith. I will ask one of the learned monks here, if he is willing to talk to us. Let us all go to that shaded area just beyond the Temple."

Mohan Lall and the driver secured a quiet spot, and invited the rest of the group to sit in a semi-circle. Sundar approached an older monk, and negotiated for him to address the small assembly.

The monk sat before his audience, clasped his hands and nodded gracefully. Everyone responded likewise. He closed his eyes, and chanted quietly for a short while. Sundar and his companions remained with their hands clasped, and stared at the master. The monk then spoke.

"We Bhuddists believe that in order to achieve enlightenment, and to be free from the ills of this world, and our own weaknesses, we must continuously practice the noble eightfold paths to aryastangamarga, or enlightenment. These eight paths fall into three divisions of wisdom or prajna, ethics or sila, and concentration or samadhi. Wisdom allows us to see things as they really are. The right ethical conduct will purify our minds. The right concentration needs the right effort, and mindfulness, to secure the best benefit."

Sundar turned to look at Mustafa and the others as if to check that they were all following the monk's talk. Mustafa smiled, and nodded in assurance. The monk continued his discourse.

"The first path of the right view is about looking at the world, at life, and at nature as they really are. Ask ourselves why we exist, why do we suffer, why we get old and die. We need to understand greed, hatred and delusion. We need to clear our minds of misunderstanding, and confusion. We must think in the right way, and prepare to do the right things. This conditions us to practice the second path of the right intention. Here we aspire to get rid of any qualities we know to be wrong, and immoral. We must practice doing without worldly and material things, and commit to non-violence towards all living things."

Mustafa shifted on his haunches uneasily, and although he felt an urge to interrupt the monk, he decided to continue listening. The others sat unperturbed, and showed commendable patience. The monk continued to speak in his controlled and soft tone.

"Right speech is about abstaining from lying, from being abusive and from entertaining idle gossip or chatter. We must speak the truth at all times, be polite in our speech, and use words that are reasonable, and memorable. If we cannot indulge in the right speech, then we must refrain from speaking. Then, we must always enter into the right action, the fourth path. This means that we must abstain from taking life, from stealing, and from illicit sex. Our fifth path is about engaging in the right livelihood, the right trades or jobs which do not directly or indirectly cause harm to others."

Mustafa looked sternly at Sundar as if to tell him that he, of all members of the group, should take heed of these practices being explained by the learned one. He then turned to the monk and asked him, "Can you tell us what kinds of things we should refrain from doing?"

The monk said, "Yes, my son. We should not trade in weapons, and other devices used for killing. We should avoid slave trading, buying and selling of children or adults, and, prostitution. We should not butcher animals for consumption or sale, and make, sell or drink alcohol and drugs which are addictive. We should not produce or sell poisonous products which are designed to kill."

Sundar became a bit troubled by this, and looked across to Ishani, Mustafa and the others. They in turn, stared back at him. He put his right hand up as if to stop the monk from giving any further advice. But Mustafa intervened, and gently waved the monk to continue.

The monk smiled, and said, "The sixth path is about making the right effort to abandon all wrong and harmful thoughts, words and deeds. Then, we should pay attention to make sure that we do not forget these paths as we speak or do things. This is the seventh path of right mindfulness. We then move towards the eighth path of concentration of the mind. Here we try to meditate by clearing the mind of all distractions, including pleasure. We should then reach a stage of bliss, of full knowledge, and of liberation. Here we can reach enlightenment, and free ourselves of the ills we carry with us."

The monk bowed slightly, and still clasping his hands, he rose to take his leave from his enraptured audience. Sundar then stood up, and wearily waved everyone onwards to find a place for resting that evening. He seemed most troubled by the monk's deliberations. Mustafa smiled at Ishani, and they walked behind Sundar. The others in the group seemed to be more perplexed by the monk's explanation about reaching enlightenment.

10.

Reflection in Gaya

The dense fog of the early hours of the morning lingered on for a while, and then eventually cleared away to reveal much of the hustle and bustle of the people, and the animals, getting on with their daily lives. Mohan Lall was not keen on the prayer routines of the Hindus in the party, and Mustafa, the Muslim. He preferred to help the driver with his preparations for the continuation of the journey. The two bullocks seemed to be very aware of the routine of their early morning feed, the driver's checking of the cart, and his securing them to their pulling positions side by side.

Sundar Das emerged from his rented lodging still trying to dust his clothes which appeared more soiled, and was thus in need of washing. None of the others in the group was given adequate time to do the same, and after they all consumed a good breakfast of *daal* and *roti* with hot *chai*, they boarded the cart for the next phase of the journey.

"Today, we will go to Gaya, and then follow the Grand Trunk Road towards Calcutta," announced Sundar in his usual assured manner.

"What will we do in Gaya?" asked Mustafa. "Will we be having yet another religious experience? I think that we are all tired of this, and just want to get to Calcutta as quickly as possible."

Sundar said, "Well, Gaya is very sacred for us Hindus as Bodhgaya is for Buddhists. It will be very important for me personally. You see, I lost my father last year, and it is my duty as a Hindu, to offer some special prayers in his name. I hope that you will all join me for this special *pooja*."

Everyone nodded in approval. Even Ishani, despite her loathing of Sundar, was prepared to show some respect for the occasion. Besides, it would also give her the opportunity to pray for her late husband whom she had loved dearly.

The notion of recent personal loss suffered, made Mustafa reflect on his own beloved Chandini, and his family. He thought about what

Chandini would be doing now, as tears welled up in his eyes. The time away from her seemed to be an eternity. He was also disappointed in not having yet achieved his mission to acquire a lot of money to be able to go back to his village, and ask for her hand. He clung on to the hope that she was still waiting for him as she had promised. He could not bear the thought of losing her to another man, especially when he was not there to do something about it.

Ishani noticed the silent tears of Mustafa, and reached out to place her small dark hand on his rugged left hand that he was resting on his left knee. He wiped the tears from his eyes, and looked at her as she also did the same.

Everyone else sat quietly, staring out across the green fields as the cart slowly moved ahead. The dusty road soon became busier with more traffic of carts, pedestrians and farmers driving herds of cattle from one grazing pasture to the other. The herds invariably slowed the traffic down as right of way was always given to the cows, and their drivers. The cows never seemed to be in a rush to cross the road, and appeared to know that they were highly valued by everyone, and especially sacred to the Hindus.

Eventually, the bullock cart and its full complement of passengers rolled gently up the slight incline in the narrow road as it approached the entrance to Gaya. The terrain here was more elevated with rocky hills, and tired looking trees and shrubs barely surviving amongst the large mounds of stones and boulders. Several small one floor houses with their grassy thatched roofs, and neatly plastered clay walls, were dotted alongside the main road leading up towards the most important building in the town; the Vishnupad Temple.

At the centre and very heart of the spired Vishnupad Temple, was an octagonal stone casing protecting the large footprint of the Lord Vishnu. Non-Hindus were not allowed to enter the Temple, but could look at it from a good vantage point nearby. Pilgrims would climb up the one thousand steps close to the Temple and its surrounds, to obtain a special view of it, and the rest of the town.

All of the group, except Mustafa, followed Sundar into the Temple. He recruited a local Pandit and explained his circumstances for the *pinda pooja* in honour of his late father. He was given the task of making the seven *pindas* for his *pooja*. These were sticky balls of boiled rice mixed with milk, some sesame seeds, a few drops of honey, a hint of perfume, some sugar, and, *ghee*. Each *pinda* was carefully rolled by hand into a small circular ball, and set aside for the Pandit to use during the ceremony. The *pinda pooja* was the final act to be made by Sundar, so that his father's spirit would be released from this world, towards its salvation.

Sundar thus completed his duty as a son, having ensured that all the required *poojas* and sacrifices were undertaken over the twelve months from the demise of his father. When he left the Temple, and walked towards the *ghat* by the nearby Falgu River, for a ritual bath, all of his companions stopped to embrace him. All but Ishani, who simply clasped her hands and bowed with respect.

Sundar then obtained some new clothes, and discarded his old *dhoti* after his bath in the river. He was soon back to his arrogant self, feeling very proud, and ready to focus on the business of acquiring his fees for the delivery of the recruits to the Agent in Calcutta.

The party faced a final tough push of about two hundred miles along the Grand Trunk Road, through several villages and towns, including Aurangabad, Dhanbad and Raniganj. Then they would pass through Durgapur and Bardhaman in the State of Bengal, before reaching their final destination of Bhawanipore in Calcutta.

Sundar Das did not know the precise date in January 1845, whence the first ship was due to leave Calcutta, for either Mauritius or British Guiana. But he knew that there was a great urgency for him to get his recruits to the holding depot in good time, and to avoid unnecessary additional costs of any further stopovers along the way.

He was also wary of the presence of other ambitious and competitive agents plying the same trade. Some of these characters were known to use more devious tactics including opportunistic kidnapping of young men and young prostitutes who were very poor and lost. He was very satisfied with his recruits who were essentially very calm, and patient. They did not show any inclination to run away from him, or to dessert him. They were not outwardly happy and carefree, but they accepted their shared experiences of the spiritual places along the way. Even Mohan Lall, the Dhangar tribesman, was observing and respecting the Hindu and Buddhist teachings and practices they shared.

Sundar also reflected on whether he had approached his recruiting effort in the best way, by travelling so far west of Calcutta, to entice his clients, and then take on the risks of retracing his journey back to his base in Calcutta. Perhaps a better option would have been to hire more people from Mohan's tribe, who had been pouring into Calcutta, and other large cities, looking for work.

Mustafa was thinking of his own situation as one of Sundar's recruits. His personal dream of acquiring wealth, and his desire to return to his Chandini, drove his risk-taking to an unplanned level. He also wondered what was on the minds of all the other recruits. They were a collection of singers, carpenters, leather workers, and field labourers. How would they all cope with the demands of a sugarcane labour contract in a distant land?

They all had their individual reasons for making this journey, from escaping the clutches of unscrupulous money-lenders, personal family quarrels and disputes, lack of work opportunities in their trade, over-enthusiastic and aggressive tax collection by the *Zamindars*, and, the promise of a better life in places well away from their abodes, with more money on offer.

This long and arduous journey, despite being interspersed with Sundar's desire to show his clients some of the significant places and sites, was a tremendous sacrifice. Having withstood the discomfort of the hard wooden seats on the bullock cart, the numerous holes in the dusty road, and the sheer boredom presented by the familiar landscape, the passengers realised that there would be nothing to gain from turning back. So, they braced themselves for the next fifteen days of the same, until they reached Calcutta.

To his credit, Sundar Das tried his best to treat his passengers well, and although Mohan Lall and the driver were his security guards, they were only called into action when separating the men who had pounced on the assailant who molested Ishani.

The bullock cart slowed down appreciably as it approached the last village before the entrance to the Bhawanipore Depot in Calcutta. It was very quiet as the village headman moved forward to greet Sundar, whom he seemed to be familiar with. Sundar pressed some money into the headman's right hand, and he quickly tucked his bribe into his pocket. The smiling headman then adjusted his white cotton turban, and welcomed everyone with a solemn "*namaskaar*", and ushered them to his house which was tucked away behind some of the other much smaller buildings. A very charming young woman smiled impishly at Sundar, and proceeded to provide the visitors with refreshments.

11.

Conditions and conditioning at the Bhawanipore Depot

Bhawanipore Depot in Calcutta, during January 1845, was a well-designed compound with Tolly's Nullah, a narrow waterway, on its western perimeter. The Depot contained a series of thatched sheds forming a loose semi-circle, broken only by the one gateway entrance, which also served as the exit. The gatekeeper's thatched lodge was a moderate wooden structure just fit for his needs. The sheds were used for cooking *daal*, rice and curries, both meat and vegetables. There was a six foot high wall encompassing the compound.

There were three large bungalows intended for the recruits, with sleeping quarters mainly located on the ground floor. These lodgings were very over-crowded with the mostly male labourers. There was, however, clear separation of families, single men, and single women. The beds were similar to the structures familiar to the people from the villages, but there was no real privacy, and limited space between them. The air was rank with the smell of unstoppable perspiration in the heat. There were no means to cool the temperature in the houses, and individuals continuously flicked pieces of their cotton garment across their faces in an effort to ease their discomfort.

The living space available at Bhawanipore was just enough for one shipload, but the Emigration Agent who was the manager of the Depot, tried to squeeze in enough people for two shiploads. He had paid a good price for each recruit to the Recruiting Agent, and was keen to ensure that there would always be enough people to export, as quickly as possible. A fast turnover was critical to making a good profit out of the venture.

Sundar Das had quickly despatched his driver with a good pay, and delivered his fifteen recruits with great efficiency. He did not linger around to bid his recruits farewell, and wasted no time in guiding his assistant and new partner, Mohan Lall, away from the site. Mustafa stared at them with a degree of contempt, as they hurried out via the main gate.

He observed that his fourteen companions appeared to be very nervous, and lost. He realised that he must act on their behalf by leading them forward to the Emigration Agent, for instructions as to what had to be done next. The Agent noticed Mustafa's action, and advised him to lead the others towards the bathing area. Ishani was asked to join the women in their quarters.

The bathing area for the men was a communal space with water in buckets placed on the stone floor. Bars of soap were to be shared. The bath water ran out of the flooring straight into gutters that led directly into the filthy waters of the Tolly's Nullah. As soon as each person finished bathing, he was handed a fresh set of new clothes with his older clothes either put for washing, or discarded altogether. Then they made their way in a single orderly file, to the hospital and dispensary which were located at the far end of the compound, and well away from the cooking, and other living activities.

Mustafa and his companions were very pleased to see that there was an Indian doctor and two Indian nurses responsible for carrying out the medical and physical examinations. Other Indians were working as cooks, cleaners, washer-women, and watchmen. The recruits were each checked for the state of their eyesight, hearing, teeth, feet, and whether they were carrying any injuries. The men had to demonstrate how well they could wield a machete, or cutlass.

Mustafa was given a clean bill of health, and walked out of the examination, chest forward, and as proud as a peacock. All of his male colleagues were also passed fit, and when he did see Ishani sitting and chatting amongst the single women, he realised that she must have passed the test. He did notice, however, that some of the other recruits who were sitting around or strolling in the compound, were a lot more feeble-looking, and wondered why they were still seeking to work as labourers so far away from their homes.

He approached a small group of such individuals, and found that they conversed in Bhojpuri, having also come from his home State of Uttar Pradesh. They told him that they had been at the Depot for over two months, and were struck down with illnesses that caused severe vomiting, fever, loss of weight, and in some cases, a few of the afflicted had died. This was mainly caused by the impure water from the giant water vat in the compound, the over-crowded lodgings, the lack of good sanitation, and, mosquito bites.

The men praised the doctors and nurses for the treatment and medication they received. This contributed to their slow but welcome recovery. They however, wished that they had not accepted the offer to seek the jobs abroad. But, having survived their long and arduous journeys by road, and the conditions in the Depot, they felt obliged to carry on. Besides, walking out and facing a return journey, unpaid, and for hundreds of miles back to their villages, and to endure the ridicule of their families and friends, were not agreeable prospects.

They advised Mustafa and his companions to take better precaution when using the water, to ensure that they took regular washes, to stay clear of anyone showing signs of illness, to cover themselves well in the evenings, and, to avoid the mosquitoes as much as possible. They also indicated that the Emigration Agent and all the staff working at the Depot had treated them well, and were always keen to improve the conditions there. Their complaints were generally listened to, and in most cases, acted upon.

Mustafa valued the thoughts and suggestions shared by the fellow recruits, and recognised the importance of continuing to communicate with as many people as possible. He also pointed this out to his companions who were quick to begin their liaison with the other potential travellers, and workmates.

They learnt that their colleagues had come from several villages in Uttar Pradesh, Bihar and Bengal. They were of different religions and castes, and were keen to talk to each other. They shared their stories of how they were enticed to join the search for work, and to explain their circumstances, and hopes for the future. They were delighted that they all showed solidarity, and realised how important it was for them to stay united. Differences of religion and caste were put aside if they were to survive whatever challenges they faced in the future.

Although the recruits spoke in different languages and dialects, they began to build up a new Hindustani tongue mixed with words that were mutually recognised, including some Urdu and English. The Urdu language which was developed and used by the Moghuls, was formed in much the same way, by the officers and soldiers in their cantonments. This allowed the new conquerors the opportunity to retain their distinctiveness. The recruits, by starting to develop their Hindustani, had found a common ground towards greater understanding, and unity.

Mustafa used his superior command of English to help his fellow recruits to develop better understanding of the language, and he soon acquired growing popularity across the Depot. He was treated with great respect by most of the men. He was also admired by the women who would smile or blush whenever they saw him.

A day at the Depot would commence just before dawn with people doing their Hindu *pooja* or Muslim *namaaz*, despite not having access to dedicated spaces for their prayers. This would be followed by a quick bath which was very welcome by the people who had only been used to a traditional dip in a nearby stream or pond. This facility made them feel much better, and gave them a new sense of pride.

Cooking in the sheds started very early as well, and the enticing smell of curry being stirred with large wooden ladles, *rotis* being swiftly made on hot plates, and the smoke billowing from the crackling firewood in the earthen cooking ovens, excited everyone. They all made their way to sit at the long benches and tables, to be served most generously.

Exercise was very limited to just strolling around in the open spaces of the compound. They appeared to be like prisoners due to the similar coloured outfits they were given. It was during the free moments of strolling and sitting around in small groups, that more friendships were formed, as well as opportunities for the young men and women to flirt.

Mustafa noticed how many young men tried to catch the attention of Ishani, whose beauty was becoming more apparent as the days passed by. Her long black hair was neatly combed, and plaited like a young girl's. Her dark face was shining, and her white teeth would gleam as she smiled more confidently, and with the attention she was receiving. She had also put on some more weight, and embellished her good looks with beautiful silver studded nose rings and earrings. Her silver bangles and anklets completed a picture of a very happy and contented young woman.

He was very pleased to see Ishani improving in this way, and occasionally they would notice each other, and just exchange pleasant greetings. She did not seem to be attached to any of her young admirers who spent much of their time looking at her, making comments aimed at her, and sometimes teasing her.

There were instances where the flirting became more serious between some couples, and small ceremonies were conducted as marriage proposals were accepted, and a Brahmin would be on hand to perform the Hindu rites. Muslim marriages were much easier to complete, and any Muslim who could read the Holy Qur'an, would carry out the *nikahs*, with minimum fuss. These weddings were not recorded, but were allowed to take place at the Depot. However, with such a small proportion of women to men, this created even stiffer competition amongst the young men, to win the hand of an eligible spinster.

Mustafa did not feel the same urge to acquire a wife in this way, and was still loyal to his beloved Chandini. He avoided any flirtatious moves by the admiring women who were impressed by his natural charm, confidence, and newly acquired status of one whom others referred to for help or advice.

During the midday to late afternoon hours, everyone would seek the welcome shade of the dwellings. The men would gather around to give vocal encouragement to those who played board games such as draughts. The women indulged in darning torn clothing or grooming themselves. The small number of children played amongst themselves.

The second main meal of the day was served just before the setting of the sun, and darkness prevailing. Everyone retired to their sleeping quarters quite early in the evenings as an eerie calm descended on the Depot. The only people who stayed awake, were the watchmen relaxing in the guardhouse, by the light provided by oil lamps.

Some stray mongrel dogs roamed around the perimeter of the Depot, and would occasionally breach the calm with their frantic barking. Their noise helped to keep the watchmen awake through the night. The residents tried hard to ward off the buzzing, and blood-thirsty mosquitoes by slapping at them, and covering themselves from head to toes with their cotton sheets. The unrelenting dry heat added to the discomfort. Eventually, through sheer tiredness and fatigue, they managed to drift off to sleep.

Early one morning, there was a commotion in the single men's quarters as the body of a man was discovered. Mustafa recognised him as one of the group who seemed to be recovering well from their illness. A doctor and a nurse soon arrived on the scene, and everyone was asked to leave the area. Once the death was confirmed, the body was neatly wrapped in white cotton, and tied at the head and feet. The man must have been a Muslim, and without much fuss, he was carried off to the cemetery nearby, and buried by a small group of men, one of whom acted as the Imaam for the final funeral prayers.

Before the recruits could indulge in discussions about the man's demise, news quickly spread about a ship being made ready for departure. This was confirmed when most of the young men, women and families were selected for a final medical examination by the Surgeon Superintendent of the ship. He was an English doctor who concentrated on thoroughly examining the males, whilst the Indian nurses checked the females. Everyone selected for the ship was classified as fit, and able to travel.

Mustafa and all his companions recruited by Sundar Das, were chosen to travel on this ship, heading for Demerara, British Guiana. They had heard about this place from Mohan Lall who had related his experiences on the sugar plantation at Vreed-en-Hoop. However, they were not told about what to expect on the ship or on the sea voyage.

The ship, called the SS Lord Hungerford, which was constructed in Calcutta in 1813, was regularly being used for transporting goods and people to and from the English colonies. It was inspected by the Protector of Emigrants as to whether it was sea-worthy, had the right complement of Master and crew, adequate provisions for the purpose of the journey, was properly fitted out as to the required accommodation for the recruits, and, had a reasonable facility for treating and caring for those falling ill.

Mustafa was delighted to be chosen to lead a group of fifty men, due to his willingness to help his companions, his noted leadership, and the respect he earned so quickly at the Depot. The Emigration Agent must have observed his behaviour, and therefore, recommended him for the role.

Every adult was given an advance on their pay, and issued with a bag containing a tin plate, a tin *lota*, two blankets, clothing, and, the men were given sailors' caps. The females were given a petticoat and a *sari*. Mustafa noticed that some recruiting agents had returned to the compound a day before the departure, and some recruits had confirmed that they were forced to give the agents some of their money and belongings. So, he made sure that this would not happen to members of his group. He was pleased to note that Sundar Das had not returned to the Depot.

Soon, the time came for them to walk the short distance to the embarkation point, and to board the fleet of small boats that ferried them to the ship which was waiting in the middle of the Hoogli River.

He and his companions looked at the large vessel in awe as they reached closer and closer to its side. They had never set foot on such a large vessel before, and they felt quite nervous as they were helped aboard by the Indian *lascars*. When they were all aboard, they were made to stand side by side on the wooden deck in an orderly fashion, with their bag of their only worldly possessions, at their feet.

PART 2

VOYAGE TO BRITISH GUIANA

12.

Turbulence across the Kaala Paani

The SS Lord Hungerford presented a very impressive picture of dominance over the much smaller boats that were used to transfer the emigrants over the short distance from the harbour. Three very tall main masts towered magnificently over the beautifully carved timber vessel that settled calmly on the slowly rising waters of the Hoogli River. The ship was held firmly by its huge iron anchor which was in turn, secured by a long, thick and robust rope. The ship's fourteen sails were not yet fully extended on the masts, and the ropes attached to the canvas sails dangled loosely.

The Captain was a short, stockily built Englishman in his mid-thirties. His eyes were deep blue. His nose and cheeks were reddened by exposure over many years of hot sun, and cold biting winds at sea. His fully grey beard gave the impression of him being much older than his years, and, also a sense of authority. He emphasised this by always standing very upright, and with his arms akimbo. His main right hand man, particularly for such voyages, was the Surgeon Superintendent, who always stood beside him.

The Surgeon Superintendent was also a short, but slimmer English doctor who was mostly responsible for the health and wellbeing of all those travelling on the ship. He wore a long dark beard that also made him appear to be much older than his twenty five years. This was his second trip on the SS Lord Hungerford, and he seemed to be quite assured and confident. He wore his stethoscope loosely around his neck, and over his cream coloured jacket. The two men walked forward side by side, and everyone stopped speaking.

The Captain took up a position at the head of his crew of mostly English and Arab *lascars*. The Surgeon Superintendent and two mates stood beside him, facing the new passengers. The Captain welcomed the emigrants, and explained where their sleeping quarters were located, for the single men, the single women, and the married families. The single men, who included Mustafa as a *Sirdar* nominated to be responsible for twenty five of them, were allocated to a position below deck just under the galley. The married families occupied the space below the sick bay. The single girls were reserved a space below the poop deck at the back of the ship. Just beside the sick bay, was a small dispensary room where two compounders worked on the medications to be used on the voyage.

Below deck and the sleeping quarters, there was a large hold where provisions and other cargo were neatly stored. This area was generally just below the level of the water, and was well ventilated. The sleeping quarters were also ventilated through a series of portholes. However, the spaces were fairly dark and gloomy apart from some streaky light passing through the portholes, and from the small oil lamps attached to supporting posts.

The berths provided for each emigrant, were limited to about six feet long, two feet wide, and six feet high. This was very uncomfortable, and unfamiliar to the emigrants who were more used to the lightweight wooden *matyas* in their homes. They were expected to adjust to sleeping on bunks on top or below each other, and amongst fellow passengers in a relatively cramped and confined environment. Their experience of sleeping in an open space at the Bhawanipore Depot was very comfortable compared to that on the ship.

The Surgeon Superintendent announced the names of those nominated to work as *Sirdars*, and pointed out their duties, and responsibilities. They were expected to help maintain discipline, and cleanliness, above and below decks. Some sweepers were appointed from amongst the emigrants, and were to be paid for their work. The cooks were men from the Brahmin caste, so that the Hindu tradition for vegetarian meals was sustained. Muslim cooks prepared the non-vegetarian meals using salted meat. The Dhangar tribesmen were mostly non-vegetarian, and were generally content to eat any meal that was served.

The Captain and the Surgeon Superintendent were very keen to ensure that the emigrants were well looked after, and survived the long crossing of the *Kaala Paani* which was known as the Dark Waters of the Ocean. The emigrants needed to be in good health when they arrived at their destination, as the Captain was paid according to the number of individuals handed over alive. The two men did not disclose any details of how long the journey was, or the nature of the hazards ahead, or the hardships to be endured. They, however, explained the daily routine of having to wake up early, taking their wash, cleaning their sleeping quarters, consuming two main meals per day, using limited time for exercise and entertainment, and, obeying the rules of the ship. For instance, no males, including the crew members, were allowed to go to the female quarters without permission from the Captain.

The three hundred and seventy two emigrants stood on the deck to observe with great interest and awe, the whole operation of the preparations for the ship to be towed slowly down the Hoogli River, before it set sail into the Bay of Bengal. They were very impressed by the calm efficiency by which the Captain and his crew organised themselves with precision. They heard unfamiliar words of command from the Captain, with responses of "Aye Aye Sir!" The *lascars* were young, very fit, and hard working men who were well trained in their tasks of pulling up the sails, and rigging them to their respective positions on the masts. They shouted encouragement to each other in their Arabic language, and never flinched when the pressure to work faster and harder, was placed upon them.

The large metal anchor was slowly wrenched up from the bed of the river, and finally secured just below the raised front of the ship. Shortly afterwards, at the crisp command of the Captain, the ship began to slowly inch its way forward, and out through the middle of the river. It was aided by a wind which became stronger as it moved upstream. The wind caused the waves to become choppier, and the vessel started to pick up greater speed.

The emigrants took the opportunity to view the rapidly disappearing landscape that they were leaving behind, and although they were very sad to see this, they felt that soon they would return to India, as richer and more successful people. They enjoyed the new views of the *ghats* along the edges of the river, and the hundreds of their countrymen and women going about their daily business, with a few stopping to gaze at the large vessel quietly drifting past. The emigrants started to wave their hands, and were smiling as the people ashore responded likewise. The young children waved much more enthusiastically. This gave the emigrants some sense of comfort, and assurance that the voyage would be a good one.

As the ship picked up more speed, it began to roll gently with the waves, and for the first time, the emigrants experienced the new sensation which occasionally made them stagger a little. The prevailing wind caused the sails to assume new shapes as the sailors adjusted them expertly to take full advantage of the force. The wind also blew into the faces of the emigrants, and their cotton garments began to flutter like the ship's standard and buntings.

The Captain noticed the growing discomfort amongst the emigrants, and as the ship began to enter into the Bay of Bengal, he ordered for them to be shown to their respective quarters below deck. Although the *Sirdars* did not know the layout of the berths, they were encouraged to lead their twenty five charges to the section they would occupy.

Mustafa secured a top berth next to a porthole so that he could observe the outside as much as possible. Everyone carefully hung their bag of possessions against the wooden uprights of their berths, and proceeded to test their beds for strength and comfort by pressing down on them vigorously with both hands. They talked constantly amongst themselves, and ensured that those who had struck up closer friendships, would choose berths next to each other.

Although they did not know it at the time, these friendships of *jahaji bhais* and *jahaji behens* would help them enormously in the days and years to come. The *jahaji bhais* and *behens* were of Hindu and Muslim religions and from different castes. The *Sirdars* from each group appreciated this comradeship, and tried their utmost to work within these relationships to achieve a reasonably easy existence for themselves. Often, the close friends would be paired up to do the tasks allocated by the *Sirdars*.

The *jahaji bhais* and *behens* learnt to show each other mutual respect, and tended to regard themselves as working partners. However, this did not stop them from having occasional disagreements and rows, which would only be resolved by the intervention of the *Sirdars*.

The initial few hours of the first day at sea passed by without incident, and everyone was in good spirits. Individuals took turns to climb back up to the deck to use the nearest toilet available. Others simply kept staring out through the portholes, and to remark on their surprise to see so much water all around them. Some took short naps on their new beds.

Bells were rung to indicate that their first full meal was ready to be served on deck at about five o'clock that afternoon. The emigrants took their tin plates and *lotas*, and were directed to their seating places on the bare wooden floor of the upper deck. They sat on their buttocks with their legs crossed and folded as in a yoga position. A narrow gap was left between the rows of hungry diners so that the servers could pass through with the offerings of one *roti*, a cup full of boiled rice, some *daal* poured onto the rice, and a small portion of vegetable curry. Clean distilled drinking water was served from clay pitchers, into each *lota*.

After the meal, the team of servers and cooks took their turn to have their dinner whilst the emigrants washed and wiped their own plates and *lotas*. The men had learnt to do this for themselves whilst at the Bhawanipore Depot. Normally, in the villages, these tasks were exclusive to the women.

Everyone stayed on deck for a couple of hours after the dinner, and then as darkness began to prevail, they were ushered down to their respective sleeping quarters. They spent their first night aboard, sleeping soundly despite the fierce lashing of the water against the ship, and the creaking of the highly stressed ropes against the timbers of the masts.

At first light the next day, everyone was ordered up on deck in readiness for their breakfast or first meal of the day. As soon as they reached their positions, some emigrants started to cough and vomit violently. They tried to reach to the edge to deposit their vomit into the sea, but most of them failed and the deck was splashed with the mess. They were helped by their more able-bodied friends, and eventually led back down to their berths to recover. The others joined the sweepers to wash the soiled areas of the deck, before the meal was served. This time they were given limejuice to drink, instead of water. None of the emigrants were too ill to be treated or isolated at the sick bay at this stage.

Then, later that day, as the ship continued to press on, many more of the emigrants began to feel sick, and were vomiting below and above deck. Despite the efforts to clean the sleeping quarters, they became increasingly foul. The vomiting was followed by diarrhoea, and the smell became unbearably bad. Suddenly, the sick bay became a hive of activity as the Surgeon Superintendent and his small team began to deal with dozens of increasingly ill passengers.

Some of the emigrants were so ill they could not muster up enough strength to climb up to the deck. So they just lay in their berths as if they were waiting to die. The Surgeon Superintendent was very aware of this behaviour by the Indians, and made sure that he visited and treated them below deck. He and his team needed to wear face masks to help avoid the rank smell.

Mustafa took his medicine, and the restricted diet on offer, of biscuits, sugar and limejuice. This helped him to recover sufficiently to resume his duties as a *Sirdar*, and to try to maintain a cleaner sleeping area. His companions, many of whom had endured the long trek by road to the Depot, were also recovering well, and were able to help the others in their group. Those emigrants who were more familiar with working on boats, such as the fishermen from Calcutta, were very helpful towards their new friends, and offered them advice and comfort, towards recovery. Some of the Dhangars who were on their second such sea journey, having chosen to return to the plantations, were far better equipped to deal with the hardship, and illness.

After this first bout of illness on board, and the vomiting and diarrhoea eased, the emigrants were assembled on deck before the morning meal. The Captain and the Surgeon Superintendent told them that they were pleased to see the good recovery, and warned that such an outbreak could recur, particularly if the sleeping quarters were not kept as clean as possible. Now that they had been at sea for just over one week, everyone was to have a proper bath with soap. Many were issued with new clothes.

Sadly though, the Surgeon Superintendent announced the death of one passenger, and that his funeral would be held that afternoon after the bathing, and before the early evening meal. The women began to weep upon hearing of this loss, whilst the men stood quietly with their heads bowed in solemn respect.

The funeral ceremony came as a great surprise to all the emigrants, as the body of the deceased, wrapped in white cotton from head to feet, was simply lowered by six bearers, into the sea. A Brahmin priest had performed a simple reading of some Hindu *shlokas* without the elaborate *pooja* that would normally be undertaken. It was not viable to cremate the body on the ship. This experience was particularly troubling for the emigrants, and they were not forewarned about such events. That evening, the mood amongst the emigrants was subdued, as they huddled in small groups, and discussed the episode.

A group of Hindus gathered around in a circle, and began chanting from the *Ramayan*, whilst clapping in perfect rhythm. All those who were familiar with the glorious text of the epic story of Lord Raam and his consort, Sita, soon joined in the session. All the others, including the Captain, the Surgeon Superintendent, and the crew, stood and looked on in silence, and with great respect.

When the session was over, the *Brahmin* who was leading the reading and singing, stood up, and humbly requested for permission to perform a *havan* with a small carefully controlled fire, for any Hindu who died on the voyage. The Captain instantly agreed, and the emigrants retired that evening with a greater sense of assurance.

Mustafa was awakened by the whimpering cries of someone from the set of emigrants that the deceased man was a member of. He quietly sneaked over, and began to console the young man whom he recognised as one of the bearers at the funeral.

"Please do not cry my *bhaiya*," whispered Mustafa, as he put his arms around the young man's shoulders.

"That... that was my dear father. He has gone, and left me alone. Why did this have to happen?" asked the young man as he continued to weep.

Mustafa said, "My name is Mustafa Ali. I am also away from all my relations, and sometimes I hate myself for this. What is your name?"

"Kanhaiya Ramchand. At least you have parents and a family to go back to. I now have no one. I am so scared. I do not know what to do. I just feel like jumping into the sea, and to be with my father. He was everything to me," said the young man, wiping his tears from his eyes and face with a piece of cotton.

"I am so sorry my *bhaiya*. But you need to carry on. Your father would have wanted you to go, and to achieve your dreams," said Mustafa also wiping tears from his eyes and cheeks.

Kanhaiya said, "Mustafa, I am so ashamed that I could not read a simple *shloka* for my father who was so religious. He always wanted me to learn our scriptures, and that is why he studied for so many years. He wanted to go to Demra to teach the people *Hindi* and *Hinduism*. But *Bhagwan* has taken him. Why? Why? Why?"

Mustafa said, "Kanhaiya, God works in mysterious ways, and fate also plays tricks on us all. This is now a true test for you. God wants you to go and achieve your father's dream. You have to fulfil all of his hopes and wishes. So please start from now on, and do not think of harming yourself."

"But, Mustafa *bhaiya*, I cannot do this on my own. I need help. I have no family left. I do not even know where I am going," said Kanhaiya, still trying to wipe away his tears.

"From today onwards, you are my *bhaiya*, and no one or anything must come between us," promised Mustafa solemnly as he embraced Kanhaiya.

After supper the next day, Mustafa arranged for Kanhaiya to swop his berth with another emigrant, so that he could keep a close eye on the distressed, and grieving young man. He made every effort to ensure that Kanhaiya would be treated as his true blood brother, and the two became inseparable throughout the remainder of the voyage.

Successive days and nights passed as the ship made impressive progress through the Bay of Bengal, and into the Indian Ocean. The confidence of the emigrants grew from strength to strength as they settled very well into their new routine. The *Sirdars* asked for, and were given permission by the Captain, to have regular music and dance sessions after the evening meals, and before they retired for the night. This was very good for the morale, and physical wellbeing of those who actually participated in the sessions, as well as those who actively encouraged the performers.

Inevitably, these evenings brought closer contact between the young men, and the small number of young women. One evening, a group of the young men approached the young women, and after a brief exchange, they managed to pull Ishani out and into the ring they had created, and kept encouraging her to dance. She was in no mood to cooperate, and pleaded with the ringleaders, to let her go back to her friends. They refused, and became more aggressive in their actions towards her.

Mustafa and Kanhaiya stepped forward, and confronted the ringleaders, ordering them to let go of Ishani. They did so, but then turned on Mustafa and Kanhaiya, punching and kicking at them. A group of sailors saw the commotion, and quickly stepped into the fray. They managed to separate the young men, and arrested Mustafa and Kanhaiya.

The Captain stepped forward, and the two arrested men were brought before him. He was not pleased about the disturbance, and gave them a stern warning. He also threatened to suspend the music and dancing sessions if there was a recurrence of the fighting. Mustafa and Kanhaiya were very aggrieved at being wrongly accused for the disturbance, when they were only trying to stop it.

They were more upset to see that their fellow emigrants did not come forward to inform the Captain that they were not to be blamed for the incident. Nevertheless, Mustafa was more pleased that Ishani had come to no harm as a result of his action.

Later on, a great storm arrived in the middle of the night, and the emigrants woke up with utter fear in their shining eyes, as the ship rocked violently. The women and children began to scream as if certain death was upon them. Some older men buried their heads in their hands, and began to fervently recite their prayers. Mustafa, Kanhaiya and the other young men wanted to go above deck to help the seasoned but noisy crew who were frantically trying to carry out the orders of the Captain.

They soon discovered that they could not climb up onto the deck as the hatches were firmly battened down from above. They reluctantly returned to their berths, and just sat there to ride out the storm. The emigrants were utterly shocked by the sheer intensity of the raging winds, and the immeasurable size of the waves which seemed to lift the ship and drop it back into the water. Everyone tried hard to grab the upright posts of their berths, but yet some people were thrown from them by sudden jerks, as the ship rolled from side to side.

This continued through the remainder of the night, and when calm was restored by the next morning, everyone was allowed up on the deck. The Captain, Surgeon Superintendent and the crew appeared completely exhausted, and were in need of a good rest. As no one was able to cook that morning, the meal was limited to dry biscuits, water and limejuice. The emigrants were told to soak the biscuits into their water before eating them. The biscuits were tasteless, stale, hard, and were made worse by the need to dunk them into water. The limejuice was more palatable when mixed with some sugar, and was serving as a medicine to help control the sea sickness that many of the emigrants were once again, experiencing.

Unfortunately, during the course of the storm, two more emigrants died. One was a Muslim man and the other, a Hindu woman. Once again, the emigrants had to share in the grief. The Muslim's funeral was conducted by a *hafeez* who acted as the *Imaam*. The *hafeez* was a Muslim who could recite the entire Holy Qur'an from memory. Everyone sat down on the deck in silence as the short service was concluded and the body, fully wrapped in white cotton, was lowered into the sea.

The Hindu funeral rites were more elaborate as the *Brahmin* performed a *havan* ceremony which offered the deceased much more spiritual benefit than was given to Kanhaiya's late father. Cremation was not available, so the body was also lowered into the sea. The *Brahmin* placed a single *diya* onto it as it drifted away, and sank beneath the relatively calm water.

Mustafa and the other *Sirdars* offered to cook that evening's meal, and were allowed to do so under supervision by the regular cooks. This helped to ensure that a full and more normal meal would be available instead of the tasteless fare they had endured earlier that day. The general mood of the emigrants was one of relief that the storm was over, but they were in dread of a recurrence.

That evening, after their meal, everyone retired early to their berths, as they were not prepared to sing and dance. Kanhaiya sat up in his berth beside Mustafa, and asked about the place they were heading to.

"Mustafa *bhaiya*, tell me about this island called Demra. I have heard about Mauritius, but not about this place."

Mustafa sat up and said, "First of all, Demra is called British Guiana, and there is a place called Demerara. It is not an island like Mauritius, but a big country with very large sugar plantations. I have heard about some very bad stories from people who came back from their first contract to work there. But I decided to go on this trip because the government and the plantation owners have been forced to improve things for us. You can see that we are being treated well on this ship, and it is up to us as *jahaji bhais* and *behens* to work with our masters."

"Yes *bhaiya*. I can see why the Captain and crew show you so much respect. You are a very smart man, and I am proud to be called your *bhaiya*. I promise you that I will never let you down," said Kanhaiya as he reached out and touched Mustafa's feet.

Mustafa placed his hands on Kanhaiya's shoulders, and said, "Kanhaiya *bhaiya*, you are also a very good person, and I want you to help me to do this job, and to advise me if I do anything wrong."

Just then, one of the men came forward and complained to Mustafa that his tinplate and *lota* had gone missing. He placed suspicion on the person who had exchanged his berth with Kanhaiya.

Mustafa called everyone to attention, and asked whether anyone had taken the plate and *lota*. They were all in denial, so he asked them to check their bags, and place the contents on their berths for him to inspect. Mustafa and Kanhaiya then split up as two searchers, and confirmed each person's belongings. They had only completed checking a few when the perpetrator owned up to the theft. He apologised for his sincere mistake, and returned the plate and *lota* to their rightful owner.

Mustafa chose not to berate the man, and kept the situation under control. He did, however, advise everyone to take better care of their belongings, and to continue to support each other. Kanhaiya observed Mustafa's approach in dealing with the matter. He said, "You see, *bhaiya*, I would have properly chastised that man for his dishonesty."

Mustafa smiled, and said, "I could not assume that he stole the plate and *lota*. And, because he finally came forward to say he was sorry for his mistake, I gave him the benefit of the doubt this time. If he does something like this again, then I would ask the others to suggest how to deal with him. Now, let us go to sleep."

The SS Lord Hungerford continued to sail serenely over the next few days of relatively calm seas with less intense winds. The emigrants were allowed to spend most of the daylight hours between their meals, on deck. This was a welcome relief, as the sleeping quarters below deck were still very smelly despite regular cleaning. One disadvantage of being on deck, however, was their having to endure the sharp rays of the sun, and its painful effect on the eyes from its shimmering reflections on the waves. The few children on board seemed to be unaffected by the conditions, and just chased each other up and down the deck, screaming and laughing loudly.

The adults felt that singing, beating drums, and dancing virtually every day, was becoming too tedious. So, it was arranged that a grand wrestling match would take place on deck. One emigrant, a large man with a bulging chest and powerful arms and legs, known as Hanuman Singh from Varanasi, had challenged another similarly built young man by the name of Pathana Khan from Kanpur. One of the sailors volunteered to act as referee for the fight as he had claimed to know the rules of wrestling.

Everyone gathered around the makeshift ring, and was kept just outside the marked perimeter by the *Sirdars*, including Mustafa. Each wrestler had his own supporters who began shouting "Hanuman! Hanuman! Hanuman!" or, "Pathana Khan! Pathana Khan! Pathana Khan!" The arena became alive and extremely noisy as the Captain and the Surgeon Superintendent took up their privileged positions on the bridge overlooking the ring.

The referee, with the help of translation by Mustafa, set out the rules for the contest which would last for three rounds of two minutes each. Another sailor acted as the bell-ringer and timekeeper. There would be one minute rests between the rounds.

The first bell rang, and the two men crouched low as they cautiously assessed each other, and waited for the first move. Hanuman saw his opportunity when Pathana seemed to look away for a moment. He lunged at his opponent's legs, and with the fury of an enraged bull, he grabbed Pathana and lifted him up before throwing him unto his back on the hard floor. Pathana grunted, and dismissed any pain as he responded by kicking at Hanuman's legs causing him to trip over. The crowd gasped.

The two men continued to fight with all their might, without conceding any scores to each other. The first round ended at the same time that Hanuman struck Pathana full on his jaws with a fierce punch. Pathana staggered backwards, and fell onto the crowd who pushed him back into the ring. He struggled to get up and missed the opportunity to rest in his corner as the bell sounded for the start of the second round.

Hanuman, sensing victory, charged at his opponent, grabbed him and lifted him above his head. He spun around, preparing to slam him onto the floor when Pathana managed to twist himself, and fell out of Hanuman's grip, onto his thick neck. He locked hard and forced Hanuman onto his knees before pushing him onto the floor where he attempted to pin him down as the referee started to count "One!... Two!..." Hanuman found incredible strength to push Pathana off his chest before the final count of "Three!" The crowd applauded both men wildly, and the Captain and Surgeon Superintendent were equally impressed with the performance. They rose up, and applauded with great pleasure.

The third and final round began with both men covered in perspiration, and showing some sign of tiredness. They stalked each other with great intent, and they both grabbed each other's powerful hands trying to achieve a winning lock, and each time they managed to wriggle out of being caught. The crowd were becoming agitated at this apparent stalemate situation, and began to shout words of advice to their favourite wrestler. Then the two men broke free and charged at each other several times, one slipping the other, until Hanuman caught Pathana with a severe push that sent him flying into the crowd at one corner of the ring. The force caused Pathana to crush a few men onto the floor. He stood up and charged towards his opponent in a complete rage, and slammed Hanuman to the ground where he tried to pin him down until the bell rang out to signal the end of the round, and of the match.

The referee held both men's arms aloft as he announced a draw. This brought some applause, but others vented their displeasure by booing the result, insisting that their fighter had won. Hanuman and Pathana embraced each other, and with great smiles, raised the other's arms in a show of mutual respect, and admiration.

That evening, all the talk below deck was about the fight, and the result. Sometimes the arguments became so heated, that Mustafa called out for everyone to calm down.

Hanuman and Pathana thenceforth became immensely popular amongst the emigrants and the ship's crew. They put on shows to demonstrate their outstanding wrestling skills, and individual feats of strength. Hanuman would wrestle with two or sometimes, three young emigrants, and still emerge the winner without causing the youngsters any harm. Pathana showed how he could lift up two men, one in each arm, at the same time. The two men became even closer friends from thereon.

The Captain took the opportunity to have Hanuman and Pathana lead the daily exercise regime on deck, before the morning meal. Even the crew members and emigrant women joined in with the communal muscle stretching, and loosening up sessions.

Hanuman and Pathana were often seen helping the sailors on some tasks requiring additional muscle power. Their presence on deck also drew attention from the younger men who were full of admiration for them, and would gather around them when they were doing their own training and practice.

It became an almost comical show when, as the two strong men stood up, and walked with their powerful chests pushed forward and heads held high, the group of young men would follow them trying to ape their every movement, despite being scrawny replicas of their new heroes.

13.

Respite at the Cape of Good Hope

The emigrants were now in the middle of the crossing of the *Kaala Paani*; a journey which was feared by their compatriots. There was a belief that anyone who dared to cross the *Kaala Paani* was effectively relinquishing his or her Indian heritage, culture, religion, and the right to be considered an Indian upon their return, if and when they chose to do so. Many of the first tranche of emigrants, who had chosen to return to India in 1843, after labouring in British Guiana since 1838, had experienced much vilification from the people of their villages. The *Zamindars* wasted no opportunity to demand money from those who returned to their villages from overseas.

Mustafa and his fellow travellers, were wondering just how much longer their journey would be across the temperamental seas. Yet, no one asked the Captain or his crew, and they preferred to endure all that was happening to, and around them. Some of the men, particularly from the Dhangar tribes, were becoming homesick, and displaying signs of depression, fatigue, boredom and withdrawal.

The Surgeon Superintendent was alert to this behaviour, and he encouraged the *Sirdars* to talk to the Dhangars, and to try to lift their spirits. But this was also difficult for the *Sirdars* themselves, who had no experience of such a long sea voyage. Mustafa decided that he would approach the Surgeon Superintendent to find out how much longer the journey would last.

The Surgeon Superintendent, although irritated by Mustafa's question, informed him that they were heading towards the Cape of Good Hope, where they would stop for a few days. They needed to secure some fresh supplies, and to give everyone some much needed rest. He asked Mustafa to call the *Sirdars* together, and to tell them about the plan.

Mustafa duly obliged, and the *Sirdars* in turn, passed the message to their respective group of emigrants. They were disappointed to learn that none of them would be allowed to disembark at the harbour. They were further upset to hear that some of them would be selected to help with the loading of the supplies.

That night, without warning, a fierce wind took hold of the ship, and rocked it violently, preventing anyone from sleeping. Sea sickness struck many below deck, and by the next morning, the whole sleeping area stank with vomit. Worse still, two more emigrants did not survive the night, and the next day was dominated by the Hindu funeral ceremonies. Five unfortunate souls had now perished on this wretched mission and journey with seemingly, no known end in sight.

The wind continued to force the ship forwards, and it was noticeably colder. All the emigrants were now confronting a new hazard of coldness beyond their experience. They tried to wrap as much cloth around their shivering bodies, from head to toes. For the first time in their short lives, they felt the effects of acute cold which made their fingers and toes numb with excruciating pain. The freezing wind penetrated their defences, and their ears, eyes and heads also ached as if they were caught in the grip of some unbearable illness. The children were weeping aloud as their mothers cradled them to give them added warmth, and some comfort.

The emigrants were now more relieved to be kept below deck, as they realised that if it was so cold away from direct contact with the icy wind, it would be far worse for them above deck. Meanwhile, the tired crew continued to battle with the wintry conditions, and managed to keep the ship well within its course.

Just before dawn, one member of the crew shouted, "Land Ahoy! Land Ahoy!" and all his colleagues cheered and shouted with great pleasure, and mighty relief. The emigrants did not, at first, understand what the commotion above their heads was all about, and they looked bewildered. Then, as the hatches were opened, they were all told to go up on deck.

When they arrived on deck, some of the emigrants were still visibly shivering from the cold. The Captain, with the Surgeon Superintendent standing beside him, gladly announced that they had finally reached within sight of the Cape of Good Hope. They would steer towards Table Bay, and then obtain some fresh food and medicines. He asked them to wash their sleeping quarters, and to have baths. He offered them some clean clothes and blankets if they needed them.

The stay at the Cape of Good Hope lasted for three days and nights, and everywhere on the buffeted ship, there was a hive of activity to clean, and polish all the metal and woodwork seen above the water line. The sleeping quarters were vigorously dusted, and then sprayed with sanitary powder. The oil lamps were taken down from their positions, and cleaned thoroughly by the emigrants. There was a sense of renewed optimism prevailing on board.

A fleet of small boats ferried the ship's supplies back and forth. The tired crew were relieved to have volunteers such as Hanuman and Pathana, who lent their much needed strength to collect, fetch and pack the foodstuff which included fruits, rice, potatoes and flour, into the ship's hold.

The emigrants were very pleased to have the sweet oranges as part of their evening meal on the first night of the stopover. They sang, played rhythms using sticks, and danced, whilst many of the crew chose to seek their own entertainment on shore. When Hanuman and Pathana had rested after their labour, they agreed to put on a special wrestling re-match the following evening. The Captain invited some guests on board, and true to form, the programme was a resounding success. Hanuman had every chance to secure a victory over Pathana, but chose not to "go for the kill", as his friend had sustained an injury to his right leg, during the fight.

Later that evening, the sailors who had gone ashore, returned when the emigrants were asleep, and continued to drink rum that they had brought with them from the taverns. Soon, there was a commotion, as a few of the drunken sailors tried to open the hatch where the young women were sleeping.

Two of the sailors managed to creep down the steps from the hatch, and grabbed the first person they could reach. The woman screamed as the men ignored her pleas, and started to rip off her clothing. The assault continued for a few more frightening minutes, until a pistol shot was heard. Other sailors, who were not with the drunken mob, rushed down to the women's quarters, and finally managed to arrest the two men after a brief scuffle.

The Captain restored order, had the two men put in chains, and locked up for the remainder of the night. The next morning, before the first meal, the two prisoners were brought before the Captain as the emigrants, and the rest of the crew looked on. The woman, who had suffered the assault, was held in the sickbay, and cared for by the Surgeon Superintendent. There were some ghastly bruises to her eyes, face, arms and legs, and she was utterly traumatised by the experience.

Justice was meted out swiftly and efficiently by the Captain, who ordered the two men to be accompanied off the ship forthwith, and to be placed in the hands of the authorities on the Cape. They were effectively banished from the ship without pay. The Captain then re-affirmed his intolerance of bad and criminal behaviour by anyone on board his ship. He then ordered the crew to get back to work after announcing that no crew member would be allowed to go ashore for the remainder of that day, or, evening.

The emigrants were visibly upset by the callous actions of the two sailors, but were also assured by the Captain's firm handling of the incident, and his immediate embargo to help prevent future misdeeds. They would tread carefully in their dealings with the crew who were now held with greater mistrust than before.

Mustafa looked across towards the young women, and was relieved to see that Ishani appeared to be well. They smiled at each other. Kanhaiya saw the two exchanging smiles, and he winked knowingly at his *bhaiya*.

Kanhaiya said, "Thank *Bhagwan* that she is well."

"Yes, thank *Allah* that they are all well. I am so angry with these worthless white men who think that they are so superior to us. They are nothing but rats from their sewers in England, who still look at us, and talk to us with such contempt." Mustafa stopped his comments short, as the order came for them to prepare for their meal.

The meal that morning was decidedly better than all the previous ones, and the emigrants ate heartily. Those who chose to eat meat relished the spicy mutton curry, rice and *daal*. The vegetarians enjoyed *bhaingan* and *aloo* curry with their rice and *daal*. Tamarind chutney was also served with the meals, and the dessert was fresh ripened oranges. After a short rest, Hanuman and Pathana, along with their young and enthusiastic fans, conducted the usual exercise routines, and everyone retired for a good sleep until it was time for the evening meal.

The replacement sailors were brought aboard to take the places of the banished seamen. They appeared quite nervous at the sight of the hundreds of emigrants who simply stared at them in silence. The sailors quickly fell into their routine, setting about their tasks without the need for much close supervision.

At the end of the third day in the picturesque Cape of Good Hope, the ship weighed anchor, and began to sail quietly out of the port, and into the next phase of the epic journey. This time the Captain explained to the emigrants that there will be periods of extreme cold as the ship made its way out into the Atlantic Ocean. They were advised to make best use of their blankets to keep as warm as possible, at all times. Everyone was asked to look out for each other as they tried to overcome the expected hardships. The *Sirdars* were asked to report any signs of sickness amongst the emigrants on their watch, to the Surgeon Superintendent, as soon as possible.

That evening, as the ship rolled from a new push from the icy winds, a shrill cry was heard from the family quarters. The Surgeon Superintendent had gone down to attend to a young boy of about ten years, who had suddenly taken very ill, with coughing and vomiting. His young mother cradled him in her arms against her chest, and tearfully pleaded for him to get better. His father could do nothing but look on, silently sharing in the despair. The Surgeon Superintendent eased the patient away from his mother's tight grip, and laid him on a blanket which was spread on the floor beside his berth.

He examined the boy thoroughly, and administered some medicine orally after some resistance. The parents crouched helplessly beside their son whose life was fading fast. The mother kept mopping the boy's hot forehead with a piece of damp cotton cloth, still crying as she spoke to him. But the boy could not respond as he closed his eyes for what turned out to be the last time. He was finally at rest, and out of the misery of his pain. As soon as the Surgeon Superintendent quietly announced that the boy had died, both parents and the other families who had witnessed the event began to weep.

The funeral of the young boy was the saddest of all that the emigrants had experienced on the journey. The parents of the deceased stood side by side consoling each other, and appeared thoroughly demoralised and downtrodden. When the body was gently lowered into the sea, many of the emigrants walked over to embrace the couple, and to offer their condolences.

The other children, who were great friends and playmates of the deceased boy, were inconsolable. Once again, through the remainder of that day, the children refrained from their usual games on deck, and the adults sat around in small groups, immersed in quiet conversation.

After the evening meal, a session of chanting from the *Ramayan* was held by the Hindus, followed by a short reading of the *Qur'an* by the Muslims, before everyone quietly drifted away to the sleeping quarters. A sense of great calm descended on the ship, and even the hostile wind dropped appreciably, adding to the mournful atmosphere. No one seemed to be in the mood to talk, preferring instead, to sleep through the night, and taking advantage of the little respite.

14.

Down in the Doldrums

The ship reached a large body of sea where, due to the lack of any high winds, it was almost becalmed. The tremendous skills and experience of the crew were put to the test as they constantly sought to extract any possible opportunity to move the ship forwards. They succeeded in making the ship only inch its way along the serene waters. These were known as the Doldrums.

Some of the emigrants sought to relieve their boredom by attempting to catch fish by using a variety of contraptions, from extended strings held by hand over the sides of the vessel, to poorly constructed nets they tried to cast. They displayed remarkable patience, and optimism with their venture, but to no avail. Unfortunately, they failed to add any further option onto their unexciting menu.

The children seemed to have overcome their grief, and resumed playing their games on deck. The mothers and the single women took the opportunity to form one larger group sitting together, chatting, darning torn clothes, and grooming each other's hair. The younger men still tried to win the attention of the girls they were attracted to, with little success. Hanuman and Pathana held training classes for the would-be young wrestlers, whilst the older men spent their time discussing the journey, their expectations of British Guiana, and their hopes for the future.

The Captain, Surgeon Superintendent, and the crew were busy trying to eke out as much progress that was possible in the Doldrums, and generally kept away from the emigrants.

Mustafa and Kanhaiya joined the older men in their discussions, and also spent some time by themselves, talking about their families, their friends, and their plans for the future. Ishani was constantly at the side of the mother who had lost her son, trying to console her, and to lift her spirits. The other women also took turns to do the same, but she was still grieving deeply for her child. The father was always tearful, and encouraged Ishani and the women to continue to counsel his wife.

No one was admitted to the sickbay throughout the long hours and days in the Doldrums. But the boredom began to take hold of the emigrants despite their best efforts to entertain themselves. The Dhangars were the first to become more withdrawn, and soon preferred to go below deck and sit in solitude. Mustafa and the other *Sirdars* tried to encourage them to talk, by sharing light-hearted stories.

One evening, just after it became dark, and everyone had settled down for the night, they were disturbed by a lone sailor who shouted "Man overboard! Man overboard!" This caused a great commotion on deck as all the other sailors on duty rushed to the side of the ship where the person fell into the sea. They could not see anyone in the water as it was too dark. Thus no one jumped into the sea to affect a rescue.

The Captain, still wearing his night clothing, rushed out of his cabin to join his crew as they continued to look for the person who had fallen into the water. He summoned all the crew on deck, and after a quick inspection and inquiry, established that the person or persons overboard was or were not one of the crew.

Their attention then turned to the emigrants. All the *Sirdars* were called up on deck, and asked if any of their charges had gone missing. Then, before they were able to account for their fellow emigrants, a lone passenger emerged from the family quarters, and sobbing uncontrollably, he told them that his wife had slipped away from her berth, and jumped into the sea.

The young mother could not overcome the pain, and suffering she felt for her lost son. She blamed herself for his untimely death, and despite the help she received from everyone, she fell into utter despair, and decided that the only way out of her predicament, was to join him in his watery grave.

The Captain, who had not shown his personal religious nature, decided to lead the assembled crew and emigrants in the Lord's Prayer, for the soul of the sad mother. This was followed by a short prayer by the *Brahmin*, and a *dua* by the *Hafeez*.

Every emigrant looked blankly into the still water below, as they made their way back to their sleeping quarters. They were all in shock, and not many of them were able to sleep through the remainder of the night.

The ship had not made much progress overnight, and the early morning sunshine was decidedly warmer, with the humidity also stifling. Suddenly, a squall appeared with dry hot air and wild lashing rain. This caused the emigrants to retreat hurriedly below deck. This dramatic change in the weather made the ship jolt forward for a while, but as soon as the wind dropped, the calm of the Doldrums returned.

The dry heat caused the deck to become free of the rain water, and the emigrants finally managed to resume their seats for their first meal. They noticed that the portions of rice, curry and *daal* were much smaller than usual, and they discussed their concerns with the *Sirdars*.

Mustafa found himself once again, having to make a representation about the apparent new rationing. The Captain informed him that as they had been virtually stuck in the Doldrums for days, there was a need to conserve on the ship's provisions, should the situation become worse. He cited examples where ships had run out of their food stocks, and had lost crew members, and passengers, through starvation and dehydration. He was not prepared to put anyone on his ship through any unnecessary risks.

Mustafa explained the Captain's message to the emigrants, and they understood but remained worried. Having so far endured the stormy wrath of the seas, the recurrent sickness, the loss of some passengers, the uncomfortable and sometimes sub-human conditions, they must now face up to food rationing in the hot, and unpleasant atmosphere presented by the Doldrums.

The emigrants felt increasingly entrapped in a situation where they had no amount of control. Severe doubts crept into their thoughts and conversations. They became more restless and fidgety. Little pockets of raised voices, and petty disagreements were resolved by the equally frustrated *Sirdars*. Their fears were heightened by the lack of any positive information on their prospects of getting out of the Doldrums. Their gloom was mirrored by the ever-present large dark clouds that simply did not move away for days and nights.

There seemed to be no end in sight, of the sheer frustration that gripped everyone on board. Then, early one morning, as the sun wearily rose on the horizon, an albatross appeared and glided effortlessly above, circling in a wide area, before alighting at the furthest point on the bow of the ship. The emigrants were amazed at the size of the gracious seabird, particularly its very wide wingspan. They wondered why it had chosen to land on their ship.

The sailors knew of the significance of the presence of the albatross. It was a sign that the wind was not far away, and, as always, they were correct. A severe wind storm emerged in only a very short time, and the sailors excitedly launched into action to secure all the sails in readiness for a big push ahead. The emigrants swiftly made their way below deck as the storm began to announce itself with great thunderclaps, and a dazzling array of bright lightening cutting through the black ominous clouds. The still waters began to change into growing ripples that turned into larger waves which crashed against the ship as it lunged forward.

The Captain was visibly happy to be on the move again, and belted out his orders with a new energy, and enthusiasm. The crew responded with like urgency as they knew that the change in the weather presented them with a great chance to get out of the Doldrums. But they also knew that they needed to stay well ahead of the eye of the storm for as long as possible, and to avoid being caught up in any further danger, should the storm grow into a much more dangerous hurricane.

The Captain and his crew were also delighted to have the help of Hanuman and Pathana who had volunteered to work in whatever way they could. They were not trained *lascars*, but their sheer strength would be of good use to their new workmates. The two friends made sure that they worked together, side by side, occasionally slipping on the unsteady and wet flooring of the deck, and recovering with each other's help.

The sailors were full of admiration for the two strongmen who seemed to take orders well, and were determined to see them through, despite the unfamiliar difficulties they faced. Everyone's stamina was being truly tested as the winds picked up more power through the day. They did not have the chance to have their first meal that day, and this was bound to affect their energy levels. Nevertheless, they toiled without a break, pushing themselves to the limit.

Then disaster struck. A wooden pole broke loose and swung out of control, crashing into Pathana's back so powerfully, that it sent him hurtling over the side of the ship, and into the angry waters. Without hesitation, his best friend Hanuman plunged feet first into the sea to rescue him. Pathana sank briefly, and he was unable to keep his head above the water line. He was unconscious from the blow he received. Hanuman tried his best to grab his friend, but could not reach him as he sank without a trace.

Then Hanuman also began to flounder as he was exhausted. Three sailors had dived into the violent water to try to rescue the two friends, and as they reached nearer to Hanuman, he slipped below the surface of the water. They bravely dived under to try to make contact with him, but failed in their attempts.

The Captain and the other sailors who were witnessing the drama, shouted at the three sailors to give up their search, and to climb back on board. The storm continued to rage, and no one had any time to consider the loss of the two friends they had come to admire, and respect.

The next morning, as the emigrants emerged from below deck for their first main meal, they were devastated to learn of the loss of Hanuman and Pathana. The young fans of the two wrestlers wept inconsolably, as did everyone who had come to know and love them. After the funeral service for Hanuman and Pathana, many of the crew and emigrants could not eat their meals that day.

The Captain lavished high praise on the two men, and said that he was touched by their humility, and their willingness to help him, and his crew. They were owed a debt for helping to keep everyone's spirits up, and for their work in supporting the crew through most of the storm that eventually took them out of the Doldrums. He wished that they were members of his crew.

The ship was now well on its way towards the final destination, but the gloom stayed with all on board for much of the remainder of the voyage.

15.

The end of a voyage; the sight of a new beginning

The Captain called for all the emigrants to be assembled on deck, so that he could inspect everyone. The Surgeon Superintendent walked beside him as he stopped to look at those who did not seem to be as fit and well as they could be. A young mother lifted her daughter up to her hips, and the Captain noticed that the child's eyes were reddened, and she was dribbling at the mouth. The Surgeon Superintendent took a note as a reminder to visit the child for further checks.

The overall general condition of the emigrants pleased the Captain who was keen to ensure that there would be no further loss of life above the nine souls who had perished on the journey. With the help of translations by the *Sirdars*, he told the emigrants to keep clean, eat all their food, and exercise as much as possible as the final leg of the journey would be over in a short time.

The emigrants stood and listened attentively, and did not raise any questions. They were still mournful about the losses suffered along the way. Mustafa looked across at the short line of women, and was assured that Ishani was well. Kanhaiya saw him and smiled.

The meals served that day were once again in larger portions, and the emigrants were very pleased about this. It was also a good sign that the dangers that were presented by the Doldrums, and the storm, had been lifted.

That evening, after the late meal, the young student wrestlers of the Hanuman and Pathana school, put on a wonderful show of their newly acquired wrestling skills. The two friends would have been very proud of the young men. The Captain congratulated the wrestlers, and advised them to keep practising and improving their art.

It was late March, and the Hindus asked for permission to celebrate the festival of *Holi*. A *Sirdar* and the *Brahmin*, who had acted as a *Pandit* at the funerals, explained the significance and rituals of *Holi* to the Captain, and he allowed for the festival to be observed. However, he did not permit the burning of the *Holika*, but allowed the *Brahmin* to perform the *Holi Pooja* in the morning. No meat was to be cooked or consumed by anyone, including the ship's crew, out of respect and tolerance for the religion.

Then, during the playful session of throwing water at each other, all the emigrants participated, including the Muslims, with some gusto. *Holi* songs were sung, and although the emigrants did not have white or coloured powder or *abeer*, they thoroughly enjoyed themselves. The surprised sailors looked on with some curiosity, and at times, when they were being invited to join in with the fun, they politely declined. But this did not prevent the more excitable young men from chasing after the sailors, and dousing them with water at every opportunity.

The wonderful spirit of *Holi* brought a new surge of optimism to the emigrants. By the end of the day, they were virtually exhausted, but feeling very happy. The chains of gloom and despondency had been broken, and the bonds of renewed friendship and companionship were restored.

That evening, before bedtime, the *Brahmin* led the session of religious discourse with quotations from the *Ramayan* and *Bhagwad Gita*. Kanhaiya sat at the front of the congregation, and listened to the *Katha*, very attentively. Mustafa was very pleased with his brother who was beginning to take an interest in his religion, as he had promised.

Kanhaiya, in the succeeding days and nights, took every opportunity to converse with the *Brahmin* and others who shared his interest. His passion for learning the *Sanskrit shlokas* and *Hindi bhajans* by memorising them, was an inspiration to all around him. He also found that he was gifted with a good singing voice, and perfect sense of rhythm.

The Captain and his crew took great advantage of the very favourable trade winds of the South Atlantic Ocean, and the impressive ship with its sails fully extended, cut its way through the turbulent waters with sheer majesty. This, coupled with the light-heartedness of all on board, made the journey seem more of a pleasure cruise than a shipment of labourers, and goods.

During the daytime, large schools of whales, dolphins and fish swam closely beside the ship, presenting a spectacular display of their special acrobatics at great speeds, always seeming to race ahead of the vessel. The emigrants loved the shows, and marvelled at the dexterity of the whales and dolphins. Tropical flying fish were skipping just above the waves in their hundreds. The hot sun and prevailing dry wind, although uncomfortable at times, did not deter the emigrants from enjoying the performance.

The lone albatross had long since flown away, and the only birds accompanying the ship were white seagulls which were hovering, and always on the lookout for something to eat. They would swoop down onto the waves as soon as any foodstuff was thrown out from the galley by the cooks, and flap around in an orgy of pecking at the potato peels, and other eatables. Their squawking was quite loud, and somewhat unpleasant to the ear.

The emigrants were now presented with a better opportunity to engage in some fishing, but they seemed to be more interested in being spectators rather than catchers. Besides, they realised that the seagulls would be competing fiercely for the fish that they may catch.

The new full moon which had coincided with the *Holi* festival was a beautiful glow of almost white light every evening, and the bright stars in the cloudless skies flickered in a great cosmic dance. The emigrants loved to stay on deck after the evening meal, to enjoy the majestic display of the sky at night. But their fun would always be cut short as they were ordered to retire for the night.

This luminous tranquillity was shattered one evening, by the screaming of a woman from the family quarters. She had just witnessed the final breath of her beautiful young daughter who had never recovered from her symptoms that were noticed by the Captain and the Surgeon Superintendent at the inspection.

The Surgeon Superintendent had kept a close watch on the girl, treating her with medicines, and a diet to reduce her vomiting. But her decline continued unabated. He had asked the other families to observe the grieving mother, and to report any sign of depression or attempt at suicide. The man who had lost his son and wife, tried to comfort the woman, and they stood side by side throughout the funeral, and burial at sea the next morning.

The Captain requested even closer and more regular checks on the emigrants as he was very keen to complete his mission, with the very minimum loss of life. He sought to maximise the financial gain out of his cargo of humans and goods, upon arrival in British Guiana. He was pleased that the stream of illnesses which struck the emigrants from the outset of their voyage had virtually disappeared, and everyone was in better health and wellbeing, except those who had suffered recent bereavements.

On the morning of the 4th of May 1845, ninety-eight days after leaving Calcutta with three hundred and seventy-two emigrants, the cry of "Land Ahoy!" signalled the beginning of the end of a fateful and life-changing journey for Mustafa, and all of his companions; the *Jahajis*.

PART 3

BRITISH GUIANA

16.

The welcome in British Guiana

Finally, the hugely impressive ship was steered smoothly and efficiently into the wide mouth of the Demerara River, bearing as close as possible to the harbour front of Georgetown, the capital city of the colony of British Guiana, on the mainland of South America. The water was heavily silted and dark brown in colour; a contrast with the mostly deep blue of the Seas encountered on the voyage from Calcutta. The sky was blue, and dotted with light white clouds. The sun's sharp rays were casting their spell of fiery heat as the vessel gently passed the City.

The colony's Agent-General for Emigration, along with his assistants, a Senior Immigration Agent, and, two Immigration Agents, who were all Englishmen, stood silently on the harbour by the edge of the docking area. They were patiently awaiting the arrival of this first shipment of Indian labourers since the resumption of the arrangement. There were small groups of very curious former African slaves standing around as onlookers.

The ship slowly inched its way as close as possible as it could get to the harbour which was made of strong long-lasting greenheart timber, sourced from the vast tropical forest of the colony. The harbour chosen for the mooring was located at Pouderoyen, on the West Bank of the Demerara River. The emigrants, with their individual bags of belongings, stood on deck closely observing the actions of the Captain and his crew, as they secured the best position at which to lower the giant iron anchor into the bed of the river.

As this position was still some fifty yards away from the harbour, the emigrants were encouraged to disembark from the starboard side, climbing down very nervously on the rope ladders, onto small boats which were bobbing unsteadily in the river below. The women grabbed the rope ladder with great resolve, and inched their way down, pausing when the ladder became unsteady, until finally stepping gingerly onto the boats with great relief. The younger children were held by the stronger men who volunteered to return as soon as they secured a safe landing for their charge. The boats operated in tandem, and the passengers had to negotiate the wooden steps that led to the top of the harbour floor which was about twenty feet above the water line. The *Sirdars* waited at the top of the steps to help the climbers when they reached the final rung. The Captain, Surgeon-Superintendent, and a few of their senior sailors, took up their positions at the head of the large gathering of very nervous men, women and children, who stood upright, facing the reception committee.

Then, for the first time, they heard the word used to describe them from thence onwards; "*Coolie!*" shouted a few of the Africans in a mocking way, accompanied by gestures for them to go away. They were largely ignored by the officials, and the representatives from the sugar plantations who had arrived to receive their allotted labourers; the new immigrants.

Some of the immigrants were familiar with the term *Coolie* which was attributed to people who were labourers employed to carry goods, either by themselves or by the use of carts that they pushed or pulled. However, it was being used in a derogatory manner by the resentful Africans who were former slaves and whose places as workers on the sugar plantations were to be taken up by the Indians.

The Africans tried to present themselves as menacing as possible, standing firmly and holding cutlasses in their strong hands, and pointing directly at the immigrants as they shouted their insults. They were determined to get their message of loathing and despise as loudly as possible. The immigrants could do nothing but look on in sheer disbelief, and terror.

This early treatment made Mustafa and his companions begin to harbour grave doubts and anxieties about their new situation. They had been well treated, and well looked after on the long sea journey, despite their harrowing experiences. They were not forewarned about this type of hostility towards them.

The Agent-General and the Captain appeared to be much more concerned about conducting the formalities of their business transaction, than about the feelings of the immigrants. They greeted each other with formal salutes followed by firm handshakes. The immigrants were ushered into a large holding area which was secure enough to prevent anyone from escaping. They could still hear the taunts of the Africans who were finally told to leave the area. Apart from the word *Coolie*, the immigrants could not understand what the Africans were saying in their creole language.

Mustafa recalled Mohan Lall's account of the abuse that the crowds had given Sundar Das when he was trying to recruit emigrants in Calcutta, and the instances when the Indian onlookers at the Depot seemed to ridicule them for leaving their country to cross the *Kaala Paani*. He and his companions were now faced with more insults from strangers that they had never encountered before, except for those immigrants who had chosen to return to the colony.

The *Sirdars* were told to continue to oversee their charges, and Mustafa, along with help from Kanhaiya, gathered his group in their own corner. They began to feel more assured about their situation until they observed the individual plantation representatives strolling around, and looking them over, as in a formal inspection of troops.

Mustafa whispered to Kanhaiya and his group, "Stay together as closely as possible. Do not separate or break away from here. We are *jahaji bhais* and we must remain so."

Soon, when the selection process began, for the allocation of indentured labourers to the sugar plantations on the West Bank and West Coast of Demerara from this first shipment, Mustafa's instinctive fears were confirmed. The workers, including a small proportion of women and children, were split up into groups to fulfil the needs of each plantation at that time.

Fortunately for Mustafa and Kanhaiya, they were kept together, but with only a few others from their group. They were selected for the estate of Anna Catherina on the West Coast of Demerara. Ishani, whom Mustafa had tried to protect in India and on the voyage, was selected for another estate unknown to him. He and Kanhaiya were saddened by this.

Each set of new recruits for an estate, was herded together by whip-wielding *Drivers* of the respective plantation. Whilst Mustafa seemed assured that at least one of the Drivers was an Indian, he was unsure of the others who were white men and Africans. They took up a stance of authority about them, speaking in short English and creole commands, with their whips at the ready, or tucked into their leather belts at the waist of their khaki trousers. They also wore khaki coloured pith helmets, and were walking around with some arrogance, and a

THE WELCOME IN BRITISH GUIANA

sense of great pride of being in charge. The light and relatively friendly touch that Mustafa and the other *Sirdars* had practised on the ship was now replaced by a stricter regime that sought to impress its authority on the labourers, at the earliest opportunity.

Mustafa and his group remained quite docile and calm, obeying every instruction given to them when they understood these. When they faltered through not appearing to understand what the Drivers were saying, they were shouted at until the message was received, and acted upon. Sometimes the Drivers reached for their whips, and threatened to use them. But the immigrants tactfully tried their best to obey politely.

As Anna Catherina was located at about nine miles on the West Coast, the immigrants were placed into large four-wheeled carts where they sat back to back with their feet dangling over each side, carefully avoiding contact with the wheels. They tried to cover their heads with cotton scarves which did not give them enough respite from the blazing tropical sun. They sweated profusely as they were not accustomed to the humid conditions they were experiencing for the first time. The searing heat from the sharp sun felt more intense than that in Northern India.

The road was of similar poor quality as they had endured in India; dusty and riddled with holes which made the ride very uncomfortable. As they passed from plantation to plantation, they saw how the sugarcane was planted only on one side of the road. The northern side was uncultivated, and with abundant mangrove bushes. The mangroves were natural defences against the rampaging tides of the Atlantic Ocean to the north, and the waves of the Demerara River along the West Bank.

Occasionally, on the slow journey, they would notice a small group of Indian cane-cutters walking towards their homes, or, on their way to the fields. They did not call out to the workers for fear of being scolded by the two Drivers on each of the two carts. One sat at the front of the cart beside the cart driver, and the other sat at the back facing the passengers. The Indian workers did not acknowledge their countrymen who had just arrived, and only seemed intent on going about their business without fuss.

They also noticed that beside the edges of the road, there were neatly cut trenches which separated the track from the sugarcane fields on one side, and mangroves on the other. The trenches were linked to a network of wider and deeper canals which formed boundaries for the fields, and the main routes for taking the harvested sugarcane stalks to the sugar factory. The canal and trench system was finally linked to *kokers* which were used to control the flows of water in and out to the Ocean.

The *kokers* were built by the former Dutch colonists who ceded the colony to the British. The structure of the *kokers* was of the robust greenheart timber, with two main uprights and a crossbar supporting a movable panel which was winched up to allow the water to pass through, or down, to block the flow. The huge iron winch was normally operated by one man, strong enough to turn the wheel and pulley system, to open or close the koker. The system of canals, trenches and *kokers*, was critical for the supply of adequate water used in the sugarcane fields, and the drainage of excess water to avoid flooding.

The two carts stopped for a few minutes to allow the immigrants to stretch their legs, and some of the men took the opportunity to urinate in the nearby bushes. The few women were more circumspect, and preferred not to do the same as the men. As expected, the Drivers kept a close eye on their passengers.

Further along the road, they saw villages which were mostly occupied by Africans living in small houses that were single floored with thatched roofs, one front door and one window to each side. Each house had a small piece of land with some makeshift fencing to protect the plants, vegetables and livestock kept by the owners. The immigrants noticed that the villages were not as established or organised as their own in India. The African families stood up to look at the small procession of carts, but did not shout abuse at the passengers. All the villages on route that were not sugar plantations were effectively occupied by Africans only.

The Africans tried very hard to cultivate their allotted pieces of land with plantains, ground provisions, spinach, and fruits which they sold, or used. Many of the former slaves chose to continue working on the sugar estates, particularly in the factories, but the majority left the plantations for other pursuits in the city of Georgetown, and in the mining and wood-cutting areas, deep in the forests.

When Mustafa and his companions finally arrived in Anna Catherina, they were assembled in neat rows to meet the English manager, who was referred to as *Massa* by the Drivers. The Indian

Driver introduced himself as Ragubir, a short, dark-skinned man wearing a uniform of a neat khaki trouser and shirt which had sweat stains clearly visible under both armpits. He announced in Hindi, that he was the interpreter, and would speak for the Massa. Anyone wishing to refer their issues to the Massa must do so through him.

The Massa was about six feet tall, slender, and dressed in an elegant khaki suit, with a white pith helmet that seemed to be a little too big for his head. His thin, reddened, and clean-shaven face, narrow blue eyes, and long thin nose, were conditioned by years of exposure to the British Guiana sun. He was in his early forties, and had gained a good reputation for fair-mindedness on his estate.

The Massa duly welcomed the immigrants to the estate, and informed them about their living quarters, their supplies of foodstuff, clothing, and other provisions, and, who they were expected to report to for their allocated tasks. Mustafa listened attentively to the Massa as well as to the interpretation given by Ragubir, so that he would be assured that the message was being delivered accurately.

The Massa wished the workers well, and left the remainder of the welcome, and arrangements to Ragubir, and the other Drivers. Immediately behind the workers, were two long lines of dwellings called *logies*, which faced each other, and were within a neatly cleared area surrounded by a well-constructed wooden fence which was about six feet high. There was one large main gate that was used as the only entrance and exit to the compound.

Ragubir informed the immigrants that they would be split into two groups. The first group would be comprised of males, who were expected to do the heavier and more strenuous work of digging, clearing undergrowth, and planting the sugarcane shoots. This was called the "shovel" gang, and Mustafa and Kanhaiya were both selected as members. The second group was known as the "weeding" gang, and all the women, younger girls and the weaker looking men were allocated to this group. The shovel gang would provide the workers who would cut the sugarcane; the "canecutters". They would load the cut cane onto iron barges in the canal beside the field, and this would be transported to the factory for processing into sugar.

Mustafa and the other members of the shovel gang were to occupy one of the two *logies*, and the families and single women of the weeding gang, the other. Their welcome to British Guiana was over.

17.

Mosquito battles in the logies

The two *logies* were not newly built structures, and the complex was formerly used as the dwellings of the African slaves until they were freed. The *logies* were essentially, two long single floor houses with rooms just big enough to accommodate four adults each. The immigrants mutually agreed as to whom and how many would occupy each room, and they reached a reasonable outcome for all twenty rooms. Families were allowed priority in choosing their rooms, and the three young sets of parents with their children opted to live in rooms that were next to each other in one of the *logies*. Three single girls occupied one of the rooms next to those of the families. Mustafa and Kanhaiya were surprised to be given the choice to occupy the front room of the shovel gang's *logie*. It was a sign of the growing mutual respect that the immigrants had for the two brothers.

Each of the twenty rooms of the two *logies* had enough space for two large six foot wide beds, and a small area for cooking. The beds were made entirely of wood, and the mattresses were filled with straw. Neither was comfortable. The cooking areas were scorched black by smoke from the crude earthen stoves that were once used by the Africans. The floors were made of dirt, and were very dusty. The ceilings were also blackened by soot, and daylight could be seen through several small holes in the corrugated zinc sheet roofing.

As soon as everyone had agreed their accommodation, they set about dusting, wiping and tidying their new homes. Water, which was collected in two large iron tanks from rainfall, was to be shared by all the residents.

They carefully stored their weekly provisions of rice, onions, pepper, *daal*, salt, ghee, turmeric and dried fish. Each person had received two blankets, one jacket, two *dhotis* for men and young men, one *laskar's* cap, one wooden bowl, and one metal cup to be shared. They had brought their individual plates and *lotas*. The women and girls received two cotton *saris* each.

The great hive of activity continued well into the afternoon up to just before sunset. They sat in their rooms to share their first full meal which was prepared by the women. Each immigrant had agreed to contribute some of their provisions towards the meal. After enjoying their meal, they each took turns to wash their own plates and *lotas*, with some care not to waste the limited supply of water.

Then, as soon as they began to retire for their first night of sleep, they were visited upon by the local mosquitoes. They tried in vain to swat the insects which continued their relentless blood-sucking attacks all through the night. The victims gave up the fight through sheer exhaustion from their journeys and their exertions to make their homes more habitable. They needed to find ways of combating the new menace in their lives.

Early the next morning, Mustafa and Kanhaiya, along with a few of the other immigrants, decided to tour the compound, and noticed that a single drain that ran between the two logies, was blocked with an assortment of rubbish, and a growth of wild bushes. They cleared the drain to run out of the yard, and away into the nearest trench that flowed at the end of the settlement. This action alone could not stop the army of mosquitoes in the evenings, and the house flies which were ever-present during the course of the day. Walking around bare feet also presented its hazards with squadrons of worker ants only too willing to sting anyone who disturbed them.

The weeding gang also set to work on a general clear up of unwanted bushes and overgrown grass around the compound, up to the fence and gate. They stacked the cuttings into small heaps around the yard, safely away from the *logies*, and then set fire to them. When Ragubir and his assistants arrived at the yard, he was very surprised to see how well the immigrants had transformed their living area. He then called for them to assemble, and to hear about their allocated working times, and tasks.

Both gangs were expected to be led to a new area which was identified for preparation to become a sugarcane field within the next month. Their working days would be Monday to Friday, from six in the morning until six in the evening, just before sunset. They would break for lunch at midday, and resume the afternoon session after a two hours respite. Saturday was pay day, and Sunday their rest day. Their work would be overseen by Ragubir's assistants, and he was not expecting any idleness, as there would be penalties. Everyone was presented with a new cutlass, grass knife, shovel and hoe, which they took back to their rooms.

The next morning, at about five thirty, after another night of unrelenting attacks from their mosquito enemies, albeit not as severe as the first night, they were surprised to hear Ragubir and his assistants shouting for them to be up, and ready for the day's work. They quickly scrambled from their beds, grabbed a little left-over rice and curry which they scoffed, and presented themselves before their new masters. Ragubir gave them a little more time to pack some food for their lunch, and then they proceeded in two lines to their first tasks in British Guiana. They were not given sufficient time to acclimatise to their new environment, and the work.

After observing the new batch of labourers over the first day, Ragubir chose Mustafa as the lead for the shovel gang, and Kanhaiya, the lead for the weeding gang. Mustafa and Kanhaiya were to receive extra pay for this additional responsibility. As the workers trudged back from the field after a most tiresome and hot day's work, Ragubir walked beside Mustafa and Kanhaiya at the head of the two gangs.

Ragubir asked, "Tell me young men, where did you come from in India?"

Mustafa replied, "We both came from villages near to Kanpur in Uttar Pradesh. And where do you come from? "

Ragubir said, "I am from West Bengal and came here since 1838. I am a Dhangar. I also worked very hard, and Massa has been good to me. If you and all your gang do the same, he will look after you also."

Mustafa frowned and said, "But I heard that people who came here with you suffered badly, and that is why most of them returned to India."

Ragubir simply nodded, and did not respond.

Kanhaiya joined in with the conversation, "Our *logies* and the yard were very bad for us. Please help us to improve this, and we will work even harder. The mosquitoes are also very bad for us. What can we do to keep them away?"

Ragubir suggested that they should keep small fires burning near the *logies*, and the smoke should deter them. He also advised them to keep the drains clean, and that he would arrange for a latrine to be built for each of the *logies*.

Mustafa asked, "Tell us Mr Ragubir, truthfully, what you and your Massa do to prevent being bitten by the mosquitoes, and can we do the same?"

Ragubir said, "We all suffer from the wretched mosquitoes, and you can see how I have bite marks on my face and arms. Use your blankets to cover from head to toes. That should help. But, you will feel even hotter. Anyway, I hope that you will all have a better night's sleep." He rushed off as soon as they reached the yard.

That evening, Mustafa and Kanhaiya told everyone how to combat the mosquitoes, as advised by Ragubir, and asked them to wake up earlier so that they could eat a proper meal, and prepare their lunches in advance. The women and girls suggested that everyone should rub some oil on their faces, arms and legs, as a deterrent to the invading mosquitoes.

They tried all the remedies suggested, but they were still bitten by the blood-thirsty insects. To add to the misery, the wooden beds and straw mattresses presented a new enemy to good sleep; bed bugs. The restlessness through the night was very difficult for the immigrants to cope with, and having to wake up so early in the morning to face another hot, and arduous day in the field, was a very painful prospect. But these poor souls were determined, and very resilient.

18.

Payback on payday

The two working gangs were very excited at the prospect of receiving their first official pay for their week's work in the sugarcane field. They had laboured intensely in the alien conditions, overcoming many of the obstacles in their way, and, developing a more manageable routine of waking up on time, and sticking to the tasks required.

Most of the workers could not read the payslips they received with their cash. A few of them seemed puzzled as to the amount of money they received, and immediately referred their concerns to the two people they trusted the most; Mustafa and Kanhaiya.

When the payslips were examined by the brothers, the workers' concerns appeared justified. They were deducted pay without any explanation, and the matter was referred immediately to Ragubir. He carefully perused each payslip in turn, and when he had a small bundle of them, he held them aloft in his left hand, and called all the complainants together alongside Mustafa and Kanhaiya.

Ragubir said, "I warned you that anyone found not to complete their work on time, or to do so badly, will lose some of their pay. Unfortunately for you, my assistants reported this to the pay officers."

Mustafa responded, "This is not fair. Both Kanhaiya and I saw how hard everyone worked without even being shown how to do some of the tasks. But we all learnt very quickly, and as far as we are concerned, we have up to one month to prepare the new field for cultivation. If we fail to achieve this, then you can take some of our money. If you do not do something about this, we will report this matter to the Massa."

Ragubir was taken aback. This was the first time that his authority had been challenged, and he felt very uncomfortable, and somewhat annoyed.

"Let me tell you this," scolded Ragubir. "You can go to Massa as much as you like, but he will only believe what I say to him. If he did not trust me, he would never have given me this job. Also, you can take it from me that if you do not complete your tasks, you will receive even worse penalties, including reduction in your provisions."

Mustafa pondered Ragubir's threat, and decided to give him the benefit of the doubt on this occasion. "Alright Mr Ragubir, we will accept what you say for now, and get on with our work, and lives here."

A very relieved Ragubir sighed, and said, "Thank you Mustafa. I know that I can rely on you for good commonsense. Please tell everyone to work with me, and everything will turn out well for you all. If you choose to fight with me, you will not succeed. I would like to invite you and young Kanhaiya here, to my home for some food, and the chance to get to know each other better. Will you come this afternoon?"

Mustafa looked at Kanhaiya who nodded his acceptance. They then turned to the complainants, and explained what had happened to their pay. All the workers returned to the *logies* still feeling somewhat disgruntled.

This setback did not stop the workers from organising a grand meal for that evening, and they celebrated their first week with singing, dancing and noisy merriment. Some of the Africans from the village stood by the front gate of the yard, and looked on in wonderment.

The revelry ended as soon as nightfall arrived. Each worker took care to secure their hard-earned cash amongst their belongings, and retired for the night. Some of them tucked their money into their mattresses. Some of the women rolled the notes into a bundle, and carefully placed it inside the top of their blouses. Mustafa and Kanhaiya had missed the celebrations as they had taken up Ragubir's invitation.

Ragubir's house was located in the same compound as the Massa's, and other senior personnel of the estate. It was a very large wooden structure, comprising three bedrooms, an indoor bathroom and toilet, a large kitchen, a drawing room, and a verandah which was open to take advantage of the cooler breeze during the evenings. The house was built on sturdy timber posts about twelve feet high, thus allowing for air to flow under the first floor living quarters. This was also a potential defence against sudden flooding caused by heavy rainfall or overspill of the sea defences that were only two hundred yards away. The roof was in a classical English bungalow style, and made of corrugated zinc sheets which were painted red. The house was painted in white both externally and internally.

The three men sat in the well-furnished drawing room, on beautifully carved wooden chairs made from the local mahogany timber. Mustafa and Kanhaiya were very impressed with what they saw of the house, and congratulated Ragubir.

He said, "Thank you my friends. I have earned this by being very honest and working very hard, always pleasing Massa. He picked me out from all the others, and gave me a big opportunity to better myself. Earlier today you asked me about our treatment here, and why so many of our countrymen and a few women returned to India. Well, like you, we all came here to work for about five years, and then hoped to go back with our savings, to buy some land, and start a new life."

"Yes," agreed Mustafa. "But some people I met, said that they were beaten badly by Massa's henchmen like you, treated like slaves, forced to work harder than they could manage, and had a lot of their money taken away."

Ragubir frowned, and said, "Much of what you say is true. But the people who came here were told lies by the recruiting agents in India. Lies about how the work would be easy, and how well they would be treated. Some of them were not labourers at all, and were very unsuited to this environment. So they objected, were always arguing with the Massa and the Drivers, and always looking to run away."

Kanhaiya asked, "So, were you so different? What made you accept the situation? Why did you not rebel like the others?"

Ragubir took a handful of rice, *daal* and fish curry, and chewed quickly on the mouthful, gesturing to his guests to do likewise. He then licked the fingers of his right hand, and responded, "I had no one to go back to in India. I had made up my mind that this will be my country, and Massa encouraged me to stay after I finished five years. So, there was no reason for me to give this up for yet another start back in India."

Mustafa said, "Mr Ragubir, would you like for Kanhaiya and I to do the same here, and stay in this place? I will find that difficult to do, and my mind is still very much on my village in India. I have to return there for very special reasons."

Kanhaiya turned to Mustafa, and asked, "Is it because of a person you love there?"

Mustafa nodded, and said, "Yes, my *bhaiya*, she is all I am living for at the moment."

The men continued their discourse for another hour after finishing their delicious meal. Then, just before they were about to part company, Ragubir said, "My friends, one reason why I confided so much in you, is that I too have an unfulfilled dream. I am a very shy person, and I need your help to fix me up with one of the unmarried young women living in your yard."

"Aha!" said Mustafa. "And, which of the three young ladies are you interested in?"

Ragubir pursed his lips, and said, "The tallest and fairest of the three living together. I tried to catch her eyes, but to no avail. Could you please approach her on my behalf?"

"Well, Mr Ragubir," said Kanhaiya, seizing the moment. "If Mustafa and I are successful in this mission, I would expect you to return some favours to us!"

Ragubir nodded, smiled, and ushered his new matchmakers through the large wooden front door of his house.

"Of course, my friends. I promise that I will pay you back someday!" offered Ragubir, as he shut the door firmly behind them.

19.

Promises, promises, promises

At about six o'clock on the morning of the first Sunday, the day of rest, many of the residents of the two *logies* woke up to the usual dawn chorus of cockerels, the bright yellow kiskadee, and other local birds. Mustafa turned over lazily in his bed in an effort to catch up on as much sleep as possible. But Kanhaiya, who had a very restless night, stood up and started to shuffle around near the cooking area, occasionally causing the pot he was using to brew some tea, to rattle. This irritated Mustafa who sat up in his bed and said, "Kanhaiya, please be quiet, and go back to sleep. I need some rest!"

"Mustafa, I am sorry, but I could not sleep last night. It was not because of the mosquitoes, and bed bugs. I am so worried about our promise to Mr Ragubir," said Kanhaiya as he sat down on the edge of Mustafa's bed.

Mustafa turned wearily on his right side, and said, "What is the problem? All we have to do is to go and speak to the girl who does not have parents with her, and to hear what she says about a liaison with Mr Ragubir. What is so difficult about that?"

Kanhaiya paused for a moment, and said, "You see, the problem is that I also like that girl."

"Oh, I see," Mustafa said as he sat up more uprightly on the bed. "Are you sure that this is the girl that Mr Ragubir is interested in?"

Kanhaiya said, "Yes, she is the one. Do you remember the person who was assaulted by the two sailors at the Cape of Good Hope? She was the one who was then looked after by Ishani. She has been very sad all this week as she must be missing her friend."

"And, have you been talking to this girl?" asked Mustafa.

Kanhaiya replied, "No, not much, but as the leader of the gang, I have been watching her every move all week long. I have very strong feelings for her, and I was planning to ask you to propose to her on my behalf."

"Subhaan Allah!" said Mustafa, placing his hands over his face. "We do have a problem!"

Just then, a chirpy Ragubir appeared at the gate of the compound shouting aloud, "Mustafa! Kanhaiya! Are you up?"

The brothers and a number of the residents looked out of their windows, and saw Ragubir with a cartload of sawn wood, and four African helpers.

He spoke again with a confident raised voice, "I have brought you the materials, and some men to build the two latrines for you all! As promised! Can you come and show me where you would like to have them built? I understand that you are not happy to use the old abandoned ones."

The residents gathered around, and quickly agreed to have the new latrines built at the back of the yard, but away from the old ones which they requested to be taken down, and filled over.

The workers immediately set about digging the two new six feet deep cesspits for the new latrines. They dismantled the old wooden structures, and filled the old cesspits with the soil excavated from the new ones. The old timber was stacked up in a great pile, and set alight. The men then spent the remainder of the day building the new latrines, complete with some steps to the raised entrance doors. Some of the residents cleared, and weeded new pathways to each of the new latrines. When the project was completed, a very pleased Ragubir thanked his workers, and handed them payment in cash.

"You see, I have kept my promise to you," said Ragubir proudly. "This will improve things for you all. And you can thank our kind Massa and I for providing such nice and clean latrines for you. Please keep them clean by using them properly."

Ragubir winked at Mustafa and Kanhaiya as he left the yard. The brothers looked at each other, and frowned. How were they going to deliver on their promise? What if the girl preferred Kanhaiya over Ragubir? Will Ragubir accept such a decision? Likewise, if she chose Ragubir, will Kanhaiya ever overcome this? These and many more considerations began to occupy their minds.

Mustafa decided that the best way would be for him to approach the young lady, and to find out what she had on her mind. After all, the decision was hers to make. He did not wish to dwell on the subject any longer than he needed to, so he asked the girl to meet him in his room without the presence of Kanhaiya.

She slowly and cautiously walked to the room, and Mustafa asked her to sit down. For the first time he looked at her closely, and saw how truly beautiful she was, with almond eyes, a small nose with a silver nose ring, and a radiant smile livened by clean white teeth.

"What is your name?" asked Mustafa politely.

"Mumtaz," she replied quietly with her head lowered slightly, avoiding any eye contact with Mustafa.

Mustafa smiled warmly, and said, "Mumtaz. That is a beautiful name. You must be Muslim. Where did you come from?"

She replied, "Yes, I am Muslim, and I come from Allahabad."

Mustafa said, "Aha, I have seen Allahabad. It is a very interesting place. I had the great privilege of being blessed at the *Kumbh Mela*, and I spent many months working at the Holy Trinity Church."

Mumtaz felt more at ease, and smiled, "You are very fortunate. You are also a very special person whom everyone respects so much."

Mustafa said, "Thank you. I can see that you are alone without your parents or brothers and sisters. What made you come to this wretched place?"

Mumtaz's mood began to change, and tears welled up in her eyes as she said, "I was married to a man who already had one wife, and they both treated me like their slave. I ran away, and this made my family very angry. They threatened to kill me if they ever caught me, and I did not return to that horrible man and his wife."

Mustafa said, "I am so sorry to hear about your experience. How old are you?"

"I am nineteen years old," she said sniffing, and wiping away the tears from her eyes and reddened cheeks.

Mustafa continued, "I see that you are with two other girls about your age. Who are they?"

Mumtaz wiped some tears from her face with the end of her cotton headscarf, "They are my best friends. Their names are Gita and Mamta, who are sisters, and have the same kind of story to tell. I love them very much, and I do not wish to be parted from them. I had the chance to go with another dear friend Ishani, but I chose to be with Gita and Mamta."

"Where did Ishani go to? Do you know which estate?" asked Mustafa with some enthusiasm.

Mumtaz replied, "Yes, she went to Vreed-en-Hoop. I am so sorry that I am not with her, because she is pregnant, and she will have her baby in a few weeks time."

Mustafa was taken aback, and asked, "A baby? How... Who... When did this happen? Was it a sailor? One of the men she is with at Vreed-en-Hoop?"

Mumtaz said, "No. She told me that she was raped by the Agent who took her to Calcutta."

Mustafa raised his right index finger, and said, "Aha! That must be that scoundrel, Sundar Das!"

Mumtaz confirmed, "Yes, Ishani did mention that name. But she hates him. Do you know this man also?"

Mustafa said, "Yes, he is someone I never really trusted for as long as I was with him. That is why I tried to protect Ishani from his advances."

Mumtaz asked, "Do you have feelings for Ishani?"

Mustafa smiled, and said, "No, I feel as if I am a *bhaiya* to her, and I now wish that I was in Vreed-en-Hoop to make sure that no harm comes to her. I hope I can get to see her soon."

Mumtaz asked, "So, is this why you asked to speak to me?"

Mustafa said, "No... no... I need to speak to you about whether you are safe and well here. And, whether you would be interested in getting married, and settling down here?"

Mumtaz said, "No. I want to be with my friends, to work, to save my money, and then I will consider getting married again. I need someone who will be totally dedicated to me, and me alone. Why are you asking me such personal questions?"

Mustafa said, "I... I do not know. I... I am truly sorry to pry into your business."

"That is fine. Can I go now?" asked Mumtaz as she rose to leave.

Later that evening, Kanhaiya impatiently asked Mustafa for the news he was keenly awaiting, "Well Mustafa, what did she say?"

Mustafa replied, "Nothing. I did not ask her about you, nor did I ask her about Mr Ragubir's offer."

Kanhaiya was very disappointed, and asked, "So, when are you going to ask her? And, what will you say to Mr Ragubir?"

"Let us sleep on it. I am very tired. It has been another hard day. So much for a day of rest! I hate promises! I truly hate promises! And, I hate Sundar Das even more!" growled Mustafa as he dived under his blanket.

A very surprised Kanhaiya asked, "Sundar who?"

20.

Anything for her

The second working week for the immigrants began with them waking up a little earlier than usual, forming orderly queues to use the new latrines, and enjoying washes from a new supply of clean water to the two tanks. Ragubir made a special effort to arrive a little earlier so that he could have a chat with Mustafa and Kanhaiya, his matchmakers.

Ragubir greeted the brothers with, "Asalaam O Alaikum, my friends!"

Mustafa replied, "Waa Alaikum Asalaam to you, and Namaskaar!" He realised that Ragubir was very keen to speak to him about Mumtaz.

Ragubir asked, "Well, my friend, have you made contact with my special one yet?" Then he placed his right arm around Mustafa's shoulders.

Mustafa said, "Yes, I have spoken to Mumtaz, and the truth is, we have two problems to deal with."

Ragubir smiled assuredly, and said, "Well, I am happy to listen, and I am sure we can sort out such problems. After all, this is part of my job!"

Mustafa said, "Firstly, Mumtaz is a Muslim girl, and you are Hindu, I believe."

Ragubir straightened his stance, and placed his right arm across his chest, "Mumtaz! What a beautiful and regal name for my princess! Her being Muslim is not a problem as I am a Dhangar, and I do not practice Hinduism. I would be happy to convert, and become a Muslim for such a sweet being."

Mustafa was taken aback by this. He thought that his second problem would have to be tougher for the wily Ragubir to deal with. Then he recovered his composure and said, "That is very commendable Mr Ragubir, but the next problem is that she had a very bad experience of marriage in Allahabad, and is not prepared to re-marry as yet, until she is assured that she meets someone who will do anything for her, treat her with respect, and provide well for her."

Ragubir did not feel threatened by this, and said, "Anything for her? I will go to the ends of this earth for such a wonderful woman! Just let me know what I need to do, and consider it done!"

Mustafa said, "Well, I am glad that you are so willing to give so much for a wife, and life partner. In fact, she did ask me to obtain a pass for a day or two for herself, myself and Kanhaiya to go to Vreed-en-Hoop to meet one of our friends there. Could you arrange this for us for Saturday, and perhaps Sunday coming?"

Ragubir said, "Mustafa, my friend, consider it done. I can see how smart a fellow you are. Perhaps you will take the opportunity to talk to Mumtaz much more about me, and my devotion to her. Not only will I get you the passes, but I will also ask one of the cart drivers to take you there, and bring you back safely. How does that sound?"

Mustafa said, "That is beyond my wildest dreams. Mr Ragubir, you are a gentleman!" Then he walked off to lead his gang to work.

"Oh Mustafa!" Ragubir called out, "Remember to tell your fellow workers not to be slackers, as I do not wish to see any of you lose more pay or any of your provisions!"

Kanhaiya heard the warning given by Ragubir, and said to Mustafa, "Why is Mr Ragubir so happy? Have you made promises to him?"

Mustafa said, with a glint in his eyes, "No, he has made promises to me. He will get passes for Mumtaz, you and I, to go to Vreed-en-Hoop next Saturday. We will even get a lift as well!"

Kanhaiya smiled, and said, "Oh, thank you *bhaiya*. I really look forward to travelling those few miles with Mumtaz. At least I will be able to talk to her, and get to know her better. And, why are we going to Vreed-en-Hoop?"

Mustafa said, "To see Ishani. Mumtaz told me that Ishani is expecting a child, and we should go to see how she is coping on the estate."

Kanhaiya asked, "So, is Ishani married?"

"No, I think I know how and when she became pregnant," whispered Mustafa, for fear of being overheard.

"Do you wish to tell me more? Or, are you keeping your courtship on the quiet?" whispered Kanhaiya.

Mustafa said, "No, she has always been like a *didi* to me, and she also happens to be a close friend of Mumtaz's. Her pregnancy has nothing to do with me. I believe that she was raped by Sundar Das, the Agent who took us to Calcutta."

"That Sundar Das sounds as if he was a really nasty man," said Kanhaiya with a concerned frown on his face.

Mustafa said sternly, "Yes, I would like to meet him again, and to personally give him a good beating!"

That week, the workers continued to make very good progress in their effort to prepare the new field for sugar cultivation. The searing heat was unrelenting during the daytime, and apart from a high wind which accompanied the inward tides of the Atlantic, the nights were also unbearably hot. They were beginning to grow more accustomed to the mosquitoes through their various remedies, and actions to avoid being overwhelmed. The workers were also taking good care of their hygiene by using six inch cuttings from the black sage bush, as toothbrushes, and by keeping the drains clean as well as regularly burning their household waste at the back of the yard.

The workers began to prepare part of the yard for planting vegetables such as aubergines, tomatoes and peppers. They built a chicken coop, and purchased some hens and a cockerel from the Africans in the village.

Relationship with the Africans was still a little uncertain. This was partly due to a lack of being able to communicate in English on both sides. The Africans' creole language was completely alien, as was the Indians' broken English and Hindi. But, they were beginning to interact. Ragubir and his assistants were always willing to allow the two peoples to engage, and to explore how they could be of more help to each other. He recognised the importance of building mutual trust between them.

On the Friday morning of that week, Ragubir, true to his word, brought the official passes for Mustafa, Kanhaiya and Mumtaz, to go to Vreed-en-Hoop the next day. They would have the services of a driver and his cart, and could stay over until Sunday, if they so wished. He looked across to see if he could catch Mumtaz's eyes, but she simply glanced at him and looked away. Ragubir's heart pounded with utter excitement.

Ragubir said, "Mustafa, here are the passes for tomorrow. The driver and his cart will pick you up after you receive your pay. You do not have to pay him for the trip. I have already given him some money for this. His name is Joshua, and he was one of the men who built the new latrines. All I ask is that you treat him well. He is a true gentleman, and works extremely hard. And, do not forget to speak to my Mumtaz on my behalf. Every time I see her, I am so lost for words. Who would not do anything for a woman like her?"

"Mr Ragubir, thank you," said Mustafa. "Yes, who would not do anything for her?"

21.

No peace and hope in Vreed-en-Hoop

Everyone had special reasons to be happy on Saturday morning. No one had lost any pay due to fines, and for the first time, there was a sense of belonging to the new environment, despite the challenges being faced.

Joshua, the former African slave, carefully parked his two-wheeled cart and horse beside the dusty dirt-tracked main road which ran from Vreed-en-Hoop through several villages and plantations, for about twenty miles to Parika on the eastern coast of the mighty Essequibo River. He had also received his pay as one of Ragubir's assistants, and all-round handyman. He was about five and a half feet tall, thick set, and with strong muscular arms developed over many years of strenuous labour. Two of his front teeth were missing, and he consciously tried not to smile to expose this. He was very proud to wear a khaki shirt and trousers which were handed down to him by Ragubir. He also took great care of his very old pair of brown leather shoes. He always gave the impression of a man of few words, extremely polite, and referred to Ragubir as "Massa", and the manager of the estate as "Massa Bass".

Ragubir, always eager to present himself in such a way as to be noticed by Mumtaz, beckoned Mustafa, Kanhaiya and the young lady towards Joshua and the cart.

He said with some authority, "Come on Mustafa. Your transport awaits you. Please help the young lady to get on board. And remember, you must look after her very well. Your driver is very capable. Have a good trip, and let me know how you get on when you return."

Mustafa nodded, "Thank you Mr Ragubir. I will do so."

When the three passengers were carefully seated on the cart, Joshua took up his driving position, and cracked his three feet long whip which was made from old rope. The horse jerked into action, and quickly settled into a steady pace. The Vreed-en-Hoop estate was about nine miles east of Anna Catherina.

Mumtaz sat in the middle of the cart facing the mangrove side of the road whilst Mustafa and Kanhaiya took up the seats at the back facing away from Joshua and the horse. They did not look at, or speak to, Mumtaz or Joshua for the entire journey. However, occasionally one would point out something or someone of interest that he saw as they passed through each village or plantation, until they finally reached Vreed-en-Hoop.

"Whoa! Whoa! That's my girl!" shouted Joshua, as he pulled hard on the reins until the horse stopped. "Here we are! Vreed-en-Hoop, a Dutch word meaning peace and hope! I do wish we could find some peace and hope here!"

Mustafa and Kanhaiya leapt off the back of the cart, and instinctively turned around to take one of Mumtaz's hands each, and to help her off safely.

"Thank you both," she said as she adjusted her scarf over her head, and tied it securely under her chin. "Thank you also, Mr Joshua."

"Yes, thank you Mr Joshua," said the young men in unison.

"I hope that the ride was not bad for you," replied a pleased Joshua. "You go ahead to meet your friend. I will look after the horse and cart, and wait for you."

Mustafa wasted no time in looking for Ishani. He stepped forward smartly, and briskly. As soon as he saw someone, he enquired about Ishani's whereabouts. A young man pointed out which room she was living in at one of the *logies*. Before they reached the door, Ishani stepped out and as soon as she recognised her visitors, she exclaimed, "Mustafa! Mumtaz! Kanhaiya! Oh my God! Come, come on in! I cannot believe that you have come!"

They looked at Ishani, and could clearly see that she was in an advanced state of pregnancy.

"How are you Ishani?" asked Mumtaz as she reached out, and held her friend's hands.

"I am well. It has only been two weeks here, and it seems like such a long time," said Ishani, walking carefully just ahead of her guests.

"Are you being treated well?" asked Mustafa with some concern.

"Not at all *bhaiya*. Although I am not short of food and so on, my fellow workers do not treat me well. As soon as they knew that I was pregnant, they kept their distance from me. They think that I must be a prostitute, and have shown me much scorn. Sometimes some of the young children spit at me when I walk past them. I complain to their parents but they also insult me."

Mumtaz warmly embraced Ishani, and said, "I am so glad to see you. But I am also very sad to hear this. Maybe we should try to get you away from here, and look after you on our estate."

"That would be so good. I have asked the Driver here, and he said that will not be possible. I am at a loss, and I cry every day. The only thing that keeps me going is my baby," said Ishani, placing her hands gently on her stomach.

Mustafa said, "I think that there is a way to get you out of here. But first, let us have something to eat, and then I need to talk to the people here."

After a delicious meal of catfish curry, rice, *daal* and coconut *choka*, Mustafa and Kanhaiya went outside into the large open yard, and asked as many people they met, to assemble under the shade of a large mango tree.

Mustafa said, "My *bhaiyas* and *behens*, my name is Mustafa Ali, and my *bhaiya* here is Kanhaiya Ramchand. I can recognise some of you as our *jahaji bhais* who travelled with us, and arrived here only two weeks ago. Life here is very tough, and we all wish that we had never come to this wretched place. But, we must live together as *jahaji bhais* and help each other. We are trying to do this in our estate at Anna Catherina, and we are feeling good about this."

"Yes," added Kanhaiya. "We need each other, and as Indians, we must always try to respect each other."

Everyone was generally taken by surprise by the requests of the two young visitors. Then Ishani and Mumtaz emerged from the room.

"Our sister Ishani here, is not the vile person you think she is," pointed out Mustafa. "She has had a very unfortunate experience whilst she was travelling to the Depot in Calcutta. In fact, the Agent who recruited us was responsible for making her pregnant against her wishes. He just took advantage of a young woman who was on her own. When I return to India, I will deal with him personally."

"So what do you want from us?" asked the young man who had directed the visitors to Ishani's home.

Mustafa pleaded, "All we want from you, is to forgive our sister, and to help her live amongst you in peace, and to bring her innocent child into this world, without harm."

An older man stepped forward, and said scornfully, "Who do you think you are? We have young people and children here, and we do not want prostitutes living amongst us. It would be better if she was taken away from here."

Upon hearing this, Ishani broke away from Mumtaz and ran back to her room, slamming shut the door. The residents ended the discussion by walking away, and muttering amongst themselves.

Mustafa, Kanhaiya and Mumtaz stood bemused for a few moments, and then walked slowly towards Ishani's room. When they were allowed in, they tried to comfort her as best they could. Mustafa then asked Kanhaiya and Mumtaz to step outside, and to leave him alone with Ishani for a while.

When they left the room, Mustafa said, "Ishani, I am so sorry to imply that your baby is Sundar Das's, and, to say this in front of everyone."

"No, Mustafa," said Ishani as she wiped the tears from her eyes and cheeks. "You are right. It was Sundar who forced himself upon me. He even wanted me to stay with him in India, marry him, and work for him in recruiting more women to work abroad."

Mustafa said, angrily, "So, why did he not treat you with respect and propose to you instead of taking advantage of you? He has no decency."

Ishani, still with tears in her eyes, said, "He did propose to me, but I kept refusing him. I do not like him at all. He felt that by making me pregnant he will cause me to change my mind. I feel very hurt. He took away everything that I hold dear to me. Now, these people are adding to my unhappiness. At times, I just feel like ending it all. But, Bhagwan Raam reminds me that my unborn child is a precious soul. Otherwise, I have no peace and hope here."

Mustafa said, as reassuringly as he could, "Leave this to me, my *behen*. I will try my best to help you, and in the meantime, we will always come to visit you. At least the people here now know that you are not alone, and that you have good friends."

Kanhaiya meanwhile, took the opportunity to speak to Mumtaz whilst they were finally alone.

He said, "So, Mumtaz, what else do you think we can do for Ishani? I cannot see how she could survive this torture for much longer. I really do feel sad for her, and her baby."

Mumtaz replied, "Me too! She has already gone through so much in her life, and now this! I also feel very sad for her, and I agree that we must do something for her. What about Mustafa? He seems to be so close to her. And, he is not yet married."

Kanhaiya said, "Yes, he is very close to her, but like a *bhaiya*, not a lover. She also feels the same way towards him. They share something quite special. Besides, he is only here to work for a few years, and his big hope is to go back to his village, and to ask for the girl he promised to return to."

"Oh, I am sorry," said Mumtaz. "He must also feel great pain. Perhaps helping others is his way of dealing with his own problems. What about you? What are your hopes and dreams?"

Kanhaiya was suddenly feeling very twitchy and uncomfortable as the conversation took such a turn towards his feelings. "Well... well... I... hope..." he stuttered, trying to regain some composure. "I hope that one day I will meet someone who I could settle down with. I have no one to go back to in India. I am willing to make a new life here, and my *bhaiya* Mustafa is helping me to make this possible."

"Hmm... I see," Mumtaz said as she smiled warmly. "Let us hope that your dreams come through."

"And you?" asked Kanhaiya hesitatingly. "What are you planning to do?"

Mumtaz did not answer Kanhaiya's question, and when she saw Mustafa and Ishani emerge from the room, she shouted, "Oh, there they are! Let us go and talk to them."

22.

Foul deeds amongst the poultry

Whilst Mustafa, Kanhaiya and Mumtaz decided to stay overnight at Ishani's home in Vreed-en-Hoop, Joshua was able to stay with some of his friends in the village.

Back at the immigrants' yard in Anna Catherina late into that evening, the silence was broken by a commotion within the newly built chicken coop which housed the stock of hens and a cockerel. Upon investigation by some of the younger men armed with their cutlasses, it was not clear as to how the coop was breached. But loose feathers were scattered on the floor, and the carcass of one hen was found. A quick stock-take revealed that apart from the dead hen, one other was missing. The survivors of the vicious attack were huddled into a corner of the coop, nervously cackling in distress.

The immigrants were astonished by this loss, and discussed amongst themselves just how this happened. They assumed that it could not have been perpetrated by one or more of their number. Their suspicions were then placed at the Africans in the village. They were the only other persons who knew of the existence of the chicken coop. It was then agreed that the young men would take turns to watch over the coop for every night thence forward.

As soon as Mustafa, Kanhaiya, Mumtaz and Joshua returned from their trip, they heard about the incident in the chicken coop. Due to Joshua's presence, no one openly suggested that they suspected the Africans for the crime. They expressed their disgust, and disappointment at their unexpected loss.

Joshua saw how much the immigrants were upset, and volunteered to make some enquiries in the village. Mustafa advised him not to cause unnecessary tension between the Indians and the Africans just for the sake of the loss of a couple of hens. Nevertheless, Joshua expressed his determination to help to solve the mystery.

Several ensuing nights passed without incident in the chicken coop, or "fowl pen" as Joshua called it. Fresh eggs were in regular supply by presumably happy hens. The rota of night watchmen appeared to be working well.

Then late one night, the tranquillity of the fowl pen was once again disturbed. The duty watchmen quietly mustered up some recruits armed with their cutlasses. They crept towards the coop as stealthily as they could, taking care not to make a sound. The hens and cockerel were fluttering around wildly, and cackling loudly in sheer fear and panic.

The young men spotted the dark figure of a man trying to sneak away from the coop. The thief was clearly disturbed, and made a dash towards the perimeter fence. The young men chased hard, and as they quickly encircled the stranger, he stopped and raised his hands in surrender. He was an African who started to plead for his life as the young men raised their gleaming cutlasses threatening to strike.

"Please!... Please! Do not hit me! Please do not kill me!" begged the African.

He was marched back to the *logies* where the rest of the residents had assembled. Mustafa looked closely at the man, and quickly identified him as Joshua.

Mustafa peered closely at the man and asked, "Joshua, is that you?"

"Yes, please let me explain," requested Joshua in his creole English which Mustafa was becoming more able to understand. "I am no thief. Go and see for yourself. I killed the real culprit."

Everyone gathered around the coop, and saw the remains of a large snake with its severed head lying beside its body. A blood-stained cutlass lay abandoned next to the victim. The poultry were still rattled, and very nervous as they huddled in a safe corner of the coop.

Joshua then proudly announced, "That beast is called an anaconda. It had been attacking our fowl pens in the village for months now, and every time it digested its latest victim, it would come out from the bushes, and look for its next meal."

Mustafa said, "Joshua, you should have told us about this before risking your life here."

"I am sorry," replied Joshua. "I had to do this because people in the village have been spreading rumours that I am a "fowl thief", but I knew that the real culprit would be a snake or some other animal."

Mustafa said, "Thank you Joshua. You can go home now. Tomorrow morning we will take the dead snake to the village, and tell everyone what you have done."

Joshua took his bloodied cutlass, and quietly left the yard as everyone, except the young watchman, retired for the remainder of the evening. The residents of the coop also settled down to a more peaceful existence.

The next morning, before marching off to work in the field, Mustafa, Kanhaiya and the duty watchman carefully bundled the dead anaconda into a bag, and took it to the village. The residents gathered around their visitors who emptied the carcass onto the dusty ground in the middle of the settlement.

Joshua stepped forward, and took the lead to explain the reasons for the demise of the snake. Everyone was relieved that the mystery of the "fowl thief" had been solved, and Joshua was treated as a new hero instead of an old villain. Two of the villagers took the carcass, and disposed of it deep in the bushes from whence it came.

Joshua was pleased to hear from Mustafa, that he was most welcome to visit the Indians' yard as they shook each other's hands. He in turn, extended the same invitation for the Indian residents to visit the village.

As time passed by, the relationship between the Indians and the Africans improved steadily through greater contact, and communication. They each began to understand the other's broken English, and picked up words and phrases from each other. Joshua became a useful handyman to the Indians in the *logies*, especially with his skills as a carpenter. He would often be the first person the Indians would turn to for any help to do with carpentry, and the Indians learnt from him by observing him at work.

Ragubir and the estate's Massa were particularly pleased about the pervading coexistence between the two races of people. However, the one unresolved issue for Ragubir was the state of his quest for the hand of Mumtaz, the love of his life.

23.

A slave to love

Early one morning, as Mustafa and Kanhaiya led their gangs out to work, a breathless Ragubir jogged gingerly to catch up with them.

Ragubir called out, "Mustafa, Asalaam O Alaikum, my dear *bhaiya*!"

Mustafa said, "Oh Mr Ragubir, Namaskaar! Have you heard about the anaconda and Joshua's bravery?" He was deliberately trying to avoid a conversation about Mumtaz, the love of Ragubir's life.

Ragubir, still panting a little, said, "Yes, I told you that he is a good man. But, I must really talk to you about the other thing."

"Oh yes, about the other thing. We did have a good trip to Vreed-en-Hoop, and met our dear friend Ishani," said Mustafa, still trying to avoid speaking about Mumtaz.

"Look, I mean the young lady we talked about," said Ragubir as he held on to Mustafa's left arm to stop him from walking further away. He did, and his gang proceeded without him.

Mustafa smiled re-assuredly, and winked as he said, "Mr Ragubir, we did speak to Mumtaz again, and she has clearly set her mind to staying here to work hard, and to settle down with someone. We need to give her some more time, and I am confident that I could help her make the right choice for her future husband. You are just the kind of man who can fulfil that role."

"Oh thank you so much my friend. I think about Mumtaz every moment I am awake. I also dream about her every night. I just cannot get her out of my mind," confessed the lovesick Ragubir.

Mustafa said, "Mr Ragubir, Mumtaz and I would like you to help us with a problem we have, concerning our friend Ishani in Vreed-en-Hoop. You see, she is a lovely single woman who is expecting a child, and is being treated very badly by the people there. Mumtaz told me that you are the only one who could arrange for Ishani to be transferred to this estate."

"Does Mumtaz think so highly of me?" asked the besotted lover.

"We all know how good you are, Mr Ragubir. I am sure that this favour will be well rewarded," said Mustafa, as he nudged Ragubir.

Ragubir stepped aside to avoid any further prodding from Mustafa, and said, "This is a very difficult one for me. But, for my darling Mumtaz, I will speak to Massa, and try to get Ishani here. Normally, no one is allowed to be transferred between the estates."

Several days passed by with no contact between Ragubir and Mustafa. Until one Saturday, just after the workers had received their pay, and were walking back to the yard, Ragubir stood by the main gate, and ushered Mustafa aside.

"I have some good news for you," said Ragubir, forgetting his usual formal greeting.

Mustafa said, "Thank you. Mumtaz and I were beginning to worry a lot about this."

Ragubir smiled, and said, "I have arranged for Ishani to be taken from Vreed-en-Hoop, and Joshua has already been sent to collect her. They should be here a little later on. She had asked to stay with Mumtaz and the two sisters. Also, I have arranged for Ishani to work at my home as a housemaid, instead of her working in the fields."

"Oh Mr Ragubir, you are truly amazing! You have such a great heart!" exclaimed Mustafa, as he hugged Ragubir tightly.

Kanhaiya and Mumtaz were also delighted to hear about Ishani's transfer. Mumtaz hurried to her room to tell Gita and Mamta, and to make preparations for her friend's arrival. Kanhaiya, however, was a little troubled by the latest development, and sought clarification with Mustafa.

He approached Mustafa and said, "*Bhaiya*, Mr Ragubir will now want to have his reward for his great help. I fear that he may become bold enough to make his own proposal to Mumtaz."

Mustafa said confidently, "Please do not worry. Mr Ragubir has given me another idea that I need to work on. Just calm down, and prepare to welcome our *didi*, and leave the rest to me."

Ishani's arrival was greeted with loud cheers as all the residents stepped out to meet her in the yard. This made her feel mightily relieved, and very satisfied. She smiled, thanked everyone, and was cheerfully led to her room by Mumtaz and the two sisters. Even the very pleased Joshua forgot his pride, and smiled broadly, exposing the large gaps in his front teeth.

That night, the residents were in a great celebratory mood, and after dinner, they sang and danced with gusto. Ishani, due to her pregnancy, could not join in with the girls, and was quite happy just to watch them enjoy themselves.

Early the next morning, Ragubir arrived at the gate, and asked the duty watchman to call for Ishani. He had come to show her the way to his house, and the tasks she would undertake for him as his housemaid.

Ishani was very comfortable with the arrangement, and soon settled into a well-organised routine of tending to Ragubir's needs around the house. He was very pleased with the way she single-handedly cooked each meal, tidied the rooms, and laundered his clothes. He took every opportunity to accompany her to and from the house, ensuring Joshua or one of his assistants did so when he was unavailable.

Everyone, including Mustafa and Kanhaiya, began to notice a growing friendliness between Ragubir and Ishani, as each day passed by. Mustafa decided to chat to Ragubir about the new arrangement.

Mustafa asked, "Mr Ragubir, how is Ishani managing the work?"

"Mustafa, she is truly wonderful. She loves my home, and treats it like it is her own. I also love her cooking. I have not eaten so well since I left India!" said Ragubir excitedly.

Mustafa said, "That is really nice to hear. I can see how you are getting fatter! But she is pregnant, and should not be doing too much work now."

"Yes, I am also concerned about this. I have asked for the nurse at the clinic to check on her progress. I would not like any harm to come to Ishani or the baby," confirmed Ragubir.

Mustafa said, "Mr Ragubir, I am truly grateful to you for looking after my *didi* so well. I wonder if you will consider allowing her to stay at your home so that she is more comfortable. The room she is sharing with the girls is too cramped, and as someone expecting a baby, she needs more privacy."

Ragubir said, "I have considered this, my friend. I have asked Ishani to come and stay in one of the rooms at the house. In fact, this was suggested by the nurse, and I have also discussed it with Massa. At the moment, junior staff such as I, are not allowed to have live-in servants. But Massa is such a kind-hearted man that he has allowed me to offer this until the baby is born."

Mustafa smiled, and said, "I am so pleased to hear this. When is Ishani planning to join you?"

Ragubir said, "She said that she would like to discuss it with you, and then let me know."

As soon as Ragubir left, Mustafa hurried over to see Ishani, who was sitting with Mumtaz just outside their room.

"Ishani, I believe that you wish to tell me something," said Mustafa as he stooped down beside them.

"Yes, Ragoo... I mean Mr Ragubir, and the sick nurse suggested that I should move into a room at his house until the baby is born," said Ishani, with a most radiant smile.

Mustafa nodded in agreement, and said, "Well Ishani, I think that you should go there immediately. It is a truly kind offer made by Mr Ragubir. He is a caring man, and he is full of praise for you and your work."

"Ragoo eh! Interesting! Very Interesting!" said Mumtaz as she hugged Ishani warmly.

Mustafa chuckled heartily.

24.

Hard labour, joyful outcomes

It was early June 1845, the end of the first month for the new immigrants on the Anna Catherina plantation. They were very pleased about their achievement of the task set for them to prepare the new field for planting sugarcane. Both gangs were well established in their roles, but the shovel gang was required to move onto the cane-cutting work which presented them with new challenges.

The fields with the tall ripened sugarcane plants were chosen for harvesting, and were set ablaze in order to burn off the leaves, and to clear the undergrowth of snakes, and other hazards. The dry grass and other weeds at the base of the sugarcane plants caught afire very quickly, and soon the whole area was crackling with wild red flames. The skyline became blackened with smoke and ash rising, and flying away for hundreds of yards. The paper thin grey ash flew onto the roofs, and the surrounds of the neighbouring settlements. Anyone living within range, tried to avoid the ash by closing their doors and windows of their homes until the threat disappeared. Then the residents set about clearing the soot and ash from around them.

Ragubir advised Mustafa and his gang about their new task of working alongside other gangs of Indian and African labourers, to cut the burnt sugarcane, bundle the stalks, fetch, and load them onto the waiting pontoons which were chained together in the canals beside the fields.

This was truly back-breaking work as the labourer positioned himself carefully alongside the base of the sugarcanes which were mostly at an incline, and contorted by the powerful heat of the raging fire. He then struck the sugarcane at about six inches at the base with one mighty swipe of the sharpened blade of his cutlass whilst holding the stalk with his free hand. Each cut sugarcane stalk was placed neatly, and assembled into a bundle of just the right size and weight. The slender but strong labourer lifted each bundle, walked as steadily as he could, and, with one heave, loaded each onto the pontoons. The soot from the burnt sugarcane stalks soon stuck onto the arms, legs and faces of the tiring men. Their white clothing was also almost covered in the black soot.

Each field, or designated area within a field, had to be cut and cleared by the appointed gang whose members were expected to stay on duty until the task was completed. This often resulted in the gangs having to work well beyond the normal assigned hours of the day. Darkness would begin to set in as the thoroughly blackened, and physically exhausted men struggled to finish the day's task. They would then trudge home, try to wash the soot off their bodies, eat some dinner, and go to sleep for only a few hours before waking up to do the same over the next day. Sometimes, if the work was not completed over the week, the men were expected to toil through their rest days as well.

This constant and unrelenting pressure soon began to take its toll on the workers. Many of them tried to continue working in their gangs despite suffering from the effects of the fiery sun, small cuts and bruises which were being allowed to self-heal, and, bites from mosquitoes, ants and other insects. They were determined not to affect the performance of their gang. Inevitably, many were forced to present themselves for treatment at the sick house.

During this intense work period, Mustafa met Ragubir only briefly in the early mornings. On one such occasion, he asked Ragubir about Ishani.

Ragubir said proudly, "She is very happy and well. She is looking more beautiful each day, and we are both looking forward to the birth of the baby."

Mustafa smiled, "I am so pleased to hear this. Please tell her that we all miss her, and hope to see her soon. Mr Ragubir, I notice that you have not asked me about Mumtaz. Particularly since Ishani moved into your house."

Ragubir looked around him discreetly, to make sure that no one was in earshot. Then he said, "My friend, through you I have found what I have been looking for. I feel as if I am already married now, and I know what marriage will be like with Ishani."

Mustafa said, "Do you mean that you and Ishani are in love with each other? If so, I am really very happy for you both. Soon, for the three of you!"

Ragubir's happiness shone on his full, beaming face as he said, "Yes, we are truly deeply in love with each other. Mumtaz is now completely out of my mind."

Mustafa asked, "How do you feel towards Ishani with a baby that is not yours?"

Ragubir still wearing the broadest smile, said, "I love Ishani, and everything about her. So, it is very easy for me to accept the baby because it is part of her. Besides, the father is not here, and Ishani assures me that the baby was an unfortunate accident."

Mustafa, very relieved about this development, said, "So, Mr Ragubir, when will you marry Ishani? I am happy to act as her guardian."

Ragubir said, "Wait! Not so fast! We have decided to await the arrival of the baby, and then we will take the next step."

"Can I tell the others about this great news?" asked Mustafa with excitement.

Ragubir said, "No, not yet. Wait until the baby is born, and then I will tell you what we will do."

Mustafa went off to work that day feeling very pleased about Ishani's good fortune, and the fact that his plan had turned out to be better than expected. He could not, however, resist encouraging Kanhaiya to press on with his courtship of Mumtaz.

That evening, after they had eaten a special meal prepared by Mumtaz, Gita and Mamta, the brothers talked about Kanhaiya and Mumtaz's relationship.

Mustafa said, "So Kanhaiya, I now see that Mumtaz is preparing our meals for us. What is going on?"

Kanhaiya said, "*Bhaiya*, I did not ask her to do this, but I think that she is very fond of us and wants to look after us."

Mustafa said, "You really mean that she is being more caring towards you. And, as your *bhaiya*, I am very happy for you both. I would very much like to see you marry Mumtaz."

Kanhaiya said, "Mustafa, you are right. But I am now a very devoted and serious Hindu who everyone comes to for advice on religious matters, and who is being treated like a Pandit. Mumtaz is Muslim, and this will be very difficult."

Mustafa shrugged his shoulders and said, "Well, we will have to cross that bridge when we get to it."

The brothers retired for the evening. They were filled with all kinds of thoughts, except those of hard labour in the fields.

The three months into early August during the hottest spell, were extremely challenging for Ishani. Several times she had spent sleepless nights crying out in acute abdominal pain. Ragubir tried his best to offer comfort to her, and became increasingly anxious for Ishani, and the baby's health. They both relied heavily on the ardent sick nurse who always managed to help control Ishani's pain, and soothe her discomfort. Over this period, Ragubir relieved Ishani from her housemaid duties, and employed a very capable young African woman to take her place.

Mustafa and Kanhaiya were invited by Ragubir to have meals at the house, and to see Ishani. It became quite clear to them that Ragubir and Ishani were growing closer to each other. Inevitably, they began to discuss plans for a future wedding. Ragubir and Ishani asked Kanhaiya to conduct the Hindu marriage ceremony. The overjoyed couple both insisted that no one else should be told about their intentions, until the baby was born. Kanhaiya was most delighted to know that the path for him and Mumtaz was now much clearer.

The night that Ishani went into labour had started with a light drizzle, and cool soothing breeze that accompanied the inward Atlantic tide. Darkness set in rapidly, and everywhere was calm except for the occasional yelping of one or more of the numerous stray dogs that roamed the area. Ishani's painful cries sent Ragubir into a frenzied panic as he dashed out into the road to fetch the sick nurse.

When he finally reached the sick nurse's house, he could hardly explain the reason for the emergency, except for shouting Ishani's name several times. The first thunderclap and lightening struck as a clear sign of what was developing into a violent storm. He was completely soaked from head to toes, and the tears from his reddened eyes merged with the rain water pouring down from his head.

The sick nurse hurriedly put on a big hat to protect her from the lashing rain, and tied it securely with a neat bow under her chin. Soon however, as they fought their way against the strengthening wind, and relentless rain, the hat flew off her head, and dangled behind her shoulders as she also became completely wet. The sheer volume of rain water over-spilled the drains by the side of the narrow road, and flooded the entire route to Ragubir's house.

As they reached the outer stairway leading up to the main front door of the house, they could hear Ishani's screams. The sick nurse dashed into one of the rooms, and quickly changed into one of Ishani's dresses. Ragubir also changed into some dry clothes, and nervously joined the sick nurse in attending to Ishani, whose arms were flailing around wildly. The sick nurse told Ragubir to grab Ishani's arms, and to try to bring them under control whilst she lay on the bed. He clumsily managed to hold one arm only to be struck a mighty blow to the side of his head by the other. He reeled back, staggered and fell heavily onto the floor beside the bed.

The sick nurse shouted at him, "Come on, pull yourself together! Get up and hold her arms!"

Ragubir rose slowly up on his shaking legs, cleared his head, and then finally succeeded in securing both of Ishani's arms. He winced in agony as Ishani grabbed his wrists, and sunk her sharp fingernails into them. He screamed in tandem along with her as the sick nurse calmly tried to instruct Ishani on her breathing, and pushing. Every time Ishani took a deep breath, screamed and pushed, Ragubir would cry out in agony as her fingernails sank deeper into his wrists. He was shocked by Ishani's strength and her sheer power.

After about an hour into the labour, the new baby finally emerged, and seemed in good health. Ragubir barely glanced at the newborn, then fainted, and fell heavily onto the floor. The sick nurse ignored him, and concentrated on completing her maternity care. She carefully wrapped the baby in some cotton, and placed it into the arms of the proud, and radiant new mother. She then leaned over Ragubir, and slapped his face firmly in an effort to revive him.

Ragubir slowly rose to his feet. He felt extremely relieved, and proud to see Ishani cuddling the new baby. She looked up at him, and thanked him for supporting her through her times of need. They both thanked the sick nurse, and as she left, the storm subsided and calmness prevailed through the remainder of the fateful evening. The baby slept through the remainder of the night, beside Ishani. Ragubir went to his room, and collapsed with sheer exhaustion.

Several days followed through which Ishani, Ragubir and the sick nurse attended to the baby boy until it was clear that both mother and son had recovered from the birth, and were progressing well. Ragubir and Ishani invited Mustafa and Kanhaiya to see the newborn, and for Kanhaiya to bless him as well as to suggest a name for him.

Kanhaiya duly obliged by reciting some Hindu *shlokas* over the mother and baby, and offered the name Bharat for the child. Ishani thanked him, and accepted the name given.

Mustafa congratulated Ishani, and offered an Islamic *dua* for the new mother and son. A delighted Ragubir then set about organising a date, and some of the arrangements for the wedding.

Ishani asked, "Why so quickly? Can we not wait until the baby is stronger? I also need a few more weeks to make a full recovery."

"Ishani, my love," said Ragubir. "You are right. But I had promised Massa that you can stay here only until the baby is born. If we get married quickly, then he will accept that you are my wife, and you will not have to leave."

Ishani said, "I understand. Let us do the wedding as soon as possible. Mustafa and Kanhaiya please tell everyone in the yard, and also Joshua and the people of the village." Ragubir nodded, and looked at his bride-to-be, and her baby son Bharat, very approvingly.

25.

Bitter sweet freedom

"Aha, Mustafa! My friend!" exclaimed a delighted Joshua as he approached to greet Mustafa who had decided to meet him to extend a personal wedding invitation to all the villagers. "How good to see you!"

"And you too, Joshua! I bring some very good news for you, and all the people of the village!" replied Mustafa as he stretched out his arms to embrace Joshua.

A few of the villagers gathered around to listen to the two men's conversation. The Africans still bore a sense of general uneasiness, and curiosity about the presence of the Indian labourers on the plantation.

Mustafa said, "Joshua, I have been asked by Mr Ragubir, to invite you and all the villagers, to his wedding with Ishani whom we met on our trip to Vreed-en-Hoop."

Joshua's eyes lit up as he said, "Oh yes, I remember the lady. But she was expecting a baby. How is she?"

Mustafa said, "Ishani has given birth to a baby boy named Bharat, and both mother and son are doing very well."

"So, we have to celebrate two things! The baby and the wedding!" observed Joshua with one of his rare smiles. The onlookers also smiled warmly upon hearing the news.

Mustafa looked around, and said, "I hope that you and all the people will attend. However, there is one thing that you need to know. The wedding will be a Hindu ceremony, and there will be no meat served at Mr Ragubir's house."

"Look my friend, please tell Mr Ragubir and Ishani that we are all happy for them, and we will attend to witness the ceremony," said Joshua who turned to the growing crowd of villagers for their approval. They all nodded, and said "Yes!" enthusiastically.

Mustafa said, "Joshua, thank you and everyone here. Mr Ragubir and Ishani will be most pleased to hear this. You can all join our Muslim brothers and sisters who will be having a meal of mutton curry, rice and *daal* at the Indian yard, away from the Hindu rituals."

Joshua then invited Mustafa to his small thatched home, which was no bigger in size than the rooms at the *logies*. It was a separate detached structure with one front door, and one window on each of the three sides. The house stood towards the back of a small plot of land which was fenced with a collection of old boards, sticks, and uneven wooden poles which must were retrieved from unwanted stocks given to him by others in the village. All the other houses in the village were about the same design, and on a similar size of land. They all had neatly laid out beds planted with vegetables, including *bhaji*, tomatoes, pumpkins and squashes. The most prominent fruit tree was mango, and there were many plantain trees. Some yards had the very tall coconut trees, and breadfruit trees. Everyone kept poultry, some goats and sheep. There were a few cattle grazing freely wherever they could access grass.

Joshua offered Mustafa a cup full of fresh coconut water with some soft white jelly taken from the young nut. He said, "Mustafa, you must be a Fulaman."

"A Fulaman?" asked Mustafa with a frown.

Joshua said, "I mean Muslim. You see, I noticed that you prayed in the open when you felt that it was time for *namaaz*. And, I used to pray in the same way."

"So, Fulaman is African for Muslim?" asked Mustafa as he sipped the delicious coconut water.

Joshua said, "Yes, I come from the Fula tribe from West Africa, and we were all Muslims."

"But your name is Joshua. That is a Christian name. Did you convert from Muslim to Christian?" asked Mustafa.

Joshua said, "Yes, and I have always wished to tell you about my people and I who were fooled and betrayed by one of our leaders who took money, and a lot of bribes from some Arab traders, in exchange for us. He told us that the Arabs were our Fula brothers, and that they would take us away, and look after us. Then they would take us back to our village. We were very happy to do this, and we felt that we would earn enough to make our lives better in the village."

"So, where did the Arabs take you?" asked an intrigued Mustafa.

Joshua wiped some tears from his eyes, and said, "They took us to a port by the edge of the ocean. We had never seen this place before, and did not know what was going on until we saw other African brothers and sisters shackled in chains around their necks and ankles. They were tied to each other, and were almost naked."

"So, the Arabs sold you to the white man?" asked Mustafa, leaning forward to listen more intently.

"Yes, some of us ran away, but most of us were also shackled together. The white men ran after the ones who ran away, and we trembled with great fear when we heard shouting, and the sound of gunshots in the woods. We were so terrified, that we gave up fighting and trying to resist the chains," said Joshua, as he wiped some more tears from his eyes with the palm of his hands. Mustafa offered him a piece of cotton to wipe his face.

Joshua continued, "Then we were sold to the highest bidder as if we were cattle. We prayed to Allah to release us from this bondage, and to set us free. But our prayers were never answered. I still pray to this day, for the souls who were murdered, and also for those who betrayed us. I even pray for the white people who also bow down to the same God."

Joshua's tears subsided, and his eyes began to redden with growing anger, as he clenched his toughened fists, and banged them on his knees.

Mustafa leaned over, and held his hands, "Your story is a little like mine, and our betrayal is about some false promises made by our own Indian people."

Joshua sat upright, and said, "Yes, but you have not suffered as we have over so many hundreds of years. Your story has only just begun. We were never loosened from our chains, and were made to lie down side by side in the ship that brought us here. We vomited and messed ourselves whilst we lay next to our brothers. Just like animals. Just like wretched animals. I still cry in my sleep, and every time I recall my experiences, I feel such anger, such hatred, and such pain."

Mustafa shook his head in empathy, remembering how his own journey in the ship was difficult even though he was not chained, and was treated with more dignity as a human being.

Joshua continued, "When one of our brothers or sisters died, they would be taken out of the hold, and simply thrown into the sea. The only prayers they received were from our oral recitations from the Holy Qur'an. At least they would face the Day of Judgement without their painful shackles around their necks and legs."

"Al hamd ul Allah," said Mustafa, raising his cupped hands to his face.

Joshua said, "When we arrived here in British Guiana, we were made to parade before the Massas from the estates. We were still in shackles, and although we were half naked and beaten down by the misery, and near starvation on the ship, we were lashed by the helpers, who wanted us to stand more upright. The pain from the whip was more mentally hurtful as we were being beaten by some of our own African brothers who were working for the white man."

Mustafa, with tears in his eyes, said, "I never knew about this thing called slavery, my brother. I admire you and your people very much. I can see how deeply hurt you are, and I can also understand why your people are so suspicious of us."

Joshua nodded, and still wiping away his tears, said, "I want you to know that our suffering continued as we were always forced to work in our chains, and beaten over and over again. Anyone caught escaping would be flogged most severely in front of all of us, in order to show us what will happen if we tried to run away. Many died from the beatings they received."

Mustafa leaned forward towards Joshua, and said, "Joshua, you are all now free people. You can do what you wish. You can live without this fear of being punished for no reason. You can go anywhere you like without having to show passes."

Joshua nodded and said, "I agree. When we heard that we were freed from slavery, we laughed, and we cried at the same time. Then the white man turned on us again. They did not like to have to pay us for the work on the estate, and refused to give us proper reward for our labour. They hated the idea that we were not like their animals anymore, and refused to treat us with the dignity we expected as human beings."

"So, is this why so many of your people are not working on the estate?" asked Mustafa.

Joshua said, "Yes, I feel very sorry about this. There are people who say that they prefer to live off their piece of land, grow their produce, sell some of it, and stay away from the white man. Some of us still prefer to work in the factory and the sugarcane fields for the money we get, but we are not happy. You and your people were brought here without shackles as freed men and women. You were given the *logies*, food, water and all kinds of help. And, to rub salt into our wounds, you are being given even better pay than us. Mustafa, it will take a long time for us to forgive the white man, and to trust you Indian people. You cannot blame us for this. You are good people, and I respect you very much."

Mustafa said, "Joshua, my brother, we did not know about your people, and your sufferings. We do not wish to take anything away from you, and we all feel that one day we will return to India. That is still my dream. I hope that we can all live in peace with each other, and to help each other as much as possible whilst we are still here. I think that Mr Ragubir and Massa Bass also want this to happen, and that is why I am here with this invitation."

"Thank you Mustafa," said Joshua. "Our people are God-fearing, and want to live in peace now. We have hoped, and prayed for our freedom for a long time, and we need to enjoy this the way we wish to. Your freedom will also come when you have done your work here, and you return to your country."

Mustafa smiled, stood up, shook Joshua by the hand, and they embraced each other very tightly.

"May Allah be with you always," whispered Mustafa into Joshua's left ear.

"Yes, and may the Lord Jesus Christ bless and keep you," replied Joshua into Mustafa's right ear.

They both wiped the tears from their eyes, and Mustafa walked off in deep thought.

26.

A day of bliss, an evening of sorrow

The last Saturday of the very hot month of August 1845, was a day that began full of promise. The sugarcane harvesting, and new planting season were in full swing, and the sugar factory was constantly grinding away producing the uniquely flavoured golden brown "Demerara" sugar. The Indian labourers, and the Africans who opted to continue to work on the plantation, were toiling tirelessly over very long hours, in the fields, and at the factory.

Mustafa's and Kanhaiya's gangs from the new Indian yard, were now well-established in their environment, and contact with the Africans in the village was improving as the days, weeks, and months passed by. Joshua continued to be their main link with the villagers, and the weekly market day of Sunday, was a very popular highlight for all. Even the white people from the estate's administration were to be seen buying vegetables, fruits and other goods, accompanied by their housemaids who were mostly well-built, and well-groomed African ladies resplendent in their colourful floral dresses, and large hats.

As soon as the workers received their pay from the general office of the factory, they walked over to Ragubir's house to attend the Hindu wedding ceremony. Smoke could be seen rising from the specially tented cooking area, and as the guests reached closer to the sitting area, they were overwhelmed by the enticing smell of the vegetable curries, *daal* and rice being prepared as the main meal. At the front of the seating area of the large tent, was a *mandap* made of freshly cut coconut palm leaves tied to the four wooden pillars that held the structure together. The leaves were also spread neatly on the earthen floor, and local flowers were carefully placed amidst the four posts of the *mandap* where the elaborate wedding ceremony would be performed.

Kanhaiya, immaculately dressed in a white *dhoti*, and a saffron coloured turban, sat on a low wooden stool waiting nervously for the groom and bride to emerge. Mustafa, similarly attired, took the role of Ishani's father, and there were five workers from the Brahmin caste chosen to act as witnesses to the marriage. The Massa and his wife, both wearing formal English clothes, sat in the same yogic way at the head of all the guests. They appeared very uncomfortable in their adopted posture, and their faces were reddened by the heat as well as their sense of embarrassment.

The wedding was a two hour long curtailed version of the traditional Hindu ceremony which would normally last for several hours. The new bride and groom presented a picture of elegance and poise, as they slowly completed the obligatory walks around the sacred fire contained within the *havan kund*. Kanhaiya, who was very impressive as a Pandit, finally announced the end of the marriage ceremony, and presented the newly married couple to an appreciative audience.

All those who wished to eat the vegetarian meal, were invited to sit in a large circle, and their food was served onto large round lily leaves placed before them. They ate the hot food by using the fingers of one hand to mix the rice, *daal* and vegetable curries, and then carefully chewed a reasonable mouthful at a time. Only the bride and groom, Kanhaiya, Mustafa, the five Brahmins, and the Massa and his wife, were given their food in tin plates and silver spoons. Those guests who preferred to eat meat, were discreetly told to go to the Indian yard where they would be served by Mumtaz, and the other Muslims who had prepared the food.

Ragubir and Ishani were very pleasing hosts, and were relieved when the event concluded. The Massa told them that although their Hindu wedding was not recognised as a legal fact in the colony, they were permitted to live together with their son Bharat, in the junior manager's house. They were overwhelmed with joy.

Mustafa was very proud of his brother Kanhaiya who had handled the ceremony with increasing confidence as it proceeded. The young man had enhanced his growing reputation as a learned, and competent Pandit amongst the Hindu community on the estate. His ability to recite from memory, the extracts from ancient holy texts, greatly impressed the congregation, many of whom had travelled to British Guiana on the same ship, and knew about his interest in the religion.

After the celebration was over, Ragubir, Ishani and their son Bharat, returned to the lounge of their house to begin their new life as a family.

Ishani was advised that she was no longer an indentured labourer on the estate, and that she was now a housewife with access to her own staff.

Mustafa and Kanhaiya returned to the yard, and helped Mumtaz and the others, to clean the cooking utensils, and to clear up the debris from the feast. They stacked all the rubbish onto a pile at the back of the yard, and set it alight.

It was just before sunset, when the residents of the yard were disturbed by a young Indian woman who raced through the open gate with her arms flailing and screaming aloud, "Murder! Murder! Murder!"

Mustafa and Kanhaiya grabbed her, and tried to calm her down. Mumtaz brought a cup of water for the young woman. Then they noticed that her hands and clothes were bloodied. They were shocked to see this, and when the young woman finally settled down, Mustafa asked her what had happened.

"My neighbour... he chopped up his wife... and he ran away!" said the woman still panting heavily.

Mustafa and Kanhaiya immediately left the young woman in the care of Mumtaz, and ran over to the next Indian *logie* yard. A crowd of the residents gathered at the location of the murder. The women were wailing, and the men were standing around too stunned to do anything.

When Mustafa and Kanhaiya finally moved through the crowd and entered the room, they felt sick at what they saw. The dead woman's body was riddled with huge cuts inflicted by the killer, and the walls and floor of the room were spattered with blood. Her head was almost severed from her neck. They quickly realised that the killer who was on the loose, would be very dangerous, and armed with a bloodied cutlass.

They took a blanket, and covered the body. They then told the anxious crowd to go to their rooms, to remain alert, and not to let anyone into their homes if they did not know the person.

A few of the younger men, armed with cutlasses, formed a search party with Mustafa and Kanhaiya, and headed into the woods nearby. They each carried a lit lantern, and stayed very close together as they carefully searched the undergrowth. Shortly after about an hour, they were preparing to give up their search until the next morning, when Mustafa stumbled onto something on the ground.

It was a blood-stained cutlass, and when he looked up into the tree just ahead of him, he saw the dangling legs of a man who had hung himself. The search party looked up at the body, and their eyes were full of fear, and horror.

Mustafa and Kanhaiya decided to leave the hanged man and cutlass at the scene, and advised the search party to return to the yard. They informed the Massa about the shocking and brutal events, and returned to their home feeling tired, and emotionally drained.

The next morning, they learnt that the killer had murdered his wife after an argument following his suspicion of her having an affair with another man. Such incidents of "wife killings" were sad features of the Indian indentured labourers who had migrated to the colony with a very small proportion of women. This was a principal reason for husbands to take such drastic action against their wives for any behaviour they felt was adulterous.

27.

Reasons to go, offers to stay

During May 1850, Mustafa, Kanhaiya and their gangs of labourers had almost completed five years of indentureship on the plantation. The population of Indian indentured labourers had doubled on the estate through the continuation of shipments into 1848, whence the Indian immigration was again suspended. The production of sugar continued to flourish as well as the distilling of a very potent Demerara rum.

Although there had been many Indian labourers lost due to the dreaded malaria, and a number of other tropical diseases mostly attributable to the recurrent problem of a lack of clean water and poor sanitation, these souls were easily replaced by new Indian immigrants. A separate *logie* community was established for those Indians originating from the South of India, via the port of Madras.

The "Madrasis" as they were referred to, were very dark in complexion, and practiced a different form of Hinduism alongside their peculiar cultural habits. When for example, a new child was born, the Madrasis would weep, signifying their sympathy for such a pure soul having to enter this world of darkness, and despair. When a person died, they celebrated with *Kali Mai pooja*, folk music, and dance, as the soul was deemed to be released from this world.

The two communities of Indian labourers from the North and North-East of India, and the South of India, were kept apart from each other on the estate, primarily due to the religious, and cultural differences. They spoke different languages, and used foods prepared differently. Their clothing, although of the standard allocations, were differentiated by peculiar headwear. The Madrasis had brought their beautifully woven multi-coloured *rumaals*, which were mainly worn by the women.

The Massa and the other white drivers and administrative staff were comfortable with the separation of the Indians and the Africans. Such divisions helped to ensure that there would not be any challenging collaborations, and mischief towards them. Besides, this also kept a firm grip on the ready availability of the workforce.

Anna Catherina also received a few of the Portuguese labourers from Madeira, the Portuguese Island in the Atlantic Ocean. Madeira had a good history of sugar plantation, and manufacture until the industry fell into hard times. Unfortunately, the Portuguese could not cope with the harshness of the British Guiana weather, and the tough environment on the estates, and most of them sought non-manual work in Georgetown. They saw themselves as white Europeans who were superior to the Indians and Africans.

Mustafa had remained a bachelor as he kept his desire to return to India to seek the hand of his beloved Chandini. He had tried to send messages to her through anyone who was returning to Uttar Pradesh, and, to find out about her from anyone who had travelled from that area. However, there was no news about her or her family, and indeed his family. He had consolidated his leadership role at the head of his gang, and had earned considerable respect from the Massa and Ragubir as well as all the other Drivers on the estate. His relationship with the Africans of the village also grew into mutual respect, and Joshua became an even closer friend.

Kanhaiya, who had become an established and popular Pandit, was relieved of his role at the head of his gang, and allowed to practice and serve the community who paid him well for his services. His marriage to Mumtaz was quietly arranged by Mustafa, with the help of Ragubir and Ishani. The growing Hindu and Muslim communities, although frowning upon such inter-religious marriages, made an exception to this union through their fondness for both Kanhaiya and Mumtaz. The couple moved into their own room in the *logie* on the estate which was once shared by Mumtaz, Gita and Mamta.

Gita and Mamta became happily married to young men from another *logie* on the estate, and moved away to their new homes. Kanhaiya and Mumtaz, who were expecting their first child, had firmly decided to stay on the estate, and renew their indentureship for another five years. Mustafa, although delighted for his brother and sister-in-law, began to feel that his insistence on returning to India was being affected by this development.

He visited Ragubir and Ishani to discuss his predicament as he was now torn between his love for his brother, and the respectful way he was held by the people and his friends, against his unfulfilled desire to be with his Chandini.

"My friends, I have come to seek your advice on what I should do at the end of my five years here," said Mustafa as he placed little Bharat on his knees.

Ishani said, "You have survived a lot of hardship since you left your village all those years ago. However, as a woman, I know how you must feel for your Chandini."

Ragubir said, "Yes Mustafa. Let me tell you how much I am so grateful to you for all you have done here in helping me, and my family. I have seen how you have grown into a man of great integrity, and who commands the respect of every one on this estate."

Mustafa's eyes welled up as he said, "I am very thankful for all this my friends, but I cannot get Chandini out of my mind. She is always there, and sometimes I find myself talking to her, and asking for her advice when I have problems to deal with. I feel she is guarding over me in everything I do or say."

Ishani leaned over, and touched Mustafa's right hand gently, "I too have grown to love you as the *bhaiya* I never had. I feel for you, and really want to have you always near to me. But if you wish to go back to India, I will fully understand."

Ragubir reached over and took hold of little Bharat who was becoming unsettled, and agitated, "So Mustafa" he said, "This decision has to be yours alone because it was your determination that brought you here to make a fortune, and to go back to help your family. But even your own family have not made contact with you."

This struck a chord with Mustafa as his own thoughts had always been for Chandini almost at the exclusion of his family. Ragubir then raised another doubt by saying, "And, what if you return to India, and go to look for Chandini, and you find that she is married to someone else? That would be very difficult for you to accept, and to live with."

"This possibility has always been on my mind," replied Mustafa, wiping tears from his eyes. "I keep telling myself that she would rather die than to be with someone else. I know my Chandini."

Ishani said, "Mustafa, Chandini must be in her twenties now, and the pressures on her to get married would be very great. I do not know how she would be able to resist this. Besides, you should know that her family would never accept you."

"These are the things I do not know, and the only way for me to find out, is to go there, and to see for myself," concluded Mustafa.

Ragubir and Ishani offered Mustafa dinner, and after they ate, he left their home thanking them for their advice. He decided to ask Kanhaiya and Mumtaz for their opinions on the matter, and before retiring that evening, he visited them.

"Kanhaiya and Mumtaz, I have just returned from Ragubir and Ishani," announced Mustafa. "I need to speak to you about my decision to return to India, now that my five years are about to end."

"Go back to India?" asked Kanhaiya. "I know that you dearly wish to be with your Chandini, but what about all that you have here? We are your family here. We love you dearly, and want to be with you always. We want to look after you, and to repay you for so much you have done for us."

"And for all the people here," added Mumtaz.

Kanhaiya continued, "My *bhaiya*, you and I have more work to do here. Mumtaz and I would dearly love for you to stay here and to continue to help all the people. Look at the Madrasis. They are being kept apart just for the benefit of Massa, and his people. You and I need to work on bringing all the people together. This is what we are here for now. This must become our estate and our country when the white men leave."

Mustafa was taken aback by Kanhaiya's stance. This shed new light on his situation, and he knew that he needed to think about this more carefully.

"Kanhaiya and Mumtaz," said Mustafa. "You are the ones, along with Ragubir and Ishani and young Bharat, as well as Joshua, who can take on such responsibility. My whole being and soul are rooted in India, and this place will never become like our homeland. Besides, the Africans will always despise us, and we have the Portuguese who already think that they are so superior to us all. Now I have heard that Massa wants to bring Chinese people here as well. This is going to become very difficult for anyone to deal with."

"But Mustafa, we have already done so much to help all the people here, and helping others will not be so difficult," suggested Kanhaiya. "Besides, everyone on the estate, including Massa and all the white people, have so much respect for you. They will all be very disappointed, and upset if you left."

168

Mustafa spoke at length with his brother and sister-in-law, and then retired for the evening. He could not sleep for most of the night, thinking about his situation. Early the next morning, he sat up, said his prayers, and headed off to the Sunday market.

He saw his friend Joshua who was now a foreman at the sugar factory. Joshua was also married to a fair-skinned mulatto lady by the name of Matilda. She was in her late twenties, and a few years younger than Joshua who was very proud of his "catch". They were strolling hand in hand amongst the small stalls when Mustafa spoke to them.

"Hello my friends," said Mustafa. "How is married life?"

"Oh Mustafa, this is what us men hope and pray for! A fine woman, a decent cook, a clever mind, and a great lover!" enthused Joshua, bearing the broadest smile. Matilda just blushed.

"Yes Joshua, you are both truly blessed, and I wish I could also enjoy such a lovely experience," said Mustafa as he leant forward, and picked up a half-ripened mango from a fruit-seller.

"Come now young man, you have to start thinking of settling down. A handsome person like you will have no problem in finding the best available young lady here," advised Joshua, winking at Matilda.

Then, as they moved forward to purchase their fruits and vegetables, Ragubir, Ishani and young Bharat approached the group.

"Hello Mustafa, Joshua, and Matilda I believe!" shouted Ragubir, who signalled to Mustafa that he wished to speak to him alone.

"Mustafa," said Ragubir. "I think that I have found the answer to your problem."

Mustafa was not expecting to be "fixed up" so quickly, and interrupted Ragubir.

He said, "Look, I am not looking to get married to anyone here. So, if you do not mind, please take your proposition to someone else."

Ragubir smiled, and said, "Do you really wish for me to take Massa's offer to you to become a Driver, to another person?"

"What?" asked a surprised Mustafa.

"Yes, Massa has asked me to tell you that he wants you to become a new Driver, and to take charge of the Madrasi gang. If, that is, you do not wish to go back to India."

"Well, well, well Mustafa!" said Joshua who had managed to overhear the conversation. "That is the best thing I have heard on this estate for a very long time! Congratulations, my friend!"

Joshua moved over and embraced Mustafa so tightly, that he dropped the mango onto the ground, much to the annoyance of the fruit-seller. Mustafa quickly turned to the man, and said, "I am very sorry. I will buy the mango. I hope it is very sweet."

Ragubir said, "But not as sweet as Massa's offer!"

28.

A new heartbeat

"Mustafa Ali!" shouted the Massa on one of his weekly tours of the estate's dwellings. "Have you decided to accept my offer?"

"Yes, Massa," answered Mustafa as he lifted his bag containing his bowls of lunch for the day's labour on the plantation. "I have heard of the offer from Mr Ragubir. I have not made up my mind as yet. Besides, I need to find out more about the Madrasi gang you are asking me to lead. They may not want me, and may prefer to have one of their own, as their Driver."

The Massa said, "Mustafa, I have also thought of this, and I would like you to come with me now to meet them, and to hear what they have to say."

Mustafa said, "Massa, you should do that first, and then tell me what they say. If I am there they may not speak up, and tell you what they really have on their minds."

"No, Mustafa," said the Massa. "I do understand what you say, but everyone on this estate knows about you, and your character. You are known to be honest, and a natural leader. In fact, these are the reasons why I have chosen you over anyone else. Also, Ragubir has highly recommended you to me."

Mustafa said, "But sir, I am due to complete my five years here, and I really do need to go back to India. I may then return here in a few years time."

The Massa said, "Mustafa, what else can I do to change your mind, and make you stay? You took great trouble to come here, and to do so well after five years. Why put this at risk by another dreadful journey over the oceans and back on the road in India? It would grieve me, and so many people here, if anything should happen to you."

Mustafa had never seen the Massa become so emotional, and personally caring, in all his years on the estate. It touched him greatly, and he felt obliged to accept the offer to at least visit the Madrasis with the Massa.

"Well, let us go to the Madrasi *logie*," said Mustafa as he stepped forward. The relieved Massa strode briskly alongside Mustafa as they headed to the yard.

A few of the Madrasi men and women gathered at the entrance, and greeted the Massa and Mustafa by clasping their hands, and bowing respectfully.

"Can you gather up the workers? I have come to talk to you about this young man whom I believe you know very well," commenced the Massa as more of the residents joined the gathering.

The Massa continued to speak to the silent and very attentive audience, "I know that you all work very hard on the estate, and I hope that you are well treated, and properly looked after here. I want you to continue to stay here, and to help us build this great estate. So, I have appointed Mustafa to be your Driver who can listen to you, and then speak to me personally about any problems you have, and any other help and support you require."

One of the older Madrasi men stepped forward, and spoke directly to the Massa. "Sir, we are happy here amongst our own people, and we make no trouble for anyone. Our gang leader, Nandoo, is a strong young man, and he helps us enough. Besides, Mustafa does not speak our language, so he will never really understand us, and how we feel about our problems."

The Massa said, "I understand, and I have heard about young Nandoo over there. But Mustafa has good English, and he can help to teach and guide you all, as well as Nandoo."

Nandoo, who spoke a little broken English, raised his right hand to attract the Massa's attention, and said, "Sir, I agree with you. I like Mustafa. But his people do not like us. The African people are more kind to us."

"Thank you for your honesty, young man," said the Massa. "Mustafa will help all the people on this estate to understand each other more. He is the best person I can rely on to do this."

"Yes sir," said Nandoo who was, like Mustafa, in his early twenties, and who stood out as slightly taller than the other residents. "I too am thinking of leaving the estate to go back to India."

"I hope that you and your people do stay here," said the Massa. "The estate needs all of you more than ever."

Mustafa then realised why the Massa had approached him with the promotion. He turned to the Massa and announced, "Look, I am willing to accept the role of Driver, and I would like to have Nandoo as my assistant. Do you agree to this sir?"

The Massa was delighted, and gave an immediate response, "Of course, Mustafa. Nandoo will be a good helper to you, and I am sure that you will make a very strong team." He then shook Mustafa's and Nandoo's hands firmly, and continued on his inspection tour. Nandoo warmly embraced Mustafa, and thanked him, before inviting him to his home in the *logie*.

Mustafa sat on the low wooden *peerha* stool as Nandoo drew up another, and placed it opposite his guest.

"Well Mustafa, we need to talk about our new jobs here. But first, let us have some *chai* and food," offered Nandoo as he beckoned towards a young lady who approached the front door of the room. She was petite, short, very dark in complexion, and with long straight and neatly combed black hair. Her eyes were dark brown, and lit up her beautiful face. Mustafa was immediately taken by the young lady's presence, and poise. She quietly accepted Nandoo's order of two cups of hot *chai*, some *roti* and curry.

The special Madrasi curry was a dark green colour, with an appetising aroma, and very hot to the taste. This heat was due to the large quantity of a unique Madras curry *masala* combined with the hottest of the local peppers. Mustafa leaned forward awkwardly, and in reaching for a cup of water to soothe his burning mouth, his hand accidentally touched the young lady's, and they both smiled at each other nervously. Mustafa apologised, and she blushed as she turned her face away.

He experienced a glowing warmth in his heart for the first time since he was last in the company of Chandini. He turned to Nandoo and said, "Please tell your wife that I loved the food very much, and I am very sorry for causing her any embarrassment."

Nandoo laughed heartily and said, "Oh no, my friend, Neesha is not my wife. She is from Madras, and came on the same ship with us. She is not married, and cooks for all the single men and women in the *logie*. She is a Muslim like yourself, and very religious. We all love her as our truly kind *behen*. I will tell her that you are sorry for bumping into her, and that you liked her food."

Mustafa thanked Nandoo, and glanced at Neesha as he rose up to leave. She returned his glance in a shy way, and bowed gracefully, smiling with a soothing warmth. Mustafa began to walk away, and his heart pounded with a new excitement. He turned back at the gate, and waved at Nandoo.

Mustafa shouted, "Nandoo, I will see you and the gang tomorrow morning at six-thirty!"

Nandoo acknowledged this, and replied, "Yes Bass! We will be waiting for you!"

Nandoo turned to the smiling Neesha, and whispered, "See you early tomorrow morning. Please prepare an extra bowl for lunch. And make it a very special meal, for a very special person!"

Neesha giggled girlishly, and slipped quietly away.

29.

A new start

That day in the sugarcane field, Mustafa was allowed the luxury of almost complete rest by the gang who were very pleased that their new leader had agreed to oversee the work. He nevertheless, insisted on pulling his own weight as he had always done over the last five years on the estate. He was always prepared to lead by example.

During the break for lunch, Mustafa sat by himself under a tall coconut tree, and thought about his decision to stay on in the colony for at least another five years. He wondered whether Chandini had indeed waited for his return. Why was there no news about her or her family? Did they abandon him? Would he ever be forgiven when he eventually returned to his village in India? Will Chandini still wait for another five years?

Every time he thought about the uncertainties in India, he was able to appreciate the strength of feelings everyone had shown him on the estate. Their words of advice and encouragement rang in his ears, and brought tears to his weary eyes. The gang resumed working after their break, and did not disturb him as he eventually drifted off into a mid-day snooze.

After a short while, he awoke suddenly at the sound of his name. "Mustafa! Mustafa!... Mustafa! Help!" It was Kanhaiya running speedily towards him. "Mustafa, please come now! It's Mumtaz! She is in labour, and in great danger!"

Mustafa sprang to his feet, grabbed his bag, and without telling his gang, he sprinted off with Kanhaiya. They soon reached the *logie* where a small group of women and children had gathered in front of Kanhaiya's and Mumtaz's room. They could hear occasional screaming followed by words of calm. The sick nurse had arrived to tend to her new patient, and was trying to help Mumtaz who was in great distress.

The estate's doctor also arrived, and immediately took charge of the situation, by asking Kanhaiya and Mustafa to stand outside the room, and to await the outcome. Kanhaiya was chanting Hindu *shlokas* whilst Mustafa raised his hands, and silently uttered Islamic *duas*. Everyone knew that the survival rate for a mother and baby in a difficult birth, was poor on the estates.

Soon, more people from the surrounding *logies*, and the village gathered outside the scene of the unfolding drama. Ragubir, Ishani and young Bharat joined Kanhaiya and Mustafa to offer their support. Joshua and Matilda were allowed to stand at the bottom of the small stairway that led from the front door, and they offered the Lord's Prayer, in a hushed tone.

The door of the bedroom was opened slowly, and the sick nurse emerged with perspiration streaming down her face. She requested some more clean water, and hand towels. Kanhaiya quickly obtained this, and handed a large bowl of water and some cotton towels to her without asking about Mumtaz.

There was a long period of silence within the bedroom, and outside in the yard. Everyone was standing with their heads bowed, and hands clasped in front of them, praying almost inaudibly for the well-loved young woman, and her baby. Then they suddenly looked up when the door was opened, and the doctor emerged, mopping his brow. He announced, to everyone's delight, and utter relief, that a new baby girl had been born, and the new mother was feeling poorly, but not in serious trouble.

Kanhaiya and Mustafa hugged each other, and everyone uttered their warm congratulations. The spectators then quietly left the yard. Ragubir, Ishani, Joshua, Matilda, and young Bharat formed a huddle with the brothers. Shortly afterwards, they were all allowed to enter the bedroom to see Mumtaz and the baby.

Ragubir said, "Kanhaiya and Mumtaz, Ishani and I would like to congratulate you, and we would like you to bring the baby to our house, and for you to stay there for as long as you need to."

Kanhaiya quickly acknowledged Ragubir's offer and said, "Thank you very much. You are so kind to us." Mumtaz looked up, and despite her tiredness, she smiled and nodded in appreciation.

In the six weeks that followed, Kanhaiya, Mumtaz and the new baby who was named Meena, were well settled in Ragubir's home. Mumtaz had made a full recovery from her difficult delivery experience, and baby Meena was improving with each passing day.

With Mumtaz's absence from the *logie*, Mustafa had initially struggled to prepare his meals until Nandoo suggested that he should go to the latter's home to share the meals prepared by Neesha. This arrangement worked very well for a while until Mustafa began to experience some difficulty in having to walk back in the dark from Nandoo's house, to his own. Neesha readily agreed to cook and deliver Mustafa's meals early each morning, and to return to collect her utensils before sunset each day. Sometimes, Mustafa would accompany Neesha back to her *logie*.

This friendly liaison was noticed by the residents who set about talking affectionately about the young couple. Indeed, Mustafa began to grow very fond of the shy Neesha, and he seemed to be much happier in her company, and in his general outlook. The Madrasi gang was also very pleased with him as their Driver, and Nandoo was benefiting from his close contact with, and coaching from, his boss.

Ragubir and Ishani invited Mustafa over for a Sunday lunch, and they discussed the issue of Kanhaiya and Mumtaz's return with their baby Meena, to the *logie*.

"Mustafa," said Ragubir. "I am concerned about the baby's health on the *logie* settlement. It would be very difficult to bring up this lovely child there."

"So what are you proposing?" asked Mustafa.

Ragubir said, "I am suggesting that you should consider having your brother and his family over to stay with you at your house that is being prepared for you, just next to mine."

"I was not aware that Massa was doing this for me. Why did you not mention this to me?" asked Mustafa, looking very puzzled.

Ragubir said, "Well, I am sorry, but we all felt that you had other things on your mind, and it would be better to tell you about the house only now."

Mustafa asked, "What things on my mind?"

"Well," said Ishani. "Rumour has it that a certain young lady has been seen visiting you. She is very beautiful, and we are happy for you."

"Yes, *bhaiya*," added Kanhaiya. "You both seem to be so happy together. And, let me tell you that as your *bhaiya*, I fully approve of your choice."

"Oh! You mean Neesha!" said Mustafa smiling. "You are all so wrong about this. She has only been cooking my meals for me whilst

Mumtaz has been away. That is all there is to it. Please stop trying to arrange my life for me. And, as for the house, I must now organise my move there as soon as possible. Yes, I would be more than happy to have my *bhaiya* and his family there with me. Is there anything else you are holding back from me?"

"Actually," said Ragubir. "There is a very important issue I need to talk to you about. It concerns the education of our son Bharat, and the other young children on the estate. Joshua told me that he and a few of the villagers want to start up a school there, and would like to have the Indian children attend as well."

Mustafa said, "That is a very good idea. Who will be the teachers?"

Ragubir said, "Well, the local parish priest and his wife, and Matilda, are willing to do so."

Kanhaiya said, "And of course, Mustafa, you could teach some English on a part time basis."

Mustafa said, "I do not mind this, but I fear that the people on the estate have avoided schooling their children because they are afraid that the Christian priest will try to convert them to Christianity. Besides, they have preferred to take their children back to India as soon as they decide to return there."

Ragubir said, "Mustafa, that is why, if you go there to teach, it should help to encourage those Indian parents to send their children to the school without fear."

Mustafa said, "Well, we will need to call everyone to a meeting at the yard, and explain this to the people."

Mustafa said, "The Priest and his wife should also be there, and to promise that they would not be seeking to convert anyone."

Ragubir quickly grabbed the initiative, and said, "Let us do this as soon as possible. Ishani and I have already agreed to send Bharat to this school, and we can use this as an example to encourage the other parents."

The meeting at the yard was hastily arranged for the following Sunday after the morning's Church service had been attended by the villagers. The community's response was very strong, and after some important issues were debated, the Indian residents agreed to send their children to the new school, with the condition that there would be no enticement to convert the children to Christianity.

Mustafa, Kanhaiya, Mumtaz and baby Meena moved over to the new house next to Ragubir's, and Neesha was appointed as the housemaid. At last, Mustafa's doubts about returning to India had been resolved, as he settled into his new job, new home, and with his brother's new family.

Young Bharat and his new friends from the estate and the village also began their new adventure into the world of education.

30.

Speaking up

Mustafa was delighted with his new home, which was of similar build and style as Ragubir's. He was also pleased that he was able to share this symbol of success on the estate, with his brother Kanhaiya and family.

Kanhaiya was given one of the three large bedrooms, and a smaller private room where he kept his Hindu *murthis* of the various manifestations of God, such as Lord Shiva, Lord Raam, Lord Krishna, and Shri Hanuman. There were also beautifully carved and decorated Goddess *murthis* of Maa Durga, Maa Lakshmi and Maa Saraswati. Every morning, Kanhaiya, Mumtaz and Meena would visit this mini-temple to say their Hindu prayers, commencing with the *gayatri mantra*, and ending with *aarti*. Mustafa kept his Islamic prayer mat in his bedroom where he performed his *namaaz* five times each day. Sometimes Mumtaz would join him whilst Kanhaiya and Meena sat and listened with respect. Regular prayers continued to play a central role in the lives of all the residents of the sugar estate, and mutual respect for each other's religion, and customs was ever-present.

Kanhaiya obtained a *betel* leaf sapling, and dutifully planted it in a cool section of the small garden. He took great care in tendering the plant by watering it early in the mornings, and late in the afternoons. The *betel* leaf, also known as *paan* leaf, was an essential part of the items required for the Hindu *poojas* and *havans*. It was also used to help in the care of teeth through regular chewing. Other Hindus on the estate would visit Kanhaiya to purchase the *paan* leaves, and other requirements such as *sindoor*, *supaari* and camphor, for their *pooja* and *yajna* ceremonies. Such enterprise and the small retainers for his service as a Pandit gave him a reasonable income.

Mustafa was always happy to see Neesha arrive every morning to prepare breakfast, and the lunch pack he took to the plantation. She was always very quiet, and said very little to Mustafa, Kanhaiya or

Mumtaz, preferring to do her work without fuss. She normally took a break after lunch, to go to her room at the Madrasi *logie* to cook Nandoo's dinner before returning to Mustafa's home to do the same. Often, she would have left the house before Mustafa returned in the evenings, and his mood would be a little despondent. Kanhaiya and Mumtaz noticed this behaviour, and felt that they should do something about it.

Just as Ragubir had done with Ishani, they encouraged Mustafa to ask Neesha to move over to his house, and to work as a live-in housemaid. He initially objected to the idea, suggesting that the people she worked for, especially Nandoo, may take umbrage to the idea, and begin to mistrust him. He agreed, nevertheless, to discuss the matter with Nandoo, and then Neesha.

He met Nandoo the next morning as they headed out to the sugarcane fields, and said, "Nandoo, I wanted to ask you firstly, whether you would have any objection to Neesha moving over to my house, and to do her work there."

"I have no objection Bass," said Nandoo shaking his head. "In fact, I have been waiting for this moment, and the people on the yard have been talking to me about it."

"Do they not like the idea of Neesha working for me?" asked an anxious Mustafa.

"No, not at all! In fact, they have been saying that you should do the right thing for Neesha," said Nandoo seriously.

Mustafa said, "She has a good job, and we all treat her with much affection, and respect. So what more should I do?"

Nandoo said, "Well, for a start, you should think and act like your friend Mr Ragubir."

Mustafa said, "Come on! Stop talking to me in riddles, and spell it out!"

Nandoo said, "Mr Ragubir took in Ishani, and then married her. So, we think that you should do the same with Neesha. You know that you have feelings for her. So why do you not make her your wife? This will please all of us."

Mustafa said, "Yes, I do feel strongly for Neesha, but I have not talked to her about these matters. After all, she may not feel the same way towards me, and I do not want to hurt her, and to make myself look like a fool."

"So, why do you not speak to her?" asked a concerned Nandoo. "You are always the one who speaks for others, and here you are not being able to do so for yourself. What is stopping you from talking to her? Is it because she is one of our people?"

Mustafa said, "I have no problem with your people, and I respect that we are all Indian first, and I have been working to bring us all more together. I do plan to speak to Neesha, but preferred to consult with you firstly."

"Will you be talking to her about moving into your house? Or, about marriage?" asked Nandoo with a broad grin.

Mustafa said, "I will speak to her as soon as possible. Thank you for your support, and advice. If Neesha agrees to move to my house, you will need another cook."

"That is the least of our problems. We would be most happy for you both," said Nandoo as he shook Mustafa's hands.

Unknown to Mustafa and Kanhaiya, Ishani and Mumtaz had agreed to befriend the shy Neesha, and to broach the subject about her feelings for Mustafa. They met her one morning when Mustafa and Kanhaiya were out of the house, and Ishani initiated the conversation.

"So Neesha," said Ishani. "Are you enjoying working here for Mustafa?"

"Yes *didi*. I am very happy here. I like to come over, and also help Mumtaz and the baby," said Neesha in her usual polite manner.

"And we also like you very much," acknowledged Mumtaz. "You have been so good for us over this difficult period."

"Thank you *didi*," said Neesha quietly.

"Tell me Neesha," continued Ishani. "What do you really think of our Mustafa?"

"Well, he is very kind to me. He has never said a bad word to me, and is always polite. Sometimes I think that he is more of an Englishman than an Indian," answered Neesha, smiling slightly.

"You know, he says that he is very fond of you," said Ishani, glancing at Mumtaz.

"Yes," said Mumtaz. "He has told me this as well."

"Oh! I do not know about this," said Neesha blushing as she dusted a piece of furniture.

"And, do you also have such feelings for him? You can tell us. We will keep this to ourselves," promised Ishani, with Mumtaz again nodding in agreement.

"Look, it is getting late for me here. I must get on with my work," pleaded Neesha nervously as she moved over briskly to the kitchen. Ishani and Mumtaz looked at each other, smiled, and nodded simultaneously.

Mustafa returned home earlier than usual that afternoon, and saw Neesha completing her cooking of the dinner. Mumtaz and baby Meena were resting in their bedroom, and Kanhaiya was still out. Mustafa approached Neesha in the kitchen, and they exchanged greetings.

"Neesha, I have spoken to Nandoo, and I wondered whether you would like to move into the spare room here, and to work for us only, from now on?" asked Mustafa nervously.

"Sir, I am very happy coming over here to do my work, and also at the *logie*. I have all my friends there, and I do not think that I deserve to live in this big house," replied Neesha humbly.

"Nandoo said that he and the people at the yard would be very happy for you to do this. Of course, you will always be free to visit them, and to do as you please," reasoned Mustafa.

"Well, I need to think about this, and then I will decide what to do," said Neesha whilst she dished out his food.

"I understand, and I will wait for your answer," said Mustafa, taking his plate of food, and moving to the lounge area. Neesha followed him with a cup of water.

She then quietly completed her chores, and bade Mustafa goodbye. She left just before the sun began to set.

Mumtaz and baby Meena joined Mustafa in the lounge, and she said, "Well, how is Neesha?"

"She is fine. She has just left. She will be back as usual tomorrow morning," said Mustafa as he enjoyed another delicious mouthful of Neesha's cooking.

"Hmm! She is indeed a fine young woman. I do hope that her hard work will be highly rewarded, Insha Allah!" said a smiling Mumtaz.

"Insha Allah!" said Mustafa as he continued to enjoy his meal.

31.

Pointing the way

A few weeks later, Mustafa's and Neesha's Islamic wedding was conducted quietly at the house that they shared with Kanhaiya, Mumtaz and baby Meena. The Massa, his wife and most of the senior staff of the estate attended the simple ceremony, and thoroughly enjoyed the delicious meal of mutton curry, rice and *daal*.

The Massa, as a special gesture, donated several sheep to be feasted upon by the villagers, and the Indian labourers. Vegetarian dishes were also available at Ragubir's residence, for all those who preferred this.

The Massa gave a brief congratulatory speech at the end of the meal at Mustafa's home, and expressed his delight at how well the estate and factory were performing. He thanked Mustafa, Ragubir and all the other Drivers and Foremen for their hard work in overseeing the tasks in the fields, and the factory. He also announced that due to the success of the sugar production, there would be an increase in wages across the estate. Everyone present cheered enthusiastically.

Special praise was given to Ragubir, Mustafa, Kanhaiya, Joshua and Nandoo, for their hard work in bringing the communities more closely together. But he said that the estate now needed more labourers, and that there was talk about importing Chinese people due to the suspension of Indian immigration.

Joshua was the first member of the congregation that spoke after the Massa had completed his announcement. He asked, "Massa Bass, please tell me why we have to have yet another kind of people here? We had the Portuguese who were not able to do the work, and who just behaved as if they were in charge like you."

"Joshua, I know how you feel," replied the Massa. "But you cannot say the same about the Indian people who have come here, and are working really hard."

"No sir, I cannot argue with that. But why can you not ask my people to come forward, and give them the same good money, and all the things you have given to the Indian people?" proposed Joshua, as the audience listened to the exchange with great interest.

The Massa said, "I am still prepared to do this, but some of your people appear not to be interested any more, in working in the sugarcane fields. Some, like you, are doing very well in the factory. Some are also doing very well with growing and selling their provisions and fruits, but others just prefer to sit around drinking rum, smoking *ganja*, and cursing all day."

Joshua said, "Much of that is also correct Massa Bass. How can we convince the people who do not work, to change their habits, and to take the jobs?"

The Massa said, "Well Joshua, I need people like you, Ragubir, and Mustafa here, to continue to work with me and my Overseers, to encourage these people back. If we can do this, then we do not need to have the Chinese or any other race of people on this estate."

"Massa," said Ragubir. "I am prepared to help and perhaps we should also involve the Church and the School to encourage the wayward young men to change their behaviour, and attitude towards work."

Kanhaiya suggested, "Perhaps they could be offered training at the factory if they do not want to work in the sugarcane fields."

Joshua intervened with, "And we must make them feel that they are really free, and will never be beaten as their parents used to be when they were working as slaves. Massa Bass, these scars are still on our backs, and much more in our minds. Some of these people speak about you and all the other white men here on this estate, and everywhere else they are seen, with deep hatred and contempt. That will be very difficult to change for a very long time."

"But Joshua, you and many more like you have made that change, and are even overcoming the presence of the Indian people here. You may have all the answers. That is why I am in full support for the new school in the village. This will help to change everyone," concluded the Massa as he tried to bring the discussion to an end, and prepared to take his leave.

Mustafa thanked the Massa, and all of his other guests for attending the wedding ceremony, and encouraged all who wished to remain, to have some more food and drink. The villagers, and all those who went to have their meal at Ragubir's home, continued to celebrate the wedding with gusto until the early evening hours.

Joshua, quite animated by his brief discussion with the Massa, spoke to Matilda and they both decided to call a meeting of the villagers, to consider the offer proposed. It was arranged for after the market day, in the middle of the village when most of the people were present. Joshua and Matilda opened the meeting with the solemn rendition of the Lord's Prayer, and Joshua spoke for the first time.

"We called this meeting today, to discuss matters that concern all of us in the plantation, and the village in particular. Matilda and I are very happy that all the children are attending the school, except for some of the older boys and girls who are not working."

He was immediately interrupted by an older African gentleman who was carrying a well-carved walking stick which he brandished as he spoke, "Joshua, I hope that you have not been sent here by that Massa to stir up trouble with us. If this is so, just go back and tell him that his days of bossing us around are over. He and his kind have drawn blood, sweat and tears from us for hundreds of years, and we do not need them to tell us how to live out our freedom."

Joshua kept his composure, and said, "I agree with you my respected elder, but we all know that our young people are not helping themselves to do better. They cannot just go on living off their parents who are still trying so hard to make a living."

The old man stuck his walking stick into the hard ground, and leaning onto it, he responded, "You must know that some of their fathers are working in the bush as pork-knockers, and they earn enough money from the gold that they find, to look after their families. Their wives and young children just wait for them to return after every few weeks."

Pork-knockers was the name given to the gold mining workers who either worked independently or for mining companies, in the mining areas deep in the jungles of the colony. They enjoyed eating pork in the mining settlements near to the areas of gold prospecting, and referred to this as, "Let's go to knock pork", hence giving rise to the term. Most pork-knockers were ex-slaves, and were immensely courageous and hard-working, taking tremendous risks to travel into the jungle which they referred to as the "bush", spending most of their prospecting days sifting or panning hand-held trays whilst bending over or squatting, and trying to avoid being robbed of their finds or their money. They preferred the thrill of working for themselves, and dreaming of large fortunes. Often though, they would earn some money and just spend this wildly in the pursuit of prostitutes who were mainly Amerindian women, and, drinking "bush rum".

Joshua calmly responded to the old man, and his interested audience, "Look, we all know that when they come back to the village, they do not seem to have a lot of money. They stay for a short while, and then they are off again. How can they hope to raise their families in this way?"

"So, what do you want to happen?" asked the old man resignedly.

Joshua said, "Matilda and I would like for the older boys and girls to stop smoking *ganja* and drinking rum, and to go to the school. We also have some space at the factory for young men to go, and learn some new things. After this schooling and training, they can take jobs there. The pay is good but we have to work long hours. Nobody raises a hand to whip workers, and I give you my word on this."

The old man acknowledged this, and he turned to the crowd saying, "Well, you all heard Joshua and Matilda. I hope that you take up their offer." Then he turned back to face Joshua and Matilda and said, "Thank you for speaking up, and pointing to a better way for the future of our people. We have suffered a lot of pain and misery here, but we have to find ways of forgiving. We must look to better ourselves, and to try to remove these terrible scars we have. May the good Lord Jesus always bless and keep you."

"Amen!" shouted the gathering.

PART 4

ENTER THE CHINESE

32.

Additions to the melting pot

It was a very stormy mid-morning in January 1853, when ten Chinese labourers arrived onto the estate. They were huddled together on the cart driven by Joshua, with Mustafa also on board. The Massa and Ragubir rode on horses beside the cart as it slowly passed through the main road of the village, avoiding the large muddy puddles created by the heavy downpour. The Chinese men wore large straw hats, but these were not good enough to prevent the wretched souls from being soaked through and through. They appeared miserable, and very nervous as they remained hunched and very close together.

The party halted just in front of a newly built *logie* on the edge of the village, and within sight of the others occupied by the Indian labourers. The Chinese were greeted by Nandoo, and a few of the labourers from his gang who were specially assigned to help the men to settle into their accommodation. The Chinese men were also expected to work with Nandoo's gang, and it was the Massa's intention for them to be looked after by the well-established and highly-performing Madrasi workers.

Nandoo, who was by then, a newly married man, used some improvised signs with his hands to point the way for the Chinese men. They were to share the five rooms as they wished, and ultimately settled for two men to each room. They quickly occupied their rooms, and changed into their clean clothing. Nandoo and his helpers offered the Chinese some rice and curry. They did not appreciate the curry, and preferred to eat the bare boiled rice, using the chopsticks that they brought with them. Nandoo was amazed to see how they used the sticks to eat the rice without dropping a single grain.

The Massa, Ragubir and Mustafa had moved on whilst Joshua turned his cart around, and headed back to his home in the village.

When the rain finally subsided, and the sun burst through the clear blue sky, a crowd of Indians and Africans approached the *logie* where the Chinese were located. They were quite animated, and were talking amongst themselves in a loud enough way to warrant Nandoo's attention.

He emerged from one of the Chinese rooms, and was joined by the men who were helping him.

"Can I be of help to you?" asked Nandoo as he and his men stood in front of the crowd.

One Indian man who was holding his cutlass aloft in his right hand, immediately responded, "Yes! We want to know why these Chinese people are here!"

Nandoo raised his right hand, and said, "The Massa is not here to answer your question directly, but I will try. They are here to help us with the work in the sugarcane fields. We are short of men to cut the cane, and these men are experienced labourers from Macao."

Another Indian man asked, "But why bring these Chinese people? They could turn out to be no good. Just like the Portuguese who ran away when they saw how hard we have to work."

Nandoo said, "Look, this is not my doing. Let us give them a chance, just like our African friends did for us, and then see what happens."

One African shouted, "Massa likes to cause more confusion for us! Which other people will he bring here next? Men from Mars?"

"And how are we going to understand one another?" asked another African. "We have African, Portuguese, Indian, English, and now Chinese! You know what they say about too many cooks?"

"Yes, too many crooks!" said another, laughing aloud.

"What do you mean by too many cooks and too many crooks?" asked a frustrated Nandoo.

The older African man said, "Well, my friend here really meant that so many kinds of people in one place can cause a lot of problems. And my other friend is referring to the rumour that these Chinese people are convicts sent here to do hard labour."

"Yes Nandoo, we are having a real melting pot!" shouted the Indian man with the cutlass. The crowd broke out into great mocking laughter.

Nandoo said, "Look, can I ask you to please allow these few harmless men to do their work, and if they are not able, then Massa will do the right thing."

"And, what about their food?" asked an African woman. "I see that they have no women to cook for them. Besides, none of us know what Chinese people eat, and how to cook for them."

Nandoo said, "That is a good point. In fact, they did not eat the curry we gave them. But they said that they will cook for themselves. They use rice, and all kinds of meat. So, they will buy from you at the market place."

"Well, in that case, I better go and bring some chicken and spinach for them to buy off me," said the African woman, immediately sensing an opportunity for new custom.

A very relieved Nandoo said, "Thank you madam. This is the spirit I expect, and I hope that we can all offer help to these men. They will be working in my gang, and if you have any problem with them, please let me know. Now, please go to your business, and leave these people to get on with theirs."

The crowd gradually dispersed, and the African woman quickly returned with a few live chickens, to commence her trading with the Chinese men. Some of the villagers who were still standing around near to the Chinese's *logie*, laughed at her. Nevertheless, she was unperturbed, and was quite determined to deal with her new clients.

Nandoo gathered the Chinese men around him, and started to explain through his crude hand gestures, the working regime that he expected them to follow, as well as all the facilities available to them on the estate. Unlike the Indian labourers who were expected to start working the very next day of their arrival on the estate, the Chinese men were given one day to become more familiar with their new environment.

Dinner for the Chinese that evening was steamed chicken and fried rice, with boiled spinach. The market vendor took no chances, and returned the next evening with more provisions and poultry, including ducks, for sale. She discovered that the Chinese men loved duck through their impersonations of the quacking sounds of ducks along with frantic flapping of their arms. The men continued to buy the live poultry so that they could raise their own. They built a large coop at the back of the yard, and soon began to enjoy collecting chicken and duck eggs.

The Chinese men used their day of rest to ensure that they cleared up the rubbish from the yard, set this on fire, and prepared beds for growing their favourite vegetables. However, like all those before them, they also encountered the wrath of the aggressive mosquitoes. They used some special oil in small bowls, and lit a wick that burned slowly through the night. This seemed to work for the men who awoke very early, and were well prepared for their first day of labour in the sugarcane fields. Nandoo was very impressed with the men's punctuality, and preparedness for work.

The Chinese men worked in a small group within the gang, and launched themselves into frenetic activity, cutting and bundling the cane with great efficiency and speed. However, by noon, they appeared to be very tired, and almost exhausted. They took advantage of the rest, but their effort in the afternoon session when the sun was at its hottest, was significantly slower. Nandoo and the gang noticed this, and he tried to explain to their main spokesman by the name of Wong Yee, that they should take their time and work much more slowly over the whole day. The Madrasis intervened, and tried to help the Chinese to achieve their allotted workload.

Wong Yee was in his twenties, short, and slim with sinewy muscles developed over years of hard labouring in Macao, a Portuguese colony. He was serving a life sentence for the murder of his mother-in-law, but insisted that he was innocent. He was in a fight with a neighbour who threw a thick piece of wood towards him. He ducked to avoid being hit, but the wood struck his mother-in-law on her head. She died almost instantly, and Wong Yee was arrested, tried and convicted for murder. He was able to explain his story to Nandoo by some broken English, and hand signals.

Nandoo worked very hard to build up a good relationship with Wong Yee, and every time they spoke or tried to communicate with each other, the other Chinese men would try to listen in on their conversations. The Chinese men were very keen to mix in with the other people on the estate, and they quickly gained the confidence of their new neighbours and work colleagues. They were always neatly dressed before and after their day's work, with their almost over-sized straw hats covering their long "pigtails" hairstyle. They walked very quickly, and did not stand around indulging in idle chat, always seeming to be busy cleaning, cooking, and gardening.

Nandoo was always offering much praise for Wong Yee, and the other Chinese men in his regular verbal reports to Mustafa, who in turn, kept the Massa fully informed.

The Chinese men also loved pork, and on pay days, they would go into the village as a group, and buy specially cooked "souse" and "pepper pot" made and sold by a cheerful African woman by the name of Miss Betty. She was quite large, much taller than the Chinese men, and always wore a toothsome smile. She wore a Madras kerchief as a head scarf which she had purchased at the Sunday market. Inevitably, the close bonding of the Chinese with the Africans of the village became more noticeable as time passed by.

On their rest days, the Chinese would stay close to, or in their yard playing card and board games, such as draughts. The Indian workers would gather around the players, and observe how the Chinese played the games, and soon they gradually joined in. But the Chinese were more interested in gambling for money, and the Indian players were not too keen to compete with the experts.

Despite such activities, the Chinese were generally bored and frustrated at not having any women amongst them. Miss Betty soon provided a quick answer to the men's emotional and sexual needs. She was well-known in the village for running a small and fairly discreet brothel of four young African girls who provided a service to go with the souse and pepper pot. Some of the Indian men were also Miss Betty's regular customers.

The other main attraction at Miss Betty's was the availability of fine Demerara rum as well as the more potent "bush rum" which she called "high wine". This was not a wine, but it made the drinkers very high, very quickly. She was a very astute business woman who knew how to cater for the varying needs of all the races settled in the village.

33.

Unwelcome influences

Mustafa and Joshua had discussed the increasing influence of Miss Betty's business, and other services she offered to the Chinese men within only a few weeks of their arrival on the estate. They welcomed the supply of her special food dishes to the men, but were concerned about the prostitution, and rum drinking available to them from within the community.

They talked to Ragubir and the Massa about the negative effects of Miss Betty's establishment, and were concerned in particular, about some of the impact of the excessive rum drinking on the labourers of the estate. The Indian male workers, although having their own pastimes to entertain themselves, also began to drink rum regularly and more intensely, especially on pay day. Not only were they becoming more rowdy, they also often ended up arguing loudly, and fighting each other viciously. These quarrels and fights would sometimes result in bloodshed caused by the use of the sharp cutlasses as weapons, to inflict horrendous cuts on each other.

The Africans in the village were more content to steer clear of the Indians and Chinese who had also started to drink large quantities of rum. The Africans preferred to indulge in their smoking of *ganja*, and engaging in loud discussions amongst themselves.

Wong Yee became very fond of Miss Betty, not only because of her special pork dishes, but also her very attractive eighteen year old daughter called Molly. He was infatuated with her smooth dark complexion, her instant smile, and her warmth towards him whenever he visited Miss Betty's place. Molly was Miss Betty's only child, and she was not married to the father who was a pork-knocker, and wanderer.

At first, Miss Betty did not seem to mind the growing friendship between Wong Yee and Molly. She felt that it was good for business with the Chinese men. Wong Yee steered clear of the four young prostitutes, preferring to focus his attention on Molly, whilst the other men indulged in their own entertainment with the girls.

As a result of their discussion with Ragubir and the Massa, Mustafa and Joshua decided that they would talk to Miss Betty with a view to reducing the excessive rum drinking that was causing disruption, and greater absence from work in the fields and the factory. They approached Miss Betty on a Sunday morning when the business was closed.

"Gentlemen, what can I do for you?" asked Miss Betty most politely and with great charm.

Mustafa frowned, and said, "We have come to talk to you about your business."

Miss Betty smiled broadly, and said, "Oh! Before we do, can I tempt you with some delicious souse or pepper pot?"

Joshua replied, "No thank you Miss Betty. We do not eat pork."

Miss Betty, ever the keen businesswoman, insisted, "You are missing something quite tasty, nourishing, and very potent for your manhood."

Mustafa, still appearing serious, said, "Thank you, but I am a Muslim, and I am not allowed to eat pork."

Joshua said, "Miss Betty, we have really come over here to talk about the rum drinking, and the rowdiness that takes place particularly on Saturdays. It also affects the workers who are either not turning up for work on the following Mondays, or are not fit enough to do the work after a lot of drinking."

Miss Betty realised that her visitors were quite serious, and said, "Well Joshua, this is not my fault. The men are all old enough, and it is up to them to control their drinking, and behaviour. I do send them away if I see that they are getting drunk, or are becoming rowdy and quarrelsome. What else do you want me to do?"

Mustafa and Joshua thought for a moment, and then Mustafa suggested, "You could consider opening a little later on Saturdays, and closing a little earlier. Also, close the whore house that you are running. This is not an acceptable business."

Miss Betty glared at the two men, and said firmly, "Look, this is my business. If I offer rum for a shortened time, they will go and obtain their bush rum elsewhere. Likewise, if the prostitutes go, the men will follow them to their homes. Besides, the girls depend on me for many things, and they feel much safer here. These men are often prone to violence at the least provocation. I am sorry, but I cannot be of any help to you. Now, if you do not mind, please leave me alone."

Mustafa and Joshua left Miss Betty's establishment feeling very disappointed with her reaction, and negative attitude to their request. As they walked back towards the estate managers' quarters, they discussed what they should do next.

Joshua said, "Let us talk to Ragubir and Kanhaiya."

"Yes, they may have some other ideas on the matter," agreed Mustafa. "But I think that Miss Betty is getting too big for her boots, and she needs to be stopped. Otherwise, this could become a more serious problem for her customers, the community, and the estate."

"I agree with you my brother," said Joshua. "In the old days, she would have been shut up for good!"

"What do you mean Joshua?" asked Mustafa worriedly.

"Well, the Massa would have quietly gotten someone to sort her out, and close down her business," said Joshua, gesturing with his right hand as if to slit his throat.

"Did our Massa do this? Will he do such a thing to Miss Betty?" asked Mustafa, whispering to avoid being overheard.

Joshua said, "Let me put it this way. The estate is expected to make a lot of money for the owners. Massa Bass's job is to do everything in his power to achieve this. And I mean everything!"

They finally reached Ragubir's home, and were warmly welcomed in by Ishani. Eight years old Bharat was playing with little Meena in the lounge.

"Well Mustafa and Joshua, can I offer you something to eat and drink?" asked Ishani as she directed Bharat and Meena to leave the room.

"Oh yes please! We are starving," they both said with some relief.

"Can you please ask Ragubir to join us?" requested Mustafa. "I will go and invite Kanhaiya over."

The four friends sat in the comfortable lounge chairs enjoying their meal when Mustafa said, "Gentlemen, we have asked Miss Betty to restrict her selling of rum on Saturdays, and she is not willing to do so. Also, we asked her to stop the prostitution, and she was not happy to do so. What do you suggest we should do now?"

"Well," said Ragubir. "We have to talk to our workers about their rum drinking. On the other matter, there is a big problem for the young men in particular. There are not enough young ladies to choose from. It is worse for the Chinese men. They have no Chinese women at their *logie*."

Kanhaiya suggested, "We have to speak to Massa about bringing more women and girls to the estate. This prostitution can bring serious disease, and it is a sinful practice."

Joshua said, "Look, our priest talks about these things every Sunday at the church. But no one listens to him. In fact, the four girls also go to the church more regularly than some of us! And so does Miss Betty!"

They continued to discuss the problem for a while longer, but with no consensus as to what they should do. Then Mustafa concluded, "We have talked a lot about this, but we have come to no agreement as to what to do. I suggest that we should all go along with Nandoo and Wong Yee, to meet the Massa as soon as we can. This problem is also his to resolve."

Wong Yee meanwhile, continued his courtship of Molly, and decided to approach Miss Betty. He said in his improving but broken English, with a new and distinct Chinese accent, "Miss Betty, you know I like you velly much. I also like Morry velly velly much. So, I come to ask you for Morry. I want to mally Morry."

"To mally Morry?" asked a confused Miss Betty.

"Yes, to take Morry and baby," said Wong Yee.

"Morry... Molly and baby?" asked a shocked Miss Betty. "You mean to say that you and Molly expect a baby? This is crazy! Right under my nose? Are you mad?"

A very nervous Wong Yee said, "Yes Miss Betty, Morry is having baby. It is my baby. No, I am not mad. I am a good man, and I want to mally Morry and look after baby."

"No! I cannot allow this! Molly... Molly... come here right now!" screamed an angry Miss Betty.

Molly appeared before her seething mother, and the very worried Wong Yee.

Miss Betty, stood upright and clenched her fists. She asked, "Molly, is this true? Are you having a baby, and with this miserable Chinaman? Tell me!"

"Yes mama," said Molly quietly, as she began to cry.

The furious Miss Betty, with sweat pouring down her strained face, said, "Oh my good Father! This cannot be! What have you brought upon me? What have I done to deserve this? You with this worthless Chinaman? And this baby... What is it going to look like? No, this cannot happen! I will never agree to this marriage, and to this baby!"

"But Miss Betty," said Wong Yee weakly.

Miss Betty interrupted him, and said, "Do not but Miss Betty me! You both heard me loud and clear! No marriage and no baby! Now, just get out of here Mr Wong Yee, before I hurt you! Molly, you stay here, and I will deal with you later!"

Wong Yee felt very scared of Miss Betty. He left quietly, and hurried back to the *logie*, utterly shocked at the response he received from Miss Betty. He feared for his beloved Molly and the baby. He hoped that no harm would befall Molly. He was thoroughly confused, and did not know what to do. His other Chinese friends saw that he was very troubled, and gathered around him to offer some solace.

34.

Invitations to treat

The delegation led by Ragubir, and including Mustafa, Kanhaiya, Nandoo, Joshua and Wong Yee, met the accommodating Massa at his sumptuous home in the senior staff compound. They were served hot teas in beautifully carved, and exotic looking tea cups and saucers made of expensive China which was unfamiliar to them, except for Wong Yee. Whilst they all held their teacups awkwardly just above their saucers, Wong Yee preferred to hold his in the traditional Chinese way by cupping it in his hands without using the saucer.

The Massa, retaining an air of supreme British decorum, held his teacup's handle with the thumb and first two fingers of his right hand, and with the little finger pointing outwards, and away. The others tried to copy this, but they struggled to achieve this posture, and spilled much of the tea onto the saucers, and onto the luxurious Persian carpet. The Massa smiled nervously as he observed the clumsy attempts at aping his style. He nodded reassuringly to allow them to recover their composure.

"So gentlemen," the Massa said. "I understand that you wish to discuss a serious matter with me."

Ragubir said, "Yes Massa, my colleagues here have come along to discuss something which has started to affect the work on the estate, and Mustafa and I are very concerned about this."

"Yes sir, we are," added Mustafa in agreement.

Joshua said, "You see sir, we have a situation where our working colleagues have been drinking too much rum too often, and are behaving badly in the yards, and in the village."

The Massa shook his head, and said, "I have heard about this, but you all need to talk to your men, and try to control them. Otherwise I will have to involve the police, and this may not be the best thing to do. They do not have much entertainment to keep them happy when they are away from work."

"Aha!" said Kanhaiya. "It is also the other entertainment that we are worried about. And that is to do with the goings on at Miss Betty's place."

Wong Yee's ears pricked up when he heard reference to Miss Betty and her girls. But he remained speechless, sipping his tea with a disconcerting slurp.

The Massa said, "I have heard that Miss Betty cooks and sells some very tasty dishes, and I hope to try some of her pork sometime."

Mustafa put down his teacup and saucer with great care, and said, "Massa, I have also heard that her food is great, and everyone who has tasted it just go back for more. But the entertainment that Kanhaiya is referring to, is more to do with carnal sin."

Joshua nearly spilled more of his tea, and intervened with, "Sir, Miss Betty is running a whore house, and the men have been going there regularly. Wong Yee might wish to say something about this."

Wong Yee reluctantly broke his silence and said, in his best English, "I do not know what is a whole house. But, Miss Betty is good woman. She look after girls and customers. All my men go there for fun. But not me."

Nandoo intervened with, "Sir, Wong Yee and his people have done really well since they came to the estate. But I am most worried about my Indian gang who are drinking too much rum, and the young men who have been going to Miss Betty's girls for sex."

"Look gentlemen," said the Massa. "I understand what you are telling me. I need some time to think about how best to deal with Miss Betty. Meanwhile, you all need to go back to your workers, and talk to them about their rum drinking. I know Mustafa that your Muslim brothers are not supposed to drink any kind of alcohol, so you need to remind them. Kanhaiya and Nandoo, you need to talk to the Hindus and Madrasis. Joshua, you and I can talk to the Parish Priest. And, Wong Yee, I know that you seem to be coping without drinking rum, and fraternising with the prostitutes, but you also need to speak to your men."

Ragubir thanked the Massa, and as they all slowly stood up to leave, they tried to place their teacups and saucers on the centre table before them, as carefully as possible. But in doing so, the cups and saucers rattled noisily in their shaking hands. Eventually, and much to the Massa's relief, they were all safely placed on the table. As the delegation began to leave, the Massa said, "Thank you all for coming. Ragubir, we need to talk about Miss Betty."

Joshua looked at Mustafa, and winked at him whispering, "You see, the Massa Bass has his own way of dealing with anyone who brings trouble to the estate."

Mustafa also whispered his response to Joshua, "But, I do not want any harm to come to Miss Betty. She is a good woman who is simply trying to earn a living. If she is not doing this, then I can assure you that someone else will provide her kind of service."

Joshua, still speaking in a hushed tone next to Mustafa, said, "The problem is, this should not have been allowed to happen in the first place. It is also a bad thing for Massa Bass and others involved in this labour trade, not to have enough women on the estates. They should have known about this throughout the years of slavery."

Mustafa nodded in agreement with the wizened Joshua who had experienced living in the slavery environment, and also appreciated the latest developments.

"So," said Mustafa stroking his chin. "Do you suggest that we talk to Miss Betty once again? We can give her some kind of warning or hint that if she does not improve things as we suggested to her, then she may face some serious consequences."

"That is a good idea Mustafa," agreed Joshua. "Let us sleep on it for a few days, and then approach her."

"Yes Joshua," said Mustafa. "That is good. But I think that we need to act much more quickly before Massa goes any further."

The two men bade goodbye to Kanhaiya, Nandoo, and Wong Yee, and hurried over to see Miss Betty in the village.

"Hello Miss Betty!" said Joshua enthusiastically.

Miss Betty said, "Hello Joshua and Mustafa! You are back! I hear that you went to see the Massa. Are you so keen to see my business closed?"

The men noticed a sad looking Molly sitting in a corner of the house.

"Miss Betty," said Mustafa. "Is anything wrong with Molly?"

"No Mustafa. She is not feeling so good at the moment, but she is otherwise fine," said Miss Betty smiling at Molly.

Joshua beckoned Miss Betty to a spot on the small verandah of the house, away from Molly. He said quietly, "Miss Betty, we did go to see the Massa Bass, and he is very angry with you about the rum drinking, and the young ladies offering their services to the men."

Miss Betty clenched her fists and said angrily, "So what is your Massa Bass planning to do? Close me down? Beat me like he did when I was a young girl, and refused to have sex with him? Well, if he wants to do so, let him come here. This time I am a free, hard-working woman, and I am not going to do as he says! Joshua, why are you siding with the Massa and these people?"

Mustafa intervened, "Miss Betty, as I said, we all love you, and do not wish to see you suffer in any way. All we want is some compromise on the drinking hours, and maybe you can start charging a higher price for the girls so that only a few of the men can use their services."

Miss Betty said, "Mustafa, you must be crazy! If I do that, where will the men who cannot afford the girls, go? I am happy to compromise on the drinking hours, and will put up a notice about this, starting from next Sunday."

Joshua said, "Miss Betty, thank you for the rum drinking bit. But you really need to think about the prices for the girls as Mustafa suggested."

"All right then, give me some time," proposed Miss Betty with her fists unclenched, much to both men's relief.

"Now, you also, why do you not try some of my freshly made pepper pot?" offered a smiling Miss Betty.

Joshua stood back and said, "It is a very tempting offer and the food smells nice, Miss Betty. But, as Mustafa said, he will not use pork because he is a Muslim, and I do not because I was also once a Muslim, and I still respect my Muslim upbringing, even though I am now a Christian."

Mustafa added, "But, the good news is that the Massa has said that he will like to try some."

Miss Betty recovered her composure, and was more relaxed as she said, "Well, who knows, if he behaves himself, he might get some from me for free! And, maybe if he is still interested, and does not close my business, I may be willing to offer him something else he once craved for!"

Mustafa and Joshua blushed, and smiled at the proposition as they left Miss Betty in much better spirits. They decided not to lose any more time, and rushed over to tell the Massa about Miss Betty's promises, but not about her personal special offers.

The next working day began with everyone who turned up for work with the Nandoo gang and Joshua's factory workers, looking utterly bemused and sad. But this was not due to the rum drinking and other revelry.

Kanhaiya heard the news, and as soon as he saw Mustafa, he told him with tears in his eyes, "*Bhaiya*, they have found Miss Betty dead, with her throat cut through and through!"

35.

Love's hurt

Mustafa hailed Joshua as he passed by the manager's quarters in his cart, on the way to the sugar factory.

"Joshua, did you hear the terrible news?" asked Mustafa.

"What news Mustafa?" asked a bemused Joshua as he reined in his horse.

Mustafa said sadly, "They say that Miss Betty's body has been found with her throat cut."

Joshua raised his arms in the air, and said, "Oh my good God! Who could have done this? We left her so happy only yesterday afternoon!"

Mustafa looked around and beyond Joshua, and said, "My friend, I have not yet seen Ragubir, and he is normally up very early, especially on a Monday morning."

"You are not suggesting that Ragubir has something to do with this?" asked Joshua with a serious quizzical look on his face.

Mustafa, still looking around him nervously, said, "Well, it was you who told me about Massa's way of dealing with people who cause problems on the estate."

Joshua said, "Yes, but I cannot believe that the Massa Bass will do or arrange for something like this, especially since we told him about Miss Betty's agreement to change things."

Mustafa asked, "Well Joshua, if this is not the case, then who could have done such a vile thing?"

Just then, Ragubir stepped out onto the roadside, and joined the two men in their conversation.

Joshua said, "Oh Mr Ragubir, have you heard the dreadful news about Miss Betty?"

"No, what happened?" asked Ragubir as he acknowledged Mustafa.

"Well, Miss Betty has been found dead in her house. Someone killed her," said Mustafa, wiping tears from his eyes.

"Oh my God!" exclaimed Ragubir, putting his hands to his mouth. "This cannot be true! I cannot believe that such a thing could happen to such a nice person."

Joshua held Ragubir's arms and said, "Mr Ragubir, tell me something. When we all discussed Miss Betty and her business with the Massa Bass, he pulled you aside when we were leaving. What did he say to you about Miss Betty?"

Ragubir said, "Joshua and Mustafa, all Massa wanted to talk to me about was getting ready to receive some more labourers for the estate as more plans were being made to expand the sugar plantation."

Mustafa said, "Well, thank you for telling us this."

"You... you are not suggesting that Massa and I have anything to do with Miss Betty's death?" asked Ragubir in total disbelief.

"No... no... Mr Ragubir, you and Massa Bass are very honourable people. We could never suggest such things," said Joshua looking at Mustafa.

Mustafa said, "That is right. We need to help investigate what happened to the poor lady, and also try to keep everyone calm and alert. Her killer or killers would be very dangerous people."

Work on the estate was brought to a standstill on the day of Miss Betty's funeral. Virtually everyone from the *logies* and the village turned up to the small overcrowded Church, and then followed the makeshift hearse to the cemetery in Anna Catherina. Joshua acted as the chief mourner, and bedecked his cart with flowers that covered the large, unpainted, and beautifully constructed coffin made of mahogany.

A distraught and sobbing Molly and the four working girls of Miss Betty's business followed the hearse at the head of the hundreds of mourners who slowly and respectfully walked the route in silence. They were all still very shocked at the sudden loss of the popular figure in the village.

The Chinese men were led at the front by a tearful Wong Yee, who was constantly muttering to himself in Chinese. Then, as the pall-bearers struggled to lift the large coffin, and lower Miss Betty into her grave, Wong Yee broke loose from his group, and shouted in his broken English, "Miss Betty!... Miss Betty! So solly! I never mean to hurt you so much! Please... please forgive me!"

For a moment, there was a huge hush, and groan from everyone, as Wong Yee reached forward, and knelt beside Miss Betty's coffin as it was being lowered into the grave. He nearly slipped onto the coffin, but was firmly grabbed by Mustafa and Joshua.

"Let me go!" screamed Wong Yee. "I love Miss Betty! I am solly I hurt her! But she did not want me to mally Morry!"

Joshua looked at Mustafa for a moment, and they agreed to keep firm hold of Wong Yee. They led him away from the graveside as he continued to scream hysterically. Then they handed him to the local police who arrested him, and took him away. Everyone was utterly stunned by what they saw, and heard.

Then Molly stepped forward, and spoke to Mustafa and Joshua. "What have you done to Wong Yee? He is not a killer! You are wrong! You had no right to do this! He is an innocent man!"

"But... but Miss Molly," said Mustafa, resting his hands on the distraught young woman's shoulders. "You heard him say that he did not mean to kill your mother."

The tearful Molly pleaded, "No! No! You do not understand! He did not mean to hurt her feelings. He is in love with me, and I am having his baby. He wants to marry me, and my mother refused to accept his proposal. He is an innocent man. Please go quickly, and get him released."

The crowd was now even more surprised to hear what Molly said, and they realised that a mistake had been made to arrest Wong Yee for the murder of Miss Betty.

Soon after the burial, the mourners were advised by Ragubir, Mustafa and Joshua, to return home, and to maintain their vigilance. The three men then rushed over to the Police Station which was also the local jailhouse.

When they arrived at the Station, they could hear Wong Yee pleading his innocence, and sobbing loudly. Mustafa spoke to the policeman guarding Wong Yee's cell. "Sir, we have all made a bad mistake to arrest Wong Yee. We only handed him to you because we were worried that he might have caused a disturbance at the cemetery. Please let us take him home."

"I am very sorry sir," said the officer. "He has already been charged for the murder, and I have to keep him here until he is taken to Georgetown for his trial."

"What?" asked Joshua, angrily. "He is not the murderer, and you have no evidence!"

"Well, I heard him saying that he did not mean to hurt Miss Betty so much, and I found this specially carved knife on him," disclosed the officer.

Joshua's anger made him move towards the officer threateningly, and Mustafa and Ragubir forcefully restrained him.

"Come on Joshua," said Mustafa whilst holding Joshua's arms firmly. "Let us go home. We cannot do anything about this now. We need to go and make sure that Molly is safe, and is looked after."

They left the Station with Wong Yee's pleas of his innocence still ringing in their ears.

Molly and the four prostitutes had just returned to her home when Joshua, Mustafa and Ragubir waved frantically for her attention.

"Miss Molly!" said Joshua. "We have come to tell you that they have already charged Wong Yee for the murder of your mother. We could not get him freed."

"Do you know anything that could help Wong Yee?" asked Mustafa.

"Yes. You see, my father came back from the mining town a few days ago, and when he heard about Wong Yee and me, he went mad," said Molly, sobbing.

Ragubir asked, "What did he do?"

"He was so angry with me that he slapped me very hard on my head. I was instantly knocked out, and fell on the floor," said Molly wiping the tears on her face with her hands.

"And then what happened?" asked Joshua impatiently.

"I do not know. But when I woke up, all I could see was blood everywhere..." said Molly as she fell to her knees on the floor.

"I think that she has said enough," said Mustafa, as Joshua and Ragubir helped the girls to console Molly.

Joshua said coldly, "We have a killer on the run. The Police need to go, and look for him."

"He must be very far away now," said Molly as she sat on a chair. "He must have left as soon as he killed my mother. Please somebody, go and get hm. Otherwise I will lose my Wong Yee. I cannot take this pain any more. My whole family is being destroyed by my love for this man. And my baby, what will happen to it? Please for our sake, save my Wong Yee. I love him so much. I do not want to see him hurt anymore."

36.

Manhunt

Ragubir, Mustafa, Joshua and Nandoo, who had been asked by the Massa to speak to the workers and other residents of the estate, about controlling the rum drinking, used their individual meetings to warn everyone to be on the lookout for Miss Betty's killer on the run. Molly's pork-knocker father had been described as a very dark African man, stockily built, and about forty years old. He had a scar running down the left side of his face that was caused by a whip when he was brutally beaten as a slave on the estate. His name was Alfred, and although he was normally very quietly spoken, he was quick-tempered, and carried a specially adapted knife that he made out of a worn cutlass.

Alfred was deeply in love with Miss Betty, but she never intended to marry him because of his quick temper, and refusal to stay close to the estate instead of wandering off to the goldmines as soon as he felt the need to do so. He was also a doting father to Molly, and she could do no wrong in his eyes. As she grew older, she became a more important reason for him to return from the goldmines more frequently.

So, the thought of his sweet Molly succumbing to the charms of the Chinese Wong Yee, and to be expecting his baby, was too unbearable for the jealous Alfred. He simply vented his feelings on Miss Betty on the assumption that she should have been alert to the situation, and should have put a stop to the blossoming romance. Miss Betty's recently acquired knowledge of Molly's pregnancy and affair with Wong Yee came too late. And she paid the ultimate price at the hands of an unforgiving, and outraged Alfred.

On that dreadful night of the murder, Alfred would have had to pass by the Chinese *logie*, and Wong Yee was saved from a similar fate had he been present at the yard. So, in his haste to run away as far as possible from the scene of the crime, Alfred did not waste any further time to look for his next victim.

The local Police team was not large enough or experienced in undertaking such a testing manhunt in the bush environment, dozens of miles away from the estate. Sending a posse to track down, apprehend, and bring Alfred back to face justice, was also out of the question.

Ragubir, Mustafa and Joshua discussed the situation with the Massa, as Alfred's actions had caused everyone to be fearful and nervous as long as he was free. Rumours began to be spread across the estate, and in the neighbouring villages about various sightings of Alfred. One person told of how he saw Alfred, dressed as a woman, walking in the next village one night. Another said that he was sure that Alfred had come in the middle of the night, and stolen one of his chickens. These stories spread like wildfire, and added to the increasing fear, and anxiety that gripped the residents.

The Massa listened to the concerns of Ragubir, Mustafa and Joshua, and agreed that no one should go on the hunt for Alfred. If the rumours of sightings of him in the area were true, then the best approach would be to lay in wait for him, and then try to arrest him.

Ragubir asked, "What if he is really far away into the interior, and these stories are not true? We can be waiting here in fear, and he may never return."

The Massa said, "This may be true, but I think that he will try to harm Wong Yee, and if what I hear about Alfred's violent temperament is true, he will come back for his man, no matter how long he had to wait."

Mustafa said, "So, it is best for Wong Yee to stay in jail for a while. In fact, it is better for him to be taken away to Georgetown. Alfred is capable of getting at him even in the local Police jail."

Joshua added, "But the poor man could be condemned to death for a murder we all know that he did not commit. One way or other Wong Yee is doomed."

Mustafa thought for a moment, and then said, "Aha, maybe the best thing to do is to get a message sent out that Wong Yee has been freed on bail, and then we can set up a team of vigilantes to wait for Alfred, and then capture him."

The Massa agreed, "Yes, this is a good idea. However, people charged with murder are never given bail. But, I will start the ball rolling on the bail story, and we can set up the other Chinese men with some volunteers to lay in wait for Alfred to return."

They were all getting more excited with their developing plan, and Ragubir said, "Yes, we will ask one of the Chinese men to move into Wong Yee's room to act as a decoy."

"Well gentlemen," concluded the Massa. "We have a good plan, but we must not tell anyone about it. Now, let us get started."

The Massa contacted many of the other estate managers across the West Coast and West Bank of Demerara, and used every other method of communication to spread the false news of Wong Yee's release from prison, back to the estate. He also asked those in contact with local Amerindians in or near to the mining areas, to look for, and apprehend Alfred. The Amerindians had been used in this way, to re-capture African slaves or those Indians who had run away from the plantations.

In the two weeks that passed since Wong Yee was taken to Georgetown, and the local vigilante group laid in wait for Alfred, there was no sign of him. The rumours of new sightings had also dried up. The Amerindians had not made any progress in catching Alfred. Three of the vigilantes were detailed to guard Molly and the girls at Miss Betty's house. All of this helped to ease some of the fears of the residents, but they were still wary that the wanted man was at large, and very dangerous.

Then early one evening, as the vigilantes took up their positions around the Chinese *logie*, a stifled sound was heard coming from Wong Yee's room. A fierce scuffle was in progress, and as the vigilantes converged on the location, a gruesome groan was heard, followed by a heavy thud.

Seconds later, the front door which had been bolted shut from the inside was opened, and in the darkness, the bloodied face of a Chinese man emerged. He was holding a knife still dripping with blood, in his right hand. He stumbled forward, and collapsed into the arms of two of the vigilantes.

The other vigilantes stormed into the room, and saw an African man lying face down in a pool of blood. They turned his body over, and he was instantly recognised as Alfred. Then they saw another Chinese man huddled in a corner of the room whimpering, and almost motionless. He was the most terrified decoy that Alfred must have mistaken for Wong Yee.

One of the vigilantes holding the Chinese man with the knife shouted, "It's Wong Yee! It's Wong Yee! How he come back?"

When Ragubir and Mustafa arrived on the scene, Wong Yee was sitting on the stairs in front of his room with all the Chinese men gathered around him in animated discussion, whilst the other vigilantes stood by in silence.

Mustafa asked, "Wong Yee! What happened?"

"I kill Alfred. Now I am murderer. They can hang me," said Wong Yee coldly.

Ragubir said, "Wong Yee, you should have been in jail, in Georgetown!"

"Yes, I was in jail. But I escape. I came for my Morry," said Wong Yee. "But too many people guard her. I no see Morry. But I see Alfred come for me, and I follow him here. I did not want to kill him, but he stab me in my leg. So, I kill him. Let Police take me now. They can hang me. My life is over."

Mustafa placed his hands on Wong Yee's shoulders, and said, "No Wong Yee. You will be freed, and we will do everything to see that you become a free man."

A tired Wong Yee said, "No Mustafa, I am done. Just promise me that you will all look after my Morry and our baby. Give them everything I have. And, please also look after my people. They are not criminals. They work hard, and want to be free to go back to China."

Wong Yee broke down in tears. He repeatedly called out for Molly.

Then, only a hundred yards away, a voice was heard screaming, "Wong Yee! Wong Yee! Wong Yee!" as the person reached closer to the scene.

Molly arrived in a desperate panic, and as soon as she saw Wong Yee, she smothered him in a tight embrace. Wong Yee, for a few precious moments, seemed to forget his pain from the stab wound in his leg, and squeezed Molly tightly, lifting her off her feet.

In the weeks that passed, Wong Yee was re-arrested, and taken back to the jail in Georgetown. The Massa, along with all the witnesses on the estate, made representations and statements at the murder trial, and Wong Yee's charge for murder, was quashed.

37.

Business is business

1855 marked the end of the second five year contract period for Mustafa, Kanhaiya and Nandoo, on the sugar estate. The plantation was flourishing under the careful watch of the Massa, and his trusted leaders such as Ragubir, Mustafa, Nandoo and Joshua.

This time, Mustafa, now with two young sons, Ahmad Ali and Rattan Ali with his beautiful wife Neesha, made up his mind to sever his links with the estate. He discussed his intention with Neesha, his brother Kanhaiya and Mumtaz, and was determined to set himself up as a local businessman, and retailer. He knew from his experiences during his journey in India, that he was capable of buying and selling goods, and provisions.

He met the Massa, and disclosed his plan to obtain a plot of land situated on the main road of Anna Catherina. He and Kanhaiya secured a license to cut and transport timber from the interior, to be used as suitable building materials for two large houses, and an integrated general store. The Massa graciously granted the plot to Mustafa, and Kanhaiya also benefited with land to build his own home. Apart from practising as a Hindu Pandit, Kanhaiya was more interested in cultivating rice, and sought to purchase two acres of an abandoned sugarcane field, for this purpose.

Mustafa could not afford the cost of completing the building of his house and store, and to stock it with the goods he wished to sell. Kanhaiya was also short of enough funds to complete his house, and to purchase the land for his rice cultivation venture. So, the two brothers decided to travel to Georgetown, and to approach an Indian moneylender who had only recently arrived in the colony, from India.

The brothers arrived at the gate of a large wooden whitewashed colonial building which housed offices for lawyers, and other business people, on Croal Street. The moneylender's office was easy to identify with a bold sign showing the name of the businessman in gold. This helped to distinguish the office and business from the other occupants of the building, whose nameplates were simply painted in white.

"I cannot believe it!" said Mustafa, as he turned to an equally surprised Kanhaiya. "It cannot be the same Sundar Das that we knew in India?"

Any doubts in their minds were removed when they recognised the security guard standing outside the moneylender's office. It was Mohan Lall, Sundar Das's assistant during the time he was recruiting immigrant labourers for the sugar plantations. Mohan Lall did not instantly recognise the brothers, and asked them whether they had an appointment to see Mr Das.

Mustafa said, "I remember you very well, although it has been ten years since we last saw each other in India. You must be Mohan Lall, the assistant to the recruiting agent called Sundar Das. I am Mustafa Ali, and this is Kanhaiya Ramchand."

"Oh yes! I can remember you Mustafa!" said Mohan Lall excitedly, hugging Mustafa. He then shook Kanhaiya's hands firmly, and welcomed them in to see Sundar Das.

"Sundar, you will not believe this, but just look who is here to see you!" said Mohan, as the two visitors were ushered into the office.

Sundar Das moved forward from behind his large mahogany desk, and greeted Mustafa and Kanhaiya with warm hugs. He was now bald, wearing a larger than normal red *tikka* on his forehead, and smartly robed in a saffron coloured *dhoti*. He still held onto a favourite, well-carved walking stick, although there were no signs of him being lame or dependent on this aid.

"Come, come, *baitho* my *bhaiyas*! *Baitho!*" offered Sundar, as he returned to his large executive chair behind his desk.

Sundar continued, "So tell me Mustafa, how are you? How has it been here in Demra?"

Mustafa said, "I am very well, Inshallah! And so is my *bhaiya* Kanhaiya. We have survived some very hard times on the estate. But, we have been treated well by the manager, and all the people working there."

"And what about you?" asked Kanhaiya. "Why have you come here?"

Sundar paused for a moment, and then said, "Well, I continued to do the recruiting work with the help of my good friend Mohan, but things were getting very hard back in India. People were even talking about getting rid of the British, and all the people who were helping them. I was threatened by some angry people, and was told that when India is free, people like me would be lucky to survive. I did not wait for this, so Mohan and I left as quickly as possible." Mohan Lall nodded in agreement.

Mustafa asked, "But how come you are here working as a moneylender, and not as a labourer on an estate?"

Sundar reached over and offered his visitors some water, and said, "Well, I was offered to work as a Driver on an estate, but my British contacts helped me to set up in this business. Besides, I know that more people like you are not going back to India, and would prefer to settle here permanently."

Mustafa looked at Sundar curiously, and said, "Sundar, you have not changed. Come on, tell me the truth as to why you are here. I can see that you are hiding something from me."

Sundar said, "Well, I am still not married, and I have come here to find my Ishani."

Kanhaiya said, "Aha! Now you are beginning to make sense!"

"Do you know where Ishani is?" asked Sundar twitching at his curled up moustache whilst opening his eyes bigger, in anticipation.

"Well, that is a big question to ask, and for us to answer," said Mustafa sipping his water. "Why do we not talk about the reason why Kanhaiya and I are here? We are looking to borrow some money for about two years, when we are sure to repay you."

Sundar said, "My *bhaiyas*, lending you money is no problem for me. I can give you whatever amount you want, and you can repay me anytime and anyhow. Only one favour I wish to ask of you. Can you help me find my Ishani?"

They discussed the amount of the two separate loans, how much interest they were expected to pay, and the length of time for the closure of the transactions. Sundar Das gave the brothers very generous terms for the loans in recognition of their promise to help him in his quest to find Ishani, and, their long acquaintance.

Mustafa and Kanhaiya then signed their individual loan agreements, shook hands with Sundar Das and Mohan Lall, took the loans in cash, and hurriedly left the office. They took great care to be very watchful as they rushed to the harbour, and made the journey across the Demerara River. Upon reaching Vreed-en-Hoop, they boarded Joshua's cart, and headed back to Anna Catherina. They were relieved to reach their home in the managers' quarters, with the large sums of cash still safely in their possession.

The Massa had generously given Mustafa and Kanhaiya enough time to build their new homes in Anna Catherina, and allowed them to continue sharing the house in the managers' quarters.

Kanhaiya, having respected Mustafa's cautiousness in not speaking about their business plans and conversation with Sundar Das, in the presence of Joshua, asked him upon their return home, "Tell me, Mustafa, why did you not disclose our knowledge of where Ishani is? That man will not forgive us if he found out that we were not telling him the truth."

"Kanhaiya," said Mustafa seriously. "We did not have to say whether or not we knew where she is. This is a very delicate matter for our sister to handle. Also, there is Sundar's son Bharat to consider, not to mention Ragubir's feelings. After all, ten years is a very long time for Sundar to just appear, and to claim what he thinks is his. We need some time to think as to how to deal with this matter."

Kanhaiya listened carefully, and responded, "But what if he, through his British contacts, manages to trace her here? And for him to find Ishani living just next door to us?"

"Look," said Mustafa. "Let us get on with building our houses and setting up our businesses, and start repaying his very high interest charged on the loans. If he happens to trace Ishani, then we will deal with that when the time comes. Meanwhile, let us keep quiet about this, and do not tell our wives or anyone else about Sundar Das, and his search for Ishani."

"Agreed my *bhaiya*," said Kanhaiya. "But I feel very uncomfortable with being accused of deception."

Mustafa smiled and said, "Kanhaiya, in business, we have to be able to deal with truths, lies and promises carefully. I understand your feelings, especially since you preach about the ills of lying, and acts of dishonesty. But in this case, we have to balance between people like Sundar, and the feelings of people we treat as close friends. Business is business, and business must come first. Especially in a situation such as this."

As soon as Mumtaz and Neesha entered the lounge, Mustafa and Kanhaiya quickly changed the subject of conversation. They told their wives that they had a very fruitful trip to Georgetown, and would now be concentrating on building their new homes, and businesses.

Mustafa and Kanhaiya organised and led a small team of experienced Indian and African woodcutters into the forest area, a few miles further inland from the estate. They carefully selected the type and size of trees to fell. They cut the crabwood timber into long strips nine inches wide and one inch thick. These were to be used for the walls, flooring, and ceilings of the two buildings. The greenheart trees were chosen for the base pillars and beams due to their strength, toughness, and longevity. The rafters were also to be made of greenheart. It took over four weeks of hard labour, for the team to have secured the wood they needed for the build.

The lumber was loaded onto large pontoons or punts which Mustafa had hired from the estate. Two mules were also hired to pull the laden punts along the canals out to the nearest point for final transport to the building sites. Joshua's cart was used to take the cut wood to the respective plots. Mustafa and Kanhaiya were not architects or carpenters, but they made some rough drawings of the designs for the houses. They appointed two local carpenters from the village, to undertake the building works.

Simon and Samuel were African twins who were responsible for building most of the *logies*, houses and other buildings on the estate. They had a good reputation for hard work, and good results. They were quite remarkable builders who, apart from having good saws, hammers, shavers and crowbars as their main tools, never used spirit levels or rulers. Yet, they skilfully adapted the straight edges of their saws as rulers, and used their excellent eyesight to check for balance and straightness to build the robust, and neat structures. One brother would often be seen standing in the middle of the main road, opposite a building under construction, and guiding the other in adjusting a plank. "Move it a little to the left. A little to the right. Up a bit, down a bit. Right, stop there!"

Simon and Samuel hired a number of men from the village as their assistants, and once they started on one building project, they would see this through to its completion and handover, before moving on to the next construction. Mustafa's house was the first to be built with a large space on the ground floor to be used as the general store. Behind the store, there was a dining area, kitchen, and a lounge. Unusually, an indoor toilet and bathing facility was built, with the waste routed through to a septic tank adjacent to the house. Overflows from the septic tank and the bath tub ran into gutters emptying out into the open drain beside the main road, which led into the trench that linked through to the koker at the sea wall.

The first floor comprised three large family bedrooms, a sitting area, and a veranda at the front. All the windows and the doors were made of wood initially. In later years, when glass became more available, the wooden windows were replaced by windows with glass panes. The roof was made of corrugated zinc covering, and the water from rainfall was collected via gutters leading into a large iron vat. There was a constant supply of water for the occupants. The iron vat caused the rainwater to be kept very cold, and refreshing.

Whilst Mustafa's house and general store was being built, Kanhaiya secured the land for his rice cultivation business. With the help of Nandoo and other workers from the estate, he cleared the two acres, tilled the tough soil, and flooded the field to help nourish the young plants which were planted by hand. The workers, who included some of the Chinese men from Nandoo's gang, had given Kanhaiya their help during the slack time on the estate. The Chinese men possessed good knowledge of rice cultivation, and Kanhaiya took every opportunity to learn from them.

Mustafa, Neesha and their two sons finally moved into their new home, and accommodated Kanhaiya, Mumtaz and their daughter, Meena. Joshua left his job at the factory, and became the full-time cart driver for Mustafa's business, transporting the provisions for the general store, and continuing to act as the family's transport provider on the main road, and other locations on the West Coast and West Bank of Demerara.

Whilst Mustafa dealt with negotiating the best prices for the goods purchased from the wholesalers of Georgetown, Neesha quickly became the expert at handling customers at the store. Her growing reputation was not only attributed to her business acumen, but also through her willingness to listen to peoples' problems, and to offer sound advice to them. She managed to find a good balance between her business transactions, and the personal needs of her customers. She was always able to maintain a level of neutrality and fair-mindedness in her relations with people.

Whilst the young rice plants were growing, Kanhaiya and Mumtaz concentrated their efforts on the building of their large family house at the front of their plot of land. At the side of the house was a ten feet wide private road that led to a rice factory, and a large open space for drying the paddy. There were two iron punts used for soaking the paddy before the drying and sifting process. The milling was aided by manual labour, and the final rice product was bagged in readiness for the market. The waste from the paddy was used as fuel, and also sold to the villagers for this purpose. Any broken rice from the process, was sold as feed for poultry.

The brothers, having laid out more capital funds to set up their businesses, found that the initial incomes from their ventures were not always sufficient for them to pay Sundar Das's loan interest, and to run their households. Often, they thought of going back to Sundar for more borrowing, but Mustafa always resisted this, and would sometimes help to pay Kanhaiya's debts. Likewise, if Mustafa was short of funds, Kanhaiya would give him the help he needed.

They continued to resist any temptation to tell Sundar about Ishani's whereabouts, preferring to deal with him on a strictly business basis only.

38.

Warding off evil

Wong Yee's marriage to Molly took place at the small Christian Church in the village, on a quiet Sunday morning. He was baptised as a Christian, much to the surprise and annoyance of his fellow Chinese labourers, who decided to stay away from the ceremony. They nevertheless accepted Molly on their *logie* as someone who needed their help through the remaining months of her pregnancy.

The newlywed couple was soon blessed with the birth of a son they named Andrew Yee. The baby was also baptised as a Christian. Wong Yee then moved into Miss Betty's home with his new family, and within weeks, the baby became ill. Neither the estate's doctor nor the sick nurse was able to diagnose the cause, and rumours began to spread in the village, about the house being haunted by an "*ole haigge*". Some attributed the illness to the presence of the ghosts of Miss Betty and Alfred. Their spirits were deemed by the villagers, to be unhappy due to the sudden and violent nature of their deaths, and would roam around until they were freed.

Wong Yee and Molly took the baby to meet Joshua who had recommended a local African *Obeah Man*, to try to remove any evil spirits or curse from the house, and the baby. The *Obeah Man* spoke very little broken English, and insisted on communicating through his African tongue which gave his presence a sense of greater mystique, and awe. He opened his large eyes widely as he spoke in a slow, gruff voice.

The ritual began with a slow drum roll by the *Obeah Man's* assistant who was also wearing a headdress made of string, and chicken feathers. There were chains made of multi-coloured *buck beads* round their necks and upper arms. Oil made from coconut, was liberally spread over their naked torsos, arms and legs, and this provided an eerie reflection in the flickering light from two small oil lamps placed in the centre of the otherwise dark room.

The gradual build up of the pulsating rhythm extracted from the taut goat skin at the top of the hollow wooden drum, was irresistible. Molly's feet were tapping out the beats almost involuntarily, and she rose up from her small stool to sway, and move in a circle around the room. The dance was not seen by Wong Yee before, and his eyes were transfixed on his beautiful wife as she continued to become fully absorbed in the drumming, and the unrecognised chanting of the *Obeah Man*, and his assistant.

After nearly half an hour, Molly's dance led her into a trance. She collapsed onto the wooden floor, and began to make unintelligible sounds in a voice that did not sound as hers. Wong Yee, holding baby Andrew closer to his chest, became increasingly nervous and concerned for Molly, as she continued to writhe, and groan. Then, as the drumming and chanting stopped, Molly lay still until the *Obeah Man* asked her to get up, and sit on her stool. He seemed to have her in his control, and this power over Molly impressed Wong Yee greatly.

Still looking dazed and confused, Molly obeyed the commands, and Wong Yee was asked to place the baby in her arms. Andrew began to cry, and Molly instinctively placed her fingers of her right hand, on his lips. He immediately stopped crying, and the *Obeah Man* gave her one of the *buck bead* chains to place around Andrew's neck, and one for her own use.

Joshua looked on in respectful silence, and when the *Obeah Man* completed his ritual prayers, he handed over a live cockerel. Wong Yee thought that this was the payment for the ritual until he saw the drummer remove a knife with a sharp glistening blade, and severed the bird's neck without fuss. The head was placed in a plate where it moved about for a short time until it stopped. The body of the bird fluttered until it stopped moving. The blood was collected in a small bowl, and the *Obeah Man* invited Wong Yee and Molly to take a sip. Wong Yee felt disgusted, but Molly still in a partial state of trance, seemed not to be affected by the taste of the blood. The drummer then dipped his right index finger into the bowl, and touched Andrew's lips with some blood. They all rose together, and the *Obeah Man* raised his arms aloft, and chanted the final pronouncement commanding all the evil spirits to leave the body of the baby, and go on their way to their own world.

The drumming and the chanting finally stopped, and a strange calm descended on the participants of the ritual. Molly slowly regained her composure, and her normal way of speaking, and voice returned, much to Wong Yee's relief. The *Obeah Man* sat on the floor with his legs crossed, and stared into the light of the two lamps. This was his way of signalling to his clients that the session was over, and that the victim was cured and freed of the evil spirits that had overtaken him. The drummer ushered Molly and Wong Yee who was carrying Andrew, out of the room.

The following Sunday, as Wong Yee and his family entered the main door of their Church, the priest, a short and stocky Englishman, took them aside.

He said, "Mr Yee and Molly, thank you for coming to Church today. I heard that you visited the local *Obeah Man* for some remedy for Andrew."

"Yes sir," said Molly who was cradling Andrew across her left shoulder. "We did go there, and now Andrew is well again."

The priest said, "You do know that you can come here for the right healing of the Lord Jesus Christ. The *Obeah* is mumbo jumbo, and dangerous. We as Christians frown on this practice, and I ask you in the Lord's name, to refrain from doing this in the future."

Molly bowed slightly in acknowledgement, and saw Joshua smiling. She smiled at Joshua, and took a pew next to him. Wong Yee followed suit.

Joshua whispered to Molly, "Look, don't worry about the reverend. He preaches to us about how the Lord Jesus was sacrificed for us all. When the Lord was put on a cross, he bled for our salvation. We have our own customs, and rituals which also involve sacrifice which works for us. We must never lose our customs. These are all we have left."

Wong Yee shook his head in agreement, and whispered, "Father cares about his way, but we also have many ways to skin cat." They smiled, and bowed their heads to the call for prayer.

At the end of another busy day at the store, Neesha, Mustafa and the boys settled down to a meal of chicken curry, *roti* and *daal*. She talked about the latest gossip in the village, concerning the *Obeah Man* and the miraculous cure of Andrew.

She said, "If people believe that the baby's health was improved by the *Obeah Man*, this will cause quite a problem."

Mustafa said, "Well, every religion has some kind of practice which deals with removing evil spirits, and making people better. These

African rituals have been with the people for centuries, and as long as they do not force their beliefs onto others, I do not see this as a problem. But I can see how *Obeah* can become part of the folklore across British Guiana."

Neesha nodded gently, and said, "You are right. I even heard someone say that the Massa should use the *Obeah Man* to cast a spell on the Africans to go back to work, and to break their strike for more pay."

Mustafa laughed, and said, "No, I think that Massa will continue to hold out for as long as the Indians and Chinese continue to work, and refuse to join in the strike action. Besides, the *Obeah Man* will not want to place himself in an awkward position against his people. If he did this, he will lose business!"

Neesha said glumly, "I hope that something or somebody will end this strike very soon. It is causing a lot of tension amongst the people. The worst thing that can happen is for both sides to mistrust each other. There should be more unity, and we will all benefit from this."

Mustafa finished his meal, and said, "Neesha, you sound like a politician. I fully agree with you about us all pulling together. We must also remember who holds the power over us all. Massa can cause this estate to close, and that could destroy our whole community, and our own business."

"So what!" exclaimed Neesha. "If he does this, we can all pack our belongings, and go back to our countries!"

"I understand your feelings Neesha," said Mustafa. "But going back to India is becoming a bad option with so much unrest building up there. The talk of mutiny and rebellion is bringing some fear to the people. It may all end with terrible bloodshed on all sides."

Neesha frowned, and said, "Mustafa, how do you know about this?"

Mustafa coughed slightly, and said, "I spoke to some people in Georgetown, and they told me about the unrest. If and when a rebellion starts, there will be only one winner. The British have a better armed and trained army, and not all Indians will support the rebels."

"Well, I hope also that the white people here do not start to take action against us for what happens in India," said a worried looking Neesha.

Mustafa said, "No, I do not believe that plantation owners here will do such a thing. Besides, it will be very bad for their production if the Indian labour force is suppressed."

"You may be right Mustafa," acknowledged Neesha. "Our community is growing here, and we must work harder to build ourselves up, and to share this country with everyone else. We can prove to the white man that we are good, hardworking people who are working together to make this place into a good country."

Mustafa smiled, and said, "Yes Neesha, we are trying to do our share of good for this new mixed community of Africans, Indians, Portuguese, Chinese, Amerindians and White people."

"Yes Mustafa, and you have to add to the melting-pot, the mixed races. We now have a Chinese mixed with African, along with the other mixes," pointed out Neesha as she gathered together the plates and cups from the table.

"And, that will become British Guiana!" said Mustafa. "A new country, with new people!"

"Our religions and customs are also blending. Although, I for one will find it difficult to accept certain practices such as *Obeah*," said Neesha, clutching at the *tabeej* she wore around her neck.

Mustafa said, "Neesha, we have to be careful, and to be able to recognise things which are not so very different from what we know, and do. Your *tabeej* has a quotation from the Holy Qur'an, designed to protect you, and to ward off evil. The buck bead necklace that Molly and Andrew are wearing, are for the very same reasons. Kanhaiya wears a *tilak*, an ancient Hindu marking on his forehead for the same kind of purpose. Joshua and Matilda wear necklaces with silver crosses, and the Amerindian man wears his native headband to display his pride, and strength drawn from his ancestors. We all need some protection from evil."

Mustafa leaned over, and warmly embraced his two sons. Neesha stood up, and joined in the tender family hug. He then said proudly, "Let this be our own family symbol for unity and love!"

39.

Debts and threats

Sundar Das and Mohan Lall were always happy to greet Mustafa and Kanhaiya at the start of every month. It was the time that they received the monthly payments of interest on the loans to their clients. Sundar was also very keen to hear any news about the search for Ishani, particularly since all of his attempts to find her had been unsuccessful.

"Mustafa and Kanhaiya, my *bhaiyas*!" said Sundar as he embraced the two visitors. "How is business? I hope that you have been doing very well!"

Mustafa said, "Well, Sundar, I buy the goods from the merchants here in Georgetown, and supply the customers with what they need. But, they end up with a lot of debts, and sometimes they fail to pay me the monthly instalments. Unfortunately, many of them have taken to rum drinking, and as soon as they get their weekly pay, they start drinking and wasting their money. Many of them eventually reach home, very drunk, and with none of the money they earned. I do not charge them interest on their debts, and I cannot deny their families the goods and provisions they need."

The wily Sundar shook his head, and advised, "Mustafa, my *bhaiya*, you need to be more strict with these people. Maybe you should have someone to collect the payments due from the workers as soon as they get their payslips. They can then do as they please with the money they have left. You should try this."

Mohan said, "I am more than willing to go to your estate, and do the collecting, at least one Saturday payday every month."

Kanhaiya intervened, "*Bhaiya* that will not be necessary. You see, we have a good community, and this kind of action may be seen as too openly aggressive. Debt is a personal thing for most people, and they may feel ashamed to have to do this in the open, and in front of all their friends and neighbours."

Sundar said, "This is a problem for you, and as long as you both pay me regularly, then I am happy with my business, and customers. I understand how you feel about your customers. Now, have you any news about my Ishani? I found out that she was allocated to the Vreed-en-Hoop plantation in 1845."

"Vreed-en-Hoop? In 1845?" asked Mustafa. "That was a long time ago. So, have you been there to look for her?"

"Yes," answered Mohan. "We went there, and no one seemed to know about her or even heard about her. All we heard was that most people who arrived there, had returned to India or died or gone to other places in this vast country."

"Hmm," pondered Mustafa. "This is very possible. Do you plan to go to the other estates? Or to ask your British friends?"

Sundar took the two bundles of money received from Mustafa and Kanhaiya, and gave them to Mohan to count, and record in the ledger.

He said, "We have been going around to the estates, but so far, we have had no luck at all. We have not visited your estate as we feel that you are there, and you will tell me if you had any information about Ishani."

"Yes Sundar, we will let you know when we have information for you," said Mustafa, looking at Kanhaiya, who nodded in agreement.

Mohan said, "Mustafa, do you know a man by the name of Ragubir from your estate?"

Mustafa and Kanhaiya's hearts skipped beats, but they tried to conceal their surprise.

"Yes, we do know Ragubir. He is a Driver at the estate," said Mustafa confidently. "What would you like to know about him?"

"Nothing really," answered Sundar. "He came here last week, and asked about a loan. But we could not do business as he felt that we are charging too much interest. I told him about you and Kanhaiya, and he seemed to know you both very well. Perhaps you may be able to encourage him to come back, and do business with us. We never like to turn customers away."

"That will be no problem Sundar," said Mustafa. "We will ask Ragubir, and let you know."

Shortly after leaving Sundar's office, Kanhaiya asked Mustafa, "*Bhaiya*, here you go again! If Ragubir goes back to Sundar, there is a great chance that he may take Ishani with him, and anything can happen."

"Hmm," muttered Mustafa. "Leave this to me. I will resolve this. Let me think of a plan."

Kanhaiya smiled nervously, and said, "You and your plans! I do hope you can come up with something really good!"

Mustafa wasted no time, and as soon as they arrived at the village, he rushed over to meet Ragubir at the managers' quarters. Kanhaiya accompanied him but had no idea as to what Mustafa had in mind. They were warmly welcomed by Ragubir and Ishani who laid out some light refreshment, and a snack of pieces of fried fish. Homemade biscuits were placed on the lounge table for Kanhaiya.

"Ragubir and Ishani," said Mustafa. "We met Sundar Das in Georgetown today, and he said that you wanted to borrow some money from him. You did not do any business with him because of the high interest he charges."

"Yes Mustafa," said Ragubir with Ishani looking at him in surprise. "He is the man we talked about a long time ago. The Recruiting Agent from India. I did not know that he was the moneylender, and as soon as I saw him, I knew that I should have nothing to do with him. He even offered me a better deal if I could help him trace Ishani. I felt very angry towards him. But I did not disclose anything about Ishani. So I refused to take the loan, and made no promises to him."

"And I am very happy about that!" said Ishani with a tinge of anger. "I said to Ragu, that we should go, and confront that vermin, and to tell him to get out of here. He should go back to India to carry on with his crookedness. But Ragu does not want to do this. What do you think?"

Mustafa said, "I fully understand how you both must feel at this time. I am quite happy to lend you some money without interest, and I am sure that Kanhaiya will support this." Kanhaiya nodded in agreement.

"Then," continued Mustafa. "We do not need to go back to Sundar for another loan. We will just keep him guessing, and looking for Ishani."

"Well, thank you both for your kind offer," said Ragubir. "But we must agree on some interest payment."

Mustafa shook his head, and said, "No Ragubir, we do not charge anyone interest in Islam."

Ragubir shook Mustafa's and Kanhaiya's hands firmly, and said, "Thank you Mustafa and Kanhaiya. I am sure that Ishani and I will repay you the loan very quickly, and in kind as well."

He frowned, and said, "Ishani and I will still go to see Sundar to tell him to stop looking for her, and to stay out of our lives."

Kanhaiya said, "Ragubir, I do think that you need to consider this move again. Sundar is a very desperate man, and he is quite capable of doing stupid things."

Ragubir asked, "Like what?"

"Well," said Mustafa. "He was well used to kidnapping people or tricking them into coming here."

"Mustafa, if he lays a finger on Ishani or Bharat, I will personally deal with him and his ugly henchman," threatened an irate Ragubir.

Kanhaiya said, "Maybe we should tell Massa about this problem, and if he cannot help, we should go to the Police."

"Kanhaiya," interrupted Mustafa. "I do not think that we should get Massa involved in this. Besides, what could he do?"

Ragubir thought for a moment, and then said, "I agree with Kanhaiya. Massa has always looked after our interests. He may be able to get a strong message to Sundar, with enough threat to put him off."

Ishani gritted her teeth, clenched her fists, and said, "I would love to put him back onto the next ship to India. He is rotten to the core, and I will never rest easily here as long as he is still in this country."

Mustafa finished off the fried fish snack, and he and Kanhaiya left Ragubir and Ishani to ponder over their problem.

Ragubir met the Massa as he had intended, and was promised some action. The Massa decided to write a letter to Sundar, and to advise him and Mohan not to visit the estate or to try to make contact with Ishani. Ragubir took the sealed letter to Sundar.

"Oh, namaskar my *bhaiya*!" said a smiling Sundar. "I see that Mustafa and Kanhaiya must have spoken to you, and I am happy that you have come to do business with me. So, how much money do you wish to borrow?"

"Not so fast Sundar," said Ragubir firmly. "Just read this letter I have brought from the Manager of our estate."

Sundar was somewhat taken aback, and cautiously opened the white envelope. He read the letter quietly, and then crunched it up in a fury.

He shouted, "How dare he threaten me like this?"

"I do not know what the Massa wrote, but let me personally advise you to stay away from me and my family," said Ragubir firmly, banging Sundar's desk with both his fists.

"And, as for this *bandar* you have here," continued Ragubir. "If he gets in the way, I have very many people who would willingly beat both of you. So, take my Massa's advice, and avoid any further contact with us! *Samjhe?*"

Ragubir stormed out of the office, brushing aside Mohan with his right hand so hard that he stumbled back onto Sundar, and they both fell back on the desk. Sundar and Mohan slowly stood up, and stared at the agitated Ragubir with utter shock. They then looked at each other, shrugged their shoulders, and stepped cautiously out onto the street looking in the direction of the disappearing Ragubir.

40.

Gold nuggets

The appearance of the short, half naked, bronze coloured, bare-footed tribal man in the village, caused much curiosity amongst the Indians and the Chinese. The man stood by the side of the main road, and was looking at Wong Yee's and Molly's residence. He became visibly nervous as a small crowd gathered around him. No one was prepared to get too close to the stranger, but they kept staring at him without trying to communicate with him.

Joshua stepped forward, and greeted the man by stretching out his right hand for a handshake. The man obliged but shook Joshua's hand limply.

Joshua asked, "Can you speak English?"

"Little," replied the man.

"What is your name? Who are you? Why have you come to this place?" asked Joshua as more people gathered around.

"Me Arawak," said the stranger quietly.

"You are an Arawak Indian," said Joshua, indicating to all around that he knew something about the native Amerindian people of British Guiana.

"Yes, me name Iwaana. Me Arawak," confirmed the stranger.

"So Iwaana, why have you come? How can I help you?" asked Joshua with some respect.

"I come look for Aafred. He pork-knocker. He my friend. He my brother," explained Iwaana as best he could.

Joshua asked, "You mean Alfred. The pork-knocker. How is he your brother?"

Iwaana replied, "Aafred marry my sister. He my brother."

Joshua said, "Oh I see! Alfred is your brother-in-law!"

"Yes, I come. Aafred say I come when he not come back home in bush. So, we not see him. I come look for him," said the proud, and brave Amerindian.

"Well my friend Iwaana, I have some bad news for you. But come with me to meet the people who know Alfred, and we will tell you what happened," said Joshua as he led the way for Iwaana to follow.

"Wong Yee and Molly!" called out Joshua. "Are you home? I have someone here to meet you!"

Wong Yee and Molly who was holding Andrew Yee in her arms, came to the front door of their house, and ushered Joshua and Iwaana inside. They sat together in the small lounge chairs, and Iwaana was offered some water to drink.

Joshua then introduced Iwaana to the family, explained who he was, and why he came to the village. Iwaana further explained that his sister had a son by Alfred, and she became married to him soon after the baby was born.

Molly said, "So, Iwaana, I have a step-mother who is Amerindian, and a half-brother who is half-African and half-Amerindian. How are they?"

Iwaana said, "Me sister name Kuku, and her son name Sam. They stay in bush. No like your village. You Aafred child?"

Molly smiled, and said, "Yes, me. I am Alfred's daughter, and Wong Yee is my husband. Andrew is our son."

Iwaana pointed to Andrew, and said, "Boy look like Arawak!"

Joshua could not resist commenting on the family relationships being clarified, and said, "Well, this is one very mixed up family! You are adding to the new people of British Guiana!"

Iwaana said, "No Mr Joshua. All my tribes are true people of Kaywana!"

"Kaywana?" asked Joshua.

"Yes, Kaywana! Land of many waters!" said Iwaana proudly.

Joshua was fascinated by Iwaana, and said placing his hands on the bare shoulders of the guest, "You are right. We are strangers here, and we must always respect you, and your people for allowing us to stay here. Please have something to eat, and feel free to rest here for as long as you wish."

Iwaana gratefully accepted the offer of food, and the invitation to stay at the house. Then Joshua persisted in asking for the real reason why he came to the village. "Iwaana, can you tell us why you came here? You see, Alfred is dead, and that is why you have not seen him for so long."

"Yes, I hear Aafred dead. People say he was killed," said Iwaana coldly.

Wong Yee suddenly felt very nervous, and began to wonder why Iwaana came to the village armed with his bow, arrows and hunting knife. He kept a clear distance from Iwaana, and looked at his every move, just in case he launched an attack.

Iwaana stared at Wong Yee, and said, "I hear you kill Aafred. But Aafred did bad thing. He kill Miss Betty. Aafred try kill you. You are good man. You look after Molly and son."

He then reached into his pouch which was attached to a string around his neck, and across his back. He took out a small leather purse, and handed it to Molly who accepted it with both hands. She untied the string, and opened the purse. There were several pieces of pure gold nuggets.

"Oh my God!" exclaimed Molly with tears welling up in her eyes, but with a broad smile.

Iwaana reached out and embraced Molly, saying, "I come here give you this gold. Aafred tell me give you this when he die. He love you very much. He very good man."

A very relieved Wong Yee stepped forward, and joined in the family embrace. Joshua looked on with admiration, and smiled as he wiped some tears from his eyes and cheeks.

He said, "Wong Yee, Molly, little Andrew, and my new friend Iwaana, Alfred was indeed a good man with a big heart. Please forgive him in your hearts, as I have now done. If only he had shown the true patience of a dedicated pork-knocker, and controlled his temper, he would now be celebrating his wonderful family."

Iwaana said, "Aafred spirit here. He see this. He now very happy. He happy with me. He protect us. He good spirit."

Wong Yee looked at Molly, and they both picked up Andrew. Although they were wearing the *buck bead* necklaces, they realised that from thence forward, everything would be fine. Their healing was well underway. Their belief was unshaken. Their wellbeing was protected.

Joshua waited for Iwaana to finish his meal with Wong Yee and his family. Then he asked him whether he wished to stay in the village before returning to the bush.

"No, Iwaana go back home," said the quiet Amerindian as he prepared to leave.

Joshua said, "We will give you work here, and a house to live in. You will get good money, and maybe you will bring your sister Kuku and Sam to live with us."

Wong Yee and Molly nodded in agreement with Joshua's suggestion. Wong Yee said, "Iwaana, we all respect you as one of us. You, Kuku and Sam can live at our house, and we will look after you."

Iwaana shook his head, and said, "You people happy here. This not for my people. I see how you people drink rum, and do bad things. Same at mining village. My people no like this."

Joshua said, "My friend, I agree with you wholeheartedly. Our people are spoiling your lives in your villages near the mining towns. But Iwaana, we are grateful to you, and will always welcome you, and your people here. We will always look after you when you come to visit."

Iwaana picked up his bow, arrows, knife and parcel with some food, and bade everyone goodbye. He moved quickly, and some children of the village walked alongside him as he headed back into the bush. The children stopped following him, and waved excitedly at him before turning, and making their way back to their own homes. The setting sun lit up the horizon with a magnificent display of red and golden light, which soon gave way to complete darkness.

41.

The first Strike

The population of Indians grew rapidly year after year, and they became the majority group on the plantations across British Guiana, despite indentured labour immigrations from China and Portugal. Leonora became the dominant sugar estate on the West Coast of Demerara with a more sophisticated sugar factory, a growing administration comprising many local Indians, increasing acreage of viable and productive sugarcane fields, hard working sugarcane labourers, and vibrant communities in the surrounding villages of Anna Catherina, Cornelia Ida and Hague in the east, and Stewartville in the west.

Leonora's newly acquired status as a sugar estate was principally due to the establishment of the sugar factory there. This effectively relegated Anna Catherina to being referred to as one of the villages surrounding the estate.

These village communities of Indians, Africans, Chinese, Portuguese, and the various mixed races, became more populated as longer serving indentured labourers moved out of the old *logies*, and took up the offer of housing lots along the single main road, and within some new allocated housing schemes behind the main road. Over the fifteen years to 1869, the well-established residents built bigger and better houses, grew vegetables and fruits in their sizeable yards, kept livestock and cattle, and some developed profitable retail general stores, rum shops, and extensive rice cultivation and production.

Each of the villages around Leonora had a Christian Church, a Primary School, and the estate continued to provide the local Community Hospital, Dispensary, and Post Office. Plans were being considered to introduce a railway service along the twenty miles of the West Coast of Demerara, from Vreed-en-Hoop to Parika.

Mustafa and Neesha, now in their middle age years, had worked very hard to build their grocery store into a bigger general store supplying goods to cater for the wider needs of the growing population.

Their two teenage sons, Ahmad and Rattan had completed their education at Primary School level, and taken on the greater responsibilities of helping to run the business.

Kanhaiya, Mumtaz and their daughter Meena, had settled in their house, and, with increasing success, the rice cultivation and production business grew rapidly. Kanhaiya had purchased twenty more acres of land for rice cultivation, and introduced bigger and better milling facilities at the factory which was built behind his yard. One of his main customers for rice was Mustafa's general store, and many other such establishments along the West Coast and West Bank of Demerara. The business employed labourers during the planting, harvesting, and milling periods through the year. The rice was transported on large four wheeled dray carts pulled by donkeys, and driven by their African and Indian owners.

Joshua was retired from the sugar factory, and continued to provide assistance to Matilda at her own Preparatory School which was established at the ground floor of their house. Everyone living in the villages showed the couple much love, and respect. Matilda was affectionately known as "Teacher Matilda", and Joshua was often referred to as "Sir", especially by their young pupils, and former students. Every child that passed through Teacher Matilda's Prep-school was given a good grounding in manners, etiquette and respect for others. They also learned basic reading, spelling, writing and arithmetic, which was referred to as "Sums". Teacher Matilda was also popular for her special homemade ice-cream called "ice blocks" which she gave to the pupils particularly when they behaved well. She refrained from hitting the children with canes, and often referred to such form of punishment as "slave beatings" which she did not tolerate.

Joshua was always willing to lend a hand to his old friends Mustafa, Kanhaiya and Ragubir, doing odd jobs or acting as their driver to take them on their business or pleasure trips with his well-preserved, and well-presented horse drawn coach.

The Massa, although well past normal retirement age, was still running the estate, but was much more reliant on his trusted group of Drivers, such as the loyal Ragubir whose son Bharat was also now a Driver. Ishani spent much of her time managing the household, and meeting friends for various leisure pursuits, and religious evenings of discourse on the Ramayan and Bhagwad Gita. With the help of Pandit

Kanhaiya, she set up a thriving Hindu *satsang* and charitable group, to serve Hindus and all other local people. Every main religious festival such as *Diwali, Holi* and *Krishna Janamasthmi*, was celebrated with great gusto, delightful music and dance, and, grand feasts. The popular three-day *yajnas* were attended by most of the villagers. Nandoo and his family became excellent exponents of Hindi songs and *bhajans*, and were the main attractions at all the great festivals, weddings, and multi-cultural events in the villages. He still worked as a Driver on the estate, but had moved out of the Madrasi quarters into a large family house which he constructed.

Wong Yee, Molly and Andrew Yee lived in an extended property that was once Miss Betty's establishment. The main business was a Rum Shop and Restaurant serving mostly Chinese dishes such as chowmein, fried rice, and fried "chicken in the rough". Wong Yee was always subject to some scrutiny, and suspicion by his customers who felt that the rum being sold from the bottles without seals, was watered down. Unfortunately, this did not prevent the local men from abusing alcohol, which contributed to untimely deaths for many souls.

By this time, more Chinese families had arrived in the villages, and each household had grown by several children. More Chinese girls of marriageable age were now available to single Chinese men, and this community began to be more settled. Many Chinese established grocery businesses and restaurants, and became keen rivals of the Indian and Portuguese businesses in the villages, and in the towns such as Georgetown.

Sundar Das and Mohan Lall had given up the quest to find Ishani, and after encountering more hostility from disgruntled borrowers, they decided to leave British Guiana, and return to India. More legitimate and controlled banking, and lending services were being introduced in Georgetown, as the proceeds from gold mining grew, and wholesale and retail businesses flourished in the colony. The excellent business acumen, and enterprise of the Portuguese, Indian and Chinese people in particular, was showing signs of a colony becoming economically viable in addition to its main trade on sugar.

However, in 1869, the living and working conditions on the estates were still not good enough, and there was a growing disquiet amongst the labourers in the Leonora estate. The practice of withholding wages as a penalty for the slightest misdemeanour or fall in a person's or gang's productivity, was still actively pursued by the over-enthusiastic Drivers and administrators, who were nearly always Indian or African.

Some of the new immigrants from India were fighting men who had been involved in the anti-British rebellion in Northern India, and were very easily agitated. They were brave, vocal and always willing to confront superiors, and the Police. The shovel gang in Leonora became the first to lead a Strike against the estate's owners, in July 1869, for the withholding of their wages.

Several other such incidents took place in the colony over the next three years, with the loss of five Indian men who were shot by police in 1872, at a plantation on the Essequibo Coast. The first Strike at Leonora was deeply regretted by the Massa, who finally retired from the estate in 1871. His tenure had been over a very long period in which he tried to serve his masters well, but also tried to improve the wellbeing of his workers, and those who were once slaves. As is often the case, the local people who were placed into positions of authority, tended to exceed the limit of their position, and were generally seen as harsher than the British Overseers or Drivers. They were either held in great respect, or loathed for their perceived over-strictness. The Indian labourers had experienced this kind of attitude in India, from the *Zamindars* placed in authority over them in the villages from whence they came. Now they had to endure a similar fate in the place they felt that would be better for them.

The Massa tried to negotiate with the leaders of the shovel gang on strike, but found stern resistance, and surprisingly shrewd responses. The workers had endured the various punishments delivered to them over many years, but in July 1869, their patience ran out as the deductions and pay withheld were very significant for each person. The other Indian and African workers were sympathetic to the forty men who were protesting against their unfair treatment. However, they continued to do their work in the fields and factory, and voiced their support for the strikers as they passed them on the way into work, and on their return from work.

The wives of the strikers joined them on their vigil outside the factory gate, and the managers' compound. They were much more vocal than the men, and shouted for what they wanted with great enthusiasm, and compelling sternness. The strikers and their supporters were not armed, and wanted to demonstrate their grievance peacefully.

The Police, who were armed with rifles and hand-guns, stood nearby, and watched the crowds in such a way as to ensure that they were prepared to respond to any disturbance or aggressive behaviour.

The Massa called upon some of the ex-Drivers such as Mustafa and Kanhaiya, and the retired Joshua, to speak to the leaders of the Strike, and their supporters. The three men stood quietly before the crowd, and tried to reason with them, but in their frustration many of the impatient workers began to throw insults at them.

The three men patiently absorbed all of the negative words said to them, and finally began to be listened to. They promised the strikers stronger representation of their grievances about the punishments imposed by the Drivers, and on the habit of withholding their pay. They also sought further basic improvements to their living areas, better access to the new Community Hospital and the medicines, and the removal of those Drivers who were accused of bullying behaviour towards the workers.

The Massa listened to the representation by Mustafa, Kanhaiya and Joshua, and after concessions were mutually agreed, the Strike was called off. Ragubir, who was not implicated in the complaints about bullying, retired from his position, and Bharat took his place. The family continued to use the house in the manager's compound.

Bharat, who was only in his early twenty's, was seen as a new rising star in the estate. Ragubir and Ishani were very proud of him as he built up a reputation for being very strict, but fair in all his dealings with the workers. He quite uncannily like his biological father Sundar Das often took up a striking pose with his left wrist on his hip, and with a large umbrella doubling as a walking stick which he held in his right hand. He also wore a newly formed black moustache, again in the style of Sundar. Some of the older workers would show their respect for him, but would mutter curses that Bharat did not understand. He would naively smile at the men, thinking that they were actually praising him.

The new generation of young people such as Bharat, Meena, Andrew, Ahmed and Rattan, were beginning to take on considerable responsibilities as their families established themselves as residents of their new country. Thoughts of returning to India were becoming less frequent, except for the occasions when workers and their families had good reason to protest, and vent their feelings against injustice, and at those who represented the perpetrators of such wrongs.

42.

Rumination about rum

Following the sugar Strike at the Leonora estate in 1869, and the retirement of the Massa in 1871, Mustafa, Ragubir, Kanhaiya, Nandoo, Wong Yee and Joshua, agreed to meet at Mustafa's house in Anna Catherina. Mustafa was worried that people in the community were tense, and that some feelings of mistrust were becoming evident once again. The Africans were seeking to blame the Indian workers for causing the unrest on the estate. The Indians, who were on Strike, were not happy with the lack of support shown towards them, by the Africans and the Chinese. The Chinese did not seem to care about the strikers and their cause, preferring to go about their lives quietly.

In addition to this, Mustafa felt that there was a growing problem of bad behaviour amongst the younger generation who were taking to abusing alcohol. He was particularly concerned about the rise in the number of rum shops in each of the villages in the district. The discourse began with this issue.

Wong Yee, whose English was much improved, commented on the rum shop businesses, by saying, "I agree that we now have too many rum shops, but we also have too many drinkers! I see fathers encouraging their young sons to drink rum in their company, and boasting about how their boys can hold their liquor! We need to talk to these fathers first."

Ragubir said, "I agree with Wong Yee. My son Bharat has told me about young workers he has had to turn away from their gangs simply because they had not fully recovered from their drinking sessions. Besides, it is a matter of their own safety, and the safety of the people they work with, that they should not be allowed to work when they are not fit to do so."

Joshua said, "As you all know, we talk a lot about this at the Church every Sunday. But, boys will be boys, and unless they can find something else to do with their free time, they will continue to drink rum heavily. Maybe the rum shops should make it more difficult by putting up their prices. We did this during Miss Betty's time, for a while after she died. Wong Yee and Molly had successfully done what Miss Betty had promised."

Mustafa nodded in agreement, and said, "But we did find that raising the prices only helped for a short time. We do not want to see the drinkers go away and, distil their own, more powerful bush rum. We also tried to reduce the hours of drinking, and that worked for a while. The drinkers only began to drink more quickly, and in greater quantities! But Wong Yee is right. We need to educate everyone about the dangers of alcohol. It is also a great sin, and I am also disappointed to see how many of my Muslim brothers drink so much rum."

Kanhaiya intervened with, "And, our Hindu brothers should not only avoid drinking alcohol, but also the use of meat! I have preached about these things at every *pooja* and *yajna*, but whilst those who are present seem to understand, the others sitting at the rum shops do not hear the *kathas*."

Wong Yee then asked, "So, my friends, what must we do? I will speak to my fellow countrymen who own the rum shops, and agree to reduce the opening hours. We will also look to discourage very young boys from drinking rum on our premises. But we will not put up the prices."

Mustafa said, "Wong Yee that is a very good start. We also need to talk to the fathers who should not be encouraging their young sons to drink rum. The mothers should also be told about what their boys are doing, and they can influence them. I also think that this matter should be discussed at the school, and we should all work even harder in our congregations, to spread a message about the harm that rum drinking is doing. Perhaps we should take our message out and about in open public gatherings as we did in our villages in India."

Nandoo broke his silence, and said, "We are not in India where we only have to deal with two religious groups. Here we have different races and religions, and we have to tackle the problem in more ways. I have been very strict with my gang members, and I never allowed someone who was drinking a lot to work in the fields, wielding their cutlass and grass knives. I think that we Hindus, and the Muslims, should try to build our own Mandir and Mosque so that our people could go to these places where the message about rum drinking, and other matters can be delivered. I know that Joshua will say that the Church sermons fall on deaf ears, but people do listen, and act on what they hear."

Joshua said, "I agree with Nandoo. The more religious centres we have, the better the chances of spreading Godliness to all concerned. I think that the Hindus and the Muslims should help each other to build your Mandir and Mosque. And, if you allow us, my Christian brothers and sisters could also help. After all, some of the best carpenters are from my community! This will also help us all to continue to live well with each other, and to understand each other better!"

Mustafa smiled contentedly, and said, "Thank you Joshua. That is a great idea! I am sure that Ragubir, Kanhaiya and Nandoo and other people can work on the building of our first Mandir and Mosque. I am very willing to help to fund both. Joshua and Wong Yee, I am also happy to pay for some repairs to the Christian Church. I hope that we can all start on these projects as soon as possible. The more that our communities see that we are all working together for everyone's benefit, then this will go a long way to ease any tensions we may have seen."

Kanhaiya, Ragubir, Nandoo and the others, shook their heads in agreement. Joshua smiled and added, "Having your own places of worship will also help to keep the "Coolie Missionary" away from this estate and district!"

"Coolie Missionary?" asked a surprised Mustafa. The others also looked at Joshua with curious frowns on their faces. They had not heard of the term.

Joshua said, "The Church of England has someone specially assigned to oversee the conversions of Indians to Christianity, in British Guiana. He is based in Georgetown, and travels around the country to win over people to Christianity. He is called the "Coolie Missionary"."

He continued as the others listened in shock, "The good news is that he has not yet managed to come to our estate, otherwise you would have heard of him. I know that if and when he comes here he will have a very hard time to convert anyone. I am a converted Christian, and I still wish that it never happened. I believe that you should stay with your own religions, and live in harmony with everyone."

"Well," sighed Mustafa, "If the Church of England is so keen on conversions, as they have been trying to do back in India, then we must work even harder, and faster to build our Mandir and Mosque, from this moment onwards! I do hate these terms they use. In India, they were keen to convert us "Heathens", now in British Guiana, we are "Coolies"!"

Ragubir suggested, "Mustafa, we should meet the new Massa of the estate to put forward our ideas, and to secure some land from him, and any other help he may be able to give. It will also be a good thing for the new estate owners, Sandbach Parker and Company, to show that they really do care about the needs of the community."

Nandoo said, "Ragubir that is a great idea! I suggest that we should all go together as a responsible group, to propose these ideas to the new Massa. In this way he will see that we are all willing to be united, and to work together for the good of everyone in the community."

"You are right," agreed Mustafa. "And as Ragubir has said, this will help the new owners and the new Massa, to achieve their goals. They will always need a very stable, and reliable workforce on the estate, and, living nearby. This will be good for all parties!"

"Except for the "Coolie Missionary"!" laughed Wong Yee.

"Yes," said Mustafa. "Except the "Coolie Missionary". I wonder if they also have a "Chinee Missionary" as well!"

Joshua also laughed, and said, "I would not be surprised my friends. Our British masters are known for their administration and organisation from the Governor right down to the smallest clerk. They have some white man for every aspect of our lives. They even have someone in charge of Lepers in the Leper Asylum!"

"Yes!" added Ragubir. "They have someone in charge of a Lunatic Asylum in Berbice!"

"Well my friends," said Mustafa. "All the more reason for us to do the right things to stop our people from suffering badly due to the heavy rum drinking. We also need to stop the wife beatings, the wife murders, and the depression that lead people to that Mad House!"

The group, led by Mustafa, managed to secure a meeting with the new Massa at his office at the estate. They took turns to explain the problems on the estate, and the surrounding villages, and the new Massa listened with heightened interest. The outgoing Massa had told him about the workings and problems on the estate, and the people who lived and worked there.

The new Massa told Mustafa and the group, that he was intending to meet some of the prominent residents, and he was very pleased that the delegation had taken the initiative. He promised to consider the request for suitable plots of land for a Mandir and a Mosque, and was pleased that these would be built from money provided by members of the community.

True to his promise, and within a few months, the new Massa allocated plots of land for the Mandir and the Mosque, and whilst Kanhaiya oversaw the Mandir project, Mustafa led on the building of the Mosque. Mustafa also paid for the renovations at the Christian Church, and the Priest praised his generosity in front of the whole congregation who were truly overjoyed to have received the help.

These gestures and actions went a very long way towards rebuilding confidence, and mutual respect amongst the residents, and the workers of the estate. The new Mandir, Mosque, and refurbished Church, were shining examples of solidarity for all to see, and they were quickly recognised as symbols of a God-fearing people who were followers of the different faiths. There was now a sense of realisation for Mustafa, Kanhaiya and all the people of the estate that this was their home, and country.

PART 5

THE NEXT GENERATION

43.

Matchmaking

The big surprise event for everyone associated with the Leonora estate, and living in the surrounding villages, was the betrothal of Bharat to Meena in July 1872. Both sets of parents were pleasantly surprised as there were no signs of a courtship between Bharat and Meena. Ragubir and Ishani were very quick to accept Bharat's suggestion for them to approach Meena's parents, Kanhaiya and Mumtaz for the hand of their beautiful daughter, Meena.

Bharat was continuing to enjoy his work as a Driver, and was building a good reputation amongst the workers. He was seen as an eligible young bachelor, and Ragubir and Ishani were approached by several parents of young girls, keen to win over the young man. There were promises of substantial land, cattle, money, and, anything that Ragubir and Ishani wanted, for the hand of their most handsome son.

Meena had matured into a most delightful young lady, who caught the eyes of everyone wherever she happened to be. The young men of the estate and the villages were infatuated with the way she looked, walked, and spoke. Kanhaiya and Mumtaz were extremely proud of her, and naturally very protective towards her. They never allowed her to go anywhere unaccompanied. Whenever Bharat saw her, they would only exchange warm smiles with each other.

The Indian community retained their custom of arranged marriages which would normally be set for children as young as ten years old. Bharat and Meena, in their early twenties, would therefore be regarded as well overdue for marriage. So, a quick arrangement was completed, and a grand Hindu marriage ceremony and celebration was planned.

The wedding ceremony was set to take place at the new Mandir, and the feasting and entertainment was organised for the Ragubir house, and extensive yard. A grand tent was erected at the back of the yard, as was done for Ragubir's and Ishani's own wedding, but with accommodation for very many more guests, and casual attendees.

On the day of the wedding, Bharat wore a finely decorated costume including a traditional yellow turban. He and his parents who were also resplendent in their costumes and gold jewellery, stood proudly beneath the wedding *mandap* which was specially constructed in the Mandir. The invitees sat on the neatly polished floor which was covered with white cotton sheets. Rose petals were strewn all along the clear walkway from the main entrance to the *mandap*.

Meena, was resplendent in a beautiful ornate red sari, and wore a veil made of strings of fresh flowers that partially concealed her face. She stood between her proud mother, who also looked like a queen, and her father who wore an elegant white *dhoti*, and turban.

They slowly walked towards the *mandap* as the congregation rose, and cheered. Nandoo and his family chanted appropriate Hindu *shlokas*, and when the bridal party reached the entrance to the *mandap*, they embraced each other. Kanhaiya, somewhat unusually, took on the role of the officiating Pandit, and he invited Mustafa to act as Meena's father. Mustafa duly obliged, and took his place with great pride.

The wedding ceremony lasted for about two hours, and when all the rituals were completed, the bride and groom exchanged their places to demonstrate that they were now man and wife. The entire congregation, which also included the new Massa and his wife, moved forward in an orderly and dignified manner, to shower flowers, rice, and money on the couple.

The wedding party and guests then walked the short distance from the Mandir, along the main road, to Ragubir's house, led at the front by two drummers playing a beautiful rhythm on the *tassa* and *dhol*. Many of the Indian women in the procession could not resist the tantalizing beats, and started to dance as they moved forward. Some of the African ladies just joined in with their own interpretation of the music, and danced with their usual gusto. People who had not attended the wedding ceremony lined the roadside, and applauded with great pleasure and enthusiasm as the wedding party passed by. It was the biggest parade ever seen on the estate or in the villages.

Some of the male guests took the opportunity to visit Wong Yee's rum shop on the way, and after downing several small measures of rum, took the remainder of the rum in the bottles with them to the reception tent in Ragubir's yard. A grand feast of various vegetable curries, rice, *daal* and *laddoos* was enjoyed by all. Then the music from the drummers accompanying Nandoo and other singers took hold, and everyone danced through the night into the early morning.

Fortunately for most of the revellers, the next day was Sunday, and they had enough time to recover from the celebrations before returning to work on Monday morning. Many of the Africans wisely decided not to attend the Sunday morning worship at the Church, as they would have had to listen to another strong sermon on the ills of drinking rum.

Ragubir and Ishani had invited Kanhaiya, Mumtaz, Mustafa, Neesha, Joshua, Matilda, Wong Yee and Molly, to lunch at their home on Sunday after all the rubbish had been cleared from the house, and yard. They discussed the wedding, and inevitably the question arose as to which of the other young persons should be tying the knot.

Wong Yee said, "Our young man Andrew is still in his teens, and needs a few more years of experience of managing our business before he can take a wife."

Joshua said, "Come on Wong Yee, we need another great celebration even bigger than yesterday's!"

Molly smiled shyly, and said, "At least we now have a lot of choices for Andrew. There are quite a number of pretty Chinese girls in the villages!"

Joshua said, "Oh yes! That Mr and Mrs Ching have fourteen children, and I think that ten of them are girls. I do not know how they manage with so many mouths to feed. Mr and Mrs Ching will be only too happy to marry them off, sooner rather than later."

Mustafa said, "Why are you assuming that young Andrew will only be looking at Chinese girls? He may be interested in others, and there are many more to choose from."

Wong Yee nodded, and said, "I see what you mean Mustafa, but I personally would like him to marry a good Chinese girl. Molly does not always agree with me. So, we just have to wait and see what Andrew does in the future."

Kanhaiya observed, "This is going to be a problem in the future for all of us. We now have so many mixed-race people belonging to the three main religions in our community; it will be very difficult for us to choose."

Mustafa said, "Well, perhaps we have to cast the net a bit further, and go to other villages, even as far away as the counties of Berbice and Essequibo!"

Matilda said, "You may be right Mustafa. I assume that you and Neesha will be looking far away for your very eligible boys, Ahmed and Rattan."

Neesha nodded in agreement, and said, "Yes, in our situation, we would like to find girls who are very interested in running a business like ours. There are not many to choose from in our area."

Wong Yee was a bit taken aback, and asked, "Does that mean that the daughters of business people here will not be the right sort for your boys?"

Mustafa intervened, "No, Wong Yee. What Neesha is referring to is the fact that we prefer to keep our business rivals as friends, and not to have to relate to them as new members of our family, through marriage. This can become complicated for us as far as doing business is concerned."

Joshua said, "But Mustafa, I thought that you business people like to keep everything amongst yourselves, by marriage and so on."

Kanhaiya observed, "Well, this happens a lot in India, and to some extent here in British Guiana. But Mustafa and Neesha would like to see their business grow how they wish, and an in-law or in-laws could complicate matters, and cause problems for the business and the marriages."

Mustafa added, "In fact, Neesha and I have already been asked by prospective in-laws for our boys. They are from far and wide, and the families have been promising so many things for the boys."

Joshua said curiously, "Like what Mustafa? Lots of land, money, houses? Are they trying to buy sons-in-laws as if they are merchandise?"

Matilda said, "Joshua, you told me that in Africa, the matchmaking was done by the village elders, and there was a lot of very serious negotiations and bargaining involving property, livestock and money. People were more consumed in the bartering, and at times they seemed to forget that they were supposed to be arranging for two young and inexperienced people to share their future lives together."

Neesha answered, "Yes, it is not so different here in British Guiana. The bidders do not seem to care about us. All they want is to offer these crazy gifts for the boys. We do not believe in dowry, and we are not interested in their money and land. All we want is a good, intelligent and well-mannered girl for each of the boys."

Ragubir said, "Aha! So you do not mind if the girl comes from a poor family. You will consider her."

Mustafa said, "Yes. Look at us. We all married the person we loved, and money was never a part of our decisions."

Joshua smiled and winked at Matilda saying, "I agree. My Matilda is still worth all the gold in the world to me. Besides we were both poor, and the greatest wealth we had then and still have now, is our deep love, and respect for each other."

Neesha agreed and said, "Yes Joshua, we women also need to be in charge to make sure that you men do not go astray, and spread those deep feelings with other women!"

Just then, the newlywed bride and groom emerged from their room, hand in hand, and greeted the luncheon guests with hugs.

Mustafa said, "Let us all wish you both everything that is good for your future lives together! And, may Allah bless you with many children!"

Joshua intervened with, "And lots of everlasting love, and care for each other! God bless you both! God bless your parents! And may God bless us all!"

Matilda led the joyful chorus of "Amen!"

44.

Secret love

Village life in the colony was becoming increasingly more tranquil, and peaceful. The communities of mixed races, religions and cultures, were unintentionally creating their own new sub-culture with the emergence of a more colourful creole language mixed with pigeon English, African words, Hindi and Urdu words, and Mandarin Chinese words. Certain foods were being shared with the Indian curry masala used in African and Chinese dishes, alongside subtle changes. African soups and Chinese noodles became popular amongst the residents either through the local restaurants, or by experimentation at home.

Everyone would join in with the African masquerades which were very popular processions at Easter time, and the Christmas to New Year period. Likewise, the Hindu festivals such as *Pagwa* or *Holi* were enjoyed by all the villagers irrespective of their faiths. They took every opportunity to splash water, mud or powder upon each other. The Muslims celebrated the ending of the *Ramadan* month of fasting with the festival of *Eid-ul-Fitr*, sharing food with the poorest in the community.

The different music of the Africans and the Indians did not quite merge in the same way, but there was a mutual understanding, and appreciation of the rhythms. Indeed, as was seen at the wedding procession for Bharat and Meena, the Africans showed great versatility, and improvisations when they danced to the rhythms of the *tassa* and *dhol* drums.

The people mixed freely, and shared in each other's games and pastimes. The young children and youths were fond of the localised version of *Kabadi*, the Indian sport, which was given the name "*Ketcha*" taken from the English "to catch you". They also invented their own version of "Hide and Seek" with some players going to extraordinary lengths to hide so successfully, that they could not be found for hours.

It was during a "Hide and Seek" game that Ahmed, when aged eighteen, had managed to hide from all the other players in a well-disguised hole he had carefully carved in the undergrowth within his backyard. All the players thoroughly searched in their own yards and houses, calling out for him, but in vain. They re-assembled at the starting point feeling very frustrated, and disappointed. He then suddenly appeared before them to claim his victory. They would all go home before night set in, having exhausted most of the time on the only game that they could play that day.

On another occasion, his secret hiding place was discovered by the eighteen year old daughter of Mr and Mrs Ching. She was beautiful, petite, fair and with long straight black hair tied in a pigtail at the back. She was always smiling, and very pleasant. When she spotted Ahmed heading for his favourite hiding place, she expertly encouraged the other players to search elsewhere by giving them clues that she craftily created. Her name was Pansy, after the delicate flower.

Ahmed was totally surprised that anyone could find his hiding place, and Pansy had other ideas than to win the game by shouting out his name aloud. She approached the well camouflaged, neatly arranged bunker with her index finger over her lips to signify silence. Ahmed signalled to her to enter his den. She looked around once more to make sure that no one was looking in their direction, and then crawled in to sit quietly beside him.

She whispered in his ears, "Let us just sit here and talk."

Ahmed said, "Are you not going to claim this victory?"

"Oh no!" she said, "I have a bigger victory in mind. I have always looked at you, and I have come to like you very much."

Ahmed was taken aback by Pansy's boldness, and he began to feel a little uncomfortable, but excited, as he was able to look at her much more closely than he had ever done before.

"I like you very much as well," whispered Ahmed, as he held her soft and tender hands in his. She did not flinch, and shifted closer to him.

He continued, "I have always noticed when you came into our store with your family, you would ask me to show you goods."

Pansy said, "Yes, I love the way you look at me, and yet you are so shy, you would try to avoid serving me on my own."

They stopped whispering or moving as two players walked very closely to their hiding place without locating them. When the players moved on, Ahmed looked at Pansy, and said quietly, "Shall I give up now, and give you your victory in this game?"

Pansy placed her arms around Ahmed's shoulders, and whispered in his left ear, "No, let us be here together, forever."

Ahmed's heart was thumping, and perspiration began to drip down his face. He hugged Pansy tightly, and was too nervous to say anything. Pansy's fair face was reddened with utter excitement, and her heart was also throbbing wildly. They had never before experienced such an emotion, and locked each other in their warm embrace without moving.

After about an hour had passed, they ended their first secret meeting, and Pansy walked away stealthily, taking great care not to be noticed by the other players. She returned to the starting point, and several minutes later, Ahmed emerged to declare himself as the winner of the game once again. Pansy glanced at him shyly, and winked at him knowingly.

The secret hiding place became the regular meeting point for himself and Pansy especially when they were not playing Hide and Seek. It was here that they developed their love affair intimately. No one from the village or their families knew about the young couple's love for each other.

They took every care to avoid any contact in public view, and Ahmed was even more careful to avoid serving Pansy when she visited the store. One evening, after the store was closed, Mustafa, Neesha, Ahmed and Rattan discussed the day's business, and as usual Neesha shared some of the gossip she heard from the women customers.

"That Mrs Ching," she began. "I think that she is such an elegant lady. She would come into the store with some of her beautiful daughters, and not make any fuss about the clothes she wanted to buy. She seems to love sewing dresses and skirts for the girls. And they always appear to be so pretty and presentable when they come here. Do they not boys?"

Rattan shook his head in agreement, and Ahmed coughed slightly. Neesha continued her discussion without waiting for further reactions from the boys.

Neesha said, "I really like the one called Pansy. She is such a beautiful girl. She must be about your age Ahmed."

"Ahm,,,I do not know Maa," answered Ahmed a little nervously, wondering whether his mother had an inkling about his affair with

Pansy, or had heard any gossip about it, or was just probing with a mother's instinct.

Rattan looked across at his brother, and offered, "I think that she is Ahmed's age. Maa, why are you asking about this?"

"No reason *beta*," said Neesha smiling. "It is just something that mothers look out for. I see all the young ladies from the district when they come into the store, or at the functions. When I speak to them I gather some indication as to their personality, manners, and general disposition. Besides, you boys are now at an age when we have to start looking for good matches."

Mustafa, who was always the one that spoke the least in such family gatherings, said, "Well, I have been approached by someone who said that he was acting for a good family in Mahaica on the East Coast of Demerara. They have a beautiful daughter, and they are looking for a suitable boy."

Ahmed said worriedly, "Oh no Paa, not another one of those people making silly promises, and offering the world for their daughter!"

Mustafa said, "Actually, the family have not made such an offer, and are only keen to have their daughter married to a most suitable boy. They are also Muslim, and the girl is beautiful and very smart."

Rattan could not resist having fun at the expense of Ahmed. He said, "Aha, so they are looking for someone as intelligent as our Ahmed! I am so glad that he is the more intelligent one in our family! Ahmed *bhaiya*, this is sounding like a very good prospect for you!"

Ahmed became irritated by the jibe, and said, "Maa and Paa, please tell Rattan to shut up! I am not yet ready to marry anyone!"

Mustafa however, ignored Ahmed's plea, and said, "Well, there will be no harm if I went there to see the family. Do not worry either of you. I am always very careful about these matters."

Neesha said, "I do hope that I will be going along with you, to make sure that you do not make any mistakes. Why not arrange the trip for a Sunday when we are closed?"

Despite the reassurances given by their parents, the boys looked very worried as they excused themselves to go to their separate rooms.

Ahmed spent that evening half-asleep just thinking about the trip that his parents were about to embark on. What if the girl and her family prove to be the best match? How will he be able to refuse to accept any arrangement for his marriage? Should he disclose his own secret love? If so, will his parents ever accept a Chinese girl for him? How will Pansy react to this? How could he abandon the first, and only love in his life? The more he pondered these questions, the more he became confused, and distressed. At times, he shed tears as he sat up on his bed, unable to sleep.

45.

Reflections on the way to Mahaica

The Sunday morning intended for the trip to Mahaica, was very warm and bright as usual. Neesha was particularly excited about the prospect of meeting her prospective daughter-in-law. She had always wished to have at least one daughter to raise along with her two loving sons. She made the breakfast for the family as the *aaya* was on her day off. In addition, she prepared some extra chicken curry and rice for the boys' lunch.

Mustafa had hired his old friend Joshua's cart for the first leg of the long journey, from the village to Vreed-en-Hoop. Joshua would leave his cart at the harbour, and then join Mustafa and Neesha on the boat crossing of the Demerara River to Georgetown. The agent would then meet the group at Georgetown harbour, and then they would take the railway to Mahaica.

Joshua as usual, was prompt on time to collect his two passengers, and he was also very smartly dressed in a new grey suit, a black hat, and well-polished black leather shoes. Mustafa said jokingly, "Good morning Joshua, you look very smart, but we are on a wedding mission, not a funeral!"

Joshua said, "Oh Mustafa that is uncalled for! I have looked forward to a day like this for a very long time. Which one of these two fine young men are we going to fix up?"

Neesha was wary of the tension brought onto the boys, and tried to diffuse the situation by saying, "Joshua, nobody is going to be "fixed up" today. We are just going to meet the people in Mahaica, and then consider what to do."

Mustafa and Neesha hugged their sons before they took up their seats on the horse-drawn cart. Joshua had designed a special covering made of canvas, to add some protection to his passengers from the hot sun. The two sets of wooden seats built into the sides of the cart were covered with leather to help cushion the bumpy ride. The vehicle was pulled by a young black stallion which was well-groomed, and raring to go.

With one simple command of Joshua's, the horse arched up its head proudly, and moved forward in a graceful trot. Mustafa and Neesha waved to Ahmed and Rattan, and soon they were out of sight as the cart headed out of the village. Very good progress was made over the nine miles of the dirt road, and they reached Vreed-en-Hoop in sufficient time to negotiate their boat trip across the calm looking Demerara River.

When they reached the Georgetown harbour and looked for the agent, he was nowhere to be seen. This immediately cast some doubt in Mustafa's mind. He sought out people who were waiting at the harbour, and asked if anyone was from Mahaica. Joshua was very concerned, and asked whether Mustafa knew the name of the agent or the people they were visiting in Mahaica.

A worried looking Mustafa said, "No Joshua, the man told me his name but in my haste, I failed to write it down. The family we are due to meet is a Mr and Mrs Khudabaksh."

Neesha said, "Well, we can still travel to Mahaica, and ask the people when we get there. We do not need an agent to take us there. So I suggest that we take a chance and go. We can at least enjoy the day out. Let us take the next train."

Joshua agreed with Neesha, and said, "Look, the next train to Mahaica is standing at the station. Let us take it as there is not another one going there today."

As the train began to pull slowly out of the Lamaha Street Terminus in Georgetown, the steam from the powerful engine rose high. Thick black smoke belched out of the funnel at the front of the engine as the large iron wheels screeched loudly, and the train slowly eased forwards. The carriages were full to the brim with passengers sitting very close to each other, thus allowing for some excess to the train's official capacity for the journey.

The three new passengers thoroughly enjoyed the entire train journey over the twenty-six miles to the Mahaica Village station. This extended portion of the East Coast Railway was completed, and opened only a few years prior, in 1864. The railway line ran parallel to, but further inland away from the main road. Much of the scenery along the coast was of either lush sugarcane fields, or rice fields.

The people living near to the railway line were always keen to pause from whatever they were doing, and wave at the passengers who also returned their greetings in like manner. Occasionally, the great and powerful steam engine would be slowed down when the driver spotted a grazing cow or donkey ambling across the line ahead. He would pull vigorously at the engine's loud whistle in an effort to scare the beasts away.

Some people would also be seen walking along the railway line ahead of the train, and striding briskly across the sleepers, until the engine's whistle would cause them to step safely aside. Another disturbing practice was younger passengers moving to the exits of the carriages, and jumping onto the platform as the train slowed down towards its stopping point. Sometimes they would jump off the train at a point which was not a recognised official stop.

Joshua noticed that Mustafa and Neesha were very quiet all along the journey, and felt that he should break the silence. He said, "Look how green and fertile our country is! This must make you feel good!"

Mustafa looked up at Joshua, and spoke above the noise of the train, "Yes, it is beautiful. It reminds me of India. Just like in the Punjab, Uttar Pradesh, Bihar and Bengal. I was thinking of my long journey along the Grand Trunk Road all the way to Calcutta. I wish that we had a train like this back in 1845."

Joshua said, "Well, in Africa there was nothing like this. Only jungles and small villages within them. Maybe they now have such things like trains."

Neesha asked, "Joshua, do you wish that you were back in Africa?"

"No my sister," said Joshua with a tinge of sadness. "I cannot dream anymore. That has been beaten out of me. I know that the reality is that I will die here, and will be buried in this land. It will never feel like Africa to me. But I have had to learn to love this place. Besides, I have my Matilda to live for. I would not have found such a person in Africa. Just as Mustafa has been fortunate to find you here."

Mustafa smiled at Neesha as he acknowledged Joshua's statement. "Yes Joshua, I am truly blessed to have found such a beautiful person here in British Guiana. She has given me so much to be proud of, and thankful for. She has always been by my side. Although, sometimes she can be a thorn in my side!"

Neesha laughed, and playfully poked Mustafa in his ribs, which made him giggle.

"All right!" said Joshua. "No need to show me how much you two lovebirds care for each other!"

Mustafa said, "Joshua, this lady is very special. She is a great wife and mother. And, she is the best businesswoman I have known!"

Neesha blushed with all the praise being showered upon her so openly. She urged Mustafa and Joshua to stop talking about her in this way. So she quickly changed the conversation by asking about the people they were visiting.

She said, "I wonder what Mr and Mrs Khudabaksh are like. We do not know anything about them. Where did they come from in India? What business are they doing? And of course, what their daughter is like?"

Mustafa said, "That is what we will try to discover. The agent did not say much apart from his suggestion that they were a very good family, and are well respected in their district."

Joshua said, "I like the mystery. We were all brought up in mystery. None of us knew what this country was like when we were on our dreadful journeys. I could not believe how flat the land was, and how everything was cut, and shaped so neatly. But the heat was a great shock to me!"

"Yes Joshua," said Mustafa. "I could not imagine what this place would be like. But as I said, it was not so bad as these fields were like those back in India. The sun and the heat felt different to that which we knew. But you are right. Our lives have been full of mystery after mystery."

"Look Mustafa!" exclaimed Neesha excitedly. "There are so many coconut trees in this area!"

Mustafa said, "Yes, this means we must be getting closer to Mahaica. I heard that they plant a lot of coconut trees there, and do good business with them."

"Out of coconut trees?" asked Joshua.

"Yes, the coconut tree produces the coconut water we like to drink. They use the dried nuts for making coconut oil which we rub on our skins. And the leaves of the palm are used to make baskets and brooms," said Mustafa as he peered out at the hundreds of trees along the way.

"That is really good business," acknowledged Joshua. "This is something we should try out in our village. The plantains we grow are not as profitable as coconuts. And we have to wait so long every season to reap a few bunches of plantain. On the other hand, these coconut trees always seem to have lots of coconuts!"

"I agree Joshua," said Mustafa. "The other problem we have is that too many people in our district are trying to produce plantains and vegetables for a very small Sunday market. This does not make for good business sense, and that is why too many of our families are not making enough money to have a better life. But, mind you, I do love my plantain in hot soup, or fried ripe plantain, or even boiled plantain along with boiled potatoes, boiled cassava, boiled eggs, and some fried salted fish!"

"Hm, Mustafa that is a typical African meal! Very wholesome and filling!" said Joshua proudly. "But you are making me feel very hungry. I do hope that we get something very nice to eat at our host's house in Mahaica."

Neesha said, "Yes, we will most likely get some curry, rice, *daal*, and coconut choka!"

Joshua licked his lips and said, "Ah! This is what I really love about our British Guiana. We have created so much variety in our food. We can never starve in a country like this. Mind you, I can never understand why we saw so many people begging in Georgetown!"

Neesha said, "Joshua, we also have some beggars in our district. Some people are just too lazy, and cannot seem to be able to help themselves. When you add the rum drinking to the laziness, then you get to see the worst in human beings. This reminds me that we are due to invite some of our poorest to attend our Annual Qur'an Shareef as part of our *zakaat* giving for this year."

Joshua said, "Neesha, just leave that to me. I know most of these people in the village, and I will ask one of the beggars to go around and invite the others. Just tell me the date and the time that you want them to attend."

Joshua always loved the notion that he was put in charge of any task or action. He took great pride in his appearance, and walked with much purpose in his stride. He also loved to volunteer for work offered by Mustafa and his friends in Anna Catherina, and elsewhere.

Mustafa said, "Thank you Joshua. This is a very important thing for us as Muslims to do each year. We are also keen to help all kinds of poor people, and not just our Muslim brothers and sisters."

Joshua nodded in approval, and said, "I know that you also give generously to the Church, the Hindu Temple, and the Mosque. This is one reason why the people from near and far love you so much. I can see that any future wedding that you plan will have to be very big as all these people will expect to be there!"

"Well Joshua," said Neesha. "So be it. We are in business to serve our community, and not just to get rich. We are always thankful to Allah, and the people who come to buy from the store. Without them, we would not have food on our table, and shelter over our heads."

Mustafa said, "As for the wedding, we are prepared for a very big event. Perhaps if we see two suitable girls today, we may do two weddings on the same day!"

The train finally began to slow down as it approached the station at Mahaica. Its large iron wheels screeched noisily, causing the carriages to press against their connectors amidst a flurry of white steam, black soot, and the ear-piercing noise of the engine's whistle. The signaller on the platform waved his red flag frantically to indicate that he was giving his permission for the driver to stop the train at that specific spot. But the soot and steam engulfed him as the train still eased past him to its final stop further up the platform.

The station suddenly became very busy with people dashing to and fro, offloading their baggage, helping the women and children to climb down the two steps of the carriages onto the platform, and calling out to porters and cart drivers to help with any luggage, and other goods. There were many traders on the platform offering their goods aggressively to the passengers still sitting at the windows of the carriages. They worked very quickly exchanging their goods for their hard earned money. The signaller also tried to prevent the traders from breaking any rules by pleading for order. Then the short opportunity to trade came to an abrupt end when he raised his green flag, and blew his whistle to signal the clearance for the train to move on. This time he took great care to be well away from the steam and soot as the engine pressed forward.

Then as the train moved out into the distance, the station became very quiet. The only persons on the platform were those who were still looking for help to move on to their final destination. Mustafa, Neesha and Joshua saw a weary looking driver who approached them, and asked them where they were heading to. Mustafa mentioned the

Khudabaksh's and the driver instantly recognised the name, and invited them to travel with his cart.

The cart was rickety, bereft of shelter, and comfortable seats. It was being pulled by a sad looking, and reluctant donkey which did not respond much to the promptings of its master. When the passengers were on board, the driver lazily climbed up to his driving seat, and cracked his whip whilst shouting, "Go Thunderbolt Go!"

But "Thunderbolt" just continued to move at the pace that it was most comfortable with. The only semblance of thunder was when the donkey relieved itself shortly after it began to move off with its load. The strong and pungent smell nearly choked the passengers, but the driver said, "Good boy! You needed that! Now, move on!"

They eventually reached in front of a very imposing house with a general store at the ground level. The design was very similar to Mustafa's and Neesha's premises. A short, neatly dressed middle-aged man with a small white beard, and wearing an Islamic hat, stepped forward with his arms outstretched to greet his visitors. It was Mr Khudabaksh. Mustafa quickly slid off the cart, and held out his hands to support Neesha. He then paid the driver for the ride, and gave him some more money. "Take this and get some medicine for the donkey!"

Joshua advised the driver, "Try some molasses! That will make thunderbolt move like lightening!"

Mr Khudabaksh hailed his visitors, "Assalaam O Alaikum! Come, you must be Mustafa Ali and Neesha Ali! Who is your companion?"

"Waalaikum Asalaam!" replied Mustafa and Neesha. Mustafa said, "This gentleman is our dear friend Joshua who has always been with us!"

"Good afternoon to you sir!" said Mr Khudabaksh.

"Asalaam O Alaikum! May the Lord be with you sir!" answered Joshua, delighted at being so respectfully greeted. He rubbed his stomach with both hands.

Mr Khudabaksh said, "Let us go in, and have something to eat. You must be very tired and hungry after such a long journey!"

"Thank you Mr Khudabaksh," said Mustafa, as the visitors followed their host into a well decorated, and charming guest room. They sat on the large Persian carpet in the centre of the room, and a female *aaya* brought in some refreshment. It was cold coconut water with some soft jelly. The visitors then settled into a sumptuous meal of chicken curry, *roti, daal,* rice, and spicy coconut *choka* just as Neesha had predicted. Joshua could not resist asking for some more food whilst Mustafa and Neesha tried their best to restrain their urge for more.

Mustafa and Neesha had noticed that Mrs Khudabaksh was not there to greet them or to share in the meal. However, Mr Khudabaksh finished his meal hurriedly, and stood up to announce the entrance of his wife and daughter who were both dressed in elegant *shalwar kameez* costumes with white embroidered *ornis* covering their heads, and much of their faces.

The two women bowed gracefully, and softly said, "Asalaam O Alaikum" together. Everyone, including Joshua replied with "Waalaikum Asalaam!" They then took their places beside a proud Mr Khudabaksh.

He said, "My friends, this is Aminah my wonderful wife, and that is Soraya, the eldest one of our three daughters."

Joshua was most impressed with the natural beauty, and simplicity of the two women sitting before him, and for once he was speechless. He nodded respectfully, and noticed that Mustafa was also in awe. Neesha smiled at her hosts with feelings of great joy, and expectation. She instinctively knew that she had seen her future daughter-in-law.

46.

A surprise visit

Whilst Mustafa and Neesha were away on their mission in Mahaica, Ahmed and Rattan spent much of their time together on doing odd jobs around the store, house and yard. They wiped the accumulated dust and overspills of flour, rice, sugar and other provisions on the shelves and floor areas of the grocery section in the store. Then they cleaned the glass of the showcases, and serving counters which were located at the back of the main display areas. After their lunch break, they wiped and waxed the furniture and floor of the living quarters before going outside, and sweeping the yard around the building.

The brothers were both very surprised to see Mr and Mrs Ching approaching them. Mr Ching was a small, slim gentleman wearing neat brown slacks, and a white short-sleeved shirt. Mrs Ching was fairer in complexion, slightly shorter than Mr Ching, and wearing a neat floral cotton dress. They both wore comfortable sandals.

"Which one of you two young men is Ahmed?" asked Mr Ching in a quiet and gentle voice.

"I am sir," answered Ahmed respectfully.

"Are your parents home?" asked Mr Ching.

"No sir," said Rattan. "They have gone on a trip to Mahaica, and should be back by early this evening. Can we be of help to you?"

Mr Ching thought for a moment, and then said, "Yes, can we come into the house? I need to speak to Ahmed."

Ahmed, looking a bit perplexed, said nervously, "Of course sir and madam. You are most welcome to our home. Do follow us."

Mr and Mrs Ching were ushered into the family drawing room, and the boys offered them some tea and biscuits. Rattan slipped into the kitchen area, and started to boil some green tea leaves in a pot on the manmade earthen stove.

"Well, Mr and Mrs Ching," said Ahmed quietly, almost in a whisper. "What would you like to discuss with me today?"

Mr Ching sat forward slightly on the comfortable "Berbice" chair which was made of beautifully carved mahogany. He said, "You know our daughter Pansy very well, don't you?"

"Yes sir," answered Ahmed almost choking. "We have been going to school together, and have always played with many of our friends here. Why, what's the matter?"

"Well, you see, she is very upset at the moment," said Mrs Ching with tears in her eyes.

"Is it something my brother and I have done?" asked Ahmed looking across towards the kitchen to check that Rattan was still there.

Mr Ching said, "Yes young man. She came to us this morning saying that she was feeling sick. Mrs Ching knew immediately what was the problem."

Ahmed frowned, and said, "I am sorry to hear that Pansy is unwell. We are very close friends."

Mr Ching said, "The problem is that Pansy is not really unwell. She is perfectly healthy."

Mrs Ching added, "Pansy is pregnant."

Just then, Rattan entered the drawing room proudly carrying a tray with his well-brewed green tea, four teacups in saucers, and a small plate with some biscuits. "Here everyone, tea is served!"

Rattan happily poured the tea for everyone, and invited them all to enjoy his special brew. Then, much to his surprise, Ahmed said, "Rattan, could you please take some tea and biscuits, and leave Mr and Mrs Ching and I alone for a while?"

After Rattan duly excused himself from the meeting, Mr Ching continued speaking about Pansy. "You see, Ahmed, she told us that you and her have been more than just friends, and the baby that she is expecting is yours."

Ahmed fell back in his chair, and began to wipe away the first signs of perspiration from his forehead and cheeks. His heart was pounding harder, and he responded shakily, "Mr and Mrs Ching, I am very sorry for this. I fully accept that Pansy's baby is mine. It must have been an accident, but I do love her very much. I know that she also loves me."

Mr Ching looked straight into Ahmed's eyes, and said, "Young man, I am not happy about my daughter's condition. But since I know your parents well, and you are ready to accept this situation without trying to lie to me, Mrs Ching and I are very willing to accept you."

Ahmed mustered up some more courage, and said, "Mr and Mrs Ching, I respect you very much. I will never tell you a lie, particularly since I care so much for Pansy and thank you for not being angry with me, or her."

Mrs Ching smiled, and said, "We live very simple lives, and we respect honesty. Pansy did not hide the truth from us, and she clearly loves you very much. Mr Ching and I now need to talk to your parents, and to see what needs to be done."

Shortly afterwards, Mr and Mrs Ching thanked Ahmed for the tea, and quietly left the house. Rattan caught up with Ahmed, and asked him, "*Bhaiya*, what is the matter? You are sweating so much!"

"Nothing... nothing's the matter Rattan. It must have been the hot tea. It was too hot, and it made me perspire a lot," said Ahmed, trying his best to avoid telling Rattan what transpired between him, and the Chings.

Rattan said, "Mr and Mrs Ching left very suddenly. They did not seem to be happy. Are you sure that you do not want to say anything to me?"

"Yes Rattan," said Ahmed abruptly. "Mr and Mrs Ching are fine. But they were in a rush, and will come back later on to meet Maa and Paa."

"Aha!" exclaimed Rattan. "Now I see it! They will come back to see whether you will marry their daughter Pansy! I knew that there was something going on between you two. But my *bhaiya*, I like her very much, and you will make a good husband and wife!"

"Look here Rattan," said Ahmed. "I do not know what the Chings have in mind. Let us wait and see. Meanwhile, let us continue with cleaning the yard before Maa and Paa return home."

The boys continued with their cleaning of the yard, and hardly spoke to each other. Ahmed was deep in thought as he wielded his cutlass against some overgrown grassy areas of the yard. What will his parents say when they hear about Pansy's pregnancy? What if they liked the girl and her family that they were visiting in Mahaica? How will they deal with Pansy's situation, and their own preference for a daughter-in-law? Should he defy his parents if they insist on him marrying the girl of their choice?

He was becoming increasingly confused as he began to realise how complicated this situation had evolved. Rattan, meanwhile, happily carried on with his work, blissfully unaware of Ahmed's dilemma. He whistled along merrily chopping and sweeping away some wild and unwelcome weeds and shrubs.

Soon, everywhere was clean and tidy, and a large bonfire of the debris was set alight at the back of the yard. The flames grew, and crackled noisily until the rubbish had been burnt to ashes. The boys doused the residual hot ash with several buckets of water. They then looked at each other, and smiled with satisfaction at having worked so hard together. They sat down for a well-deserved rest on some steps at the back of the house, and drank some cool water.

They took turns to have a bath under a standing pipe attached to the base of a large metal tank which was used to store rain water that was directed from the roof of the house. The water was very cold despite the warmth of the weather on the outside of the tank. The boys loved the water as it brought an instant cooling effect on their hot bodies.

"Ah, that was so good!" said Ahmed breaking the silence between the two. "I can now do with a nice rest on my bed, until Maa and Paa come home."

"Yes *bhaiya*," agreed Rattan. "I am also very tired, but you go ahead and rest whilst I wait for them to return. I just cannot wait to hear their news! Ahmed, you are so lucky to have people making proposals for you!"

Ahmed recognising his brother's sarcasm, smiled and said, "Who knows? Maybe Maa and Paa might bring home a proposal for you as well!"

This helped to wipe the smile off Rattan's face, and he frowned. "Oh no, *bhaiya*. You and I know full well that the matchmaking is for you alone! I am quite happy to wait for my turn!"

The troubled Ahmed quietly stepped into his bedroom, and shut the door behind him. He lay on his bed looking up at the ceiling thinking about Pansy, and the wonderful surprise she was carrying. He felt a cosy warmth at the thought of her, and wished that he was with her. He wondered what she was doing, and thinking about at that moment. What would she say to him when they meet again?

He was relieved at the way Mr and Mrs Ching had dealt with the situation, but was worried about what they would say to his parents, and what his parents would say to them. He soon drifted into a deep sleep when he was suddenly awoken by the sound of someone banging at his door. It was Rattan shouting excitedly, "Ahmed... Ahmed are you awake? Get up now! Maa and Paa will be here soon!... and so will Mr and Mrs Ching!"

47.

The right match

Mustafa could not avoid looking closely into the eyes of Aminah, the wife of Mr Khudabaksh, as if he was searching for something he had lost a long time ago. Then, when the young Soraya smiled at him, it sent a chill right through him. She was the embodiment of the beautiful Chandini that he knew, loved and left in India nearly thirty years before.

He could not ask Aminah directly whether she was his long lost lover, as it would be most inappropriate, and disrespectful. Occasionally, he felt that Aminah was looking at him as if she was also wondering whether he was her Mustafa.

Mr Khudabaksh said, "So tell me Mr and Mrs Ali, how is business these days? I understand that you also have a large general store on the West Coast of Demerara."

"Yes Mr Khudabaksh," said Mustafa whilst running his left hand by his clean shaved chin as if he had a beard like Mr Khudabaksh's. "We have a fair sized general store like yours, and business is very good. Our two sons Ahmed and Rattan help us with the running of the store. Does Soraya do the same here?"

Aminah spoke quietly, and said, "Yes, our three girls help to manage the home, and run the business. In fact, Soraya is so good with our customers, she takes the lead at the front counter where she is able to meet and greet everyone who comes into the store. She is very popular, very bright, and knows the prices of nearly all the items we stock and sell."

Aminah's soft tone, sweet smile, and dancing eyes made Mustafa's heart skip a beat every time he looked at her or heard her speak. He was most certain that she was his Chandini.

"I like that very much," said Neesha. "Soraya is a beautiful girl, and reminds me of myself when I first became involved in the business. I was keen to meet the customers, to talk to them, to listen to their problems, to advise them when I could, and, I have found that they come back to the store more often. A good customer is one who encourages others to come to the store. This is what makes a good business. I can really appreciate just how much of an asset Soraya is to you, and the business."

Mustafa, thinking of how to confirm that Aminah was Chandini without asking her directly, asked Mr Khudabaksh, "So, where did you come from in India?"

Mr Khudabaksh explained, "Oh, I came from a small village in Uttar Pradesh about twenty years ago. My family were small farmers, and we lost everything in a big flood which followed one of the worst famines we ever suffered. We were very lucky to stay alive until the waters finally disappeared. By then our rice crop was wiped out. I heard about emigrating to work on five year contracts here in British Guiana, and I just took a train to Calcutta."

Joshua asked, "And where did you meet your lovely wife?"

Mustafa was very pleased with Joshua's question, and was relieved that he asked Mr Khudabaksh about Aminah.

Mr Khudabaksh's face lit up with great pride, and he said, "Oh, where can I start? I was the luckiest person in the world to meet this beautiful lady on the ship that we both travelled on. It was a very rough journey, and many of our fellow passengers perished. I helped to protect her, and the other women who were having a bad experience. Anyone would do so. Then when we finally landed here we were lucky to be selected for this estate. Soon after we came, we got married."

Neesha asked Aminah, "Where did you come from *didi*? Were you also from Uttar Pradesh?"

Aminah said, glancing at Mustafa, "I came from a village near to Kanpur. I had a very large house, and family. Both of my parents died within months of each other. One of my brothers who was always ready and willing to defend our honour and village, was killed in the uprising against the British. Our closest family friends, Hussein and Batool Ali, also passed away through grieving for all our losses suffered. I was still young and not married, and felt that I had to leave that place to search for work, and maybe return to help rebuild our home and village. I also heard of the offer of work overseas, and took the train to Calcutta. Hundreds of our people had done such a journey in the past, and continue to do so today."

Mustafa could not withhold his tears as he immediately realised that Aminah had just given him enough information to confirm that she was indeed his Chandini he had parted from. To hear about the losses of his and her parents and siblings, was also unbearable. He looked up, and as he wiped the tears from his eyes, he could see that Aminah was also crying.

Neesha said solemnly, "I am so sorry to hear of your experiences. Mustafa and I have tried very hard to find out about our loved ones we left behind, and have not heard much from anyone. We even went to see if we could recognise anyone from many of the ships that have been coming here. We both dreamt of going back to India, but our lives here began to change very quickly, and we heard about great hardships being suffered by people back in the villages. So, we finally gave up that hope. Do you also feel this way?"

Aminah said, "Allah has been kind to us now, and I do not think that we will ever go back. Our life is here now, and I think that I have seen a part of my dream right before us now."

Joshua said, also wiping tears from his eyes, "Well my friends, enough of this sadness. I am so happy to think that you are all coming to an agreement here. I do not know whether you have to see the boy Ahmed, but I can assure you that he is as handsome as my friend Mustafa when he was much younger and with more hair on his head! And, your beautiful daughter Soraya is just the perfect match for Ahmed. I only wish that we had brought him here with us. We could have done the wedding here and now!"

"Not so fast, Joshua!" warned Mustafa. "We need to discuss this further, and if Mr and Mrs Khudabaksh and Soraya agree after they have met Ahmed, then we can do the rest."

Mr Khudabaksh said, "Yes, I agree. Let us visit your home soon, and if Ahmed likes our Soraya, and she likes him, then we can proceed to a *nikah*."

Aminah smiled, and cradled a very shy Soraya in her bosom.

Joshua, thoroughly enjoying his unofficial role as adviser to the matchmaking, then said, "Mr and Mrs Khudabaksh, I believe that you have two more daughters. Perhaps we could see them, as my friends here have another bright and handsome son called Rattan. Who knows, we may be able to do a double wedding!"

Without much fuss, Aminah asked Soraya to go and fetch her two younger sisters to meet their guests. Shortly after, the two girls appeared with Soraya, and they were equally stunning. Neesha was immediately impressed, and suggested that the whole family should make the visit to their home.

As the time available was too short for this meeting, the parties decided to end their discussion, and they embraced each other before Mustafa, Neesha and Joshua took their leave. When Mustafa embraced Aminah, she whispered in his left ear, "I am Chandini." He squeezed her more tightly, and whispered in her left ear, "I know. I am so sorry. I am so sorry to let you down."

Neesha said, as they were leaving the house, "Mr and Mrs Khudabaksh and girls, thank you so much for your kind hospitality. I do look forward to the day when we are joined as a family. I feel in my heart that you are all closer to us than family. I only wish that we had met before now. Do you not agree Mustafa?"

"Yes Neesha," said Mustafa wiping more tears from his eyes and cheeks, "I too wish we had met before now. You are all so close to my heart."

Joshua said, "Well, it looks like we are already one big, happy, and loving family! Come on Mustafa and Neesha, we have a very long journey ahead of us! We need to get back home before dark!"

Their transport vehicle was waiting to start the return journey, although "Thunderbolt" the donkey, and the driver did not appear to share Joshua's urgency. As soon as everyone was on board, Joshua yelled at the donkey which startled the animal and the driver momentarily. Yet the beast almost reluctantly just stepped forward at the pace that it was always used to; very short of thunderbolt or lightening!

They eventually reached the train station, and luckily caught the last train to Georgetown. The donkey cart driver waved triumphantly at Joshua, Mustafa and Neesha as they took their seats on the train. The driver was very happy that once again he and his trusted thunderbolt succeeded in delivering their passengers on time. They slowly turned around, and disappeared into the distance as the train lurched forward.

Mustafa was very quiet throughout the long train journey to Georgetown. He simply slumped to his side resting his head on Neesha's shoulders, drifting in and out of sleep. Joshua was still full of energy and enthusiasm. He tried to engage in conversation with

Neesha. She was mostly unresponsive through her own tiredness, and her desire to allow Mustafa as good a chance to get some sleep, and much needed rest. Eventually, she also fell asleep.

Joshua looked at his two friends, and said quietly to himself, "Ah, this has been a hard trip. I am so happy that I am here to look after them. What would they do without me?" Shortly afterwards, he also fell into a deep slumber.

When the train arrived at its final stop in Georgetown, the sharp screeching of brakes on the metal wheels, and the sudden jolt into the protective barrier at the end of the line, awoke the three friends.

They rushed to the harbour, and took the first available boat across the river. The tide of the Demerara River was moving in, and the small ferry rocked uncomfortably over the swelling waves. They were very relieved to reach the Vreed-en-Hoop harbour, and Joshua hurriedly collected his horse and cart.

The sun was a flaming red that lit up the horizon in one final display of magnificence at the end of the day. Neesha looked at Mustafa who sat opposite her in the cart. She asked him if he was alright.

He said, "Yes, I am fine. It has been a long and hard day."

Neesha agreed, "Yes. But we should be happy that we have found people we can grow to love as family."

Mustafa said, "I am sure that they feel the same way about us."

She smiled, and reached across to touch Mustafa's hands which were resting on his knees. She said, "Mustafa, thank you for everything you have given to me. For everything you have done for me, and the boys. You are so special to us. We cannot bear to see you hurt in any way."

Mustafa looked at Neesha, and replied, "I too love you all, and care for you with all my heart. I hope that I will never walk away from the people I love so dearly. Never!"

Joshua shouted at the stallion, "Come On! Get moving! You have rested all day!"

The horse, ever willing to respond to his master, lifted up its proud head, and jerked forward with force. He kept up his gallop without the need for further promptings until they arrived in front of Mustafa's and Neesha's house.

48.

Walking away

Mustafa gingerly stepped down from the cart, and reached out to help Neesha safely onto the roadside. He paid Joshua generously for his service, and thanked him for his companionship and very helpful advice over their mission to Mahaica. Joshua waved goodbye as he ordered his horse to complete the final stage of their journey in greater haste.

Neesha, despite her tiredness, could not wait to embrace her two sons who had stood waiting by the main gate of their home. Mustafa then took his turn to give the boys a big hug with great passion.

The four of them walked together, and before they shared the outcome of their visit to Mahaica, Mustafa and Neesha took turns to have a most welcome wash, and a change into clean clothes. Ahmed and Rattan then warmed the food left over from the lunchtime, and served their parents.

Neesha was most keen to tell the boys about the Khudabaksh family and Soraya in particular. She was utterly convinced that they had found the most suitable match for Ahmed.

"Well boys," she began. "Your father and I met a most loving family with no less than three beautiful daughters! Mr and Mrs Khudabaksh came from the same part of India as your father. They were so warm and loving to us. It was as if they knew us for many years. Is that not so Mustafa?"

Mustafa replied, "Yes, it was a happy and sad experience for me personally. Happy to meet people from Uttar Pradesh, and sad to learn how bad the situation became there."

Ahmed said, "Paa, did they talk about your family? Did they know them?"

Mustafa said, "We did not get into details, but I heard enough to make me feel that if we ever go back to India, it may not be pleasant. Our people are still suffering great hardship there. That is why so many of them are still leaving to come here, and to go to places like Trinidad,

Mauritius, and other colonies. I am very saddened by this. India is a beautiful country, and it seems that every invader brings their own brand of rule that only suppresses our people more and more."

Rattan said, "Maa and Paa do not worry. Everything will come good one day, and we will all go back to India."

Neesha nodded, and said, "Yes *beta* that may happen, but for now let us talk about the girls we met in Mahaica. Soraya is so beautiful, and very intelligent. She is just the daughter I have dreamt about. Her two sisters are also very beautiful, and the whole family will be visiting us soon to meet you both. Then, if everything is alright, we will proceed."

Ahmed asked worriedly, "Maa, does this mean that you have not made any promises or arrangement with these people?"

Neesha answered, "No, we felt that although the family is suitable, and the girls are so attractive, we should allow you both to meet them first."

Rattan also became more worried, and asked, "Maa, are you thinking that both Ahmed and I should choose from these three girls? You know full well that I am not yet ready for marriage. Surely, you should be thinking about getting Ahmed married first?"

Ahmed, not being able to conceal his anguish, said, "Maa and Paa, before we go too far on this matter, I need to discuss something else with you."

Just then, there was a knock on the front door. Mustafa wearily rose up, stepped slowly across the room, and opened the door.

He said, "Oh, hello Mr and Mrs Ching! What can we do for you at this time?"

Mr Ching said, "Mustafa, can we come in please? We have a serious matter to discuss. We were here earlier in the day, and your sons treated us very well. They told us that you were away, and that we should return when you came back."

Mustafa invited Mr and Mrs Ching into the drawing room, and offered them some refreshment. They chose to have tea, and Rattan volunteered to brew a pot of green tea for everyone.

Mr Ching began speaking directly to Mustafa and Neesha. "Did your son Ahmed here, tell you about our discussion today?"

Mustafa said, "No Mr Ching. We have only just returned from a very long trip to Mahaica, and are very tired."

Mr Ching said, "Well, thank you for allowing us to talk at this time. We are quite happy to return tomorrow. But we need to mention something that is very important to us all. We will not take up much time. You see, we have a daughter by the name of Pansy. I think that Neesha must have seen her in the store."

Neesha confirmed, "Yes Mr Ching. I have seen Pansy. She is a lovely girl."

Mr Ching then delivered his bombshell. "Mustafa and Neesha, our Pansy and your son Ahmed have been lovers, and she is now expecting a baby that they both agree is Ahmed's."

Neesha was totally shocked to hear this news. She exclaimed, "Subhan Allah!" Then she placed her right palm onto her forehead, and said, "This cannot be true! How can this happen?"

Ahmed covered his face with his hands, and began to weep.

Mr Ching said quietly, "Neesha and Mustafa, both Pansy and Ahmed have admitted their love for each other, and of having this affair. You can ask him now."

Mustafa asked Ahmed, "Tell me son, is this true?"

Ahmed, still holding his hands against his face, and with tears flowing from his eyes said, "Yes Paa. I was just about to tell you and Maa when Mr and Mrs Ching arrived."

Neesha said with bitter disappointment, "Son, why did you not tell us about this before? Look at all the trouble we have taken to find a girl for you. And now this!"

Mr Ching intervened, "I am very sorry, but it was only today that we found out. I think that Ahmed did not know about Pansy's pregnancy until we told him about it today. So, please do not be harsh on him."

Mustafa said calmly, "Mr and Mrs Ching, thank you for bringing this matter to our attention. It is not good news for us to hear at this moment. But we need to do something about it, and I am happy to hear what you have in mind."

Mr Ching said, "Well, for us it is very straightforward. We believe that Pansy and Ahmed love each other, and we do not mind them getting married. Especially for the sake of their baby."

Neesha said, "I respect you both, and I happen to like your Pansy. But this news has come as a great shock to us, and before we agree on anything we should take a little time to think about this matter. We cannot decide here and now until we have discussed this as a family.

Besides, both Mustafa and I are very tired now, and we need to retire for the night."

Mr and Mrs Ching shook their heads in respect, and left quietly. Rattan returned to the drawing room with a tray containing a pot of his special green tea, tea cups and saucers, and some biscuits. He looked surprised as he saw the Chings leaving without having their refreshment.

He asked, "Maa and Paa, what is the matter? Why are Mr and Mrs Ching leaving so quickly? This is the second time in one day that they have left before having my tea!"

Ahmed remained seated with his hands still covering his face, and Mustafa responded to Rattan, "Sorry son, but I do not think we will be having tea for the moment. Mr and Mrs Ching are fine. We will discuss everything in the morning. Come on, let us all do our *namaaz*, and then go to sleep."

After the prayers, Mustafa and Neesha retired to their room, and Ahmed and Rattan to theirs. They all found sleeping very difficult that night. Mustafa and Neesha tossed and turned restlessly for most of the night. When one began to sleep, the other would accidentally disturb him or her. Ahmed had spent much of the afternoon thinking about the consequences of the situation, and Rattan was restless through a concern as to what was happening around him.

Mustafa's thoughts were a mixture of his brief encounter with Chandini after so many years, and the dilemma of Ahmed's own forbidden love. How can fate play such a trick on him? Must he still keep his secret love for Chandini locked in his heart forever? What must Chandini be thinking right then? Will they ever be able to keep their secret if and when their families became related through marriage of their children? How must young Ahmed be feeling? Would he want to walk or run away from the love of his life? From his own child?

Neesha's anguish also caused her to turn and twist in the bed, occasionally accidentally hitting Mustafa with her arms or legs. How will she be able to face the Khudabaksh's? What will they think of her family with one of her sons having an illicit affair with a Chinese girl? With a girl expecting his baby? What shame will this affair bring onto her family? Should she just call off the Khudabaksh's' visit?

Ahmed's thoughts were more about his Pansy, and what will become of them both as well as the baby. He knew that he wanted to be with her, but he also felt for his parents' wishes, and that of his brother whom he loved dearly. He could not just walk away from his family if they did not agree with his liaison with Pansy. Likewise, how could he abandon his first and true love for someone he had not even seen or met?

Rattan's thoughts were more about his personal desire to remain single. But with two visits from the Chings, and Ahmed's friendship with Pansy, did this mean that they would be married, and he would have to be considered for one of the Khudabaksh's girls? He was feeling increasingly annoyed with Ahmed.

When they all finally fell asleep, through the sheer weight of the stress and over-tiredness, it was inevitable that their normal early rise to prepare for the opening of the store on the following Monday morning would be passed. They were all awoken suddenly by a frantic banging at the front door. It was the *aaya* who had turned up for her early morning chores. Rattan was the first to reach the door, and when he opened it he apologised to the *aaya*, and told a small group of customers to wait for a few more minutes whilst he prepared for the opening of the store.

Rattan undertook to run the business single-handedly that morning until closing time for the lunch break. He then placed a notice for the public on the front door of the store, to say that it would be closed for the rest of the day. Mustafa and Neesha thanked him for his actions as they prepared for the lunch that the *aaya* had prepared before she ended her work for the day, and left.

The four sat quietly at the table, and ate most of their food through sheer hunger, having missed their normal breakfast. Mustafa then said, "Well my family, we have to discuss a great problem, and I hope that we can arrive at a good solution. Rattan, I am sorry that you were not told about what is going on. But your brother has feelings for Pansy and she is pregnant with their child."

Rattan immediately looked at Ahmed in surprise. Then he said, "I knew about Pansy, but not about a baby. This is disgraceful!"

Neesha could see how Rattan was becoming furious, and said calmly, "No Rattan. The baby is your brother's and Pansy's. Like it or not, but it will be your niece or nephew, and you will be its uncle."

Rattan said, "But Maa and Paa, you cannot promise one girl for Ahmed, and then tell her and her family that the wedding is off because your son has made someone else pregnant!"

Mustafa said, "Rattan, I understand how you feel. But we have not made a promise for anyone to marry you or Ahmed. We need to decide what must be done about Ahmed and Pansy."

Neesha pointed out, "And the baby!"

Rattan said, "Maa and Paa, I think that they should get married for the baby's sake. Also, I think that Mr and Mrs Ching have been very understanding, and decent about this affair. They are good people just like us, and we must do the right thing."

Ahmed listened intently as the conversation developed. Neesha then said, "You are right *beta*. We have our own standing in this community to think about. Ahmed, you have been quiet. What do you think?"

Ahmed looked up with his eyes still reddened from his lack of sleep, and constant crying. He said quietly, "Maa and Paa, and Rattan, I am truly sorry for bringing this disgrace to our family. I love you all very much. I also love Pansy and even more so because she is expecting our baby. No matter what you decide, I cannot bring myself to walk away and abandon them. That is not the way to treat someone you love dearly. Whatever the hardship, I will stand by her, and our baby. I have made up my mind about this. Please let me marry Pansy, and leave us to make our own lives together. If we are away from you all, people will soon forget us, and everything will be fine."

He broke down in a flood of tears, and then Mustafa and Neesha stood up and comforted him. Mustafa, with tears running down his cheeks said, "Now *beta*, do stop crying. I love you. We all love you very much. I will not let you walk away from Pansy and your baby. That will bring much more hurt than we can all imagine."

Neesha said, also crying, "I accept what your father says. No one's heart should be broken like this. I do like that young lady, and we as a family must welcome her and her family here, as our own. It is Allah's wish for our family to be together, and to stay together as one."

Rattan also stood up, and put his arms around Mustafa, Neesha and Ahmed. Their tears then turned from sadness into joy.

Someone banged loudly at the front door. Mustafa opened it, and saw that it was Joshua.

Joshua said, looking rather puzzled, "Mustafa, what has happened? Why are you not opening the store this afternoon? People are talking. What is going on?"

Mustafa said quietly, "Joshua, please come inside. Nothing has happened. We felt so tired after yesterday's trip that we over-slept."

"Oh, I see," said a relieved Joshua as he took a seat in the drawing room. "You know what our people are like. They get very concerned about this family."

Neesha said, "Yes Joshua, we do know. Thank you for coming over, and showing your concern. We have something very important to share with you, and it will also be good news for everyone."

Joshua's face lit up with the broadest, and most toothsome of smiles. "Tell me all about it! I am not walking away from here!"

49.

The 4th of May

The next day, Ahmed and Rattan were left to run the store as Mustafa and Neesha walked over the three hundred yards to the home of Mr and Mrs Ching. The Chings' house was made of timber, and was a similar design to the others on both sides of the main road. It comprised of three good sized bedrooms on the first floor which was accessed by an external stairway at the front, and another at the side of the building. The ground floor was mostly opened at the front section, and had a small kitchen at the back. There were three hammocks hung from the beams beneath the first floor, and located in front of the kitchen so that the users could enjoy any cool air that passed through.

The Chings, like most of the other villagers, kept some poultry and livestock at the backyard which was enclosed by a neat and sturdy six feet high fence. The front yard was neat and tidy with small beds of flowers including "jumping jacks" and "turkey tails". The front yard was also fenced around with a combination of old zinc sheets, old pieces of timber, and barbed wire. The front fence was recently whitewashed, and so was the main gate.

Mr Ching promptly answered the knock at the front door, and was very surprised to see Mustafa and Neesha. He said, "Good morning. Do come in. Please excuse our lack of space. Do sit down. Mrs Ching, please come here. We have some very important visitors."

Mrs Ching emerged from the main bedroom with a coconut broom in her hands, and wearing a simple apron. She put the broom aside, took off the apron, wiped her hands nervously on her skirt, and shook Mustafa's and Neesha's hands. She said, "Can I offer you some real Chinese tea?"

"No thank you," said Mustafa. "We just had our breakfast. Do please come and join us."

"Well," said Mr Ching in anticipation. "I expect that you have come to discuss Pansy and Ahmed?"

"Yes Mr and Mrs Ching," said Mustafa. "My wife and I have discussed the matter with Ahmed and Rattan, and we have decided to ask you for your daughter Pansy, for our son Ahmed."

The Chings smiled with great relief, and excitedly called out Pansy who was sharing the front bedroom with her parents. The other children were occupying the other two bedrooms, and had remained quietly in their rooms. Pansy, who must have overheard the brief conversation, stepped out of the room, walked straight over to Neesha, and embraced her as she began to cry with sheer joy.

Neesha said, "Do not worry my child, may Allah always bless and keep you."

Pansy then sat beside her parents, facing her future mother and father-in-law. She painted a beautiful picture of a very simple, contented, and happy person in the prime of her pregnancy. Her broad smile was charming, and exposed a set of fine teeth. She wiped away a few pearl-like teardrops from her dark oriental eyes.

Mustafa said, "Mr and Mrs Ching, before we discuss the wedding arrangements, there is one thing that we need to agree on. You see, we are Muslims, and it is expected that a non-Muslim girl must be converted to Islam before she marries a Muslim boy. I do hope that you and Pansy will not object to this."

Mr Ching looked at Mrs Ching and Pansy, then said, "Mustafa and Neesha, we are very poor people and have only recently converted to Christianity. I do not know what rules we will be breaking if we refused, but for the sake of Pansy's future, I do not object to your suggestion." Mrs Ching nodded in agreement.

Mustafa then turned to Pansy, and said, "My daughter, are you agreeing to this?"

Pansy shyly replied, "Yes sir. Ahmed and I had already discussed this. I hope to be a good Muslim like him, and I hope that our child will also be so."

Mustafa clasped his hands, and said, "Well, that is it then. Let us make the arrangements. I would also like to tell you that we will pay for all the costs of the wedding. Unfortunately, we will not be serving pork, and Pansy as a Muslim, will not be using pork in the future."

Mrs Ching said very politely, and softly, "We will respect your wishes, and thank you very much for your kindness. We were willing to pay for our costs of the wedding, but we are happy to accept your generosity."

Neesha said, holding Mrs Ching's hands, "From today, you are my sister, and I promise to look after you, and your entire family here. I have seen how you have struggled to raise such a large family. How you have kept your dignity, and have never complained about your circumstances. You always offered to pay for everything you could afford at the store. Now, you are free to choose whatever cloths you need to make your wedding outfits for Pansy, and all the family."

Mr and Mrs Ching thanked Mustafa and Neesha, and said that they would work with them to ensure that the wedding was a great success.

As the visitors rose to leave, all the young Ching children emerged from their rooms, and stood before their guests in an orderly manner as if they were on parade. Mustafa and Neesha shook each of their hands as Mr Ching called out their respective names. Mustafa and Neesha repeated the names as they were announced, but almost immediately forgot who was who by the time they shook the hands of the last and smallest one in the line.

Mustafa and Neesha left the Chings' house, and a family who were suddenly made to feel very happy with their good fortune. Pansy's siblings gathered around her, and giggled with sheer delight as they each took turns to hug her tightly. She stooped down, and picked up the two youngest children holding one in each arm. The entire family walked to the front landing and stairway waving excitely to Mustafa and Neesha who turned around, and returned the gesture.

When Mustafa and Neesha reached the store and told Ahmed and Rattan about the wedding, the boys shouted in sheer delight. A very dark cloud of uncertainty and despair had been lifted, and was replaced with an atmosphere of hope and joy.

Mustafa and Neesha invited their closest friends to their home for dinner on the Friday evening that week, after the *jummah namaaz*. They made a substantial donation to the Mosque, and confirmed the date for the wedding based on the availability of the Imaam. Joshua, Matilda, Ragubir, Ishani, Kanhaiya, Mumtaz, Wong Yee, Molly, and Nandoo and his wife, Sangita, arrived at the home bearing gifts as tokens of their appreciation for the host family's good news.

Mustafa said happily, "Thank you all for coming over this evening. You need not have brought these wonderful gifts for us, as your very presence here is much more important and valuable to our family. The main reason why we invited you over is to tell you personally about the wedding arrangements, and to avoid rumours and gossip about what will happen to Pansy. She will be converted to Islam as is our practice, and she was not forced to do so in any way. In fact, I think that she is so keen on the religion, that she may very easily become a better Muslim than all of us in this family! She is also expecting a baby, and we want to tell you that we are happy that Ahmed has accepted that he is the father. We are all looking forward to receiving our first grandchild!"

Joshua said, "Mustafa, thank you very much for clarifying this to us all. As you will no doubt know, the village has been buzzing with all kinds of rumours as to who is the father. Now, I am sure that we are all very happy for you and your family, and I for one cannot wait for the celebrations! God bless you all!"

"Hear! Hear!" echoed all the guests.

They all took their turn to embrace Mustafa and Neesha. Ahmed and Rattan then entered the crowded room with trays of tea and biscuits.

Ragubir said, "Mustafa, this is a very important decision you and Neesha have made. Our community will look back upon this marriage with some satisfaction and pride."

Ishani said, "My friends, I am so proud of you. We were beginning to hear whispers about Ahmed and Pansy, and are now so happy to hear that this matter will be resolved in the best possible way!"

Kanhaiya agreed and added, "My *bhaiya* and *bhabi*, you are both God-fearing people, and Mumtaz and I prayed for you. I hope that this wedding will be the biggest ever!"

Nandoo and his wife Sangita, took their turns to say a few words by singing a couple of lines from one of his Hindi songs, and offered a translation, "Come everyone, today Raam is with his Sita, and Krishna is with his Radha. Let us all share their happiness!"

Wong Yee smiled graciously, and said, "Sorry I cannot give you a Chinese song, but please accept heartiest congratulations from Molly, Andrew and I. Also, sorry for starting this trend of Chinese mixed marriages. But, we are all in this world together, and it is up to us all to live as one!"

"Praise be to the Lord!" said Joshua. "Matilda and I are so happy for you and your family. I know that she cannot wait to receive yet another addition to her pre-school class!"

"Oh Joshua, trust you to be so ahead of yourself!" said Matilda, as she playfully pushed at his shoulders.

Joshua asked, "So, Mustafa and Neesha, what date do you have for the wedding?"

Mustafa said, "Well, co-incidentally, the Imaam was only available on the 4th of May, and I had to accept this date. It happens to be a special day for me, Kanhaiya, and Ishani. That was the date when our ship arrived in British Guiana in 1845. And none of us knew that we would still be here after all these years." Mustafa's eyes began to well up with tears.

Joshua said, "This is no time to be sad. We have all made our lives here. We have new generations to look after, and let us all give thanks to our God for all the goodness He has given us. Let us hold hands, and offer our thanks to Him in whatever way we wish to."

The friends formed a neat circle, and with each holding hands, they closed their eyes and mentally offered their individual prayers. It was a unique moment of religious tolerance, and Mustafa remembered his exposure to the Hindu, Sikh, Christian and Buddhist faiths alongside his own Islam, on his journey across North India to Calcutta, the long sea voyage, and then in British Guiana. This tolerance for a belief in the one God with so many paths towards Him was the rope that bound them together. Their new country, which they never really chose to be part of, was causing them to un-intentionally develop something new through their shared history of hardship, and their natural instinct for survival.

The group then settled down to enjoy their sumptuous vegetarian and non-vegetarian meal. Their conversations were more light-hearted, and they reflected on their own experiences before arriving in British Guiana, and over the long hard years of struggle in their new homeland.

All the friends were good story-tellers, and they loved to narrate tales which were handed down through generations of their respective, African, Indian and Chinese heritage. Indeed, some of the more recent real-life events such as the gruesome murder of Miss Betty and her killer's own demise, were being told as local mysteries embellished to make the listener experience a raft of emotions. Others were more light-hearted.

Mustafa told the story of the twin brothers, Simon and Samuel the village carpenters, who were returning from a wood-cutting mission in the bush very late one evening. As they were walking on the road beside the cemetery in Anna Catherina, the only light that they relied upon was that of a bright full moon. As a dark cloud temporarily moved across and blotted out the moon thus pitching darkness everywhere, a voice was heard to say, "Ah who da! Ah who da!"

Simon answered shakily, "Ah me Simon!" as his heart began to pound due to his feeling of increasing fear.

The voice responded, "Ah who da!" Then Samuel answered, "Ah me Sam!" as both brothers started to increase their speed of walking.

The voice became more pronounced, and seemed to be angry, "Ah who da! Ah who da!"

This time Simon and Samuel dashed off, and ran all the way to their home. When they recovered the next morning, and told everyone they met about their brief encounter with a ghost in the cemetery, most people just burst out laughing at them. The strange voice that they heard was that of an old black crow whose squawk seemed to imitate someone asking "Who are you?" as anyone passed by them, particularly in the dead of night.

Joshua said, "Mustafa that was a good one! I guess that Simon and Samuel will never be caught coming home from the bush in the dark! But joking aside, you and Neesha have not mentioned what will happen about the Khudabakshs' visit from Mahaica."

"You are right Joshua," said Mustafa. "We have to honour our promise for a visit from them. In fact, they are coming over next Sunday afternoon with their three daughters."

Neesha was quick to intervene, "Joshua, we did not make any promises or agreements for a wedding. So, we should not worry about the visit. We will just have to tell them what has happened here, and take it from there. I hope that you will come over to meet the family, as they know you."

"That will be an honour," said Joshua as everyone listened with interest.

Kanhaiya said, "Well, although Ahmed will not now be eligible to marry one of their daughters, there is Rattan who is still available."

Everyone looked across to Rattan who was sitting quietly beside his brother, and he felt obliged to say something. "With all due respect to you all, I do not intend to get married as yet. I do not wish to meet the Khudabakshs, and I think that their trip will be a waste of time. I strongly suggest that it should be cancelled. Permanently!"

Rattan stood up, bid everyone goodbye as politely as he could, and left the gathering.

Kanhaiya said, "I am very sorry if I caused the young man to be angry or annoyed. I am sure that Mustafa and Neesha will do the right thing. Let us look forward to a great wedding for Ahmed and Pansy. The whole district will remember the 4th of May!"

Mustafa said, "Yes, the 4th of May."

50.

Fated

Mustafa and Neesha were very concerned about Rattan's unhappiness, his show of dissatisfaction, and his insistence on not wishing to get married at that time. They decided to discuss the matter with him after dinner the following evening. Ahmed had gone to visit Pansy at her parent's home to talk about their upcoming wedding plans.

"Rattan," said Mustafa. "Your mother and I would like to talk to you about your future and marriage."

Rattan said, "Paa, I am very sorry for walking out on our guests yesterday. I am also sorry for what I said."

Neesha said, "No *beta*, you have a right to say what you feel about these matters. It is far better to be open, and truthful. Now tell us more about what you are thinking."

Rattan looked at his parents in turn, and said, "I love my *bhaiya* Ahmed dearly. We have grown up very closely together, and play together. We also work at the store and elsewhere together. Now that he is getting married, and will be having a family soon, this makes it difficult for the two of us. Everything will now change, and I am afraid of losing him." Tears welled up in his eyes as he paused.

Mustafa said, "These things happen in every family, *beta*. I felt the same way about your uncle Kanhaiya whom I had grown to love as dearly as you do Ahmed. We were always there for each other. Then he got married, and had to spend more time with his wife and family. But, as you can see, we have remained very close to each other, and our bond is even stronger. We do not have to say this aloud, as we understand our individual responsibilities towards each other, and to our families."

Neesha said, "Your Paa is right. I have also grown to understand and respect their brotherly love, and responsibilities to each other. That is why I am so close to your aunt Mumtaz as she is to me."

Rattan said, wiping tears from his eyes, "But Paa and Uncle Kanhaiya live in their own homes, and this will be different for me and Ahmed. I will never be able to talk to Ahmed like we do now. It will be insulting to Pansy. I know that our home is big, and Ahmed and his family can live here in comfort."

Mustafa looked at Neesha, and nodded in acknowledgement of Rattan's dilemma, and his reasoning. He said to Rattan, "I understand *beta*. Thank you for sharing these feelings. Your Maa and I have been too busy trying to arrange Ahmed's marriage, and have not given much thought as to how this will affect us as a family, and you in particular. We need to resolve this quickly."

"Paa and Maa, the only way to solve this problem is for me to leave this home, and to live away from the family."

Neesha was not prepared for this possibility, and said, "No Rattan. I cannot bear to see you leave this home. It will break my heart. I have always wanted our small family to remain together. I understand why you do not wish to be in the way of your *bhaiya* and his family. But this is your home, and there is enough room for all of us."

"But Maa," added Rattan. "I will still be in their way. I know that you want us all to be together, but then as grandchildren come along even this house will become too small for the whole family."

"So, Rattan," said Mustafa. "You are not really objecting to getting married. You are more concerned about our living arrangements. I understand this, and we will find a solution."

"Yes Paa," agreed Rattan. "The quicker we sort this out, the better for all of us."

Neesha was also relieved about Rattan's position and said, "We can assume that you will be there to meet the Khudabaksh family next Sunday?"

Rattan said, "Yes Maa. I will be here to meet them. But I do not know how you and Paa will explain why Ahmed will not be available to marry one of their daughters."

Mustafa said, "Well, we will have to tell them the truth about the matter. If they are reasonable people, then there should be no problem about Ahmed's and Pansy's situation. And remember, if you feel that you like one of the girls, then I think that they would be happy. If none of the girls likes you, then we will have to look elsewhere. Unless of course, you are not hiding any affair from us!"

Rattan smiled, and hugged his parents saying, "Maa and Paa, I love you both most of all. I have not met anyone or seen anyone that I like. I will not do what Ahmed has done. I promise you."

When Ahmed returned home later that evening, Mustafa and Neesha told him about their discussion with Rattan, and about the Khudabakshs' visit. He also agreed to be present for the meeting.

Joshua and Matilda were the first to arrive at the house on that Sunday morning. They were both immaculately dressed as if they were attending church or a wedding, and were smiling with great anticipation and joy.

Neesha welcomed her guests, and ushered them into the drawing room. Rattan as usual, volunteered to make the tea, and Ahmed presented a selection of sweet biscuits and *laddoos*.

Mustafa said, "Joshua and Matilda, we are very happy to have you here today. Joshua, I thought that you would be picking up the Khudabaksh family at Vreed-en-Hoop. What is happening?"

"Oh Mustafa," said Joshua proudly. "I feel too important to be a driver today, so I asked one of the boys who work for me, to go and bring your guests."

Neesha said, "Thank you very much Joshua," as she poured the hot and freshly made green tea for everyone. "I am also relieved that the weather is not too hot, and it is not raining."

Soon their guests arrived after a long but safe journey from Mahaica. Mustafa embraced Mr Khudabaksh, and Neesha hugged Aminah. Joshua and Matilda followed suit. The young people acknowledged each other, and they all took their seats with the visitors sitting directly opposite the hosts. Neesha informed everyone that after the tea, they will have lunch.

Mustafa, being very keen to deal with the main purpose of the visit, said, "Well my friends, our two sons Ahmed and Rattan are here, and I need to inform you of something that has happened since we last met in Mahaica. You see, Ahmed has met someone from our village, and a wedding has been set for the 4th of May."

Aminah seemed taken aback, and looked straight into Mustafa's eyes. He could not avoid her concerned look, so he addressed her directly.

He said, "You see Aminah, we were not aware of his relationship with the young lady until we arrived home after visiting you. We had no choice but to make a decision very quickly."

Neesha added, "That was because the girl is expecting Ahmed's child, and she is Chinese."

Mr Khudabaksh and Aminah sat back in disbelief, and then looked across at Ahmed and Rattan, and then to their three daughters. Joshua felt obliged to say something.

"Mr and Mrs Khudabaksh, we can see that you are good and decent people, and you may be disappointed to hear this. But it is very good for you to know the truth here and now, and I have to say that the whole community cannot wait to attend, and bless this wedding. We are all proud of Mustafa and Neesha for accepting this situation. I hope that you do so as well."

Mr Khudabaksh regained his composure, and said softly, "Thank you for telling us this. I very much respect honesty and truthfulness. My wife Aminah could not stop telling me how impressed she was with Mustafa and Neesha. She really wants our two families to come together, and to be able to meet more often."

Mustafa looked at Aminah, and clearly understood her wish. They smiled at each other knowingly, and both started to speak at the same time, until Mustafa gave way to Aminah.

She said, "I think that Neesha is very happy about Soraya, and as we had not seen or met your two sons, I hope that you could consider a possible match with Rattan."

Rattan looked up, and saw that Soraya was staring at him. She was truly stunningly beautiful, and this was embellished by her radiant smile. Ahmed playfully ribbed Rattan, and he responded with a warm smile.

Joshua, ever the master matchmaker, ceased the moment, and announced with some flourish, "Well, I can see mutual attraction from a mile! These two beautiful young people are so made for each other! It is in their eyes, their faces, their smiles! Come on everybody, this is a match made in Heaven!"

Everyone was impressed with Joshua's approach, and laughed away their polite reserve. Mustafa said to Rattan, "*Beta*, do you like Soraya?"

Rattan, relieved of some of his usual shyness said, "Yes Paa. She is nice. I like her."

Mr Khudabaksh then asked Soraya, "*Beti*, do you also like Rattan?"

Soraya lowered her head slightly, and said, "Yes Paa."

"Well," said Joshua proudly. "That is it! We have another great match! All we have to do now is to plan a date!"

Mustafa said, "Yes Joshua, we will need to plan this carefully. Before we do so, and as is customary, we all need to give Soraya and

Rattan a chance to be together alone, and to talk to each other for a while. Then we can return to have a well-deserved hot lunch. I am starving, and I hope that this wonderful couple will understand that half an hour should be reasonable. There will be more time for them to be together on other occasions."

When everyone left the drawing room, Rattan and Soraya sat for a few moments, too nervous to speak. Then Rattan broke the silence by saying, "I like your family. You look so much like your mother. She must have been a very beautiful person when she was about your age."

"Thank you," said Soraya softly, nervously adjusting her head scarf which had slipped off onto her right shoulder. "She is still very beautiful. You also look so much like your father. But you are not yet losing your hair."

They laughed together, and began to feel more at ease in each other's company.

Rattan said, "So I hear that your parents have a similar business like ours."

"Yes, it is almost the same size as your store. Ours is a general store with grocery, clothing, and other household goods," said Soraya more confidently.

Rattan nodded, and said, "Same here as well. My Maa is the real boss here. She knows all the prices, and makes all the decisions about the sales. My Paa is more the buyer who likes to haggle with the wholesale merchants in Georgetown. He would argue quite strongly for only one penny per yard of cloth. I can never understand why he does this. At times it is very embarrassing for my Maa when she is with him."

"I know," said Soraya who was becoming keener to speak about business. "My Maa does the same as your Maa. My Paa is not so keen to do the buying, so I help my Maa to do this. I go so far as to bargain on half a penny even though this is such a small amount of money which is not even in existence. But when we buy in thousands of yards, this becomes a very large amount of money. The cheaper we buy the goods, the more money we can make, and our customers can also get the goods a little bit cheaper. So everyone wins. I also know all the prices in the store."

Rattan was immensely impressed by Soraya's business knowledge. He recognised that she would be a tremendous asset to their business. He was becoming fonder of her by the minute. Not only was she so beautiful, but she was also very clever, astute and confident. Just like his mother.

The young couple continued their very friendly conversation, exchanging information about their likes, dislikes, hopes and wishes. Mustafa and Neesha took the other guests on a small tour of their home and yard.

The half hour ended too quickly for Rattan and Soraya when Mustafa led everyone back into the dining room for lunch. Rattan sat next to Soraya and Mustafa sat next to Aminah, whilst Mr Khudabaksh took his place beside Neesha. Joshua, Matilda and Ahmed sat together in a way so that they could observe the three couples. Soraya's two sisters sat facing Joshua, Matilda and Ahmed. The *aaya* had come specially to cook for the families, and she placed the sumptuous meal along the middle of the large dining table.

Joshua said, "I am so happy today. I can see that your two families are meant to be together. May God bless you all." Everyone thanked him for his good wishes.

Matilda observed, "It is so nice to see Rattan looking like a young Mustafa, and Soraya looking so much like her mother. It is as if you had met before in a previous life."

Mustafa looked at Aminah, and they smiled at each other. Neesha said, "Well, if Mustafa had met Aminah before, then we would not all be here enjoying this happy occasion!"

"Hear hear!" said Joshua. "What date will you go for?"

Mustafa said, "Well, we have Ahmed's and Pansy's *nikah* coming up on the 4th of May. I do not see why we cannot go for a double wedding on that same day. Mr Khudabaksh, how does that sound to you and your family?"

Before Mr Khudabaksh could reply, Aminah intervened with a question, "Why the 4th of May?"

Mustafa answered, "Well, that is the date that our Imaam is free, and also the date that our ship arrived in British Guiana in 1845. I am happy to consider any other date you may have in mind."

Aminah looked at Mr Khudabaksh and said, "This sounds good to me." He nodded in approval, and stretched across to shake hands with Mustafa and Neesha. Joshua raised his hands aloft, and said, "Praise the Lord! My wish has been granted! We are going to have a grand double wedding! Praise the Lord!"

Joshua's response inspired Mustafa to offer a *dua* to seal the agreement between the two families. Then they all settled down to enjoy their very special lunch.

As the guests left for their long but happier journey back to Mahaica, Mustafa caught a glimpse of Aminah. They both had tears of joy in their eyes. Their promises to each other of true and everlasting love must now be enjoyed by their Rattan and Soraya. Fate can hurt, but it can also mend.

51.

The Promenade Gardens

Mustafa had a clandestine meeting with Aminah in the beautiful setting of the Promenade Gardens in Georgetown. It was during a Wednesday afternoon when they closed their respective stores for half a day, made the regular trips to Georgetown to pay their debts to the wholesale merchants, and ordered new stock in time for the busiest shopping day on Saturday.

After conducting their respective business transactions, they met for lunch, and then strolled over to the Gardens, which was first opened to the public in 1851. They found a wooden bench located beneath an ornate iron arch which had a rambling pink rose neatly spread from its base, and over its apex. The rose bush was highly fragrant, and in full bloom.

Mustafa said, "Chandini, I could not get you out of my mind from the very first day I saw you in Mahaica. I think that you also recognised me almost immediately despite so many years, and my grey hair. Let me say that I am so sorry I did not go back to India, as I had promised to do for you."

Chandini smiled, and looking straight into his eyes, said, "I never thought that I would ever see you again after each year passed by. When you left, I knew that we would be lost to each other. But I still kept my hope alive by going to our secret place every day, then every month, and then every year, praying and wishing that you would return. But you never did, and I was so hurt by this."

Mustafa, with tears in his eyes, said, "Chandini, I was also determined to go back, and for the first five years I thought of you so much that it pained me greatly. I tried very hard to stay loyal, and single. I tried to find out information about you, and the family. I also sent messages with people who were returning to India. But I heard nothing until you talked about what happened to our families."

Chandini shook her head, and wiped some of her tears away from her eyes and cheeks. Then she continued, "Mustafa, I believe you. I also avoided getting married despite my family forcing me into many arrangements. Each time I refused they would continue to treat me very badly. I was made to feel like a prisoner in my own home. And every time I decided to run away, they would send people after me. Mahaveer was more determined than my parents, to push me into a marriage. His actions towards me made me hate him intensely."

Mustafa said, "I was always worried about how he would treat you. But at the same time, I feel sad for him as he lost his life fighting for the freedom of our people in India. I can see him standing tall in battle like our grandparents did against other invaders. Despite what he did to you, I think that we must all be proud of him."

Chandini adjusted her *odni* which had slipped off her head, and said, "Yes, he was a martyr who gave his life for us all, and I am truly proud of him for that. Then tragedy after tragedy happened to both of our families."

Mustafa said, "I was saddened when you mentioned that our parents passed away in such a short time. What really happened?"

Chandini said, "First of all, in about one year after you left, our village saw a very long dry spell which led to a severe drought. We lost all our cattle and livestock, and our crops. Then one by one, the poorer older people began to die of starvation as the stocks of rice and flour ran out. Parents gave their children whatever food they managed to scramble, and then they eventually died leaving so many orphans. It was the worst time of my life. Many people just left the village and walked away with very little, looking for work and food."

Mustafa was visibly hurt to hear of such cruel devastation and hardship that their families had to endure. He recalled how he had stumbled upon a similar village during his journey on the Grand Trunk Road, and the good fortune of a single deluge after a long wait for rain. He wished that the same kind of luck had visited upon his own village. He reflected on how lucky they all were in British Guiana, where the seasons were more predictable, alternating between rainy spells and sunny spells. He said, "This makes our suffering here, nothing in comparison to what you had to face up to. At least we had our regular seasons of rain, allocated rations of food, and some guaranteed shelter."

Chandini interrupted him, and said, "And there was even worse to come. Our prayers for rain were finally answered, and the monsoon showers came. But there was too much water, too quickly. Everywhere was flooded within two days of continuous rainfall. Villages were simply washed away. People did not have the energy to walk away, so they simply lay in wait in what they had left for shelter, just hoping that death will come sooner rather than later. Our house was still strong enough to withstand the worst of the storms, and we tried to take in as many people as we could, including your family who had lost everything."

Mustafa cried out in anguish, "Oh Allah, may they all rest in peace!"

Chandini continued, "When your mother and father died, my family made sure that they were given good burials near to where your house once stood."

"Thank you so much. Allah will always look over you," said Mustafa graciously.

Chandini said, "Yes, I know that Allah has been merciful towards me. When your father was breathing his last breadth, he whispered to me that I must go to look for you. That is why I left the village, and headed straight for Calcutta."

Mustafa said with some concern, "That must have been a difficult and very tough journey for you."

Chandini said, "No, by that time, we had a train service, and it was not so hard for me. It was on that journey that I met my husband. He was very protective towards me, and encouraged me to join him, and his friends to come to British Guiana."

Mustafa asked, "Did you stay for a long time at the Depot in Calcutta? And was your agent a crook called Sundar Das?"

Chandini said, "No, we were well looked after at the Depot for about two weeks, and then we joined the ship. I cannot remember who the agent was. But the sea voyage was like hell to us. It must have been even worse for you. At one time I felt like jumping overboard, but my future husband and his friends stopped me."

"Mr Khudabaksh is a good man. When did you get married?" asked Mustafa.

Chandini paused for a moment, and then said, "Our feelings for each other were like brother and sister. He tried to help me to find you, but we could not trace where you were. I was in more despair, and felt that I failed your father's wish. I wanted to go back to India. Then Mr Khudabaksh reminded me of how bad things were in India. Besides, I could not face up to another difficult journey on a ship."

Mustafa said, "I do not blame you for making your choice and marrying a good man. I could not suffer alone hoping to be with you again, and so I decided to marry Neesha. She reminded me so much of you, and she has been like a rock in my life. She is so fond of you, and your family."

Chandini smiled and said, "I feel the same for her, and your family. That is why I am so happy that Rattan and Soraya will be married."

Mustafa nodded, and said, "Of course, this means that you and I will at least be able to see each other from time to time."

Chandini pointed out, "Yes, but not in such a secretive manner, and place like this!"

Mustafa looked into her eyes, and whispered, "Chandini, how do you feel towards me now?"

Chandini smiled and said, "I should ask you this question first. But I will answer you honestly. I have never stopped loving you, even after I became married, and the mother of my children. You have always been in my thoughts, and that is why I agreed to this meeting."

Mustafa drew closer to her, and held her right hand, "I feel the same way, but we are both committed to two wonderful and understanding people, and we must never forsake their love and devotion towards us. We must also try our best to help Rattan and Soraya succeed in their marriage, just as if they were us."

"Mustafa, that is the most beautiful thing to say," said Chandini reaching out for his free hand. "I hope that they grow to love each other, and never part for any reason."

Their conversation was briefly interrupted by two young lovers passing by towards another secluded spot in the Gardens. The layout of the grounds was such that there were several cosy areas designed for visitors to sit, and enjoy the wide variety of exotic plants and flowers. But romantic couples became the most prevalent users for their tete-a-tete.

"So Chandini," said Mustafa. "What are we going to do from now on? Do we keep our secret to ourselves, and not tell anyone?"

Chandini said, "Mustafa, I am confused. But since we wish to see Rattan and Soraya live the love that we could not fulfil, then we should keep this as our own personal treasure forever."

They held each other's hands tightly, and smiled to acknowledge their secret pact. They had lived apart from each other for so long, they felt that there was no other choice but to continue in this vein. When they parted, it was not as hurtful as the first time. They felt very happy, and contented. As they walked through the main gates of the Gardens, Mustafa noticed that Chandini had dropped her handbag, and he shouted aloud, "Chandini! Chandini!"

He could not complete his call as he choked from a hard push on his shoulders, "Mustafa! Mustafa! Wake up!"

It was Neesha who was startled by Mustafa's cries in his sleep. She shook him again until he opened his eyes. He was perspiring profusely, and tears were streaming down his cheeks.

"Mustafa!" urged Neesha. "What happened? What is the matter? Why were you calling out for Chandini? Who is this Chandini?"

Mustafa rolled over onto his back, and wiped the tears from his eyes and face. "I do not know. I had this terrible nightmare! I kept chasing after this full moon, this *Chand*! As I reached for it I could never touch it. It was always out of my grasp."

"Oh well," said Neesha with a sigh. "Just pull yourself together! You must be very tired with all that is going on at the moment. Let us get up and get ready. We have to continue with our plans for the weddings. The boys will help us to take much of the strain, and all we have to do is to be there to offer our guidance, and support. Come let us go down for some nice, refreshing tea. And stop chasing full moons! You will never catch them!"

52.

Long live Mustafa

The morning of the third of May began with the gangs of plantation workers making their way to the fields just before the sun rose in a virtually cloudless sky. Their attention was drawn to the very loud but rhythmical beats of the *tassa* drum and the large *dhol*. The players were a very well known duo of a tall slim man rattling the small *tassa* tied around his waist, and a short fat man banging the large *dhol* which was resting just above his portly stomach and strapped in such a way that it was just below his eyes. Whenever they reached a group of people by the side of the main road they would stop playing the drums, and make their announcement. Normally, the villagers would associate the newscasters with word of one or more deaths in the district.

That day's news was already well known throughout the estates and villages on the West Coast and West Bank of Demerara. It was about the forthcoming grand double weddings, and was billed as the biggest celebrations ever to be seen at Anna Catherina. The drummers, although hired for the day by Mustafa, took the opportunity to collect money from those willing to give. At the end of their day's labour, the two friends would settle down at a local rum shop to have a meal, and indulge in some rum.

The final preparations were being made at Mustafa's house, the Ching's, and at Kanhaiya's. The latter was the venue where the guests, who were vegetarians, and strict practising Hindus, would dine on the day and night of the weddings. The grooms' home was bedecked with bright multi-coloured buntings draped on the outer walls of the house and store, all around the fence, and in the interior. A large and very spacious tent was erected behind the house, and a special cooking and outdoor washing up area was constructed beside it. The best cooks, who were mostly men from the village, were already busily preparing for the feast. The women were chopping and slicing the vegetables, and other ingredients for the curries and *daal*. Younger people were washing and setting up tables, benches, and the specially harvested *poorie* leaves which were to be used as plates. The *poorie* leaves were from the Victoria Regia lily plants grown in some trenches.

As the invitation was an open one for anyone to attend, the mass cooking of the mutton curry, *daal*, rice, and sweet vermicelli, commenced that evening so that from lunchtime on the day of the weddings, guests would be served in a continuous way through the remainder of the day.

The first wedding which was Ahmed's and Pansy's *nikah*, took place at the residence of the Chings. Ahmed was accompanied by his *baraat* which included Mustafa, the Imaam, Kanhaiya, Joshua, Ragubir, Wong Yee and Nandoo. Kanhaiya and Joshua acted as the principal witnesses to the *nikah*, which was conducted by the Imaam in a very short time of twenty minutes. Pansy graciously accepted her conversion to Islam, and was given the Muslim name of Komal. This was followed by a short reading of *surahs* from the Holy Qur'an, *nasheeds* sung by the Muslims in attendance, and final *duas* to bless the newly wedded couple.

The wedding party which included the entire Ching family, their relations and friends, then walked over to Mustafa's home, and took their places in the tent. Everyone was given an opportunity to congratulate Ahmed and Komal, before settling down for their grand meal.

Mustafa and the *baraat* joined Rattan on two beautifully decorated horse-driven carts owned by Joshua, and they embarked on their long journey to Mahaica for the second wedding due to take place that afternoon at the Khudabakshs' residence.

Their round trip was very successful, and without mishap or delays throughout. The local people from the village and district lined the sides of the main road, and in front of the house in Anna Catherina, with multi-coloured flower petals and white rice grains to shower on the new bride and groom. The Khudabaksh family had also returned with the wedding party as a special gesture by Mustafa and Neesha.

Rattan and Soraya gracefully stepped onto the specially raised stage at the back of the grand tent. The two couples warmly embraced each other, and then sat down side by side, facing their guests. Most of the attendees had already taken lunch, and were invited to stay on for the grand dinner feast that evening. The brothers and their new wives stood up, and warmly welcomed everyone. All the main family friends and specially invited guests including the new Massa and his family, offered their congratulations and gifts to the two sets of newlyweds.

The new Massa said, "Today marks the start of new lives for Ahmed and Rattan, and their most beautiful brides. I can see how proud the parents are of these young people. I can also see how joyous and happy everyone here is. My family and I are honoured to be in your company. You are a unique people. On the one hand you are all British as are my family and I. And, on the other hand, you are British Guianese people of many races who were brought here for one purpose only. That is to help the plantation owners to produce fine sugar for sale and profit. We never really thought that we would be creating a new nation here; a new nation of Amerindians, Africans, Indians, Chinese and Portuguese people and descendents. And, of course, as we can see around this gathering, quite a number of mixed race people!"

Everyone applauded heartily, and then the new Massa continued, "Yes you have a right to be here, and to forge your own destiny as a new nation. You have amongst you some wonderful people of real integrity. People like Ragubir and his family, Nandoo and his family, Joshua and Matilda, Wong Yee and his family, Pandit Kanhaiya and his family, and of course, Mustafa and his extended family!"

The crowd exploded in rapturous applause as soon as Mustafa's name was mentioned, almost drowning out the mention of his newly extended family. The new Massa continued, "My family and I hope and pray that all of you British Guianese stay united together, and build up your new communities. Your present and your future are here in this colony, and you do not have to go back to your homelands. Educate your children and grandchildren well. Live in harmony with mutual respect for each other, and most of all, work to make this land your own!"

No one had expected such a rousing speech from the new Massa, but they were awakened to a future with enormous possibilities. Then, as the applause died down, the new Massa ended with, "Thank you all. I must not forget to offer sincerest congratulations to Ahmed and Komal, and to Rattan and Soraya. And, of course, we must not forget to wish Komal a safe and happy outcome for her baby. Thank you again, and have a good night."

Everyone stood up to give the new Massa and his family another burst of applause as they gracefully made their way out of the tent.

Ragubir then took his turn to congratulate the couples, and said, "I wish to endorse what the new Massa said. I know that we have begun to build a community of different peoples here. Let us all pray that no one ever tries to divide us now, or in the future. We are much stronger when we work, and live together as we are doing now. May God bless and keep us all."

Joshua walked proudly up to the stage with Matilda by his side, and after blessing the two couples, he commented, "What has already been said here today, my wife and I are truly happy to hear. As a community, we started on very shaky ground with mistrust, and envy amongst us. But good people like Ragubir, Mustafa and Kanhaiya showed us how to respect each other. We have seen how Wong Yee and the other Chinese people have come here, worked hard, and tried to live peacefully amongst us. I also wish to mention the same thing for our Portuguese friends. But we must never forget our Amerindian brothers and sisters who have been here long before all of us, and who are the original and true Guianese people. We must always treat them with respect."

The crowd noticed Iwaana and his family amongst them, and applauded with much appreciation. Iwaana, a very shy man, simply smiled and waved his hands in graceful acknowledgement.

Joshua continued, "Finally, I want to thank my beautiful wife Matilda here, who will always be remembered in future as a pioneer of our children's education. I love every one of you with all my heart, and I wish my good friends Mustafa and Neesha everything that is blessed for now, and in the future. Ahmed and Rattan, I am very proud to be involved in your marriages, and on behalf of my wife and I, may the good Lord bless and keep you, and your new families."

Pandit Kanhaiya took his place on the podium amidst the cheering for Joshua and Matilda. He blessed the two couples and after reciting the *gayatri mantra* three times, he said, "We left our homelands a very long time ago now, and have all experienced real hardships here, not to mention the horrid, and treacherous sea voyage. We did not know what to expect here, and when the sun hit our backs we soon realised that this was not a good place to be living in. We always prayed that our nightmare would be over soon, and we would go back to our villages in India. But throughout our suffering and pain, we gathered strength and determination, and did what we never dreamt of. Now, as this is our new homeland, we have to treat it with love, respect and care. Let us also continue to show each other that we will always stand for good and do the right things. I am sure that Bhagwan Raam will continue to guide us, and protect us all." Kanhaiya then embraced the newlyweds as great applause rang out.

Wong Yee was not used to speaking in a public setting, but he took to the stage and congratulated the married couples. "Let me say that I am very lucky to be here today as you all know. My wife and our son are worth so much to me that I have never thought of going back to China or Macao. Besides, for all I know, certain people may still be there waiting to send me to my doom! I also want to say, on behalf of all Chinese people here, we do not cheat our customers, and we love you all!"

The crowd broke out into laughter and cheering as they realised that he was referring to the suspicion of doctored watered down rum being sold by the Chinese owners of the rum shops. Wong Yee continued, "I have to say that I can tell when the milk that I buy from our Indian milkman does not quite taste as full cow's milk! But, on a day like this, I do not wish to cause any friction amongst us, so I leave you with nothing but all the very best wishes, and the Lord's blessings!"

Wong Yee then took his leave from the gathering as great applause echoed around him.

Mustafa stood up, and after a short glance across to Aminah and Neesha, and the newly married couples, he began to speak in a measured way, "Today, I am very grateful to Allah for allowing this gathering, and blessed event to occur. This was never part of my dream, even before I left India. I was just a crazy young man who ran away from my village in search of something better to take back to the ones I loved dearly. My plan was to go as far away as possible along the Grand Trunk Road towards this imaginary pot of gold. I would work hard, gather as much wealth as I could, and then turn back to share this with my people. But that journey and that pot of gold became further and further away from my open arms, across a wretched and angry sea, and finally here in this hot and difficult land. I was lucky to have met some wonderful people on this long walk to this goal, and I shared all kinds of experiences. I am so happy to have met Kanhaiya and Ishani on that long sea voyage, and where we all became *jahaji bhais* and *behens*."

He paused for a moment and wiped some tears from his eyes. His audience looked up at him with concern, and compassion. Aminah also wiped tears from her eyes.

Mustafa continued, "Then my most respected friend and guide Ragubir appeared. You have been such a great help to me, and my family. We will never be able to repay you, Ishani and Bharat. Joshua, you are like an arch angel. Thank you so much for supporting me and my family over all these years. Thank you also for doing so much to bring our people closer together. You and the lovely Matilda are most respected here."

The audience applauded loudly in appreciation of Joshua and Matilda who stood up briefly to acknowledge them. Mustafa then said, "Matilda, you continue to give so many young children such a good start on their journey to learn. And your delicious ice block is something so special, I wish we had some here this evening to cool us down! But I do hope that everyone will enjoy the sweet vermicelli we have made. I also want to specially introduce our new in-laws, Mr and Mrs Khudabaksh, Soraya's parents, who have come all the way from Mahaica. And, Mr and Mrs Ching, Komal's parents, whom we all know very well!"

Again, the audience cheered wildly, and the Khudabakshs' were quite humbled by this show of welcome and appreciation. When they sat down, Aminah looked at Mustafa, and nodded in approval. He said, "My family and I will love your beautiful daughter as she is our own. She will always remind us of your family, and we will never forget the special bond we have between us. I also love someone else who I call my *bhaiya*. He is our learned Pandit Kanhaiya, with the beautiful Mumtaz and their princess Meena! Kanhaiya, you have been my younger *bhaiya*, and you have made me proud of all that you have achieved ever since you set foot in British Guiana. It was through your strength that I was able to overcome some of the difficulties I faced. You continue to inspire us all with your devotional work. You continue to lift our spirits when we are down."

The audience stood up to cheer their Pandit who humbly clasped his hands, and nodded in gratitude. Mustafa continued, "I must not forget our best singer Nandoo, and his lovely family. I know that he and Sangita will continue to entertain us with their wonderful renditions of religious songs and of course, wedding songs that remind us of our homeland. Tonight we also have our two amazing drummers who will help to spice things up. I want to thank the new Massa and his family for taking time to be with us. I hope that we can all live up to his expectations of us as a new people. I really do hope for this!"

The gathering, including the people who had been cooking, serving and cleaning all night and day also stood up to applaud. Mustafa then turned his attention to the very shy Neesha. He said, "But most of all tonight, I have to tell you about someone who is the reason for my standing here today. My wife, Neesha!"

The audience gave the loudest ovation for the evening, and did not stop until Mustafa raised his arms aloft, and told them to sit down. He continued, "Neesha is the real backbone of our family. She runs the store, looks after Ahmed, Rattan and I, looks out for all of you who come to the store, and still finds time to advise on what we need to do to develop as a better community. She is an amazing leader, and if we were politicians, she would be in charge! This British Guiana needs people like Neesha, Aminah, Ishani, Mumtaz, Matilda and Sangita, to make us all better!"

Again, the men and young men in the audience shouted their approval for all the women and young ladies. Mustafa then concluded, "On behalf of my wife and family, I wish these lucky young people the best future, and lots of grandchildren for Neesha and me to spoil! I also want to thank all of you for looking after us in this village, and for attending our function. I also want to specially thank all the people who have been preparing for these weddings, for catering such amazing food, for serving us and for helping us in every way possible to make this a most memorable event. Finally, I must thank Allah, Bhagwan Raam, the Lord Jesus, and whoever you wish to worship, for the blessings we have been given. Please enjoy everything that we have to offer here tonight and tomorrow, as there will still be more food for all!"

Everybody stood up, and shouted "Long live Mustafa! Long live Mustafa! Long live Mustafa!" Aminah smiled, and mimed, "Long live the Chosen One!"

Suddenly everyone was stunned into silence by the sound of a big bang. Mustafa put his hands to his chest, and fell back heavily onto his chair. The silence then turned into loud screams particularly from the women and children as his friends rushed to his side. More loud cracking sounds like rapid gunfire caused everyone to slump to the ground amidst louder and wilder screaming, and sheer panic. Some people scrambled to their feet, and ran out from the tent with their arms held aloft, still screaming and shouting with utter fear. No one seemed to know who was firing on them, nor where the firing was coming from. People pointed to several directions, as they ran for their lives. Very quickly, several of the wedding congregation reached a safe distance away, and lined the roadside looking on in awe at the group who were trying to revive Mustafa.

Many of the women in the large crowd began to scream out Mustafa's name with their arms stretched out in sheer anguish. They asked as to who would want to shoot and kill their beloved Mustafa. Why would anyone wish to destroy such great hopes and expectations that were just shared for all to hear.

Then Wong Yee appeared, and shouted at everyone, "Freedom! Everybody enjoy the special Chinese crackers and fireworks! Come outside and enjoy!"

Mustafa recovered his composure, much to everyone's relief as they too got up and dusted themselves down. He looked at Wong Yee, and said, "Thank you for nearly taking my life! You should have warned us about this! Anyway, thank you for your surprise. Let us all go out, and enjoy the display!"

The remaining firecrackers and fireworks were set off, and everyone enjoyed the spectacle. Mustafa looked up, and caught the eyes of Aminah. They instinctively turned and saw Rattan and Soraya in a warm embrace. The love that Mustafa and Aminah never shared, the promises that were never fulfilled, and the dreams that caused their separation, were being fatefully passed on. The great satisfaction in their proud eyes was sweeter than the special allure of the golden sugar of Demerara.

GLOSSARY

Aarti	One of the final rites of Hindu worship. It includes waving a lit *Diya* in a tray in a clockwise or anti-clockwise way according to the ceremony. This is accompanied by an *Aarti* chant.
Aata	Flour
Aaya	Maid servant
Abeer	Coloured powder mixed with water and sprayed during the festival of *Holi*
Aloo	Potato
Aloo choka	Mashed potato with several spices including crushed ginger, cumin, red chilli powder, turmeric, and salt
Aloo paratha	Indian bread with a mashed spiced potato filling
Amrit	Holy water from sacred rivers such as the Ganges
Arabic	The language of the Arabs, and the Holy Qur'an
Baitho	Sit
Bandar	Monkey
Baraat	Indian wedding procession of the groom and his entourage
Bazaar	Market of small shops
Ber	Berry
Beta	Son
Betel	Climbing plant whose leaves and nuts can be chewed as *Paan*
Beti	Daughter
Bhabi	Sister
Bhagwad Gita	Epic account of the Mahabharat battle; a holy text in Hinduism
Bhagwan	Hindu name for God
Bhai or *Bhaiya*	Brother
Bhaingan	Aubergine or Egg Plant
Bhajan	Hindu devotional song or hymn
Bhaji	Spinach
Bhojpuri	Indian language associated with the Uttar Pradesh and Bihar States
Brahmin	Member of the first group in the four Hindu social divisions of Brahmin, Kshatriya, Vaishya and Shudra
Buckbead	Common climbing plant (Arbus precatorius), found in bushy places over sandy ground in the Tropics. The Amerindian men and women of British Guiana (Guyana) wound long strings of these colourful seeds into necklaces and anklets
Buddhism	The religion founded by Gautam Budh that teaches that all suffering can be brought to an end, by overcoming greed, hatred, and delusion
Chaat House	Indian establishment that caters for teas and snacks

Chacha	Uncle
Chai	Tea
Chaiwallah	Tea seller
Chand	Full moon
Channa	Chick peas
Coolie	Derogatory word to describe an unskilled Asian labourer
Daal	Spicy Indian lentil soup. There are several types of *daal*
Dhol	Large base drum usually accompanying the *tassa*
Dhoti	Traditional wear of Indian men, usually made of cotton. It is wrapped around the waist, between the legs, and knotted at the waist
Didi	Sister
Diwali	Hindu festival of lights
Diya	Small shallow cup containing oil and a wick which is used to provide a slow burning light. It is used by Hindus in the performance of prayers, and during the festival of *Diwali*
Dua	Arabic word meaning prayer. It is associated with Muslim prayer
Driver	Person appointed as a foreman on the sugar estates
Eid-ul-Fitr	The festival celebrating the end of the Islamic holy month of *Ramadan*
Fajr	The first of the prescribed five daily prayers for Muslims
Fakir	A mendicant who leads a holy life. The Muslim equivalent of the Hindu *Saadhu*
Ganja	Marijuana; a highly potent form of cannabis, usually used for smoking
Gayatri Mantra	Universal Hindu prayer
Ghat	A series of stone or wooden steps leading from the top of a river bank to the water's edge
Ghee	Clarified butter
Hafeez	A Muslim who has memorised the Holy Qur'an
Havan	Hindu religious ceremony performed in temples or in homes, involving worship through the use of a sacred fire
Hindu	Person born of, and who believes in, the ancient Indian faith called *Hinduism*
Hindi	The Indian language derived from the ancient Sanskrit
Hinduism	Religion of the *Hindus*
Holi	Hindu Spring festival which includes devotees throwing coloured water and powder upon each other
Holika	Sacred Hindu fire ceremony during the festival of *Holi*
Imaam	Muslim priest
Islam	The faith of *Muslims*
Jajaji	Seafarer. Indian indentured labourers who travelled together by ship from India referred to each other as *Jahaji Bhai* or *Jahaji Behen*
Jeera	Cumin seeds
Jummah	Friday. Associated with Muslim Prayers, *Jummah Namaaz* or Friday Prayers
Kaala Paani	The dark waters of the seas and oceans
Kabadi	Indian sport where two teams try to catch or tag their rivals before their clearly marked out space is invaded by the opposition
Kabootar	Pigeon
Kabootar Baz	Pigeon fancier

Kali Mai	A Goddess in the Hindu religion
Katha	Hindu religious lesson
Koker	Dutch-built barrier which helped to control the flow of water into and out of canals
Krishna	An incarnation of God in Hinduism. *Krishna Janamasthmi* is the birth of *Krishna*
Kunda	Square metal container for the fire maintained through the *Havan* prayers. It is also made of bricks
Laddoo	Indian sweet made of flour, sugar and other ingredients. It is made into a small ball and cooked with some *Ghee*
Laskar	Indian seaman employed by the British
Logie	A row of wooden houses used as communal dwellings by the Indian Indentured labourers on the sugar estates
Lota	Drinking vessel or mug usually made of brass, copper, or in modern times, aluminium, steel or plastic
Madrasa	Islamic school
Mandap	Special enclosure used as an altar for Hindu wedding ceremonies
Mandir	Hindu place of worship
Mantra	Hindu prayer
Masaala	Mixture of several Indian spices including coriander, turmeric, ginger, onions, garlic, chilli pepper and salt
Massa	African slave term for Master or Boss of the plantations
Matka	Indian clay goblet
Matya	Indian wooden or cane bed
Mela	Indian fair
Moksha	Enlightenment. Spiritual upliftment
Mor	Peacock or peahen
Mosque	Muslim's place of worship
Murthi	Sculptured image representing a manifestation of Hindu deity. Once invoked, it is then focused upon during worship
Muslim	Follower of Islam
Namaskaar	Hindu greeting meaning: "I bow to thee" Also *Namaste*
Namaaz	Islamic prayer expected to be offered by Muslims five times each day. It is one of the five pillars of Islam
Nasheed	Islamic song of praise, usually sung without the accompaniment of music
Nikah	Muslim marriage ceremony
Obeah	Spiritual belief originating from West Africa, and involving the use of sorcery, spells, hypnotic trances, and sacrifice. *Obeah Man* is a practitioner of *Obeah*
Odni	Embroidered scarves worn by Indian women
Ole Haigge	Creole term for witch
Pagwa	See *Holi*
Pandit	Hindu priest of the *Brahmin* caste
Paratha	Indian bread or *Roti*
Peerha	Low-level wooden bench for one person
Pinda	*Pinda Pooja:* Hindu prayer ceremony performed for the benefit of a deceased person using *Pinda* made of boiled rice and a number of ingredients

Pooja	Hindu ritual prayers normally conducted by a *Pandit* for the benefit of the participating devotees. A *Pooja* normally ends with *Havan* followed by *Aarti*
Poorie	Type of Indian bread or *Roti*. *Poorie Leaves* are the Victoria Lily leaves used to eat *Poorie* and other foods
Punjabi	A person from the Punjab State of India. Also the language of Punjab
Qur'an	*Holy Qur'an*: The holy book of Islam
Ramadan	The holy month of fasting in Islam
Ramayan	Epic poem about the life and times of the Lord Raam, a manifestation of God in Hinduism
Roti	Indian bread
Rumaal	Indian headwear for women. It is similar to a handkerchief or bandana
Saadhu	Hindu Holy Man
Sahib	Indian term of respect usually accorded to a European man
Samjhe	Hindi for understand
Sanatan Dharm	The ancient or eternal way of life based on truth and selfless service to all
Sangam	The convergence of rivers. The most notable *Sangam* in India is that of the Rivers Ganges, Yamuna and Saraswati
Sanskrit	Ancient Indian language
Sari	Elegant Indian woman's dress made by wrapping five yards of cloth around the waist, to the shoulders
Sati	The now illegal practice whereupon a widow was expected to die on the funeral pyre of her deceased husband
Satsang	Hindu gathering to discuss religious issues
Shivalingam	The stone representation of creation attributed to the Lord Shiva
Shlokas	Verses in Sanskrit
Sikh	Follower of *Sikhism* founded by the Guru Nanak, the first of ten Gurus
Sindoor	The vermilion powder used in Hindu worship, and placed on the parting of a woman's hair to indicate that she is married
Sirdar	A person chosen to lead
Supaari	Ingredient used in Hindu pooja
Surah	A chapter from the Holy Qur'an
Tabeej	A message, usually a quote from the Holy Qur'an, worn in a necklace, and designed for protection and to ward off evil
Tassa	Small kettle drum played with two sticks, and usually accompanies the large *dhol* drum
Tilak	A red mark placed at the centre of the forehead, and worn by Hindus
Wuzu	The prescribed cleansing ritual that every Muslim is required to perform before prayers or *namaaz*
Yajna	Hindu commitment to public prayers that could last for three or more days
Zakaat	Annual obligation for Muslims to offer a proportion of their wealth for the benefit of those in need
Zamindar	Indian landlord or landowner who is often the head of a village or district